IT LIVED TO KILL

It was a man, but it was like no man Ben had ever seen. It was huge, with mottled skin and huge, clawed hands. The shoulders and arms appeared to be monstrously powerful. The eyes and nose were human, but the jaw was animal. The ears were perfectly formed, but the teeth were fanged.

A terrified young girl stood between Ben and the . . . whatever in God's name the creature was. It towered over her. Ben guessed it was an easy seven feet tall.

Ben didn't hesitate. He whipped out his .45 just as the creature lunged for the girl. He got off one slug; the big shot hit the mutant in the shoulder. It screamed in pain and spun around. All three hundred pounds of it were mad—and now it was coming right at Ben . . .

ANARCHY
IN THE
ASHES

WILLIAM W. JOHNSTONE

PINNACLE BOOKS
Kensington Publishing Corp.
http://www.kensingtonbooks.com

PINNACLE BOOKS are published by

Kensington Publishing Corp.
850 Third Avenue
New York, NY 10022

All Kensington Titles, Imprints, and Distributed Lines are available at special quantity discounts for bulk purchases for sales promotions, premiums, fund-raising, and educational or institutional use. Special book excerpts or customized printings can also be created to fit specific needs. For details, write or phone the office of the Kensington special sales manager: Kensington Publishing Corp., 850 Third Avenue, New York, NY 10022, attn: Special Sales Department, Phone: 1-800-221-2647.

Pinnacle and the P logo Reg. U.S. Pat. & TM Off.

ISBN-13: 978-0-7860-1959-5
ISBN-10: 0-7860-1959-X

First Pinnacle Books Printing: July 1997

10 9 8 7 6

Printed in the United States of America

To Charles and Rosemary

The enemy say that Americans are good at a long shot, but cannot stand the cold iron. I call upon you instantly to give a lie to this slander. Charge!

—Winfield Scott

PROLOGUE: A NEW BEGINNING

It looked good.

Yes, Ben Raines thought as he drove the area of the nation known to a few as the new Tri-States, it did look good. As he drove he gazed out at the fertile land that would soon bring forth beans and cotton and corn and the many hundreds of small gardens that would feed the people.

Ben smiled.

For the first time since the arrival of Ben and his Rebels in portions of Arkansas, Louisiana, and Mississippi, Ben felt some degree of optimism for the future of those who chose to follow his dream.

The spring of 2001 was, Ben felt, a long way from what most science fiction writers of his generation had envisioned. Those writers envisioned robots doing much of the tasks formally relegated to the unskilled. They imagined numerous space shuttles to faraway worlds, an easing of the world's hunger, great strides and breakthroughs in the field of medicine—and so very much more.

Instead, the world now hung by a slender thread: on one side a chance for civilization to flourish; on the other, anarchy, barbarism, a return to the caves.

We've got to make it, Ben mused as he drove. Some group of people must show the rest of the world that civilization and order can once more prevail over chaos.

We've got to make it.

It's up to us, and I know it. But I don't have to like the heavy yoke of responsibility that hangs like that stinking albatross about my neck.

But, he sighed, we almost made it. We came so close, so very close to crawling out of the ashes of nuclear war. 1988 was not the end. It could have been a glorious new beginning. But 1988 blew up in our faces and very nearly destroyed the entire world.

His thoughts drifted back to the beginning of his dream: Tri-States, a section of America in the west, after the horror of germ and nuclear war; a society of free men and women of like mind, like dreams, like hopes. A society where people of all races could live and work and be content. And live free of crime. And Ben Raines and his Rebels did it. Social scientists and social anthropologists and assorted liberals and bleeding hearts had always maintained it could not be done, but Ben and his people had proved them incorrect. Grossly incorrect. Those men and women who were the founders and the foundation of Tri-States had succeeded against all odds. They had made their dream work.

And for almost a decade they had lived in peace and harmony and contentment, in a land where good schools — free of nit-picking and government interfer-

10

ence and unions and leniency—had done what schools were meant to do: educate the young, mold their minds, teach them reading and writing and math and science and discipline and respect.

Tri-States had shown the world—that world which remained—that a government does not need to be top-heavy with bureaucracy and dead weight and hundreds of unfair and unworkable laws and pork-barrel projects and scheming politicians and massive over-spending and dead-heads.

But the Central Government—then located in Richmond, Virginia because D. C. had taken a nuke dead-on back in '88—with a lunatic at the helm of state, could not bear the success of Ben Raines and his people. President Hilton Logan had ordered the destruction of Tri-States—and all its inhabitants.

Only three years ago, Ben thought, waving to a Rebel standing by a fence, talking with a neighbor. The men returned the wave.

"Hi, General!" they called. Both men wore side arms belted around their waists. And they would have automatic weapons close by, not just because they were citizen soldiers, regulars in the Rebel army, but because the world was still tumbling about in fear and chaos and violence and near-anarchy.

Citizen soldiers, Ben thought, driving past the talking men. That is why we survived and so many others did not. I insisted that *all* my people be a part of the armed forces, with all the training and discipline contained therein. And we survived the holocaust, came through it, due in no small part to the fact the people were armed and trained and disciplined.

That should tell the world something.

11

But what world is left to hear it?

So much has happened in only three years.

Ben wondered, if history were ever written about this tragic period of the world, if anyone would believe that one man, Ben Raines, could go from novelist to guerrilla leader to the founder of a separate nation within a nation back to guerrilla leader, and from there move on to the office of the president of the United States, and once more back to guerrilla leader — all in the short span of only twelve years?

Unbelievable.

Ben smiled. It would have made a hell of a book, he thought, the writer in him once more surfacing. He missed writing, missed the long hours of solitude, missed the exercising of his mind as he grappled with plot and dialogue, missed the deadlines he used to curse.

Reading, he thought, the smile still on his lips. That's the key. That is what we have to stress with the young people. The nation, Ben knew, had begun slipping in the reading department — really took a beating from 1960 to the big blow-up of '88. Can't let that happen again. Got to stress reading and math and science. For those will be the keys to picking up the pieces of civilization and putting them back together once more.

Thank God the mindless inanity of much of prime-time TV was gone. His smile turned grim. The only good thing to come out of being nuked.

Ben lost his smile as his eyes picked up the reflection of his constant shadow in the rear-view mirror of his pickup: his bodyguards.

Sgt. Buck Osgood would be at the wheel of the rear

12

vehicle. With another Rebel riding shotgun, armed with an automatic weapon, and a third Rebel in the rear of the vehicle, ready to grab the big .50-caliber machine gun.

By nature a loner, Ben could never become accustomed to the idea of having a babysitter wherever he went — not even after all these years.

And ranging a half mile ahead of him, always trying to stay out of his sight, for his bodyguards knew how Ben felt, would be another Jeep or APC, with more Rebels in it, all heavily armed.

What price fame? Ben silently mused, the mental question laced with sarcasm.

But Ben knew the precautions were necessary, for there had been sightings of mutants. However, the mutants for the most part left humans alone as long as they were not provoked. In addition, there was the need to guard against roaming gangs of thugs and paramilitary groups. At least several times a month they would attempt to slip into the new Tri-States, to steal or rape or burn or kill, or all of those things.

They would be put down hard; if not killed on the spot, they would be hanged the next day.

For that was the order of day now — around the battered globe. Nowhere else that the Rebels knew of was there social order — only the new Tri-States, which set rules and behavior and morals.

In this late spring of 2001, worldwide, it had come down to the survival of the fittest. Humankind had reverted very nearly back to the caves. And in some cases, had indeed returned to the caves, although Ben and his people would not learn of that for months to come.

For now, in the new Tri-States, Ben Raines and his six thousand survivors, men, women, and children, were attempting to rebuild some sort of workable society out of the ruins of war and anarchy and a worldwide plague. Hopefully, they could fan a spark from the ashes.

Ben thought that just maybe they could pull it off. Maybe.

God knew they had to try.

Ben didn't think humankind would have another chance.

PART ONE

ONE

May, 2001

The men and women of the IPF, International Peace Force, had landed quietly on Canadian soil, on their way to the United States. Their route had been long and often tedious. They had waited and trained and studied for ten years before making their move. They had planned well.

They had sailed from home port in March — not the easiest month to leave — and skirted south of Cape Farewell, into the Labrador Sea. They sailed into the Hudson Strait, passed around Mansel Island, keeping to the east, then angled south by southwest until the mouth of the River was in sight. There, they offloaded boats and equipment for the river trip.

They followed the Nelson into Lake Winnipeg, then began a torturous trek overland. But most were young and strong and the trip was nothing compared to the training they had been undergoing for the past decade.

All came through. Anything for the Motherland and for the development of a *meister rasse*.

The IPF picked up Highway 10 in Canada and procured vehicles from the abandoned cars and trucks. They headed for the United States border, dropping off small contingents of IPF personnel along the way. They saw very few people alive in Canada. Those they saw seemed more curious than hostile.

Had the people in Canada known what type of monster mentality they were facing, they would have turned hostile in a hurry.

But by the time they discovered the truth, it was too late for the few Canadians left alive in the areas where the IPF landed.

In the United States—the late, great United States—the IPF set up base camp in Minnesota and radioed back to home port they were at their objective. They were told two more ships had set sail and had steamed near the mouth of the Nelson. There, they were awaiting orders to offload men and equipment.

In Minnesota, the IPF broke off into teams and fanned out into the countryside, testing the mood of the people. In a great many cases they found men and women—entire families—who were just barely hanging on to life, victims of the many roving gangs of thugs in the land.

The men and women of the IPF spoke grammatically correct English, with only a very slight accent. They were very polite: the men were often courtly in their dealings with American women, straightforward and open with the American men. At first. But conditions and deportment among the IPF were subject to

18

sudden and drastic changes — very soon.

An American man asked where the people had come from.

"Originally, Eastern Europe," came the reply, always with a smile.

"That would account for the accent."

"Yes."

"And you want?"

"To be your friend, and for you to be our friends. To live in peace in this troubled world. To try and find the cause for the terrible tragedy that has befallen us all, and to correct it."

"Isn't that what we all want?"

"Yes," Gen. Georgi Striganov said with a smile. He was a strikingly handsome man, tall and well-built, with pale blue eyes, fair skin, and blond-gray hair. "Indeed it is."

The American stuck out his hand. "I'll tell you what the problem was. The goddamn niggers wanted everything given to them and the goddamn Jews went along with it. Every time you looked at the TV there was about a million greasers comin' across the border, grabbing up jobs that should have gone to Americans."

General Striganov listened with a sympathetic smile on his lips.

"Taxes kept goin' up and up and up; it never seemed to stop. Everything for the minorities and to hell with the taxpayers. I said it, and by God that's the way I feel about it."

Striganov shook the man's hand. "My name is Georgi. I think we're going to get along very well. Now tell me: How can we help you?"

* * *

Ben watched Ike pull into his driveway and get out of the pickup. Ike walked up to Ben, resting on his hoe handle in his garden.

"El Presidente," Ike said with a grin, "it is time, I believe, for me to speak."

"Quote the Walrus, 'Of shoes—and ships—and sealing wax.' Maybe I don't want to hear it, Ike."

The grin never left Ike's face. "Hell, Ben, that never stopped me before."

The two men had met down in Florida, back in late '88, the ex-SEAL and the ex-Hell-Hound. They had been close friends, like brothers, ever since.

"That certainly is true, Ike."

"You need a woman, Ben."

"Oh, hell!"

"Hear me out, ol' buddy. Things are lookin' pretty good around here, thanks to you. You somehow put some steel in the backbones of those who follow you. I personally didn't believe you could do it—but you did. With any kind of luck, pal, we'll make it here."

The usage of the informal noun brought memories rushing to both men of Pal Elliot, a black man who had been instrumental in shaping the original Tri-States. Pal, his wife Valerie and their children had been killed in the governmental assault on Tri-States.

Ben shook away the memories of people dead and events past. "I am perfectly content with my life as a bachelor, Ike."

"That's bull and you know it, Ben. You got too much he-goat in you for that." He grinned. "Have you seen the twins?"

20

"Which set?" Ben asked sourly.

Ike laughed and punched the man playfully on the shoulder. "Rosita's set."

"No."

"They got their momma's good looks and your eyes. You know what she named them?"

Ben had to smile at the memories of Rosita. "Ben and Salina. Not very subtle of her, I'd say."

"Have you seen Dawn?"

"Get to the point, Ike," Ben said wearily. "If there is a point." He knew very well what the point was.

"That's your baby, Ben." It was not phrased as a question.

"Yes," he admitted. "She said she was going to have it and nothing I could say would change her mind."

"And now you're alone and have been for some months."

Ben shrugged.

"What are you going to do: put a rubber band around it and become celibate?"

Ben laughed at just the thought. "That would be painful, buddy."

"The rubber band or celibacy?"

Ben tried his best glare on Ike. It didn't work, bouncing off the stocky man. "Ben, you've been rattlin' 'round in that big ol' house like a pea in a dry pod. For all you've been through, you still look like a man forty years old. I know—a lot of us know—you're restless. Would like to take off and ramble. But you can't do that, Ben. You're the glue that holds us together. You was to take off, Tri-States would collapse."

Ben did not like to think of himself as being that

important to the society. It bothered him. "And you think a woman would help settle me down, is that right, Ike?"

"It's been known to happen."

"I read Roanna's newspaper every week. Maybe I should advertise?"

"It isn't funny, Ben." Ike was serious.

"And I'm not treating it as a joke, Ike. Damn it, Ike, I don't want a harem. And I'm not liking the feeling I get when I leave the farm. That's why I've been keeping a low profile, and why Cecil is being groomed—not that he needs any grooming—to take my place, and the sooner the better."

"Cecil's a good man," Ike said guardedly.

"Drop the other shoe, Ike."

"Nobody can take your place."

Ben felt temper building in him. He fought it back. "And I don't like that crap either, Ike. Damn, buddy, nobody is indispensable—you should know that. Nobody!"

Ike stood quietly, waiting by the fence. Finally he waved his hand and sighed. "All right, Ben, let's don't fuss about it. Too much to do without putting that into it. Two reasons I came out here. You won't discuss number one, so here's number two: Intelligence keeps picking up some strange radio transmissions. They came to me with it 'cause, well . . ."

"They're afraid to come to me with them," Ben finished it. There was a flat tone to his voice.

"I reckon that's about the size of it," the Mississippi-born-and-reared Ike admitted.

"That really makes me feel swell, Ike."

Ike spread his hands in a gesture of "what can I

say?" When he spoke his voice was soft. "You know you're bigger than life to a lot of people, Ben."

"And I get the feeling it's getting out of hand."

"Maybe. Anyway, we pinpointed latitude and longitude. Coming from just south of the Arctic Circle. Twenty degrees west longitude, sixty-five degrees north latitude. They're coming from Iceland, Ben."

"Iceland! But Iceland was supposed to be destroyed, Ike."

"You got it. And the transmissions are in a funny language. It's almost Russian—but it isn't. It is a Russian dialect, though."

Ben nodded his head thoughtfully. "Could be one of a dozen or so. Latvian, Croatian, Georgian. What do you make of it?"

Ike shook his head. "Strange, Ben—weird. You remember that we got reports back in '89 that Iceland was hot, took several nukes nose-on."

"Yes," Ben's reply was thoughtful. "We damn sure did. And as I recall, I wondered why they would—or should. OK, they've got to be broadcasting to somebody, Ike."

"Right. To a base in northern Minnesota."

"Now that is interesting."

"I did a little checking 'fore I drove up to see you, since you never seem to leave this raggedly ol' place," Ike added dryly. Ben ignored that dig. "Doctor Chase says it would have been highly unlikely the plague would have hit that far north. Extreme temperatures, hot or cold, seem to at first stall it, then kill it."

"Wonder why he never told me that?"

" 'Cause you don't never leave this goddamn place!"

"Uh-huh. You have someone attempting to translate

23

the language?"

"Right. Ben, what are you thinking? Man, I don't like the look in your eyes."

Ben slapped his friend on the back, his mood suddenly lifting. "Ike, I want you to personally get me a full platoon together."

"Now, damn it, Ben!"

"I want supplies for a sustained operation. Full combat gear. Mortars and light howitzers."

"Goddamn it, Ben!"

"At least two APCs and rig .50s on all the Jeeps, no telling what we'll run into."

"If I had known you were gonna pull this kind of crap I'd have never come out here!"

"And have one of Doctor Chase's doctors accompany us. No telling what we'll find. Get on that right away, will you, Ike?"

Ike stood for a moment, glaring at his friend. Ben returned his gaze sweetly, blandly, the picture of all innocence. Ike finally turned away, muttering under his breath.

Ben rubbed his hands together, a grin moving his mouth. Ben Raines did not like inactivity. He liked to be on the move, liked action.

This was just what the doctor ordered.

Sam Hartline looked like the stereotyped Hollywood mercenary—when Hollywood existed, that is. Six feet, two inches, heavily muscled, a deep tan, dark brown hair graying at the temples, cold green eyes, and a scar on his right cheek.

Cecil had summed up Hartline several years back.

"Sam Hartline is a goddamned psychopath. And one hard-line nigger hater. He was with Jeb Fargo outside Chicago back in '88 and '89."

"Mr. Hartline," General Striganov greeted the mercenary warmly, with a smile and a firm handshake. "How good to meet with you at last. Did you have a pleasant trip up?"

"Very nice," Hartline replied, his eyes taking in and silently appraising the Russian. The man looked to be about the same age as Ben Raines, and in just as good physical condition. Hartline wondered if the Russian was as tough as Ben Raines. He'd damn well better be, he concluded, if he's thinking of tangling with Raines.

"You have laid claim to the entire state of Wisconsin," General Striganov said, not losing his smile. "Don't you find that a rather ambitious undertaking, Mr. Hartline?"

Hartline's smile was as cold as the one greeting him. "Not at all, General. The people seem to be coming along splendidly."

Striganov leaned back in his chair. "You know, of course, who I am and what I represent?"

Hartline shrugged his heavy shoulders. "You're a former member of the KGB." He smiled. "The Komitet Gosudarstvennoy Brozopasnosti."

Striganov's eyebrows lifted slightly. Then the rumors concerning Hartline's linguistic abilities were not exaggerated.

"A general in the Russian Army. Or what is left of that army."

The smile did not quite reach Striganov's eyes. "I assure you, Mr. Hartline, we are of more than ample number. Ah, well, shifting away from me for a time, Mr. Hartline — may I call you Sam? Thank you. Sam, it is quite obvious to any intelligent being that communism — that type of order advocated and practiced by my superiors over those long decades — simply did not work. It was much too repressive. Would you agree?"

"Yes, General, to a point, I would."

"Ah, good. We are of like mind already. Half the battle is won, I believe. Sam, I have some excellent English tea; would you care for more? Good!" He ordered more tea sent in. "You see, Sam, I was one of those who led the rebellion — for want of a better word — against the Politburo back in '88. I was a colonel then, but with quite a following." A look of anguish mixed with regret passed over his handsome features, quickly disappearing.

"We failed," Georgi said simply. "The world exploded in nuclear and germ warfare. You know all that — ancient history. We shan't fail again. Not if you agree to help me instead of fighting me."

Hartline had no intention of fighting the Russian. But he saw no point in revealing his hole card just yet. "I'm still here, General, listening." Hartline sipped his hot tea. It was very good tea. The best he'd had in months. "Earle Gray?" he asked.

"But of course. None finer. Before you misinterpret my previous statement, Sam — I am still a communist. I was born a communist, I shall die believing in that ideology. But I lean more to the socialistic aspects of the philosophy, and away from the harshness — more or less — of hard-liners."

Hartline knew the man was lying. But he decided to

26

play the game. "But you do believe in the caste system."

"But of course! And so do you, *nyet?*"

"Da," Hartline replied, his eyes locked to the cold gaze of the Russian. "I speak fluent Russian, General."

"I know," Georgi said.

Hartline began musing aloud. "Divide the people into classes. At the second level, the doctors and scientists and legal minds and upper-echelon executives. At the third level, the farmers and ranchers and foremen and supervisors, people of that ilk. The fourth level will be the workers. The fifth level, the really menial jobs. Am I close, General?"

"Very. But you left out the top level, Sam."

"Why . . . that's us, General."

"Yes." The Russian smiled. "Go on."

"We need to purge the races. Make the races pure, so to speak. Niggers, spics, Jews, Indians, Orientals — we can dispose of them."

Georgi Striganov laughed, a big booming laugh. "I think, Sam Hartline, we are going to get along very well. Very well, indeed. Oh my, yes."

June, 2001

Ben longed for the day when Cecil would take over the reins of responsibility so Ben could just roam. But for now he was leaving Cecil in charge only temporarily. As Ben made ready to pull out on Sunday, June tenth, he felt better than he had in weeks. He drove a Chevy pickup with four-wheel drive capability if needed, and all the vehicles in the column had PTO winches on the front. Four deuce-and-a-halves carried spare parts, ammo, food and other equipment. Ben had planned very carefully, leaving nothing out: medical supplies, walkie-talkies, bull-horns, clothing and dozens of other small but likely-to-be-necessary items.

Ben had cut his platoon down to forty for mobility purposes, but the forty were, for the most part, all combat vets, and all of them 110 percent loyal to Ben Raines and his desire to rebuild from the ashes.

James Riverson, the ranking NCO in the Rebel army, and a longtime member of Ben's recon team, sent out two of his people to take the far point. They would range several miles in front of the column, always staying in radio contact.

Although everyone was against Ben's leading the column—directly behind the point vehicle—no one dared say anything about it.

Except Lt. Mary Macklin.

"Pardon my impudence, sir," she asked, standing by his pickup truck, driver's side, moments before pulling out. "But are you trying to prove something?"

Ben looked at her, blinked. Tried to place her. Then it came to him.

Back in Tri-States after racing to escape the plague, arriving there in a raging blizzard, Ben had slept a few hours in the motel Ike and his people had prepared for the Rebels from the east, then had walked downstairs for breakfast.

Over bacon and eggs and a huge stack of flapjacks, Ben asked, "How's it looking, Ike?"

"Fifty-eight hundred, Ben."

Ben could not believe it. "What the hell happened to the rest? We had more than ten thousand six months ago."

"They just didn't make it, partner. Word is still pretty sketchy, but from all reports, we lost a full battalion of people coming out of Georgia. We were in contact one day . . . next day, nothing. A couple of companies were ambushed up in Michigan. We lost a full platoon of people in Wisconsin, and we don't know what killed them."

"What do you mean, Ike?"

"Just that, Ben. We don't know what happened. The two people who survived died on the way here without ever regaining consciousness. They were, well, mangled all to hell and gone. I got the pictures if you got the stomach for it."

Ben thought he knew what the pictures would reveal; he had seen something very similar to it on a lonely, windy highway in Illinois.

He said as much.

Ike toyed with his coffee cup. "And?"

Ben shook his head. "We deal with it if or when we see whatever killed those people with our own eyes."

Ike grunted softly. "Probably be best. Keep down the horror stories, I reckon."

The large dining room was silent, only a few of Ben's Rebels from the east up and about. It had been a harrowing and dangerous journey, with nerves stretched tight most of the way.

Ike mentioned that Jerre would like to have her babies as soon as possible. He suggested a chopper.

Ben agreed.

Ike motioned for a uniformed young woman to

29

come to the table. Lt. Mary Macklin. After receiving her instructions, she saluted smartly and left.

Ben smiled. "Getting a little rigid on discipline, aren't you, Ike?"

"That ain't my idea," the ex-SEAL replied glumly. "It's hers. She was regular army 'til about six months ago. I can't get that damned salutin' out of her. Drives me up the wall."

"I beg your pardon, Lieutenant?" Ben shook himself back to the moment.

"I do not mean to be out of line, General, or to overstep any chain of command. But all concerned would feel much better if you were in the middle of the column instead of leading it."

Ben smiled at her. He took a closer look with a man's eyes. Light brown hair, hazel eyes, about five-seven. Nice figure. Erect military bearing.

"Thank you for your frankness, Lieutenant. Noted and appreciated. Your name?"

"Lieutenant Mary Macklin. I was a rigger with the Eighty-second Airborne prior to OCS."

"After that?"

"ASA, sir."

"Well. Lieutenant, if you're so concerned with my well-being, why don't you ride with me and protect me?"

"Is that a joke, sir?"

"Not unless you want to take it as such."

She met his eyes. "Then may I take it as an order, sir?"

This lady was all military, Ben thought. "No. But if

30

you like I can make it an order."

"That won't be necessary, sir. I'll just get my gear and put it in the bed of your truck."

Ben watched her walk away, his eyes on her reflection in the side mirror. Might be an interesting trip in more ways than one, he thought.

Hard eyes, Mary thought as she walked away. She knew, with a woman's awareness, that General Raines was watching her. She tried very hard to walk with a military bearing. She failed miserably.

The column pulled out shortly afterward. They skirted Little Rock and picked up Highway 67, taking that all the way to the northeast corner of Arkansas. They stopped for the night in Piggott, Arkansas, a small town just a few miles from the Missouri line.

The town had been looted, but as in most cases of looting, the looters did not take essentials such as food, clothing and medicine.

"Another reason I have always advocated looters being shot on sight," Ben muttered, driving around the courthouse square.

"Beg pardon, sir?" Mary asked.

"Muttering to myself, Mary. Nothing of importance, I suppose."

"Looters, sir?" she guessed, for she knew how Ben Raines felt about lawbreakers.

"Good guess, Mary. Yes, looters. Two-legged animals."

"And you feel that they should be?"

"Shot on sight."

She stirred beside him and Ben hid a smile, knowing a full-scale debate might be only moments away. He nipped it short.

31

"Hemingway lived here for a time, did you know that, Lieutenant?"

"Ernest Hemingway? Here?"

"Yes." Ben laughed at her expression. But he was thankful that at least one person of her generation had heard of the writer. All was not lost, he supposed. "We'll get the people settled in and I'll try to find the house."

Col. Dan Gray was the next-ranking officer under Ben and Ben gave the Englishman orders to pick a spot to bivouac.

"We'll be in radio contact, Dan," Ben said. He dropped his pickup into gear and pulled out. He smiled as Buck Osgood tore out after them.

Mary looked at his smile. "Do you enjoy worrying people, General?"

Ben glanced at her. The lady was smart as well as pretty. "Is that what I do, Lieutenant? How about if I call you Mary when we're alone?"

She met his brief glance. "All right," she said softly. "Yes, you worry people. And you do it deliberately. Just like right now. You knew damn well Buck would be after you; it's his job."

Ben thought about that and slowed his speed, allowing Buck to catch up. The sergeant was frantically flashing his headlights off and on, signalling Ben to slow down.

"You're right, Mary." She was mildly astonished to hear the admission from his lips. "I'm a loner at heart, and I've been taking care of myself for a good many years. And doing it quite well without a nanny. I've never gotten used to being bird-dogged."

"I've heard so many stories about you, General.

32

How did you get into this . . . this position of authority?"

Ben laughed aloud. "Did you ever hear what John Kennedy said about him being a hero in World War II?"

She blinked. "Was that the president, or what?"

Ben sighed. "How old are you, Mary?"

"Twenty-four."

Ben did some fast math. Odds were good that her parents had not been born when Kennedy was sworn in, back in '61.

"Depending on how one counts it, Mary, JFK was either the thirty-fourth or thirty-fifth president of the United States. He was assassinated in 1963. As to his being a hero, he said, 'They sank my boat.'"

She smiled, then laughed as the humor of it struck her. "Thank you, but that doesn't answer my question."

Ben was thoughtful for a few moments, as he skillfully twisted and turned the wheel, avoiding the many obstacles in the road: abandoned cars and trucks, fallen trees, skeletons of humans and animals, tin cans and garbage containers, and an occasional fresh body.

How to tell her? How to tell anyone? How to tell a stranger that Ben had this dream of a free society, free of crime and bigotry and hatred, with jobs for those who wished to work, and those who didn't could either leave voluntarily or be kicked out.

"I'll tell you someday, Mary," he said. "When you have several days to listen."

Ben drove and drove and finally gave up. "Well," he said, "I can't find the house. Crap. I saw it once, back in the seventies. It was beautiful."

"That's right!" She looked at him, "I almost forgot. You used to be a writer, didn't you?"

"About a hundred years ago," Ben said dryly.

"I'd like to read some of your books."

"I assure you, Mary. I have many copies."

They drove the streets of the small town once more. They could find no one alive. But Ben knew from past experience that was probably not true. In a town this size, so his statisticians had told him—and Ben was still a writer at heart and wanted to know those types of things—from five to eight people would have survived. But they would have become very wary of strangers, especially uniformed, armed strangers.

He told Mary that. She asked, "I wonder how they survive—get along?"

"Many of them won't make it for any length of time. Only the very toughest will stand the test—usually. Of course there is always the exception; but the exceptions find out they'd damn well better get tough or die. The ones who will come out will be those who will not hesitate to shoot first and ask questions later."

"So we have come to that." Her words were softly spoken, just audible over the hiss of the tires against the pavement. "Then we have gone full circle."

"Back to the caves? No, not yet. Not if I have anything to say about it. We're on the right track, Mary, but we still have a very long way to go before we get home free."

"Optimistic, General?"

"Only at times, Mary. Other times I hit new lows."

She looked at his profile in the waning light of evening. She had heard all the talk about his being some sort of god, that he could not be killed, and all that. That shrines had been secretly built in his honor by some of the people who followed him. She wondered if he knew about those places of worship. She decided he did not. Everything within her being wanted to reject any notion of a higher being, for Mary was more agnostic than believer — at least she felt that way most of the time. She had heard about General Raines's sexual escapades and the children he had sired. She wondered if Ben was attempting to repopulate the world single-handedly. That brought a smile to her lips. And an idea to her brain.

"Tell me the joke?" Ben asked, glancing at her Mona Lisa smile.

"I don't think you would appreciate the humor, General."

"Perhaps not, Mary." He pulled up, parking in the center of a street lined with Jeeps and trucks. "Let's see about getting something to eat."

She came to him later that night, after the area was silent, with only the guards maintaining their lonely vigil. He did not seem at all surprised to see her appear at his door.

"Mary," he greeted her, motioning her inside the lamp-lit home. "What's on your mind?"

"Can I level with you, General?"

"Of course."

"I have a boyfriend back in Tri-States. We plan on getting married in a few months."

"My best wishes, Mary." Ben looked at her, a puzzled expression on his face.

"But I've been trying to get pregnant for six

35

months."

"Oh?"

"Jim thinks the bombings back in '88 made him sterile."

"That's certainly possible."

"But I want us to have a child."

The expression on her face and the look in her eyes told Ben everything else he needed to know.

"You sure Jim wouldn't mind?"

"Like me, General, he would be honored."

Ben took her hand. "It's a strange world we live in, Mary."

"You'll make it better, General," came her response.

TWO

It was as if the incident had never occurred between the man and woman. Mary was her usual military self the next morning, and Ben never brought up the subject. It was the first and last time she was to share his bed.

The small contingent of Rebels hit their first armed resistance in southeast Missouri, while they were on state Highway 53, angling northwest toward Poplar Bluff.

"Trouble up ahead, sir," a scout radioed back.

Ben pulled the column up short and walked forward, his Thompson SMG in hand. Mary walked one step behind him, her M-16 at combat arms.

"Ever killed a man, Mary?" Ben asked.

"Yes, sir."

"More than one?"

"Yes, sir."

"Ever cut a throat?"

"No, sir."

"You'll probably get the chance if you hang around

37

me long enough."

"I can hardly wait," her reply was dryly given.

Ben laughed at her. His smile vanished as one of the young scouts hurriedly approached.

"What's the problem?" Ben asked.

"About fifty motorcyclists have blocked the road a half mile ahead, sir. They're all armed."

"Were they hostile to you?"

"Yes, sir. Said if I tried to push through they'd kill me."

"Well, that makes my job easier. What do they want, son?"

"Women, sir. And guns."

Mary tensed beside Ben, her hands tightening on her M-16.

"Tell them to clear the road and get out of the way, or we will forcibly remove the blockade, and them with it."

"Yes, sir." The scout used a bull-horn to relay the message.

"You don't own the goddamn road!" The shout was electronically hurled back to Ben. "We got you out-numbered anyways. Give us your women and guns and you can drive on through."

Ben looked behind him. Colonel Gray was standing in the center of the road, calmly reviewing the situation.

"Colonel Gray?"

"Sir?"

"There is a pile of garbage in the road ahead. Please remove it, if you will."

"Sir."

The Englishman saluted, gave an order, and a team

began readying 81mm mortars.

Colonel Gray put down his range finder. "Nine hundred meters," he called over his shoulder. "Fire for range, adjust, then fire for effect. HE and WP. Go."

The mortars thonked and delivered Ben Raines's reply. The highway ahead exploded as range was found and clicked in. Saddle tanks on the motorcycles exploded as Ben's Rebels opened up with mounted ring-type .50-caliber machine guns, spraying the area.

"Cease firing!" Colonel Gray yelled.

The morning grew hot and still once more. Moaning and screaming from up the road drifted to the men and women of the Rebel contingent. Snipers began firing, stilling many of the cries.

Ben glanced at James Riverson. "Clear it out, James. We don't have time to jack around with prisoners."

APCs rolled forward. After a few moments of automatic weapons' fire, no more moaning was heard. A deuce-and-a-half with a front-mounted scoop rolled forward, lowered the scoop, and unceremoniously cleared a wide path through the smoking, bloody rubble.

Mary was outwardly calm, but her pale face betrayed her inner feelings. "I was told you don't believe in fucking around, General."

Ben smiled. "That depends entirely on the connotation one places on that vulgarity, Mary."

Her mouth closed with a snap.

"Let's roll it!" Ben yelled.

At Poplar Bluff, Missouri, the Rebels found two

dozen or so survivors. They were not in good shape.

"Can you help us?" a man asked. There was a whine to his voice that cut at Ben's nerves.

The group consisted of nine men, fourteen women, and half a dozen young people and babies. They all looked to be in sad shape.

Ben's first emotion was pity — but only for the children, not for the adults. Every good man has his fault, and that was Ben's. He could not work up pity for a grown man that did not know how to survive. It was his flaw, and he knew he possessed it.

"What do you want us to do?" Ben asked, his tone harsher than he intended.

The speaker appeared to be in his early-to-mid-thirties, in reasonably good physical shape. Indeed, most of the men appeared in good physical shape. But they were dirty and stank of filth and body odors.

Don't be too harsh, Ben silently cautioned himself. You don't know what they've been through.

The question seemed to confuse the man. "Why — help us."

"In what way?" Ben asked.

The man backed away several steps. "You're just like all the rest," he said, an accusing tone to his voice. "I — we — thought the government would help. But they haven't. You look familiar. Who are you, mister?"

Ben ignored the question. "There is no government." His words were deliberately harsh. "How long does it take for that to sink into you people? Goddamn it, you've got to help yourselves this go round. The government doesn't exist. It was suspended some months ago, along with the Constitution and the Bill

40

of Rights. It probably will never exist again, not in the way you people remember it. You survived the bombings of '88, what the hell happened to your guts this time around?"

The man began crying, the tears cutting trenches down his dirty cheeks.

They disgusted Ben.

Ben looked around for Colonel Gray. "Dan, we'll bivouac here in the city. Doctor Carlton—" he glanced at a young M.D. — "after these people have bathed this filth off, check them out—all of them. Then see to it they are fed. They all appear not to be able to take care of themselves." The last was said very sarcastically.

"Hey, mister!" a woman with a small baby in her arms yelled to Ben. Anger was evident in her voice. "Just who in the *hell* do you think you are, anyway? And what do *you* know about what *we've* been through these past months? Yeah, we look pretty bad, I know all that. But we've been on the run for two months. A gang of motorcyclists have been killing and raping and kidnapping around here. They're all armed with guns. Then over at Lake Wappapello there's about fifty or sixty people that blew in here from I don't know where. They're murderers and rapists and scum. Mister whoever-you-are, the government collected all the guns some years ago. Where have you been, under a rock? What in the hell are we supposed to fight *with*, you bastard!"

Ben smiled at her outburst. Here was one with some guts. He looked at her without speaking. She would maybe hit five feet—ninety-five pounds to a hundred, if that much. But definitely female. She had more fire in her than all the others combined.

41

Ben walked over to her. She stood her ground and met his gaze without flinching. "What's your name?"

"Gale Roth. And that's G-A-L-E."

Ben chuckled. "I can damn sure see why it's spelled that way. Your husband among these tigers?"

"I don't have a husband. Never been married. You going to make something out of that, too?"

Ben laughed openly as he studied her. Black, angry eyes, very short dark brown hair, a sensuous mouth. And a dirty face. Made her look like a tomboy. From the neck up.

She glared at him. "If you're quite through undressing me, mister—what's your name?"

"Ben Raines."

The woman paled, stepped back, opened her mouth, then closed it without speaking. She appeared to be in mild shock at the mention of his name.

"A speechless Jew," Ben needled her, and from somewhere in the ranks of the Rebels came a laugh. The laugh sounded suspiciously like Leon Lansky's laugh. "I believe I've met a first."

Gale stuck out her chin. "Well . . . fuck you!"

Ben laughed and held out his hands and the baby came to him. Of them all, Gale and the baby appeared to be the cleanest, but neither of them could be called a rose.

"Is the child in good health?" Ben asked.

"As well as could be expected. I'm a nurse, so I know something about health." She was still very defiant. "Are you going to take my baby, Mr. President?"

"Don't be ridiculous, Gale. Of course I am not going to take your baby. And I am not your president."

"Don't be ridiculous," she mimicked him, "of

42

course you are. I haven't heard of anyone calling any special elections to replace you."

Everyone within hearing range could feel the electricity popping back and forth between the man and woman. Especially the man and the woman.

And neither of them could really understand it.

Not yet.

Ben looked around him, meeting the staring eyes. "What the hell is everyone looking at? You have your jobs — get moving!"

"Right-o, General," Colonel Gray said with a smile. "All right, lads and lassies, get cracking, now. Step lively. You civilians over there." He pointed.

Ben turned back to Gale. The baby reached for the woman and Ben let him slip into more familiar arms. "Mrs. Roth . . ."

"Ms.," she quickly corrected.

"I never would have guessed," Ben muttered, *"Ms.* Roth, I will not apologize for coming down hard on men who will not fight."

"They don't have any guns!"

"Then they should have killed those who did have access to guns and then fought."

"Now how in the hell does one go about that?" Out came the chin.

"One goes about that, Ms. Roth, by the use of booby traps, Molotov cocktails, dynamite, punji pits, C-4, rocks, clubs, bottles, chains, wire, ambushes. . . ."

*"Aw*right *aw*ready — enough!"

"But first one must possess enough guts to do the deed with any or all of the aforementioned articles. And where are you from? *Aw*right *aw*ready?"

43

"I was born in New York City. Moved to St. Louis with my parents when I was thirteen. I'm twenty-nine years old and this isn't my kid. He belonged to someone else."

"Is Gale your real name?"

She smiled. She was very pretty. Reminded Ben of an NBC correspondent he used to enjoy watching. Rebecca something-or-another. He couldn't remember her last name.

"Of course not. It's a nickname."

"Well?"

"Well, what?"

"What is your real name?"

"Why do you want to know?"

"Oh, forget it. Leave it Gale. It certainly fits. You said the baby *belonged* to someone else?"

"She's dead." Gale did not elaborate.

Ben let it slide. "How'd you get hooked up with this bunch of losers?"

Out came the chin. She glared at him for a few seconds. "Mr. President, sir, General, whatever in the hell you're called, has it ever occurred to you that not everyone in this world is as tough as you?"

"Ms. Roth, there are varying degrees of toughness. There used to be a football player, a giant of a man called Gorilla Jankowski. Gorilla could have, on any given day, without working up a sweat, broken me in about thirty-seven different and separate pieces, and then kicked my head the length of a football field — providing he could catch me. That's one degree of toughness. But put us both on a jet on a HALO/ SCUBA mission, where we had to drop in from about thirty-five thousand feet, free-falling down to seven hundred before our 'chutes opened in order to avoid radar, use tanks and wet suits to swim ashore from about three or four miles out, crawl ashore on an unfriendly beach, slit a few throats, blow up a bridge or two, then successfully complete a silent op—a body snatch . . . all without being detected by the enemy. That is another degree of toughness. Do you understand the parallels I'm drawing?"

"He was trained to do one thing, you were trained to another."

"Right on target, Ms. Roth."

"But those men I was—am—traveling with, they weren't trained to do . . ." She paused, a slight smile touching her lips. "Ben Raines—sure. You wrote a book one time—one of your best, if not the best, I think—called *When the Last Hero Is Gone*. In it you advocated compulsory military training, for everyone, male and female, starting immediately upon completion of high school, and you would have made a high school education mandatory. The length of service would have lasted three years. After the military, the government would then finance a four-year college plan, picking up the tab for all expenses for those who went into math, science or English, and stayed with teaching for a minimum of ten years. You maintained that in ten years the nation would no longer have a shortage of those teachers. I did a book report on that novel in the tenth grade. I got a C on it because the teacher didn't like the other books you wrote."

"My apologies. Doctor Carlton is motioning for you to come over to that aid station just set up. He'll check you out and also the baby. I'll see you later."

Gale seemed hesitant to leave. Something about the man exuded confidence and safety. "Those . . . animals from up at the lake sent word to us that they might be back tomorrow to . . . get the women. What are you going to do if that happens?"

"You mentioned a gang of motorcyclists that had been bothering you?"

"Yeah."

"We killed them all about ten o'clock this morning. Just west of the St. Francis River. Does that answer your question?"

She blinked. She had very pretty eyes now that the anger had vanished. Eyes that looked as though they could dance with mischief. "I guess you are as tough as people say."

"I guess so, Ms. Roth."

He stood and watched as she walked away. She looked exhausted. Colonel Gray walked up.

"What are we going to do with them, General?"

Ben shook his head. "I can't leave them to be killed, Dan. We could arm them, but without proper training, they would still get killed. Those civilian men aren't exactly man-hunters."

"I will certainly agree with that, General."

"Send out a team to round up some vehicles. We'll outfit them and take them with us."

Dan smiled. "Yes, sir."

Ben looked at the Englishman. He could not understand the smile. "What are you smiling about, Dan?"

"Nothing," the colonel said innocently. "Nothing at all, General." He walked away, chuckling softly.

"Crazy Englishman," Ben muttered.

Had he but noticed, everyone in his command was

grinning.

Eight more ships from Iceland had put ashore personnel and equipment: two ships every four days. The IPF troops based on American soil now numbered ten thousand, and they had spread out into Wisconsin from northern Minnesota.

The IPF teams used no force in dealing with the survivors they found. They left food, clothing and medical supplies; they worked with the people in repairing equipment and restoring such services as electricity and running water. The doctors with the IPF treated the sick and consoled the elderly and despondent. They promised that conditions would soon get better. They promised they would restore order and a government. They promised they would have jobs for everyone. They promised proper medical treatment and better living conditions. If one had been a farmer before the holocaust, then you could again be a farmer; if you had been a mechanic or a carpenter or a teacher or whatever, that job would soon be opening for you. They promised a lot. They did it all with a smile and a gentle pat on the arm. They were such nice people. So considerate. They never fussed or snapped or became angry or upset. They never used force.

They didn't have to.

Yet.

Lenin would have been so proud.

Ben stood on the outskirts of Poplar Bluff and stared out into the darkness, his thoughts busy. Gale had told him her group was not the only group of survivors in the small city. She said there were others, but their numbers were smaller, and they were much more elusive. And they were well-armed. She didn't know where they got the weapons.

Ben didn't have the heart to tell her guns were easy to find.

Being a curious sort, Ben had prowled through what remained of the local library, his heart sore at the sight of the books ripped and rotting and torn and gnawed by rats and mice. He had located a World Almanac — circa 1987 — and looked up Poplar Bluff, Missouri. Population 17,139.

Gale had told him that maybe — maybe — there were 150 people left in the small city. There had been more, but about 50 had died during the winter. Mostly old people, she said.

"The nation's elderly have been getting crapped on for years, Gale," he said. "Right up to and including 1988." He spat on the littered sidewalk. "A goddamned criminal gets better treatment and has more of his rights protected than the nation's elderly."

She had looked at him in the fading June sunlight and replied, "Maybe you're not so tough after all, Ben Raines."

He had not replied. But his thoughts had been flung back to the spring of '89, when he had been traveling with a very idealistic young lady by the name of April. He had found her in Florida and gotten rid of her in Macon, Georgia. He had been relieved to see her go. But before they had parted company, never to see each other again — and Ben did wonder, occasionally, what had happened to April — they had happened upon a small gathering of elderly.

"As to our troubles, Mr. Raines," Ms. Nola Browning, an elderly schoolteacher had told him, "it seems we have a gang of hoodlums and roughnecks roaming the countryside, preying on the elderly—those who survived God's will, that is."

"They've been here?" Ben questioned. "Bothering you people?"

Ms. Browning, who had been an English teacher for fifty-five years, then told Ben and April that yes, the hoodlums had indeed been bothering the elderly. They had raped and tortured some of the members of the small group. And they were coming back to perform some, well, perverted acts on the person of one Mrs. Carson, a very attractive woman of sixty-five. There were fifteen hoodlums, and only one Ben Raines. So what could he hope to do?

Ben smiled, and Ms. Browning noted that his smile was that of a man-eating tiger who had just that moment spotted dinner.

"Oh, I imagine I can think of something suitable for them, Ms. Browning."

Ben had killed all but two of the punks; the elderly had hanged them.

Ben wondered how long the old people had survived after he left them.

Ben pulled his thoughts to the present as he continued to stare into the darkness. The darkness seemed void of any life. He wondered about the people left

49

alive, not just in Poplar Bluff but around the nation. How many had made it? He did some fast math. Was a half million shooting too high? Only a few percentage points of the population. And was it the responsibility of Ben Raines to take every damned one of them under his wing like helpless chicks to raise?

Resolution stiffened within him. No, it was not. Then compassion touched him. If he—or someone like him—did not do it, where was civilization heading?

Back to the caves? Probably. Already, Ben knew, the nation was well into a generation of young men and women whose education was spotty, at best.

Ben Raines could not attempt to educate the entire nation. But he could start with his own people. If time would allow it.

And he had doubts about that.

He sighed, the soft expelling of breath lost in the whispering of the night wind. Again, his thoughts drifted back in time, bringing a smile to his lips.

All he wanted to do was travel the nation after the bombings, as a writer, from coast to coast, border to border, chronicling the events, talking to the people, putting their opinions and his views down on paper, in the hopes that someone, sometime in the future, would take the time to read it.

Instead, he had found himself as the leader of a people. And he had not wanted the responsibility.

But maybe it was his responsibility. Perhaps that was his purpose in life. But as he thought that, the ageless question rose silent in his mind, as it had done so many times: Why me?

As usual, he could find no answer.

Ben hefted the old Thompson, shifting the weapon from right hand to left. The submachine gun, modeled after the old 1921 Thompson with several improvements added over the years had been called the Chicago Piano in its heyday. It was as closely identified with Ben as the FBI had been with J. Edgar Hoover. Ben did not know, could not have known, that the Thompson was held in almost as much awe as the man who carried it, that youngsters believed the weapon held some special power. There was not a child in the entire Rebel-controlled areas who would have touched the weapon.

And quite a few adults felt the same way.

Ben Raines did not look his true age, nor did he feel it — except in memory. Discounting the light touch of gray in his hair, Ben looked years younger than he was. And he was in excellent physical shape, just as randy and horny as any young buck.

He fought back a smile in the gloom of night. Perhaps his true mission in life was to procreate the earth.

He turned at the sound of footsteps behind him. Doctor Carlton.

"I've checked out the survivors here as best I could, General," the young M.D. informed him. "They're scared and suffer from lack of confidence — life's beaten them down pretty badly — but surprisingly, their physical condition is good."

"Do they know how they beat the plague?"

"No. But Ms. Roth took the same type of medicines we took." He laughed softly. "That, General, is one feisty lady."

"I've noticed. Thank you, Wes. Oh, by the way, do you know if the teams found suitable transportation for the survivors?"

"Yes, sir. And they are eager to join us." He hesitated for a moment. "General, the people are scared, sir. Even after the bombings of '88, we still had some form of government, some hope, if you will. Now they have no government, nothing to look forward to, no one to tell them what to do, and they don't know what to do."

"The de-balling of America," Ben muttered under his breath, the words tossed unheard by the breeze.

"Beg pardon, sir?"

"The government got what it wanted," Ben told him. "The goddamn liberals and the goddamned lawyers and the goddamned courts succeeded in de-balling the American people."

"That's a sexist remark if I ever heard one." The voice came out of the darkness.

Neither man had to turn around; they both knew who it was. Ben said, "You wander around out here in the dark, Ms. Roth, around my people, and you're very likely to get your butt shot off."

"The de-balling of the American people, Mr. President?"

"Ms. Roth," Ben said patiently, "I am not your president."

"For a fact. I damn sure didn't vote for you," she told him.

"I don't recall *anybody* voting for me, Ms. Roth."

"Do you always carry that gangster's gun around with you, Mr. President?"

Ben kept his patience. He sighed heavily. "I've found it to be the wisest thing to do, Ms. Roth."

Dr. Wes Carlton found his cue. "I think I'll say

goodnight," he said. He quickly disappeared into the darkness.

"Coward," Ben muttered to his fast-vanishing back.

"What if I don't want to accompany you and your Rebels, Mr. President?" Gale asked. She stepped closer to Ben. A very slight figure in the dark.

"Then you may stay here."

"You'll leave troops behind to protect me?"

"Hell no!"

She stamped a foot. "Mr. President, I think you are—"

Ben cut her off. It would turn out to be one of the very few times he would be able to do that. "Goodnight, Ms. Roth. Go to bed, Ms. Roth. We pull out at 0700, Ms. Roth."

"What the hell is oh-seven hundred, Mr. President?"

"Seven o'clock in the morning, Ms. Roth."

"Where are we going?"

"Why don't you just let it be a surprise?"

"I don't like surprises."

Ben turned to walk away. "Give the old college try, Ms. Roth. Boola-boola, and all that."

Ben did not see her tongue sticking out at him or the perfectly horrible-looking face that she made next. Neither did he see her toss the bird at him.

Then she smiled gently.

THREE

The convoy took Highway 60 out of Poplar Bluff, staying with it until they came to state Highway 21 angling off to the west. Ben wanted to stay with the lesser traveled roads, feeling more survivors would be found in the less-traveled areas. He was right.

As they slowly traveled through the small towns of rural Missouri, slowly edging northward, the Rebels found survivors: ten in Ellington, a half dozen in Reynolds, twelve in Bunker, four in Stone Hill.

"Do you know of more who stayed alive around here?" Ben asked a middle-aged man outside Stone Hill. The man had been hoeing in his large garden. He wore a .45-caliber pistol around his waist, and had picked up a bolt action .30-06 upon first sighting the small convoy. He looked as though he was perfectly able and willing to use either weapon.

"A few more," he replied, relaxing when he learned who he was speaking with. "We're trying to gather up as many as possible and rebuild. That is, providin' the IPF leaves us alone."

"The what?" Ben asked.

"Call themselves the IPF. International Peace Force. They talk funny, with kind of an accent. Can't rightly place it. You ask me, they're just too damned nice. Ain't nobody that nice to a perfect stranger 'less they want something in return, or they're tryin' to hide something."

Ben kept his smile a secret. He thought: Leave it to a farmer. Rural folks could spot a ringer a mile off.

"They say where they were from?"

"Nope." The man shook his head. "And I asked them flat out." He spat on the ground. "Personally, I think they're communists."

"Why do you say that?"

" 'Cause you can ask the same damn question to every damn one of them. The answer don't never vary. It's down pat—like they've been drilled over and over. A few folks around here have taken a shine to them." Again he spat on the ground. "Personally, I don't like them worth a shit!"

"Are they armed?"

"I'll say they are. Well-armed." He described the weapons.

"AKs," Colonel Gray spoke. "Or AKM-74s. Maybe the AKSs. Soviet bloc weapons."

"Did they give you any names?" Ben asked.

"Yep. But first names only. No last names. And I got the feelin' they was lyin' about the first names. I don't like them people."

A sergeant standing nearby mused aloud. "How in the hell did they manage to keep it a secret for so many years?"

"By careful planning," Ben told him.

55

"Well," the civilian said, "you probably right about that, Mr. Raines. But I'll tell you this—all of you. We're organizing around here. So far, it's comin' along slow, but it's comin'. We've got about a hundred people so far, and we're all reasonably well-armed and know how to use the weapons—and will use them. I've defended this place several times since the rats and fleas come last year." He pointed to a graveyard in back of the house. "Them's the ones who come to steal and rape and kill. They didn't make it but just that far. Anyways, it's them damn young people up to Rolla that's playin' footsie with the foreigners."

"Young people?" Ben quizzed.

"Bunch of them have gathered up there at the old college. My cousin over to Dillard says his boy went to one of the lectures given by the IPF, come back home sayin' it was communistic. The workers this and the workers that—free this and free that. I'll be goddamned if I'll see this nation go back to that kind of crap; fucking unions damn near ruined us back in the sixties and seventies. Quality workmanship was hard to find back then. Time the eighties rolled around, if it was made in Japan, buy it. If it was made in America, odds were good it wasn't worth a shit." He looked hard at Ben. "You still the president, Mr. Raines?"

"No," Ben said. "No, I'm not."

"Shame. You might have been the one to pull us all back together. I think you might have been the only one able to do it. You're a hard man, but you're a fair one. But now . . ." He shook his head.

"But now what, sir?"

"Come on, Mr. Raines—we've had it. Oh, *I'm* not giving up. Don't you ever think that. But I've been

56

doin' some arithmetic. Say, on the average, and this might be shooting high or low, ten percent of the American people made it out alive from the rats and fleas and plague. What does that leave us, Mr. Raines? A half million folks? A million? Most of them scattered all to hell and gone in little groups of twenty and thirty. No organization, no goals, no plans except survival of the fittest. No nothing. And the young folks!" He laughed bitterly. "Hell, you know how a kid's mind works: They're easy prey for anyone with a slick line, holding out a carrot, preaching love and peace and an easy time of it. We're old enough, Mr. Raines, you and me, to remember the peace and love movement back in the sixties. The hippies and the flippies and the Yippies. No, sir. If the IPF people can reach our young, us older folks can bend down, put our heads between our legs, and kiss our asses goodbye."

"I've got some three thousand fighting men and women who just might have something to say about that, sir," Ben told the man.

"I don't care if you've got thirty thousand," the man stated flatly. "If a time has come, it's come. Mr. Raines, you ever seen a young person — any young person of any generation — who would rather work than play? I haven't, and neither have you. That's why they're young folks; they have yet to learn the work ethic." He tapped the side of his head. "The IPF people, now, they're smart — give them credit for that. I think they're evil, but they're smart. They're sending kids into the countryside — nineteen, twenty years old, good-lookin' young people. The young people are all blue-eyed and blond, and they're pulling in our young folks faster than eggs through a hen."

Something ancient and evil stirred within Ben. That remark about blond and blue-eyed triggered something . . . a memory recall. But he couldn't pin it down. It would come to him.

The man was saying, "Now you on the other hand, Mr. Raines, you're the picture of toughness, discipline, hard work — a fighting man. Many of the young people — not all of them, but many — won't be able to relate to you, sir. They've had enough of war and disaster. And if these IPF people can convince them you stand for war and they represent peace, we've had it.

"Now, your people know what you're doing is right; I know it and most people my age know it. But you're going to have one hell of a time convincing a lot of the young people."

Earthy wisdom, Ben thought. Plain, old-fashioned common sense. Why in God's name did the American people ever turn their backs on this type of thinking?

"Are you suggesting I don't even try to talk with them?" Ben asked.

"Oh, no. You can try. But I recall tryin' to talk to my youngest boy back in '87. Like tryin' to talk to a fence post. His mind was made up, and there wasn't nothing I could say or do to change it. He pulled out one morning to see the world. I guess he seen it, 'cause I damn sure never saw him again."

Caught up in the hell of global warfare, Ben mused. "Anything else you can tell us about these people from the IPF?"

"Not a whole hell of a lot more to tell. I heard one of them talk about Iceland, wonderin' how things was goin' back home. But if these folks is originally from Iceland, I'm a Baptist preacher." He smiled. "And I've

58

been a Methodist all my life. Their leader is a man calls himself George. But I heard some of his people call him General Strogonoff. That's not the right way to pronounce it. Something like that, though."

"How do they conduct themselves?"

"They're well-trained and polite. But I get the feeling they'd as soon kill a man as look at him. And the few black people left around here walk real light around them, as if they can sense something nobody else can."

The memory recall leaped strong into Ben's brain: Hitler. The master race. He kept that to himself.

Ben thanked him and the man returned to hoeing in his garden. Ben turned to Colonel Gray. "Dan, get Judy Stratmann and Roy Jaydot. Have them dress in jeans and tennis shoes—like the young people. Get them duffle bags or knapsacks and tell them to look trail-worn. We'll pull back and bivouac in Greeley, keep our heads down. Tell Judy and Roy to find out what's going on up at Rolla. We'll sit back and wait."

The Englishman saluted and left.

"James," Ben waved to Riverson. The six-foot-six ex-truckdriver walked over. "When we get to Greeley and settled in, pass the word for a low-alert status. These IPF people are sure to have patrols out—if they're smart. We don't want to be spotted."

James nodded and called the four squad leaders together.

Lieutenant Macklin came to Ben's side. "The International Peace Force, General? What in the world do they represent?"

"I . . . I'm not sure, Mary. But I think it's one hell of a threat to whatever future this country has left it."

Mary shivered, although the day was quite warm.

The young man was fair-skinned, blue-eyed and well-built. The blue in his eyes was of the piercing type, cold. Almost all the young ladies gathered at the long-abandoned branch of the University of Missouri at Rolla thought him handsome.

Judy Stratmann thought his smooth line just a bit too oily and well-rehearsed. He reminded her of an old movie about Southern Californian used car salesmen. Those old, old clips she'd seen of that guy named Johnny Carson.

Roy Jaydot thought that if all the members of the IPF were as smooth-talking and good-looking as this dude, the country was in trouble.

And both Judy and Roy had immediately noticed one thing: There was no blacks, Indians, Orientals, Jews or any other minority on the old campus.

Roy was a Ute Indian and Judy was half Jewish. It made them feel just a bit uncomfortable.

And the young ladies with Mike—Mikael, Roy felt would be the correct way to spell his name—they were all just as pretty as Mike was handsome.

On the second day of their roles as wandering young people, one of the young ladies with the IPF zeroed in on Roy.

"Hi," she said, walking up to where Roy was sitting on the grass. "My name is Katrina."

Roy looked up at her. Very pretty. About five-five, blue eyes, blond hair, fair-skinned. Very well endowed. No makeup. He wondered if she spelled her name with a C or a K? "Roy," he said, getting to his

60

feet.

"How do you like it so far?" Katrina asked.

Roy returned her smile. The opening was just too good to let slide by. "I don't know," he said, "yet."

She looked puzzled for a moment, then the double meaning came to her. She smiled, but the smile did not quite touch her eyes. They remained as cold as the land she reportedly was from. "Yes," she said, "I see. A joke. That's funny." She laughed.

Roy thought the laughter sounded very false. "I'm sorry if I offended you."

"You didn't," she was quick to reply. "A society without humor would be very drab indeed. Tell me, Roy, what are you going to report to General Raines?"

Roy felt the first mild clutches of panic grab at his guts. He kept his expression bland, but his face felt hot and he knew he was flushed. He thanked the gods for his dark complexion.

"Don't try to deny it, Roy." She stood calm and self-assured. "You and Judy were not on the campus six hours before we discovered you both were not what you pretended to be."

Roy decided to level with her. There was something about the young woman. He kept picking up strange vibes that suggested—he hoped—she was not really happy with her role in the IPF.

"Very well, Katrina. I will report to General Raines that you and the others in your party are here spreading communist dogma."

She cocked her head to one side and looked at him. "Dogma. A good word. I like it. I shall retain that word for usage. Aren't you in the least interested in how we discovered your secret?"

61

Roy shrugged. He wondered if he was going to have to shoot his way out of this bind. He had a 9mm submachine in his kit, and could feel the weight of the .38 pressing against the skin of his belly. He wondered where Judy was.

"I noticed the minute we arrived we didn't exactly fit in with the crowd."

"How?" she asked politely.

"Other than the fact I'm Indian and Judy is Jewish, I think we are too well-fed, too healthy, and that we walk with a military bearing, perhaps. Is that good enough for you?"

"Yes. That is correct. That is totally accurate. Thank you."

She sounded like a computer. "Are you a clone, or something?" Roy asked her.

She cocked her head to the other side. Roy felt something soft touch his heart. Oh boy, he thought. Feelings of gentleness for a goddamned Russian, he berated himself. Roy, you're coming unwrapped. But she sure was pretty.

"Clone? I do not understand that. What is a clone?"

"Your speech is perfect. Your dress is perfect. Your posture is perfect. Your hair is perfect. Are you real?"

This time the smile touched her eyes. "Would you like to touch me to see for yourself?"

Roy smiled, mischief in his eyes. If, the young man thought, I'm to be hanged anyway, I might as well make the best of a bad situation. He reached out and cupped a soft breast.

Katrina did not pull away. But her eyes darkened a bit.

"I guess you are real," Roy said, removing his hand

62

reluctantly.

Katrina licked her lips. "Why . . . what was the purpose of touching me there?"

"Because I wanted to touch you there."

She looked confused for a moment. "In your society, does one always do what one wishes to?"

"No, of course not. What I just did was wrong. It would be considered very rude and I'd probably get slapped for doing it."

That only seemed to confuse her more. "Why, I mean, it felt . . . nice."

Now Roy was confused. "You're, ah, you've never been touched, I mean, like that before?"

She shook her head. "Oh no! Any type of . . . sexual touching is not permitted before the committee chooses a marriage partner."

"What? I mean, Katrina, are you supposed to be telling me all this?"

"That is correct. I am not."

"Then why are you telling me?"

Again she shook her head. Her eyes, once so cold, now seemed troubled. "I . . . don't know why. You're . . . different, I think."

Roy had been correct: The girl was not happy with her life. "How old are you, Katrina?"

"I believe I have seventeen years of age."

She believes? Jailbait, Roy thought. But if we have no nation, then we have no laws. And if we have no laws . . . He shook that thought away.

"What do you mean, Katrina, that bit about a marriage partner being chosen? I never heard of such a thing."

"How many years do you have, Roy?"

"I'm twenty-three. Don't you want to answer my question?"

She hesitated, cut her eyes toward a group of people gathered a few hundred meters away, then took his arm. Her touch was warm to his skin. "Let's walk around some, Roy."

They walked the weed-filled campus, heading away from the crowd.

Katrina said, "I was chosen to confront you with the news of your discovery. Your deception. I was instructed to let you run if that was to be your choice of action."

"The IPF would have killed me?"

"No. I do not believe so. That is not supposed to be our mission. But with Mike one never knows. There are members of the IPF surrounding this institution. They would have stopped you."

"Judy?"

"The Jewess? She would have been taken alive. She would probably have been . . . would have become one of the pleasure women."

"Beg pardon?"

"Male/female contact in any sexual manner is strictly forbidden in our society. To preserve the races. But males over the age of twenty-one are allowed to satisfy themselves with selected women who have been altered."

Roy looked at her, not understanding any of this.

"Altered women cannot bear offspring," she explained matter-of-factly.

"I see. I think. Let me see if I can put the rest of this . . . story together, Katrina. You people—your leaders—practice selective breeding among humans?"

"That . . . is one way of putting it, yes. We—they—are attempting to purify the races."

"Blond hair, blue eyes, fair skin?"

"Yes. Most of us."

Something yanked gently at Roy's mind. Something he had read or heard or seen about some other person or group, a long time ago, who had strived for the same thing. He couldn't bring the person or group to mind. He thought it had something to do with Europe. Long time back. Before his parents were even born.

"There are no people of color in your society?" he asked.

She looked at him as though he had asked a very stupid question. "No. That is why we chose Iceland. Theirs is practically a pure race."

Germany! The word leaped into his consciousness. It had something to do with Germany. And some guy with a funny name. But history had never been one of Roy's favorite subjects, and like so many others his age, his education was erratic at best.

"What will you—your people—do with the different races here in America, Katrina?"

She shrugged. "Over a period of time, we shall breed all colors out. That will take many generations, but our leaders believe it can be done. Our learned people have said so."

Hitler. Roy found the man's name. More flooded into the light of consciousness. The Gestapo, the SS. Concentration camps. Extermination. Gas chambers. The horror he had seen in old movies. He looked at Katrina. He just could not believe she could do such things to another human being.

65

But he also knew that looks could be very deceiving.

Katrina said, "Our people have taught us that people of color are inferior to us. From what I have seen — or have been allowed to see — I tend to believe it." She seemed eager to talk and Roy wondered if he was being set up for a fall. For some reason, he didn't believe so.

"People can't help what color they're born with, Katrina."

"That is certainly true, at this time. But we can change all that, our leaders say. And when we do, the world will be a better place to live."

"Katrina."

"Most call me Kat. That's with a K."

"All right, Kat. Why are you telling me all this?"

They had come to a small wooded area, just off campus. They sat down on a bench by a broken walkway.

Kat was deep in thought and silence for a few moments. Roy did not attempt to break into her reverie.

"What do you know about Iceland, Roy?"

"Very little."

"Icelanders are — were — great readers. They loved literature. When I was younger, I found a huge wooden box of books in the basement of the home where I lived."

"With your parents?"

"No. I don't even know who my parents are. I don't know whether I was born in Russia or Iceland. I am just *here*. That is all many of us were told. That is the way. Parents are not important after the birthing. Children are kept in special places called communes until they are six years of age. During that time they are taught, beginning at an early age. After intelligence is tested and determined, the child is placed in a home-setting appropriate to the intelligence of child and male and female sponsor. The environment is tightly controlled. One is trained to do one thing and that is what that person will do. That, forever.

"But I was talking about books. I never knew there were so many different books. Our reading is selected for us—we have no choice in the matter. But these books . . . oh my, they were wonderful. They were about everything. Life and love and mystery and adventure and romance and, oh, just about everything!

"I had never seen anything like it, and I knew because I had never seen them before that the books were forbidden. I said nothing about them, for in our society you never know who will report you to the committee for some infraction of the rules."

"The committee?"

"Each street in all cities have committee persons living on it. One or two people. No one ever knows exactly how many. You don't have them?"

"No!" Roy was both horrified and fascinated.

"Then how do you keep order?"

"By rules, Kat. We all know the rules and we obey them."

"But what happens if you don't obey the rules?"

"If you get caught you get punished."

"*If* you get caught?"

"That's right."

"That seems a rather lax way of doing things."

"Freedom requires some degree of looseness, Kat."

"You are free?"

"Oh yes."

"You can do whatever you like?"

"Within reason."

"Who sets the reason?"

"Common sense."

"That must be interesting. Anyway, I found about a dozen books—paperbacks—by a writer named Ben Raines."

Roy smiled.

"Did I say something amusing?"

"No, Kat. Go on."

She looked at him strangely. "This writer, of the same name as your general, he wrote of many things, of monsters and werewolves and fighting men—the only true heroes—and love and honor and, oh, everything! One person did all that. That is not permitted in our society."

"I don't understand, Kat."

"One person is designated to write of one specific subject, be it history, philosophy, whatever. He will devote his life to that subject matter and nothing else."

"Kat, that sounds awfully boring to me."

She sighed. "I . . . feel the same way, Roy."

"You're not happy with your life, are you, Kat?"

"Happy is unimportant. It is the state that matters."

"But you don't believe that anymore, do you, Kat?"

She put her head on his shoulder and began to weep. Roy didn't know what to do.

FOUR

"They should have been back by now," Ben said to Colonel Gray. "You told them to return in two days, right, Dan?"

"Affirmative, General. And not to take any chances. They should have been back by last night."

"Mount up," Ben said. "We'll just leave the civilians outside the campus and just roll right in—face these people. That might be the one way to make the kids come to their senses."

"And it might backfire, General."

"There is that to consider, too, Dan. But I'm not going to toss Judy and Roy to the wolves without a fight. Or to the bears, as the case may be. Just to be on the safe side, Dan, when we get to the outskirts of the campus, you take a team and infiltrate the buildings, give me a backup."

"Will do, General."

They were on the outskirts of Rolla two hours later, with Ben trying to convince the new members it would be in their best interest to stay clear of the college area. None of them bought his plan, especially Gale. She puffed up, stuck out her chin and marched up to Ben.

Ben braced for a confrontation.

"Mr. President, General — whatever. Are you trying to dump us?"

"Ms. Roth," Ben said patiently. "I have a great many things on my mind right now, and you are not making any of them any easier to resolve with your stupid goddamn questions."

"I only asked one."

Ben looked toward the sky as if seeking some advice from a higher power.

Gale shifted the kid from left to right hip. Ben still didn't know the kid's name. Woman and baby glared at him.

It must be contagious, Ben thought.

"Ms. Roth, I have absolutely no intention of leaving anyone behind. But if matters deteriorate to the point where fast, violent action is the only way left us, I do not want a bunch of helpless civilians mucking about, getting in the way, hollering and bawling and being what they are: useless in any type of fire-fight. Now, Ms. Roth, is that perfectly clear?"

"It sure is. We're going with you." She turned to leave.

"Your ass, baby," Ben said.

Gale spun around, off balance with the child perched on one hip. She almost fell. Ben caught her.

She jerked away from his hands and said, "Don't call me baby!"

"OK, honey."

She glared at him then walked off, muttering about

sexism still prevailing among men who should know better. But, she concluded, just loud enough for Ben to hear, anyone who wrote shtup books for a living couldn't be anything but a sexist. And a male chauvinist pig, too. And other things that a lady should never even think, much less mention aloud. In public.

Ben laughed at her. "Are you any relation to Gloria Steinem?"

"I wish," she called over her shoulder. "Were you any relation to Hilton Logan?"

"Bite your tongue!"

Ben grinned, thinking: Things sure had gotten livelier since she joined the parade.

Over the loud and sometimes heated protests of his people, Ben went into the campus alone, ordering his Rebels to dismount and prepare for a fire-fight, but hoping it would not come to that. Yet. Colonel Gray had his orders and, with a carefully selected team, quietly set about carrying them out.

Ben walked slowly up the weed-grown and cracked drive of the long-deserted college, toward a group of young men and women gathered in front of a building. They fell silent at his approach.

"President Raines," someone muttered.

"Aw, come on. No way," another young person said.

"Yeah, ain't no way *he'd* be here."

"That's General Raines," a young woman said, her eyes on the tall figure walking toward them. "Believe it."

"Wonder what he wants with us?"

Some of the young people began backing away, to

71

the left and right. Ben's reputation of shooting first and asking questions later had preceded him.

"President-General Raines," a voice called from the steps of the building. "What an honor to have you join us. My name is Mike. What can I, or we, do for you?"

Ben looked at the young man. Tall and blond and well-built and blue-eyed. His eyes picked out many more like Mike. They looked as though they could have been brothers and sisters.

"Just looking for a couple of young friends of mine," Ben told him, his voice carrying over the now-silent crowd. The butt of the Thompson rested on his right hip. A thirty-round clip was stuck in its belly, another thirty-round clip taped to that, for fast reloading. "Judy Stratmann and Roy Jaydot. Perhaps you've seen them?"

Mikael smiled. He had been well-trained, and was highly intelligent. He felt he could probably convince the general he had not seen either. But what he wasn't sure of was how many troops the general had backing him up. And any convincing would have to be done privately; to lie now—openly—in front of the American young people would destroy everything he had so carefully constructed over the past two weeks.

"Yes, of course, I've seen them. They are here now, studying and learning."

"Well, then," Ben said with a smile. "You won't mind if I speak to them, will you?"

Mikael's smile had not wavered. "Of course not." He turned to a young lady and spoke quietly. He swung his gaze back to Ben as the young IPF member walked away. "They will be along presently, General."

"Fine. Don't let me interrupt your lecture. You must be quite a speaker to hold the attention of so many young people. My speeches used to bore a lot of them."

Small laughter among the crowd.

Without losing his smile, which, to Ben's way of thinking, was a cross between a smirk and being downright smart-assed, the young man said, "Perhaps, sir, with all due respect, you did not speak to them on the right topic?"

"That might well be true, young man," Ben said sagely. "But then, perhaps it was because I didn't tell them everything they wanted to hear."

Some of the young people looked at one another, shaking their heads in agreement with Ben. Their accord did not go unnoticed by Mikael. I will lose some of them, he thought. Perhaps ten or fifteen percent. But no matter. The majority will still be with me.

Ben's mind was one jump ahead of the young Russian. He said, "We're going to be camped just down the highway. Be there for a time. Perhaps Mikael would agree to debate me sometime? Then we could all have a question and answer session. That might not only be fun, but interesting and informative."

The bastard! Mikael silently raged. He would have to contact Base One concerning this unexpected development. "Perhaps," he said, his voice losing some of its confidence. "I will let you know tomorrow."

"Why not now?" Ben challenged. "Or do you have to first speak with your superiors to get their permission? Isn't that the case—*tovarich?*"

Mikael knew his face was suddenly flushed. He fought to control his temper and struggled to keep from balling his hands into fists of anger.

Before Mikael could retort, a young woman in the crowd stood up and faced him. "What did General Raines mean, Mikael? What does *tovarich* mean?"

Mikael's eyes were decidedly mean as he faced the questioner.

Ben said, "It means comrade, young lady. Your nice, friendly Mikael is a Russian."

The young woman's face drained of blood. "Is that true, Mikael?"

The Russian shrugged his shoulders. Silently he was damning Ben Raines to the pits of hell—if that place existed, and right now he hoped it did. "There is no Russia, Denise. Most of it was destroyed by nuclear warheads back in 1988. They were sent by NATO countries, and supplied by—"

Denise shook her head impatiently. "I didn't ask for a political lecture, Mikael." She stood with hands on hips. "Are you a Russian?"

His bright, hard blue eyes shifted from young lady to Ben. "Yes," he said softly, with many straining to hear. "I am."

A young man stood up. "Well . . . that don't make no difference to me. I like what Mikael and his friends are all about and what they've told us. I believe what they say is true. I'm sticking with them."

About two-thirds of the young people present agreed with that. It did not surprise Ben.

Ben said, "You young men and women who have not yet made up your minds about Mikael's . . .

ideology, come with me when I leave. Just walk with me to where we're camped and talk with those with me. I promise you no pressure will be exerted upon your minds. Let's just talk. Isn't that what a democracy is all about?"

A mixed group of young people—a few more than Ben expected—rose and walked to where Ben stood. Denise said, "We'll listen, General. But we'll make no firm commitments."

"That's all I ask, young lady."

Denise looked at the man. She was standing beside a true living legend and it filled her with strange, unexpected emotions. She had thought President-General Raines would be an old man. But he looked to be in his mid-forties. But he had to be older than that. Maybe, more than one person in the group thought, there is something to his being more than a mere human. There just had to be.

Roy and Judy came out of the building. Both of them appeared to have been roughed up and then hurriedly patched up.

They stopped beside Mikael. Ben called, "Mikael and his buddies hammer on you two?"

"Yes, sir," Roy called. "And Judy was raped."

Ben looked at her.

"I'll be all right, sir," she said grimly. "Much better, in fact, in about a minute."

"What happens then?" Ben asked.

"This," Judy said. She spun, driving her elbow into Mikael's stomach. He doubled over, gagging. She brought her knee up into his face, smiling with satisfaction as his jaw popped like a gunshot and teeth rolled and bounced on the concrete steps. She brought the knife edge of her hand down hard on the back of his neck, and Mikael dropped to the steps, bleeding, hurt, and out of commission for a time.

Judy stepped back and, stone-faced, drew back her right foot and kicked the Russian squarely in the balls with the toe of her heavy combat boot.

A dozen IPF members appeared on the steps, automatic weapons at combat ready.

"Now, now, boys and girls," Colonel Gray's voice rang from the top of the building. "We don't want this situation to turn into a sticky wicket, now, do we?"

The IPF members looked up into the muzzles of M-16s and AK-47s. They heard the roar of engines racing up the broken blacktop. Jeeps swung around, .50-caliber machine guns leveled at them, the muzzles menacing.

"Holster or sling your weapons," Ben told the IPF troops.

They did as ordered, handling the weapons gingerly.

"One more person I have to get, General," Roy said. "Give me a minute?"

Ben nodded. "Go." He was curious as to the third person.

A number of young women had gathered around Judy, asking her questions, their distaste for this newly discovered side of the IPF very evident. And they were all curious as to how she had learned how to fight like she did, and if they could learn it.

She said they could, just join up with Raines's Rebels — if they thought they could cut it.

Roy reappeared, a very pretty young woman with him, holding onto his hand. The young woman had obviously been beaten. There were bruises on the side of her face and her hands were swollen from her wrists being tied too tightly.

Ben looked at the crowd of young people. "Any of you young folks want to leave with us? Don't worry, the IPF won't try to stop you."

Almost half the crowd silently made up their minds to pull out.

Ben ordered a team to escort them to the edge of the campus and to arrange transportation for them. He smiled at the young woman called Denise; she seemed to be some sort of spokesperson for the young people.

"I think it best that we hold our discussions some miles from this place, don't you, miss?" Ben said.

She returned his smile. "Yes, I do, General. And that's ms. if you don't mind."

"Right," Ben said dryly. "What else?"

One young member of the IPF allowed courage to override training and common sense. He grabbed for his pistol and leveled it at Katrina. "You traitor!" he screamed at her.

Ben stitched him from belly to face, left to right, with a short burst from the Thompson. The young man's feet flew out from under him and he slammed back against the brick wall, bloodying the old bricks as he slid slowly downward, his brains leaving a gray trail edged with crimson.

"James?" Ben called.

"Sir!"

"Gather up all the weapons and ammunition you can find. Take as many people as you need to do it in a hurry. Search all the buildings. I don't believe these

77

people represent all the IPF personnel here. If your team comes in contact with any armed men or women, shoot first and ask questions later."

"Yes, sir."

Colonel Gray yelled from the top of the building. "You IPF people! Down on your bellies, hands behind your head, fingers interlaced. Move!"

The dozen young people obeyed instantly. Ben thought: well-trained and well-disciplined. The Russian equivalent of the German *Herrenvolk* may consider themselves to be the master race, but they damn well want to survive in order to prove it.

Ben motioned Judy, Roy and Katrina to his side. "What was done to you?" he asked the young Russian girl.

"They beat me," she said softly, her accent giving her voice a pleasing lilt. "They made me take off my clothes and then beat me. They were going to rape me but they were afraid of what might happen to them should they do that. Tell your men they are wasting their time looking for more members of this contingent of the IPF. They are gone. At the arrival of your people, they would have assessed the situation, decided they could not defeat your troops, and pulled out. Do not construe it as any act of cowardice, it is merely good sense."

"Mikael is the leader?" Ben asked.

"Yes." She looked at the unconscious young man. Blood streamed from his broken mouth and from one ear. "What is left of him, that is." She added, "He is a pervert."

The young people who had elected to remain at the school with the IPF, who had decided to adopt the philosophy of the IPF, now sat sullenly, defiantly, silently. Katrina gave them little more than a quick glance of dismissal.

"They are what we call hard-core recruits. They needed very little persuasion. You could not reconvert them now, no matter what you said. So far, we have found many like these."

Ben suspected as much. "All of them young?"

"Oh, no," the girl replied. "Many people, of all ages."

"And you?" Ben asked her.

"I have not been content with General Striganov's views of matters since I found books," the seventeen-year-old said. "I read books. In them I found a much different world than my superiors described. I began to think—and that is something our leaders and cell coordinators do not like for us to do. They do not like for us to think about anything other than what we are told to think."

"Education, then," Ben prompted, "is what swayed you?"

"Oh, my, yes. As much of a broad education as I could give myself with the crate of books I found in Reykjavik." She smiled. "And some of the books were authored by you, President-General Raines." She met his gaze. Even badly bruised, the girl was beautiful. Her pale eyes held one.

"And how do you know I am the same Ben Raines, young lady?" Ben smiled at her.

"Two reasons, President-General. One: When I mentioned the name to Roy, he smiled. Two: Your picture was in one of the books. It was, I believe, taken some years ago, but it was you."

"Don't compliment him too much," Gale said, standing just outside the group. "It'll go to his head and he'll be more impossible than ever to live with."

Katrina shifted her pale eyes. "You live with President-General Raines?"

"God, no!" Gale said. "That's a figure of speech."

Katrina smiled. *"Bot kak!"*

Walking away, Gale asked Colonel Gray, "What did that girl say to me back there?"

Dan smiled; he spoke some Russian. "Let's just say she questioned the validity of your statement."

"I wonder why?" Gale asked innocently.

"You three get to Doctor Carlton," Ben told Judy, Roy and Katrina. "We'll pull out as soon as James is through."

"He won't find a thing," Katrina predicted.

She was right.

The convoy took Highway 63 out of Rolla and rolled to just outside of Jefferson City, pulling into a motel complex in midafternoon. They had seen a few survivors, but Ben knew more had seen the convoy from hiding places along the highway. The people were wary and scared. The great unknown had reached out and slapped the nation twice, hard, in little more than a dozen years, knocking those that survived to their knees. He knew that many of those slapped down would never get to their feet.

Ben gathered the seventy-five or so young people from the campus around him. "If any of you want to go home, I'll try to find some type of transportation for you."

80

No one did. Denise explained, "We don't have homes, General—none of us."

"For how long?" he asked.

"Years," she said. "I've been on my own since I was ten. You don't know there are large groups of young people on both sides of the Mississippi River?"

Ben shook his head.

"Yes, sir. The western group is headed by a young man named Wade. The eastern group is headed by a young man named Ro. Both groups live in the woods. They are, well, rather wild, but they've never hurt anyone to the best of my knowledge."

"I see," Ben said, not sure if he saw or not. "Well, Denise, you and your people have homes now, if you want them."

"With you and your Rebels, General?" a young man asked.

"That is correct."

"If we decide to stay with you, General," Denise said, "what would we do?"

"Stay with us until we can check you out with weapons and survival tactics. Although—" he smiled—"if you've been on your own for all these years, I don't believe you need any lessons on survival.

"After we check you out, you would then move out in teams, attempting to convince other young people that the way of the IPF is the wrong way, that we—Americans—have to rebuild this nation. We have to rebuild with education and hard work, compassion when it's needed, and toughness tempered with mercy in many cases. How about it?"

The young people thought they liked that plan.

They would stay.

"Tell me about these groups of young people, Denise," Ben asked.

"I . . . really don't know much about them, General, other than what I told you." She looked at him strangely. "Except, well, their religion is not quite like what the rest of us, well, practice."

"I don't understand. They worship God, don't they?"

"In a manner of speaking, yes, sir."

"Explain that, Denise." There was a sinking feeling in the pit of Ben's stomach. He braced himself for what he knew was coming.

"They worship you, sir."

Jefferson City contained more than four hundred survivors, but as was the case in most areas, Ben and his Rebels found organization lacking. People had splintered off into little groups, each with their own leaders, with their own varying philosophy as to what should be done and how to go about doing it. In some cases the people were fighting each other.

And Ben did not know how to bring an end to the fighting.

It was what Ben had been afraid he'd find.

He spoke with a few of the survivors—those that would let him get close to them—and tried to convince them they had to get off their butts and start working, straightening matters out. And to stop warring between themselves. Many times he would turn and walk away in disgust, leaving before anger got the best of him. Of those he spoke with, Ben figured he got through to maybe ten percent.

Clearly disgusted, Ben ordered his people mounted up to pull out. He told Dan Gray. "To hell with these people. Let them kill each other off. They've lost the will to survive in any type of productive society."

"I concur," Colonel Gray said.

It was then Ben noticed that Mary Macklin was reluctant to ride with him. He did not understand it. He thought it might be due to their brief sexual encounter—but he did not really believe that was it. When they reached Fulton, Missouri, just prior to stopping at a small college there, Ben pulled the growing convoy off the road and walked back to where Lieutenant Macklin was sitting in a Jeep alone.

"I say something to offend you?" he asked her.

"No, sir. Not at all."

"You maybe don't like my deodorant?"

She laughed. "No, sir. It's nothing like that. Believe me."

Ben didn't believe her. He felt she was holding something back, but he decided not to push. "Finally decide I could take care of myself, eh, Mary?"

"Something like that, sir." You'd better be able to take care of yourself, General, she thought. Because when you and Gale stop spatting and hissing at each other like a cat and dog, things are sure going to pop.

And Mary really wasn't all that certain how she felt about that.

Ben nodded, not believing a word he had heard. "All right, Mary. Right now, I want you to take a team over to Westminster College. Check it out for survivors. Shouldn't take you more than a couple of hours. We'll wait for you here."

She nodded and pulled around the convoy, stopping twice to pick up people. With four in the Jeep, she headed out.

Ben ordered his people to dismount and take a rest.

"I'm surprised you would delegate that much authority to a woman, General Raines," the voice came from behind Ben.

"Ms. Roth," Ben said, turning around. "I really don't—"

He cut off his sentence at the sight of her. He could hardly recognize her. She had done something to her hair, cut it maybe—something was very different. Maybe she had simply combed it, Ben thought. But he decided he'd best keep that a thought and not put it into words. For safety's sake. His own. She wore jeans that fitted her trim figure snugly, and what looked to be a boy's Western shirt. However, Gale would never be confused for any boy. Ben stared. She was somewhere in between pretty and beautiful.

"A speechless gentile." She tossed his words back to him with a smile. "My goodness, I believe I've found a first."

Ben ignored that. "Where's the kid?"

"With the new people from the college. One of the young women had just lost her baby—a couple of weeks ago. She asked if she could take care of the baby. I told her that was fine with me. Baby's probably better off with her, anyway."

"Why would you think that?" Ben looked into her eyes. She really had beautiful eyes.

She returned his open stare. "You really ask a lot of questions, you know that, General?"

"Perhaps. Why would . . . what is the child's name,

anyway?"

"I haven't the vaguest idea. I found him in Flat River when I was traveling south. Believe me, I don't know from nothing about babies. Well, not all that much, anyway."

Ben sensed she was putting up a brave front, but had decided the child would be better off with someone else. "The mother who lost her baby—she still in the nursing stage?"

"That's right."

"And fresh milk is hard to come by these days."

"Right."

"I see."

"I doubt it. What do you know about nursing babies? Nothing," she answered her own question.

He stepped closer. She stood her ground. Out came the chin.

"*Ms.* Roth, would you do me the honor of riding with me in this parade?"

She seemed taken aback. For a very brief moment. "Why in the world would *I* want to ride with *you?*"

"To harass me, to annoy me, and to be a constant source of irritation to me."

"You talked me into it."

FIVE

Westminster College was deserted except for one senile old man and several young ministers and their families who had elected to stay behind and care for the elderly man.

Some young people had been through, Mary was told, but they had not stayed long. Seemed like nice young people, but rather distant, one young minister said. He thought they might have all been related, they looked so much alike. Blond and blue-eyed, mostly. But, he told the small unit of Rebels, something about the young people had frightened them all, and none were sorry to see them leave.

Ben pointed the column toward Columbia. He wanted to check out the University of Missouri.

Columbia was a dead city, seemingly void of human life. But Ben, standing on the outskirts of the city, picked up a slight odor in the air, the breeze blowing from west to east. He knew what that odor was.

He shook his head in disgust. "Mutants," he told his people. "I know that smell very well."

A Rebel looked at Ben. "You killed one of them once, didn't you, General?"

Ben was conscious of Gale's eyes on him. "Yes, months ago."

"Close up, General?" one of the new people from the campus at Rolla asked.

Ben smiled. "About as close as you can get without getting intimate with the thing." He tried to brush off the question as lightly as possible. He knew only too well his battle with the mutant had only served to strengthen the belief among many that he was somehow more than a mere mortal.

When he moved off, walking down the center of Interstate 70, Gale asked, "What happened, Ben? I mean, the mutant."

Ben had walked out of the communications shack and toward a thick stand of timber. He wanted to think, wanted to be alone for a time. More and more, since leaving Idaho he had sought solitude.

A young woman's scream jerked his head up. Ben sprinted for the timber, toward the source of the frightened yelling.

Ben reached the edge of the timber and came to a sliding halt, his mouth open in shock.

It was a man, but it was like no man Ben had ever seen. It was huge, with mottled skin and huge, clawed hands. The shoulders and arms appeared to be monstrously powerful. The eyes and nose were human, the jaw was animal. The ears were perfectly formed human. The teeth were fanged, the lips human. The eyes were blue.

Ben was behind the hysterical young woman — about fourteen years old — the child of a Rebel couple. She was between Ben and the . . . whatever in God's name the creature was.

The creature towered over the young woman. Ben guessed it was an easy seven feet tall.

Ben clawed his .45 from leather just as the creature lunged for the girl. She was very quick, fear making her strong and agile. Ben got off one shot; the big slug hit the mutant in the shoulder. It screamed in pain and spun around, facing Ben. Ben guessed the thing weighed close to three hundred pounds. And all three hundred pounds of it were mad.

Ben emptied his pistol into the manlike creature, staggering but not downing it. The girl, now frightened mindless, ran into its path. Ben picked up a rock and hurled it, hitting the beast in the head, again making it forget the girl. It turned and screamed at Ben. Its chest and belly were leaking blood, and blood poured from the wound in its shoulder.

Ben side-stepped the lumbering charge and pulled his bowie knife from its sheath. With the creature's back momentarily to him, Ben jumped up on a stump for leverage and brought the heavy blade down as hard as he could. The blade cut through skull bone and brain, driving the beast to its knees, dying. Ben worked the blade out and, using both hands, brought it down on the back of the creature's head, decapitating it. The ugly, deformed head rolled on the grass, its eyes wide open in shocked death.

Ben wiped the blade clean on the grass and replaced it in leather. He walked to the young woman and put his arms around her.

"It's all over now, honey," he spoke softly, calming her, patting her on the shoulder. "It's all right, now. You go on and find your mother."

A young boy stood a short distance away, holding hands with his sister. Both of them were open-mouthed in awe. "Wow!" he said. "He is a god. He can't be killed."

"He fought a giant and beat it," his sister said. "Just wait 'til I tell Cindy over in Dog Company about this."

By now, many Rebels had gathered around. They stood in silence, looking at the beast with some fear in their eyes, looking at Ben with a mixture of awe, fear, respect and reverence.

Ben looked at the silent gathering. "You see," he told them. "Your bogey men can be killed. Just be careful, travel in pairs, and go armed. Now go back to your duties."

The crowd broke up slowly, the men and women and kids talking quietly among themselves—all of them speaking in hushed tones about Ben.

"Maybe it is true."

"Heard my kids talking the other day. Now I tend to agree with them."

"A mortal could not have done that."

"So calm about it."

"Tell you, gods don't get scared."

"Kid prays to General Raines before bed. Maybe it's not such a bad idea."

Ben heard none of it.

Ike stepped up to Ben, a funny look in his eyes. He had overheard some of the comments. "Are you all right, partner?"

"I'm fine, Ike."

Ike looked at him. Ben's breathing was steady, his

hands calm. Ike looked hard at the still-quivering man-beast. "I wouldn't have fought that thing with anything less than a fifty-caliber."

"It had to be done, Ike. Don't make any more out of it than that."

Ike's returning gaze was curious mixture of humor and sadness. He wanted so badly to tell Ben that feelings about him were getting out of hand; something needed to be done about them.

But he was afraid Ben would pull out and leave for good if he did that.

Afraid! The word shocked Ike. Me? he thought. Afraid? Yes, he admitted. But it was not a physical fear — it was a fear of who would or could take Ben's place.

Nobody, he admitted, his eyes searching Ben's face. We're all too tied to him.

"That was a brave thing you did," Gale told him.

"I was there and it had to be done." Ben stood, looking down at her. "I was lucky."

"Maybe," she replied cautiously. She did not tell Ben that all during her travels since the plague struck the land, she had heard of Ben Raines's powers. At first she had dismissed the talk as the babblings of a hysterical popu-lace seeking something to believe in, something to grasp during this time of upheaval. Now she wasn't so sure.

"Let's get rolling," Ben told her.

The convoy backtracked, picking up Highway 54,

heading for Mexico, Missouri, where they would spend the night.

Ben and Gale rode in silence for a time, with Ben finally breaking the uncomfortable tension between them.

"Tell me about yourself, Gale."

"I'm boring. I'd rather talk about you."

Ben smiled.

"And keep your ethnic cracks to yourself."

Ben laughed. "I wasn't going to say a word."

"Sure. We're friends, right, General?"

Ben pretended to mull over that for a few seconds, pursing his lips and frowning.

"Come on!"

"OK. But only if you call me Ben."

She pretended to think seriously about that, frowning and pursing her lips.

Ben laughed at her antics.

"All right," she said. "Tell me more about the monster you killed single-handedly, Ben."

Ben had hoped that episode was past history. "It was a matter of necessity, Gale. It was there and I was there. Believe me, I would have preferred to have been elsewhere."

She doubted that. The general, she had concluded, thrived on action. "But you didn't run?"

"No. But a young girl's life was at stake. Gale, don't make any more out of it than it was. Too many people are doing that now, I'm afraid."

"You're afraid? I don't believe you're afraid of anything, Ben Raines."

"I meant that as a figure of speech."

"I know it. I still don't believe you're afraid of anything."

They were again silent for a few miles, and again Ben wondered if his staying with the Rebels was the right thing, both for himself and for the people. He knew Gale had heard the stories and tales and myths and rumors about him. He wondered if she believed any of them. He hoped not.

He glanced at her. She looked so small and vulnerable. But he knew for her to have survived she had a deep well of toughness in her. He suddenly wanted to put his arm around her; but he wanted to avoid having his arm broken even more. He resisted the impulse.

The town of Mexico, Missouri, once a thriving little city of about thirteen thousand, appeared deserted. After pulling into a large motel parking area, Ben sent a team into town to check it out. He had detected that odor in the air and had ordered the rest of his contingent to stay mounted up. He was bracing himself mentally for what he hoped the recon team would not find.

Col. Dan Gray reported back to him. From the look on his face, Ben knew the news was not good.

"It's rather grim, General," the Englishman reported. "Looks like the beasties have used this place to winter and to breed. The stench of them is strong."

"What do you think, Dan?"

"I think it's very unsafe, General."

"Very well," Ben said. He turned to his squad leaders. "We're pulling out. It's about sixty miles to Hannibal. We'll bivouac there."

The column rolled and rumbled through the town. Downtown Mexico looked as though a pack of wild kids had trashed the streets and stores. Not a window remained intact; filth was strewn everywhere. Once, Ben stopped to retrieve part of a heavy metal gas can from the street. The can appeared to have been physically ripped apart, torn open, much like a huge bear would do, with superanimal strength.

Ben silently showed the can to Gale.

For once, she had nothing to say.

Unlike Mexico, Missouri, Hannibal appeared untouched by time or mutants. There were a few rotting skeletons to be seen, but the Rebels had long months back grown accustomed to that sight.

Ben ordered the people to dismount and clean up the Holiday Inn; they would use that for a base while in the area. Ben wanted to spend several days in this part of Missouri. He wanted to search for any original manuscripts of Samuel Clemens and as many of his artifacts as possible. Ben felt that something had to be preserved—some link with the past, when times were better and life was easier. Before the bomb.

Gale mentally prepared herself for the proposition she was sure was forthcoming from Ben Raines, for his sexual antics were almost legend among the Rebels, and she had been subtly warned to prepare herself.

She went to sleep in a chair in her room, still waiting for Ben's advances. When she awakened at one o'clock in the morning, her back hurting and her neck stiff from sleeping in the chair, she smiled ruefully at the white, almost virginal nightgown she had picked up from a store in Fulton, Missouri. The gown lay across the foot of the bed.

She carefully folded it and replaced it in her duffle. "Another time, another place," she said, adding, "Shit!"

Doctor Carlton took several Rebels with him right after breakfast. Said he wanted to prowl around a bit, see what he might discover. The others took the two-day lull to wash clothes, lounge about, rest or sightsee. Ben and Gale visited the many landmarks in that part of Missouri: Hannibal's Cardiff Hill; Lover's Leap, overlooking the Mississippi River; the old lighthouse, built in 1935 as a monument to Mark Twain.

"I don't understand," Gale said, as she and Ben sat eating lunch, "how one town could be virtually destroyed by those . . . things, mutants, and another town could be almost untouched." She looked at the can of C-ration and grimaced.

"I can't answer that," Ben said. "Maybe a scientist could, but I don't know of any in this area. I don't know of any scientists—period. So much has been lost, and it doesn't appear that too many people really care. I can understand it, but I don't have to like it."

"Explain then, please. Take my mind off this horrible food."

Ben laughed at her. "I lived off that stuff for months, Gale."

"No wonder your disposition is so rotten."

Chuckling at her, Ben said, "I think many who survived the bombings of '88 somehow found the strength to bounce back. Maybe the world would have survived if the rats had not brought the plague. Just seems like it knocked the props out from under most who made it through that sickness."

"It didn't knock the props out from under you," she observed.

"No, it didn't. But we're different, the Rebels and me."

"I."

"Are you sure?"

"Damn, Ben—you're a writer!"

"Me still sounds correct."

"Ben!"

"Whatever. We had a goal, we were organized, we had a dream of a better society. Maybe we were just stronger people. Sometimes I wonder if it's all worth it."

"Hitting those new lows you told Mary Macklin about, Ben?"

"No, not really." Ben shook his head. "The fact the IPF is here shows that we have survivors from around the world, shows that somebody other than myself is going to try to pull this world out of the ashes. Even if it's just a small part of the world. Walk before you run," he quoted the old saying.

"If you don't mind, Ben." She looked at him, putting her hand on his thigh. "I'd rather it be *us* than *them*."

"So would I, Gale."

"Then let's do it, Ben Raines."

He met her gaze. "All right, Ms. Roth. Let's do it."

"It was only a matter of time," General Striganov spoke to Sam Hartline. "But Ben Raines need not disturb us all that greatly. Neither he nor us is strong enough to mount any type of sustained attack against the other. Perhaps, really, we might never need to fight. If he will keep to the south, and we to the north, perhaps we could work out some kind of peaceful coexistence plan. I think that would behoove both of us."

"Don't count on it," Hartline said. "Raines is a communist hater out of the old school. And he is one tough bastard."

"I do not want a fight at this time." The Russian was adamant. "Let us attempt to converse with President-General Raines. During the meeting—if he agrees to it—we shall attempt to work out some dividing line that would separate his form of government from ours—a physical line." He turned to an aide. "Have leaflets printed and order a team sent out to find General Raines. No contact at this time. Later we shall have a pilot do a fly-by and drop the leaflets. Raines is slowly progressing northward, taking his time, according to our people just in from Rolla." A look of disgust passed quickly over his face at that thought. The general had already seen to Mikael. "Iowa would be a good place to locate him and for us to meet, I believe." He studied the map on his office wall. "Yes. Ask Mr. Raines to meet me at, ummm, ah, Waterloo." He smiled. "Yes, Waterloo, Iowa. That should be a very appropriate place, don't you think, Sam?"

"For one of you," Hartline grunted his reply. The Russian did not know Ben Raines as well as Sam. Ben Raines would never permit a communist form of government to exist alongside his own. At least Hartline didn't believe he would.

Not for any length of time.

But . . . maybe it was worth a shot.

On the morning of the third day in Hannibal, the column pulled out, rolling northward on Highway 61.

Ben had cautioned his people to be careful, for he remembered only too well the incidents last year, when the Rebels were moving west out of Richmond, when the government collapsed.

The scouts had failed to report in at their given time. Ben and the convoy waited impatiently on the cold, wind-swept highway. The bridge at Fort Madison had been plugged up tight with stalled and wrecked cars and trucks. The scouts had radioed back they were going on to Hamilton, taking a secondary road. Ben waited a long half hour past the time they were supposed to have radioed in. He turned to Cecil.

"I'm taking a patrol," Ben told him. "I'll call in every fifteen minutes. Anything happens, you're it."

"Ben . . ."

"No. It's my show. Maybe the radio conked out. Could be a lot of things. I'll be in touch."

Back in his pickup, Ben looked at Rosita. "Out," he told her.

She refused to leave.

"Do I have to toss you out bodily?"

"That would look funny," she calmly replied.

Ben closed the door and put the truck in gear. "Your ass," he told her. He pulled out, leading the small patrol.

Rosita smiled at him and said something in rapid-fire Spanish. It sounded suspiciously vulgar.

"Check your watch," he told Rosita.

"Ten-forty-five."

"Call in every fifteen minutes. It'll take us forty-five minutes to an hour on these roads to get to Fort Madison. That was their last transmission point. Whatever happened happened between there and Hamilton. You've got the maps. What highway do we take?"

"96 out of Niota."

At Nauvoo they found the pickup parked in the middle of the highway. One door had been ripped off its hinges and flung to one side of the road.

"What the hell?" Ben muttered.

Rosita's face was pale under her olive complexion. She said nothing. But her eyes were frightened.

Ben parked a safe distance behind the pickup and, Thompson in hand, off safety, on full automatic, walked up to the truck. Thickening blood lay in puddles in the highway.

"Jesus Christ!" one of Ben's Rebels said, looking into a ditch. "General!"

Ben walked to the man's side. The torn and mangled body of the driver lay sprawled in the ditch. One arm had been ripped from its socket. The belly had been torn open, the entrails scattered about, gray in the cold sunlight.

A Rebel pointed toward an open field. "Over here!" he called.

The second scout lay in a broken heap, on his stomach. He was headless. Puddles of blood spread all about him.

"Where's his head?" the man asked.

"I don't know," Ben answered. "But we'd damn sure better keep ours. Heads up and alert. Combat positions. Weapons on full auto. Back to the trucks in twos. Center of the road and eyes moving. Go."

Back in the warm cab of the truck, Ben noticed Rosita looking very pale and shaken. He touched her hand. "Take it easy, little one. We'll make it."

He radioed in to Cecil. "Cec? Backtrack to Roseville and 67 down to Macomb. Turn west on 136. We'll meet you between Carthage and Hamilton. Don't stop for anything. Stay alert for trouble."

"What kind of trouble, Ben?"

Ben hesitated for a few seconds. "Cec—I just don't know."

"Ten-four."

Ben honked his horn and pulled out, the other trucks following.

They saw nothing out of the ordinary as they drove down 96. But Hamilton looked as though it had been sacked by Tartars followed up by hordes of giant Tasmanian devils.

"What the hell?" Ben said, his eyes taking in the ruins of the town. Bits and scraps of clothing blew in the cold winds; torn pages of books and magazines flapped in the breeze, the pages being turned by invisible fingers. Not one glass storefront remained intact. They all looked as if they had been deliberately smashed by mobs of angry, sullen children.

There was no sense to any of it.

Ben said as much.

"Perhaps," Rosita said, venturing forth an opinion, "those that did it do not possess sense as we know it."

"What are you trying to say, Rosita?"

"I . . . really don't know, Ben. And please don't press me."

"All right."

Ben cut to the bridge and saw it was clear except for a few clumsily erected barricades. They looked as though they had been placed there by people without full use of their mental faculties.

Again, he said as much aloud.

Rosita said nothing.

Ben radioed back to the main column. "Come on through to the bridge at Keokuk, Cec. But be careful."

"I copy that, Ben. Ben? We just passed through a little town called Good Hope. It looked . . . what was it the kids used to call it? It looked like it had been trashed."

"I know, Cec. The same with Hamilton. Just no sense to it."

"We'll be there as quickly as possible, Ben."

"Ten-four."

With guards on the bridge, east and west, Ben and the others cleared the structure in a few minutes. Beneath them the Mississippi River rolled and boiled and pounded its way south, the waters dark and angry-looking.

"They look like they hold secrets," Rosita said, her eyes on the Big Muddy.

"I'm sure they do." Ben put an arm around her shoulders, pulling her close.

They stood for a time, without speaking, content to be close and to look at the mighty flow of water rushing under them.

"General?" one of the men called. "Take a look at this, sir, if you will."

Ben and Rosita walked to where the man stood. Painted in white letters on the bridge floor, close to the railing, were these words:

GOD HELP US ALL. WHAT MANNER OF CREATURE HAVE WE CREATED? THEY CAME IN THE NIGHT. I CANNOT LIVE LIKE THIS.

It was unsigned.

"He was talking about the mutant rats," Ben said.

100

Rosita looked at him, eyes full of doubt.

"I wonder what happened to the person that wrote this?" the Rebel who discovered the message asked.

"He went over the side," Rosita said.

"Probably," Ben agreed.

No more was said of it until the column rolled onto the bridge. There, in the cold January winds, Ben told his people what had happened to the scouts.

Roanna told Ben of the AP messages she had received, and of her sending Jane Moore to Michigan.

Ben was openly skeptical. "Mutant beings, Roanna? Are you serious?"

"Yes, I am. Same copy that told of mutant rats. Received the same night from AP."

Ben could but stare in disbelief.

"It's entirely possible, Ben," Cecil said, as the cold winds whipped around them. "I recall hearing some doctor say that after the initial wave of bombings that God alone knew what type of mutations the radiation would bring in animals and humans."

When Ben spoke, his words were hard and firm. "Now I don't want a lot of panic to come out of this. None of us know what happened to our scouts. They were killed. By what or by whom, I don't know. What I do know is this: We are going to make Tri-States. Home, at least for a while. We've got some rough country to travel, and we've been lucky so far. I expect some fire-fights before we get there. So all of us stay alert.

"We'll be traveling through some . . . wild country, country that has not been populated for some time — more than a decade. So it's entirely possible that we'll see some . . . things we aren't, haven't witnessed before. I hope not. But let's be prepared for anything. When we do stop at motels, we'll double the guards and stay on our toes. But I won't have panic or any talk of monsters. Let's move out. Let's go home."

And now, more than a year later, as the Rebels traveled northward, they began to see more and more evidence of the mutants' existence: destroyed stores that looked as if bands of madmen had descended upon them; absolutely no sign of human life; and that awful odor that was the trademark of the mutants. For a time, it was a drive of utter desolation. And it was making the Rebels nervous.

"Steady down, now," Ben spoke calmly over the radio. "Keep your weapons at the ready and your eyes open. But stay calm and keep your cool."

His voice and words and relaxed attitude seemed to do the trick.

"Keep your cool?" Gale looked at him, a smile on her lips. "Boy, that sure dates you, old man."

"Wanna hear my imitation of Chuck Berry?" Ben asked.

"Who?"

"Forget it," Ben told her.

"Was he a singer or what?"

Ben ignored her. She grinned at him.

A few miles south of where the highway turned due east, Ben halted the column and put out guards while he consulted a roadmap.

"I was going into Keokuk," he said to Colonel Gray and Lieutenant Macklin. "But now I don't think I'll take the chance. We'll pick up this secondary road here and take it up to Highway 2, take that all the way until we junction with 63. Then we'll cut right straight up the center of the state. Stay on 63 all the way into Minnesota."

"You want me to send out advance recon, General?" Colonel Gray asked.

"No," Ben said. "I think, if what Kat said is true, and I have no reason to doubt her, this General Striganov will probably attempt to contact us."

"And then?" James Riverson asked, the M-16 looking like a toy against the hugeness of the big ex-truck driver.

"We'll have to play it by ear. But unless provoked, we are not hostile. Let them open the dance." He looked around for his radioman. He thought of Gale. He smiled as he realized his radioman was a woman. All right. Radioperson. "Corporal, get in touch with Ike back home. Tell him to put two companies on stand-by and have planes standing by ready to go." He glanced at Colonel Gray. "Do we have two companies of personnel who are jump-qualified?"

"Only by stretching the point, sir, and by pulling them all in from the three-state area."

"Mary?" he looked around for Lieutenant Macklin.

"Sir?" She stepped forward.

"You know of more riggers down home?"

"No, sir."

"Well, that's that," Ben said. "Good idea while it lasted. Colonel, when we get back, I want you to personally train at least two companies of airborne."

"Sir."

To the radio operator: "Tell Colonel McGowen we can't risk a jump if his people are needed. The pilots will just have to land the planes on a strip or in the damn road."

"Right away, sir."

103

Fifteen minutes later, Ben ordered the column out. A half hour later, they rolled into Iowa.

"Radar O'Reilly," Ben remarked with a smile as they approached Ottumwa, Iowa.

Gale laughed. "I remember watching that show when I was a little girl. But mostly I remember the reruns. It was funny."

"What did you do directly after the bombings of '88?" Ben asked.

Gale thought for a time. She was so long in silence Ben asked, "First time you've talked about it?"

"Yes," she replied, the word just audible over the highway rush.

"If it bothers you, don't speak of it."

"No. I think it's time. It's not all that great, anyway. I mean, as compared to what happened to a lot of other people."

Ben let her gather her thoughts.

"I was sixteen," Gale began. She cleared her throat and spoke louder, firmer. "Sixteen. I didn't know crap about the real world. I was still going to a damn summer camp when I was fifteen years old. That summer I didn't go to camp. Raised so much hell with my parents they finally threw up their hands and told me I was impossible.

"On the day . . . the day it . . . happened, I was out driving with a girlfriend. We went into a panic. We just couldn't believe it was happening. We were way out in the country, miles out of the suburbs. But when we tried to get back into the city, all the highways and streets were blocked for miles. I tried shortcuts, got lost. Then I calmed down some and pulled an E.T. Managed to call home. My mother said my father was at the hospital, working. I remember she was very calm. She told us not to attempt to enter the city, but to drive into the country-side—even further out than we were—get miles from St. Louis. She said to get food and bottled water and cloth-ing—if I didn't have the money to buy them, steal them. I was shocked. Really. This was my mother telling me to steal. She said to find a sturdy house or barn, hide the car, and hide ourselves. Don't come out for anything or anybody. She said it might take days for this thing to wind down. Something like that."

"Your father was a doctor?"

"Yes. A surgeon. A very good one. My mother was a psychologist. I still remember how incredibly calm she was over the phone. Anyway, the girl I was with, Amy, she became unglued. Said she wasn't going anywhere ex-cept back into the city. She jumped out of the car. I tried to stop her. I yelled at her and screamed at her. She just kept on running. I never saw her again.

"I drove . . . I guess maybe thirty miles from the city. Then I stopped at a country store and got gas. No one was there. It was eerie. I mean, the place was deserted. I rummaged around and got all sorts of food and bottled water and pop and clothes and stuff. I felt so . . . so *guilty* about just taking it. So I put all but five dollars of my money on the counter and left.

"I drove. Just drove aimlessly. Ben, to this day I can't tell you how long I drove, but it was fifty or sixty miles further from the city. And I can't tell you where I finally hid. It was terrible, though, I can tell you that. I hid like some animal in this barn. I mean, I never *left* that place. I had hidden my car, a little Chevy, in some kind of stall thing and covered it all up with straw and hay and stuff. Except to go to the bathroom and to wash my face and hands, I stayed the whole time up in the second floor."

"The second floor of a barn?" Ben questioned, looking at her.

"Whatever you call it."

"The loft."

"Thanks. I'll treasure that knowledge forever, I'm sure. What do *I* know from barns? Anyway, it was scary. There were rats and snakes up there at first. How do snakes get up that high? I don't know. Anyway, I killed them with a handle off some kind of tool. It was broken when I found it.

"Then the men came prowling around. They were looking for whiskey and women. Not necessarily in that order. The first group of men—I don't know whether they were black or white or green—had a little boy with them. They did . . . disgusting things to him. I don't want to talk about it. Then they left, took the little boy with them. Then some white men came in and looked around. One of them even climbed up the ladder to the second—to the loft—and looked around. But I was hidden really well in the hay and he didn't see me. This bunch said now would be a good time to get together and kill all the niggers. They left. Then some drunk black men came around and I overheard them talking about how would it was a good time to get together and kill all the honks. But first they wanted some tight white pussy. They left and some guys came in and had this woman with them. Woman isn't correct. She was a young girl, maybe fourteen or fifteen. I never saw her, but I could hear her begging them to stop . . . what they were doing. It got pretty . . . perverted. They raped her—among other things. Took turns with her. It was awful.

"When they finally left, they took the girl with them—said they could swap her for guns, maybe. I was alone for two or three days. I don't remember; the days kind of all ran together. Maybe it was longer. Then it got real quiet, like I was the last person left on earth. You know what I mean?"

Ben nodded, remembering his feelings of being alone when he finally left the house after being so sick for so long.

It was his birthday. It was a Sunday. 1988. It was a day the survivors would remember all their lives. Ben had started a new book, writing for three hours. It was the first time he'd felt like writing after being stung repeatedly by a swarm of yellow jackets. The stings had dropped him into shock. He did not know at the time how long he'd been out—days, surely. But now he felt fine. The mood was not to last.

He drove into town. Just outside of the small town in Louisiana, Ben cut his eyes to a ditch and jammed on the brakes.

There was a body in the ditch.

Ben inspected the dead man. Dead at least a week—maybe longer. The corpse was stinking and blackened.

He tried his CB. Nothing. He turned on the radio, searching the AM and FM bands. Nothing.

With a feeling of dread settling over him like a pall, Ben drove into town.

There, he found the truth.

"Yes," he told Gale. "I know the feeling quite well."

"I guess maybe you do," Gale said. "But you're tough. With me, it was different, believe it. Anyway, I finally ran out of food. I went through it like Grant took Atlanta."

"Sherman," Ben said automatically.

"Who's telling this story, anyway?"

"Sorry."

"I had eaten like a starving person. Ate from fear, I suppose. Gained about ten pounds, at least. I had to leave to find more food. And, I guess, even though I was still scared, I wanted to see what had happened. I just couldn't believe there had really been a war. Well, my damn car wouldn't start. I lifted the hood and looked in. Talk about a shock. There wasn't any motor. I finally figured out the motor was in the rear. I am not mechanically inclined, believe it. What I knew then about engines and stuff was nothing. But I could see where the rats had chewed a lot of wires and things. I sat down by the car and bawled and squalled.

"I finally got it together and stepped out of the barn. The sunlight blinded me for a few moments. Gave me a headache, too. Then I stepped right on a body. Talk about freaking someone out. I almost lost control at that point. Maybe I did lose control for a time. I ran. Boy, did I run. But it didn't do any good. There were bodies *everywhere*. Like in a movie, you know, after a big battle? And animals and birds were *eating* the dead people. It was the worst thing I had ever seen in my life. Period.

"Well . . . I stopped at this house—fell down in the front yard would be more like it, collapsed. Then I went inside. Luckily, the shape I was in, emotionally, the house was empty. No people, I mean.

"Ben, I know how you feel about liberals, and my mother and father were liberals, the whole bag. Gun control, civil rights, opposed to capital punishment, everything, you know?"

Ben nodded his head in agreement.

"OK, so they were liberals. But they taught me how to *think*. They taught me to sit down, be calm and rationalize things out. So that's what I did. I sat in a chair, calmed myself and thought. I thought myself right into a headache—that's all I accomplished."

Ben laughed at the mental picture of her doing so, then he apologized for it.

She smiled. "No, it's all right, Ben. I feel better finally being able to talk about it. And I understand, really, I do. Looking back, some of the things I did were funny— but not at the time. So I went looking around in this farmhouse. It was set way back from the road, in a bunch of trees, and had been left alone by the looters. I found a rack full of guns. I took out a shotgun and then found a box of shells that said twelve gauge. The double-barrel gun was a twelve gauge—said so on the metal. So I thought: By God, there isn't anybody going to rape this kid. I'll get tough.

"I finally figured out how to open the damn gun—that thing was heavy—and loaded it. I went outside to fire it. Damned thing knocked me down. When I hit the ground the other barrel went off and almost took my foot with it. I decided right then I'd better find me some other kind of gun.

"There were some other shotguns in the rack. I got the smallest one. A 410, it said. Wonderful. Personally I found it all rather confusing. It was smaller than the twelve gauge, but it had a bigger number, so thinking logically, it should have been more powerful, right? I mean, there's three hundred and ninety-eight things difference between the two, right?"

Ben was trying desperately to maintain a straight face.

"Go ahead, laugh, you big ox. I know, I know, klutzy little girl from the city trying to figure out how to work guns. But Ben, my parents wouldn't even let my brother play with *toy* guns when he was little. Me? I had Ken and Barbie. Fantastic. Really helps a girl prepare for disaster. Doesn't help you prepare for anything. Ken had been neutered and Barbie didn't have nothing. It was a big disappointment.

"The 410 was OK. It kicked, but not much. The keys to a pickup were on the kitchen table. The electricity was still working. I took a long, hot bath. I mean, I was *gamy*. I washed my clothes, fixed something to eat, and slept in a real bed.

"The dreams were kind of bad."

She was silent for a few miles, gazing out the window at the barren landscape, at lands that were once among the most productive in all of America.

Gale said, "When I got up the next morning and dressed, I looked out the living room window. There were some guys walking up the gravel road. I loaded both guns and walked out onto the front porch. I just knew bad trouble had found me. The twelve gauge was as big as me. The men laughed at me. I told them to stop and to go away. They laughed and one of them asked me what I was. I told him I was an American. He said that wasn't what he meant. I knew what he meant. Then he said some things I'd rather not repeat. Finally he said he'd never had any Jew pussy.

"Ben—" she glanced at him, her eyes seeking support

110

and condonation of what she was about to say— "I got so mad I lost control. I became so angry I didn't even feel the shotgun kick, and it didn't knock me down when I fired it. I shot the man right in the stomach. Then I fired the other barrel and hit a man in the leg. There was maybe thirty feet between us. Took his leg off at the knee. Just blew it off. I dropped the big shotgun and grabbed up the 410. I fired both barrels of it. I don't think I hit anyone, but the other two men were really running up the road. I heard a car or truck start and never saw them again. I went in the house, packed my stuff, and put it in the pickup, along with both shotguns and all the shells I could find. I walked out to where the guys were lying on the ground. One was dead. The other one was bleeding really bad. I vomited on the ground.

"I stood right there and watched that man die, Ben. I felt . . . I felt lots of things. But Ben, I didn't feel any pity for him. I . . . felt like he deserved what I had done to him."

She sighed heavily, as if the telling had lifted a load from her slender shoulders.

"One of the men had a pistol in a holster, and some bullets for it in loops. I took all those. I got in the pickup and drove off. Kind of. It was one of those four on the floor types. I knocked the whole porch down before I figured how to get the damn thing out of reverse. It was embarrassing.

"I found some people a little while later and they were very nice. They told me they heard St. Louis had blown up. So I headed for Columbia. My parents had friends there that taught at the university. They took me in. There's a whole lot more, but that's the high points. Except for this:

111

"I am tired of running. I am tired of being alone. I am tired of being scared. I do not want to be alone *ever again*. Do you understand what I am saying, Ben Raines? I mean, really understand it?"

He looked at her and full comprehension passed silently between man and woman.

"Yes, I do," Ben told her.

"Fine." She smiled and mischief popped and sparkled in her dark eyes. "Then keep your eyes on the road, Ben. You're not the best driver I've ever ridden with, you know?"

SIX

Ottumwa contained more people than Ben had seen theretofore in any one place. And Ben noticed that most of them were armed, with both side arms and rifles.

He ordered his convoy to a halt and got out to speak with some of the people. He was greeted courteously, if not, at first, warmly.

So spotty were communications throughout America that some of the people did not even know Ben had been in and out of the White House at Richmond.

Ben commented on the highly visible arms.

"Had to go to it," a man told him. "First those awful things were around — you know what I'm talking about, don't you?"

Ben nodded. "Mutants."

"Yeah. Then the IPF came nosing around, spewing that communistic bullshit. We ran them out of town, but they just spread out all around here, all around us. They got a firm hand and hold on Waterloo, conducting classes at the college, and lots of folks are being taken in by that line. But not us."

"How far up north do they extend?"

"All the way up into Canada, so I hear tell. But it's a funny—odd—type of communism. Not like the way it was in Russia before the bombings."

"Yet," Ben said.

The man smiled. "Yeah. Say, why don't you folks spend the night here? We have running water, electricity, all the comforts. Well, most of them. We can talk about what to do about the IPF."

"I'd like that," Ben said with a smile. He stuck out his hand. The man shook it.

"You're sure you won't reconsider and make the move down south with us?" Ben again asked. "Join up with us."

Dinner had been delicious. The people of Ottumwa had opened up their homes to the Rebels, eager for company and for some news of happenings on the outside. The days of turning on a radio or TV for news and entertainment were long gone . . . and for many would never return.

The Iowan smiled and shook his head negatively. He refilled their cups with hot tea. Coffee was now almost unknown. The tea was a blend of sassafras root and experimental tea leaves grown in South Carolina and in hot houses.

"I don't believe so, General. This land around here is still some of the best farm land in the world, and me and the wife have been farming it for some years now. Think we'll just stay on."

"And if the IPF returns?" Ben asked. "In force, with force?"

"We do try not to think about that, General Raines." the man's wife said. "But we're not always successful in doing it."

The farmer said, "If that happens, General Raines, look for us to join you."

"I'll stay in contact, try to warn you in time to get out."

"We'd appreciate that, General."

"But if you see it coming at you, don't wait until it's too late," Ben cautioned.

"There's about three hundred of us rebuilding around here," the man said. "And we're all armed and know how to use the weapons."

"The Russians have between five and ten thousand troops," Ben replied.

The man paled. "Then we'll have to give your suggestion some heavier consideration, General."

The convoy pulled out the next morning, rolling northward. They halted at the junction of Highways 63 and 6 while a team was sent into Grinnell College to inspect.

Ben stood beside Gale, both of them leaning against the fender of the pickup. They heard the plane coming and looked up at the twin-engine prop job as it dipped lower, coming out of the north.

"It's unarmed, General!" a spotter called, viewing the plane through binoculars. "But its markings show it's an IPF aircraft."

"Stand easy," Ben told his people.

Paper fluttered through the air as the plane did a slow fly-by. The pilot waggled his wings, banked to the north, and was gone before the bits of paper had fallen to the earth.

Gale snagged one of the falling leaflets and handed it to Ben. After she read it. Ben waited patiently.

TO: PRESIDENT-GENERAL BEN RAINES
FROM: GENERAL GEORGI STRIGANOV
MY DEAR MR. RAINES: I AM WAITING IN WATERLOO TO MEET WITH YOU. I WILL MEET YOU ON THE OUTSKIRTS OF THE CITY, SOUTH SIDE, AT THE CITY LIMITS SIGN. IF YOU WISH, COME ARMED. I WILL NOT BE ARMED AND NEITHER WILL ANY OF MY PEOPLE. LOOKING FORWARD TO MEETING WITH YOU AND SHARING SOME INTELLIGENT CONVERSATION.

GEORGI

"I wouldn't trust a goddamn Russian any further than I could spit," a Rebel said.

Colonel Gray smiled, anticipating Ben's reply. He was not disappointed.

"I think that probably has a great deal to do with the shape of the world at the present time," Ben said. "But the Russians never inspired a great deal of confidence in me, either. Colonel Gray?"

"Sir?"

"Take a team and reconnoiter the situation. Do not fire unless you are fired upon. If you meet with any of General Striganov's people, set up day after tomorrow for the meeting and report back to me immediately."

"Sir." The Englishman saluted and called for three other Rebels to join him. They left within five minutes in two Jeeps.

"Corporal." Ben looked at the radio operator. "Get on the horn and have Colonel McGowen get his people up and moving. I don't want to risk a night landing using vehicle headlights, so tell him to use the airstrip just outside of town and I'll expect him no later than 1200 hours tomorrow. I'll be waiting."

"Yes, sir."

"Dismount and make camp," Ben hollered.

"You are?" Colonel Gray asked the uniformed young man.

"Lieutenant Stolski, sir, IPF."

"Nice old Welsh name," Dan muttered under his breath. "Well, Lieutenant, are we going to be civilized about this, or do we draw a line with the toe of a boot and dare each other to step over it?"

The young IPF officer laughed and stuck out his hand. "I have some excellent tea in my quarters, sir. Would you join me for a cup?"

Dan shook the offered hand. "Delighted, son."

The four old, prop-driven planes were airborne within an hour after receiving Ben's orders. The planes were old, but in excellent mechanical condition, the motors rebuilt from the ground up. The four planes carried two full companies of hand-picked Rebels, in full combat gear.

The planes had refueled in central Missouri and spent the night there. They were circling the small airport outside Grinnell, Iowa at 1150 hours.

Ben had arranged transportation (thousands of vehi-

117

cles around the nation were still operable after a bit of servicing) and the troops mounted up and were rolling after guards were placed around the aircraft.

"You're in charge here while I'm meeting with General Striganov," Ben told Ike. "I'm only taking four people with me."

"Plus your bodyguards."

"Only four people," Ben repeated.

"Plus your bodyguards," Ike insisted, staring out the windshield.

Ben sighed. "All right, Ike. If it will make you happy."

Ike sniffed the air of the cab. "Smells like perfume in here, Ben. Have you gone funny on me?"

Ben gave him a hard look. But it was to no avail. No one could stay miffed at Ike. Ben told him about Gale.

"One good thing came of this trip anyway," the stocky ex-SEAL said with a grin. His grin faded. "We got a little more trouble down home, though."

"Oh?"

"Emil Hite and his band of kookies and fruities. They're growing, Ben. Seems people are looking for something or someone to believe in. 'Bout five or six hundred more new members just joined up with Hite and his creampies."

"Moving into our area?"

"I don't know how to keep them out, Ben. They're not armed, never make any kind of hostile move. They are not aggressive at all. What the hell can we do under those circumstances?"

"We can run their paganistic asses clear out of the area," Ben spoke through clenched teeth. Emil Hite was the Jim Jones type—only worse. Ben suspected, but had no way of proving, that Hite was having sexual relations

118

with young boys and girls ten years of age—and less. And he *knew*—having seen with his own eyes—Hite and his followers were worshipping idols. Well, they could worship a pile of horse hockey if they chose, but it was the children that concerned Ben.

Ike glanced at him and worked his chewing tobacco over to the other side of his mouth. "The mutants might not like that too much, ol' buddy."

"What the hell do the mutants have to do with Emil Hite?"

"Well—" Ike spat out the open window—"Emile Hite and his nutsos kind of worship the ugly bastards."

That so startled Ben he almost lost the pickup. He was glad Gale was not with him. "What!"

"Yeah. Our intelligence just discovered that a few days ago. Seems they—Hite and his jellybeans—have been feeding the mutants for the past year or so; kind of tamed some of them, I reckon. And hold on to your balls for this one: Every now and then, so intelligence has gathered, Hite gives the ugly things women."

"You have got to be kidding!"

"Nope." Ike shrugged philosophically. "Savage and stupid people the world over have been doing things similar since the beginnings of time, Ben. You know that."

"Yeah. The Aztecs, Mayans, hell, the Hawaiians used to toss selected maidens into volcanoes." He shook his head in disgust. "Well, I'll deal with Hite later. Right now, let's worry about the Russians."

"One thing at a time." Ike grinned.

The men stood for a full minute, each silently appraising the other. They were very close in age; no more than a year or two separated them. Both were in excellent physical shape, heavily muscled and lean-waisted.

"General Striganov." Ben was the first to speak. He extended his hand. The Russian took it.

"So good to at last meet you, General Raines. It's rare one gets to meet a legend."

"If indeed I am a legend."

"Oh, you are, sir." Georgi said with a smile. "Have no doubts concerning that."

Ben decided to pull no punches with the man. "I won't apologize for what happened to your young man in Rolla, General. He and his men raped one of my people and roughed up another."

The Russian smiled grimly. "No apologies expected, General. I personally shot him."

Ben lifted his eyes to meet the Russian's open gaze.

"Oh yes, General Raines. His orders were not to rape or physically abuse the population. And I run a very tight ship, so to speak. I will not tolerate any breach of discipline. Besides, Mikael, so I learned, was somewhat of a — how to say this — was twisted sexually. He will not be missed. His rather lame excuse about your two young people being spies had no validity. Spies against what or whom? Russia no longer exists as a government; America no longer exists as a government, a power. The world, indeed, is a free, open land, as unbridled by manmade law as the vast seas. I view it this way, General: If you have the right to set in place your own form of government, amenable to the people who follow you, then so do I. Would you argue that?"

Ben had to smile. Putting the question that simplistically, Ben could not argue the concept or the method — thus far — but he could argue and question the ideology.

And he said as much.

The Russian returned the smile, viewing the American through cold eyes. "As the Americans used to be fond of saying, General, I'm being quite 'up front' with the people. At first I was not; I will admit—openly—to some initial deceit. But no longer. I am telling the people who I *was* and what I have now *become*: a communist who has now shifted a bit to become a pure socialist in thinking and actions."

"And of the caste system you advocate?" Ben was not letting him off the hook that easily.

But the Russian was full of surprises. "But of course! Stupid and shallow people are very often quite vain, General Raines. You are a very intelligent man; I don't have to tell you about human nature. Oh no, General, I am now—much to Sam Hartline's disgust—being quite open and honest in my dealings with the people. But what is amusing to me is this: Not one of the people who now embraces my form of government actually believes he will be placed in the lower levels of the system, even though I intimate they certainly will. That, I believe, is the dubious beauty of the naive and the arrogant man who knows not that he is either. And would not believe it if he was so informed. You know those types, General Raines. The world is—or was—full of them."

The man was anything but a fool, Ben reluctantly conceded. And he would be a formidable adversary. If it came to that.

As if on some invisible signal, an aide brought them coffee—real coffee. Ben savored the rich smell and taste. He had to ask where in the world General Striganov got the coffee.

"Call me Georgi—please. And may I call you Ben?"

"Certainly, Georgi."

"Stockpiled it, Ben. Hundreds of tons of the finest coffee beans in the world, although I can't personally guarantee each bean was hand-picked by that fellow on your American TV."

Ben smiled in remembrance of that commercial: a coffee bean picker with manicured fingernails.

"And also some of the finest tea in the world, as well," Georgi concluded proudly.

"But none of that will be shared with the, ah, lower classes of your system?"

"Certainly not."

"I could attack that, Georgi."

"But of course you could! However, Ben—" the Russian leaned forward, pyramiding his finger tips in a vague gesture of praying—"do tell me this: Does an ignorant person appreciate the beauty and talents of a Renoir, a Van Gogh, Cezanne, Caravaggio?" He smiled in anticipation of an easily won verbal victory. "We both know the answer to that. If an ignorant person had a choice, which would you envision him hanging in his hovel: a print of a famous master, or some hideous cloth depicting dogs playing billards or poker?"

Ben had to laugh at that, for in that, he shared the Russian's philosophy. But he felt compelled to say: "They could be taught to appreciate fine art; are you in agreement with that?"

Striganov waggled his left hand in a gesture of *comme ci, comme ca.* "*I* can attack that, Ben. Back in the eighties, before the world exploded in nuclear and germ madness—which brought us to this point today—which TV program do you think drew more viewers, *Hee Haw* or a special from the Metropolitan Opera?"

Ben could but smile. Again, he agreed with the Russian. "We're speaking of personal choices, Georgi; that is the price a society must pay if said society is to live in freedom."

"Nice safe answer, Ben. So you are admitting that freedom can sometimes bring mediocrity to the forefront?"

"That's an interesting way of putting it," Ben said.

"And you're hedging the question."

"I learned a little about politics, Georgi."

"Of all music, Ben, which do you want to endure through the ages?"

"I think you know the answer to that, Georgi. I was listening to a tape of Tchaikovsky's *Serenade for Strings* and *Capriccio Italien* on the way up here. But I still maintain it is all a matter of free choice."

"We could argue for quite some time about this, Ben."

"Yes. But what would be the point? Unless one of us wanted to play devil's advocate?"

Georgi laughed. He leaned back, sipping his coffee. "I forbid the yowlings of hillbillies and the jungle throbbings of black music among my people."

"I don't," Ben said. "But I don't have to listen to it, either."

"You are very agile at side-stepping, Ben. But I think we are of like mind on many—no! perhaps a few—issues."

"Probably."

"How many sides do you possess, Ben?"

"Personalities?" Ben shrugged. "Several, I'm sure. I think you and I are both music snobs, Georgi."

"Yes," the Russian said. "Quite. And you are an honest man, Ben Raines. A truthful man. Diogenes the

123

Cynic would have enjoyed speaking with you, I believe. Ben, let me be quite open and honest with you. When I first . . . when this plan of mine was first conceived — and it is not original with me, I assure you — I thought at first . . . well, that I would find Americans to be more compassionate than we Russians. But do you know what I've found, Ben? The majority of the Americans I've encountered are no more compassionate than my people. So for the past few weeks, I have been very honest with those to whom I speak. I tell them up front: We are going to have a pure white race — colorless. There will be no concentration camps, no gas chambers, nothing of that horror. No torture, no starvation, nothing of that sort. Now . . . history may well perceive me as — to use a movie term — the bad guy, but historians, if they exist at all a hundred years from now, will not portray me as some sort of modern-day Vlad the Impaler or Hitler or Amin. Selective breeding — yes. It will take many, many generations, and of course, I shall not see the end results of my work, certainly, but I will die with the satisfaction of knowing I started a pure race.

"And Ben, eighty percent — at least that many — of the people to whom I have approached *agree* with what I'm doing. You don't appear to be startled at that news, Ben."

"No, I'm not, Georgi. I have thought for years that Americans are some of the most arrogant people on earth. But I also think, in spite of, or perhaps *because* of, that arrogance, we have done more for the world than any other nation in history."

Georgi reminded Ben: "You also helped to bring about the world's downfall."

"That, too."

"More coffee?" the Russian offered. "Ah—good. I shall have another cup with you. Must we fight, General Raines?"

Ben sugared his coffee. Real sugar too. "General Striganov, the historians might well condemn *me* for what I'm about to say and do, and I may—probably will—have second thoughts about it. But from what you have told me so far, at this moment, I don't want a war with you. For several reasons. I think what you are planning is wrong; I think it is monstrous. But I just don't have the troops to beat you. At least I don't believe I have. I think you carefully surveyed the situation before you came in, and you know all we would accomplish, at this time would be to annihilate each other. And I won't do that, General. I have plans and hopes and dreams for what remains of this nation. Besides, you'll fail, General, with or without me. If you think the surviving minorities in this land will just roll over and let you wipe them out as a race, you, sir, are very badly mistaken."

"They are not organized, Ben, with the exception of that little group out in South Carolina and that other group in the Southwest. And those groups are of little concern to me. *You* are a man of organization. *I* am a man of organization. And *we* know that without organization—a central government, a man in power, in full control—all is lost. How many blacks and how many Hispanics and Indians are left? Let's say a million. Spread out over more than three-and-a-half million square miles. *Nyet,* Gospodin Raines, they will present no problem. You present the immediate problem to me."

Ben knew the man was right, but damned if he was going to agree with him. "So, General Striganov, do we now talk of a dividing line?"

"In time, yes, I believe that is the only answer. But first, let us have lunch. Then we will speak of boundaries."

The lunch was excellent: thick steaks and green salad and good wine and baked potato with real butter and sour cream. Sour cream! Ben couldn't believe it. He said as much.

The Russian was amused. "I like to eat," he said simply. "And eat well."

"Do your troops eat just as well?"

"Very nearly so, yes. The steaks might not be as thick, and they may have mashed potatoes with gravy, but they are well-fed, yes. I assure you of that. I do not stint on my people's behalf."

"But there are people probably not fifty miles from where we sit, gorging ourselves, who are starving."

"Not in any area I control," General Striganov contradicted, his answer surprising Ben. "You see, Ben, we are—you and I—of very like mind. In some ways," he was quick to add. "I do not wish slavery or hunger or disease or poverty for my people. Besides, they would be so much more difficult to control should I be an advocate of those undesirable traits." He smiled. "You were correct in your statement that I have planned well. I do demand discipline, Ben, but no, there is no hunger in any area the IPF controls."

"Providing I buy all that you have told me, General, and I have certain reservations, there is still one issue—correction—*several* issues that bother me."

The Russian refilled their wine glasses. "Yes, I'm sure. Now we come to the part where I must try to match your honesty."

Ben took a sip of wine. It was a Rothschild, a very old

vintage. "White is a rather bland color, General. Black or brown or tan or yellow will almost always be dominant. You say you aren't going to kill the minorities; you aren't going to starve them out. No concentration camps, no gas chambers. Tell me, just how do you plan on achieving the master race without some form of genocide?"

The smile on the Russian's face widened. "The minorities will not have children."

Ben laughed. "Men and women have been known to engage in sex, General."

"They may engage in all the sex they wish, General. As a matter of fact, I plan to encourage that—keep them happy. I am merely saying they will not have any offspring."

"You'd better have one hell of a medical team if you're planning on performing operations on every man and woman in this nation who doesn't fit your standards of what a human being should look like."

The smile remained on Striganov's lips, but his eyes were cold. "What do you think we've been doing in Iceland for the past decade, Ben—playing cards and drinking vodka?"

"I have no idea what you've been doing, Georgi."

"When we left Russia, Ben—getting out with only seconds to spare, I can tell you that—I took quite a few very good scientists with me. Doctors, scientists, the like." He shrugged. "Many of them were Jews, I will admit, but still intelligent people. I don't like Jews," he conceded, "but they are survivors. And good scientists, too. It seems the Jew scientists perfected—and kept it a secret for years—a simple method of preventing pregnancy. One injection virtually destroys the ability to reproduce. They kept silent about their discovery for years; we found out only by accident. Then it was only a matter of, ah, well, convincing them to share their knowledge with us. How we got it is not something one would want to discuss over lunch."

"Torture."

The Russian shrugged. "The end justified the means, Ben."

"I'm sure." Ben's reply was as crisp as the wine.

"The people will be able to have and enjoy sex as often as they like. But they will never be able to reproduce offspring."

Ben stared at the man for a full moment, allowing the horror of what he had just heard to sink in to its hideous depths. "That is monstrous!"

"Calm yourself, Ben." Striganov patted Ben's hand and Ben fought to restrain himself from taking physical action for that gesture. "After all, I'm not destroying a human being; I have no gas chambers or firing squads or the like. I beg you, please don't compare me to Hitler."

Ben thought of several people and many things he would be more than happy to compare the Russian to and with. But he kept silent.

"And, Ben, there is this: We aren't monsters. If the people do not wish to have the injection, they may breed — selectively — with someone of fair skin. The offspring will do likewise, all very carefully controlled, of course. And so in time, several generations, they will conform. Selective breeding. It's all up to the individual, I assure you."

"How magnanimous can you be?" Ben said sarcastically. "And if the newborn child does not conform in color to your plans?"

"It will be destroyed for the good of the pure race."

Ben felt a small sickness within him grow larger. He looked at the handsome features of the Russian and in his mind, the man wore the face of evil, his hair that of a Medusa.

Ben heard himself saying, "It will never work, General Striganov."

"Oh?"

"When I leave here, I am going to spread the word about you."

"But of course you are. I fully expect you to do that."

"And you're not going to try to stop me from leaving?"

"No, indeed, Ben. I'm not a barbarian."

Ben could but look at the man and wonder if he was insane.

"You see, Ben, we've already injected over five thousand blacks, Hispanics and Jews. All your spreading the word will do is slow the process a bit, but really not very much. In the end, General Raines, we will be victorious."

"I fail to see how, General."

"Because a great many people simply do not like blacks and Spanish people, Ben. A like number—maybe even more—do not care for Jews. Those people will turn them in to us." He smiled at how simple it all was—in his mind.

Ben thought the smile resembled the SS death's-head insignia. "Let me guess how you plan on keeping records, General Striganov: little, portable tattoo machines."

The Russian applauded Ben. "How marvelously astute of you, President-General Raines."

Ben's lunch lay heavy on his stomach. The once-delicious meal felt as though it had turned wormy. He had lost all taste for the wine. He wanted to run outside and breathe deeply of the summer air. He felt the invisible odor of death and evil and everything hideous and unimaginable through his clothing, sinking into his flesh. For a brief moment, Ben entertained the wild thought of reaching across the table with his steak knife and slashing the Russian's throat. He rose from the table.

"I am going to stop you and your master plan, General Striganov."

"You will forgive me if I don't wish you luck, General Raines. But no matter—you will be unsuccessful, I assure you of that."

Ben's smile was grim, the smile of a mongoose looking at a cobra. "You will forgive my lack of manners by not offering to shake your hand?"

"Perfectly understandable, General Raines."

Ben walked out of the building and to his waiting troops. "Let's go," he said. "First chance you get, pull over to the side of the road."

"Something the matter, sir?" Sgt. Buck Osgood asked.

Ben looked back at General Striganov, looking at him through a window. The Russian waved merrily. "Yeah," Ben said, "I need to puke!"

SEVEN

"So you didn't speak of dividing lines?" Ike said.

"No, I blew it," Ben replied. "Got mad. Lost my cool. Almost my lunch. I wish I had. I wish I had vomited all over that bastard. He's got to be stopped, Ike."

"I agree. Al Malden time, Ben?"

"With much reluctance, Ike. I don't like Al Malden. Cecil doesn't like Al Malden. There isn't a black in all of Tri-States that likes him. He's a militant white-hater. He's as bad in his own way as Striganov." Ben shook his head. "No, he isn't. I shouldn't have said that. The man reminds me of Kasim, that's all. But I know he isn't that bad."

Ben had met Kasim back in the late fall of 1988, at a motel in Indiana. The man had been traveling with Cecil, his wife, and several other blacks, including the lady who was later to become Ben's wife, Salina. Kasim had hated Ben from the beginning, and the feeling had been more than mutual with Ben. Kasim had later been killed by Hartline's mercenaries; Cecil's wife and family, along with Salina, had been killed during the

131

government assault on the first Tri-States.

"Juan Solis?" Ike asked, shaking Ben out of the misty memories of the past. Ike had lost his family during the bloody and needless battle of Tri-States, and, like Ben, sometimes retreated into memory.

"Him I like. Yes, get in touch with both of them. Sorry to have brought you up here on a false alarm, Ike."

"Got me out of the house for a little while." Ike grinned. "You want to meet with them in Tri-States, Ben?"

"Yes. Tell them what's going down." Ben sighed. "But for God's sake, Ike, don't *tell* Malden to come in for the meeting. You'll get him mad and he'll puff up like a spreading adder."

Ike laughed and slapped his friend on the back. "Hell, Ben. Malden is just doing what you did back in '89: starting his own little country." There was a twinkle in Ike's eyes. He knew only too well he was touching a very sore spot with Ben.

Ben bristled. "Damned if that's so, buddy, and you know better." Then he smiled. "You do love to needle me, don't you?"

"Helps to keep you young, ol' buddy." Ike grinned lewdly. "And with Gale, boy, you'd damn well better stay young. That lady is a spitfire."

"Tell me. OK, buddy, you head on back. I'll see you in a couple of weeks."

So often when tragedy strikes, the first glimpse is misleading. The initial scene depicts total desolation, seemingly void of life; but there are almost always sur-

132

vivors at the second glance: men and women who somehow made it through the impossible.

Such was the case with Juan Solis and Al Malden and their followers.

Juan had surfaced only a few weeks after Ben and his Rebels and pulled into the new Tri-States. Juan had sent patrols out, looking for Spanish-speaking survivors, urging them to resettle in New Mexico and Arizona. Some eight thousand had, with more trickling in each day. Juan was building, as Ben had done back in '89, a society of like-minded men and women whose aim was to rebuild from the ashes of chaos and destruction a workable, fair society, with schools and businesses and a strong economy. Juan's was not an all-Spanish-speaking society. Just like Ben's Tri-States, there were people of all faiths, all nationalities.

Al Malden had surfaced on the East Coast, claiming parts of North and South Carolina. But unlike Juan, Al's regime was a rocky one, with many of his followers objecting to Malden's constant barrage of not-too-subtle hate directed at the whites. When Malden tried to drive the whites out of his disputed territory, most of his own people had stopped him, horrified at Malden's unwarranted actions and bitter vituperation.

Ben's intelligence corps had predicted that unless Malden changed his methods, he would, probably within a year, be assassinated, with a much more moderate black coming into power. That would be Mark Terry, a former IBM executive, Harvard graduate, class of '83. Mark was a very vocal opponent of any type of New Africa. Mark had met secretly with Cecil Jefferys several times during the past year, seeking advice from the level-headed VP of Tri-States and the first black to ever become vice president of the United States. When there had been a United States.

Cecil had told him bluntly that, "You would be doing the world in general a great favor if you would just shoot that ignorant, bigoted, biased son of a bitch and pull your followers out and into Tri-States. Then we could get on with the process of rebuilding."

But no man is totally bad, and Al Malden did have a few good points, despite his open hatred of whites. He did want the best for his people, but if the whites suffered for it, that, to Al, was of no consequence. He wanted good schools for the blacks, but he insisted upon his teachers teaching myths and half-truths instead of fact. (Cecil had once asked Malden that if indeed there ever was a "great black center of learning located at Timbuktu," where in the hell was it now — lying somewhere alongside Atlantis?)

In short, Al wanted everything for his people that he did not have as a child in south Alabama. And he did not care how he achieved that goal.

"I can't do it, Cecil," Mark had said. "Maybe Al will come around."

"Doubtful," Cecil had responded. "I had the same hopes for Kasim, back in '89 and '90, when I was attempting to build in Louisiana and Mississippi. Kasim's hatred of whites had made him crazy, just like Malden."

"We have to try, Cecil." Mark smiled. "You know that Al calls you a white man's nigger?"

Cecil's returning smile was not pleasant. "*I* am nobody's *nigger*."

Mark's smile this time was genuine, knowing he had

riled his friend. "Yeah," he said softly. "I know that for a fact."

Ben watched the planes carrying his Rebels lift off and head south. His own people on the ground were mounted and ready to roll. The young people he had gathered at the college in Rolla were ready to move out also, but they would not yet be returning to the new Tri-States. Ben had personally checked them out with weapons — rifles and pistols — and found most of them better than average with each. He had given them plenty of ammunition with which to practice and was now sending them out into the countryside, half of them to the west, the other half to the east. They would spread the word about General Striganov's IPF and their monstrous plan for a pure race. Each of them carried a signed statement from Ben Raines containing Ben's condemnation of the Russian's plan and urging all Americans to arm themselves and resist, to the death, if necessary.

"What are the odds of us succeeding, General?" Denise asked.

"I think they're better than even," Ben told her, thinking how young she was and how much she reminded him of Jerre. She wore a revolver at her waist and carried a 20-gauge shotgun.

Ben said, "Striganov was correct when he said a lot of people don't like minorities. The man did his research well; no telling how long he's had people in this country, reporting back to him. He'll get some support — perhaps not as much as he believes, but more than enough, unfortunately."

The young woman had a puzzled look on her face. "Why do people dislike minorities so, General?"

"Right and wrong on both sides, Denise. A lot of it has to do with arrogance, what the people were taught as young people in the home, and that which the minorities brought on themselves. I don't think they did so knowingly, many of them, but they did. You're far too young to remember the social programs designed to help people. They were badly misused, badly administrated and grossly over-budgeted back in the sixties through the eighties and caused a lot of resentment among the taxpayers who had to foot the bills."

"I don't understand, General," Denise said. By now, quite a crowd had gathered around Ben, not just the new young people, but many of his own Rebels.

Careful, Ben silently cautioned himself. Many of these people—maybe all of them—think your words should be chipped in stone to stand forever, and for many of them, this will be the final mental imprint of an event that history might never record with the written word.

He looked at them. They waited patiently.

But I am a man, Ben thought. Therefore I am human, with all the frailties therein. So I have to tell it as I saw it and perceived it.

"The government meant well," Ben said, choosing his words carefully, conscious of Gale's eyes on his face, listening intently. "But in their fervor to correct a centuries-old problem, they went overboard with their efforts. The government and courts meant well, and much of what they did was right and just. I will never be convinced that a racially balanced school system did one damn thing for or toward quality education. Do not — any of you — misconstrue my statement. I am not now and have never been an advocate of the so-called separate but equal philosophy. If one is equal, that is enough said. I believed very strongly in neighborhood schools. They were built so the children of that neighborhood could stay in that neighborhood and still receive a quality education. The courts changed all that by forced busing, and they created a monster; they created hard feelings and near-riots, undue expense for the taxpayer and unnecessary hardships for the kids who had to — were forced — to endure miles of riding a bus. Yes, they were forced. If the parents did not submit to the whims of the government, they faced jail. So much for personal freedom and freedom of choice.

"The government created a welfare state, up to three and four generations of people on welfare. The government took away the will to work among many people. Certainly not all the recipients, but enough of them to create one massive problem. The solution was simple to men like me: *Make* the people work if they were able to work. But the courts refused to do that. More hard feelings among many of the taxpayers who were picking up the tab — and the tab got more and more expensive. It got — along with the programs — out of hand.

"The great shame of our social programs was the way the government neglected the elderly and the very young. That was a shame I shall never forget. The government would give a community a half million dollars to build a goddamn swimming pool, yet in that same community, the elderly didn't have enough to

137

eat, proper shelter or warm clothing. I don't know how our politicians could shave in the mornings without feeling the urge to cut their throats.

"It seemed that for a while, almost everything the government did irritated somebody or some group. And sadly, rightly or wrongly, the minorities got the blame for it. Many people's dislike of Jews turned to hatred because so many of the American Jews supported the social programs, were against the death penalty, headed drives in support of gun control. That did nothing to enhance the position of Jews in rural areas — and not just in the South, for the South had become the whipping boy for the liberal eastern establishment.

"The government — in the form of the courts — moved into the private sector, into the work place. Private industry was *ordered* to establish hiring practices that would include X number of blacks, X number of Hispanics, X number of this and that and the other thing. I'm not saying it was right or wrong, just that it created as many problems as it did solutions.

"And then we had the traditional haters on both sides of the color line. Whites who hated blacks but couldn't tell you why — they just did. Blacks that hated whites and couldn't tell you why — they just did. Both sides taught their kids to hate. We had teachers in private academies who would stand up in front of their all-white classes and proudly announce they would never teach or allow a damn nigger in their classrooms. And that is fact, people, not fiction.

"And in many — if not most — of the public schools in the South, and probably all over the nation, teachers became afraid to discipline blacks, and I mean literally afraid. Fear of losing jobs, fear of having their tires slashed, fear of a lawsuit. All it produced was a couple of generations of badly disciplined and ill-educated blacks. But whitey wasn't gonna do no number on me, man. You dig?

"Now . . . that was not the majority of blacks, but just enough to leave a bad taste in a lot of people's mouths.

"Anybody with any insight at all could have and should have seen what was coming: white flight. That became quite a popular word back in the seventies.

"It may seem to you all that I am being unduly harsh on the black people. But you new people, look around you — you don't see any of the blacks in this command leaving, do you? None of them are leveling guns at me for what I just said. No, because we worked it all out. We agreed on every major issue. We of Tri-States don't have bigotry and hatred for someone of another color. We don't have it because we all realized that education was the key to removing it. Education, understanding, some degree of conformity, and patience. We understood that regardless of color, a child is going to need and get a spanking from time to time. That is up to the teacher and it begins and ends there. That is the agreement made between school and parent.

"We almost made it work in Tri-States. We came so close the taste of victory was on our tongues. But the central government in Richmond just couldn't stand it. I thought they would applaud the achievements we made: all races and nationalities living and working together without one incident in ten years. I thought the central government might learn something from our experiment. But they didn't. But we aren't giving

139

up, people. We'll make it work again. On a smaller scale, certainly; but we will make it work once more."

The Rebels stood in silence for a few moments, then slowly began to disperse. Denise stood with a wistful expression on her face. "I just want to live in peace," she said. "Yet here I am carrying guns. It's crazy, General."

"Crazy world, Denise. But it's always been my belief that the olive branch of peace only gets partial attention. Especially to people who aren't really interested in peace. It gets their full attention if the other hand is holding a gun."

"But isn't one the contradiction of the other?" she asked.

"So is the term fair fight."

She laughed and turned to leave. "Wish us luck, General."

"Break a leg, kids."

She walked away to join the other young people in one final check of supplies and equipment and weapons.

"When I first heard about Tri-States," Gale said, moving to Ben's side, "I thought what you people were doing was monstrous."

"Little liberal got all outraged, eh?" Ben smiled at her.

"That's putting it mildly, Ben."

"Our success stuck in the craws of government, Gale. They just couldn't stand our proving them wrong on nearly every social issue they had advocated and bled the taxpayer to implement and keep going for years. Government just couldn't believe we could bring it all back to the basics and make it work. But we did and it outraged them."

"And you are going to do it again, Ben." It was not put as a question.

"If I can."

The man and woman stood in silence for a few moments. Stood and watched as the young people began leaving. Gale said, "I wonder if they know what they are facing?"

He took her small hand in his. "No. No, they don't. But those that survive this will grow wise to the ways of this ravaged planet very quickly, I am thinking. Either that or die."

Gale glanced up at him, horror evident on her face. "Those that *survive?*"

"We will never see thirty to forty percent of them again," Ben said flatly.

"Knowing that, you still sent them out?" There was genuine outrage in her voice.

"It had to be, Gale. I tried to tell them what they were going up against, but I'm not sure how much of it registered on them. I really hope my words sank in. We'll know when we see the number that return."

"I can't believe you would do something like that, knowing that many of them faced death, would be sure to die."

"The survivors will make it. The rest will either get tough or die. That's the way of the world now. Those that don't have the right stuff will die along the way. There is no momma to write home to, now, honey. No USO, no Red Cross, no State Department. This nation, the very laws upon which it was founded and which the high courts and our elected leaders chose to spat upon for decades, is standing on the brink, teetering, first in one direction, then the other. A lot of people will die before any type of democratic process is ever again in force. If, in fact, any type of democratic government is *ever* again adopted. And I have very grave doubts about that. Right now, Gale, this moment, we are facing the greatest challenge since the bombings of '88. And if we don't win, we can all kiss any hope of freedom and democracy goodbye."

She looked at him. Blinked, then smiled. "Thank you, Professor Raines," she said. She rose up on tiptoes and kissed him.

The small column, now minus the young people from the college, backtracked to Ottumwa. There, Ben told the villagers what was soon to go down.

"What do you want us to do, General?" he was asked.

"I'd like for you to come with us, back to Tri-States."

The people of Ottumwa had already discussed this. The man shook his head. "No, sir, we won't do that. This is our home, and we have agreed to die defending it. We may be making the wrong decision, but we're going to stand firm."

Ben knew there was no point in arguing. He shook hands with the spokesman and pulled out, heading south, leaving them with their shotguns and hunting rifles. Against trained troops and experienced combat officers, with mortars and long-range howitzers. Maybe, Ben figured, just maybe, if they were lucky, and had the time to group before the IPF hit them, they might last six hours. If they were lucky. But Ben could understand the desire to defend homes and a free way of life.

Ben ordered his column to head west until they intersected with Highway 65, then to cut down into Missouri, staying to the west of Kansas City by about sixty miles, for Kansas City was radioactive and would be for centuries. During the trek, they found survivors in Princeton, and Trenton, and about a hundred in Chillicothe. Thirty families elected to go with the Rebels, the rest stayed, despite Ben's warnings they didn't have a prayer of defeating General Striganov's IPF.

But they would not leave their homes.

The column crossed the Missouri River and found more than a hundred people at Missouri Valley College. It was there Ben made up his mind, there Ben put the strugglings of his brain to rest.

"Get me General Striganov," he told his radio operator. "You'll have to search the bands, but I feel sure he's got people waiting to hear from me."

"Yes, sir."

She began searching the bands, carefully lingering over each frequency. She would broadcast for a few moments, then listen, seeking some reply.

Ben looked over the band of people on the campus of the old Presbyterian college. They were a grim-looking lot. Most of them wore a defeated look, and once more, that flaw appeared in Ben. He was not now and had never been the type of man to give up. No one who was ever a part of any hard-line special military unit was a quitter. One could not make it through the training by being a quitter, and very few special troops have anything but contempt for a quitter. Past training had been too brutal, too dehumanizing for a man to face failure by just rolling over and giving up.

With very rare exceptions, no man who was once a part of any tough military unit, the elite, if you will, will ever beg or quit in a bad situation. And they do not like to be associated with those that do.

Ben shoved his personal feelings back into the dark recesses of his mind and asked, "Where are you people from?"

"South Dakota, mostly," a woman replied. "Aberdeen-Watertown area. Thought we were making a sort of life for ourselves. Then the IPF came in. They suckered us, General Raines. They were nice, at first. Real nice young people. They helped us. But our minister, Ralph Dowing, he was the first to figure them out, what they were really all about and up to. He called them on it. They didn't do much about it, at first. No rough stuff, nothing like that. But we noticed that after that, they all started carrying automatic weapons. So my husband—no, he's not here, he's dead—he started carrying a pistol wherever he went. He and several other men. They—the IPF—they didn't like that. They told my husband they would rather he not wear a gun. They would protect us if the need arose. My husband told them he didn't give a jumping good goddamn what they liked or disliked or wanted." She wiped a hand across her face and sighed heavily. "Shortly after that, there was an accident—so the IPF called it. My husband was run over by a pickup truck. The IPF said my husband fell in front of the truck." She shook her head. "It was no accident, General. He was deliberately killed to get him out of the way."

"Yes," a young man standing beside her said. "Then

144

they started rounding up all the privately owned guns. That's when we started to fight them. But let me tell you, General Raines: They're tough and mean. And Lord, are they quick. Those of us you see here got out just in time, 'bout fifty of us. We picked up the other people outside Watertown. Same thing happened to them. General, what in the hell is going on?"

Briefly, Ben told them what he knew. He could see by the expressions on their faces many did not believe him, but the majority did.

"I've got General Striganov's HQ, sir," the radio-operator called from the communications van.

Ben keyed the mic. "This is Ben Raines. To whom am I speaking?"

"My dear Mister Raines," the familiar voice rolled from the speakers in the van. "This is Georgi. I trust you have had a most pleasant trip thus far?"

"Just dandy, General. But I am not contacting you to exchange social amenities. Interstate 70 is your stopping point, General. Starts in what is left of Baltimore and cuts right across the center of the country. That's your southern boundary, Georgi. You keep your IPF people north of that line."

"Are you buying time, President-General Raines, or tossing down the gauntlet?"

"Maybe a little of each, General."

"And if I don't comply with your demands?"

"Then that little war we talked about just might come to be a whole hell of a lot sooner than you expect," Ben said bluntly.

"I see," the Russian said after a short period of silence. His mind was racing as fast as Ben's. "Then may I have your word you will not interfere with my personnel north of the line?"

"I most certainly will interfere, General. If you disarm the citizens, I'll send teams in to rearm them. If you use any type of force or torture, I'll meet it with force."

There was an edge to the Russian's reply. "I don't like this game, General Raines. You're not even being slightly fair with your demands."

"It's the only game in town, General Striganov. Take it or leave it."

"I'll think about it," the Russian said.

"You do that, partner."

The connection was broken from the Russian's end. Rather rudely, Ben thought.

A crowd had gathered around the communications van. A man asked, "Is there going to be another war, General?"

"Do you want to live under communist rule?" Ben answered with a question.

"I don't care," the man replied. He had the pinched look of a man who had been born into poverty and never escaped it. His expression was sullen. "I ain't gonna fight them people. I don't think what they're doin' is all that wrong, noways. I just want to live and be left alone."

"Then you're a damned fool!" a woman cried, her face flushed with anger. Ben noticed she had a pistol belted around her waist. "Man, have you lost your courage or your senses—or both?"

"I won't fight them people," the man insisted. "So what if the niggers and the spics and Jews are wiped out? Be a better world without them people."

About a third of those present agreed with the man.

Gale stirred beside Ben, but kept her mouth shut. But if her eyes could speak, they would be speaking volumes. Her fingers dug into Ben's arm with a hard fury.

"Then why don't you take those of like mind and join up with General Striganov's people?" Ben asked the man.

"By God, maybe I'll do that little thing!" the man flared, his eyes furious. "I just cain't see what is so wrong with what he's doin'. And a lot of others around here agree with me."

"Mister." Another man stepped forward, his hands balled into hard fists. "Why don't you just take those that agree with you and carry your goddamned ass out of here? My wife is Mexican, and I don't like what you're saying or what you're all about. And if you open your fat mouth one more time, I'm going to knock your goddamn teeth down your throat."

The man who thought he might like to join Striganov's IPF opened his mouth to speak, then thought better of it. He walked out of the small encampment with about two dozen other men and women following him.

"I just can't believe Americans are really doing this," Gale said. "This is . . . unreal."

"Oh, you can believe it, dear," Colonel Gray spoke. "There is a lot of hate in this world. Or, rather, what is left of this world."

"And it will get worse," Ben cast more gloom. "Count on it."

EIGHT

Ben shook hands with Juan Solis and Mark Terry and then offered his hand to Al Malden. Malden merely looked at him and folded his arms across his chest.

Ben shrugged it off and gazed out the window. It was late June and the weather had been ideal. If these conditions prevailed, there would be a bumper crop of wheat and corn and thousands of acres of vegetables.

"So from what you have seen, General," Juan said, "you think that perhaps thirty percent of those approached are buying the garbage the Russian is spewing?"

"At least that many, Juan. There's a lot of hatred in this country directed toward minorities. Striganov is bringing it to an ugly head."

"Placing yourself amid the pus of that boil, too, I hope, General," Al said.

Cecil sighed and looked out the open window. Mark caught Ben's eye and shook his head in disgust. Ben could but smile.

"Al," Juan said, "you're a real asshole, I hope you know that."

"You'll see someday, Juan," Al replied. He smiled, but his smile was void of humor. "Big Ben Raines," he said sarcastically. "The great white hope."

Ben decided the best action he could take was none. He ignored Malden. When he spoke, his words were directed to Juan and Mark. "I don't see how any of us can sit on our hands and do nothing about this situation. Are we in agreement with that?"

"I agree with nothing you say," Al said.

Juan said, "Are you suggesting we take the fight to them, Ben?"

"Have we any choice in the matter?" Mark spoke. "My people will work with you in any way we can, Ben. You can count on that."

"Hey, *brother!*" Al rose from his chair in open anger. "I run the government of New Africa, not you—or have you forgotten that?"

"You run the political arm of the parts of North and South Carolina our people have settled in," Mark said pointedly. "But I run the military arm of it. That is a position the *people* placed on *my* shoulders—not yours. Al, are you so full of blind hate for all whites that you can't see that Ben is trying to help us?"

"Ben Raines never did anything except for Ben Raines," Al retorted heatedly. "Are you forgetting he once threw the national president of the NAACP out of his office when he was in charge of this nation?"

"No, I haven't. But did it ever occur to you the man might have deserved being tossed out? I never did learn what happened. All I got was the one side—the side the liberal press chose to report, as usual. And,

149

Al, I seem to recall that back in the early eighties, when Reagan was president, the same man, before he took charge of the NAACP, once referred to President Reagan as a California cowshit kicker. Now, Al, playing devil's advocate for a moment, I wonder how that man would have felt, being from Colorado, if President Reagan had stooped to his level, and called him a Colorado Coon?"

Cecil burst out laughing, as did Juan and Ben. Al Malden bristled with anger.

"All I'm saying, Al, is how about some fairness? That's all." He again looked at Ben. "We're with you, Ben. I'll give you all the help and personnel you feel you need."

Malden kept his mouth shut, but the hate in his eyes was intense.

"Same here, Ben," Juan said.

"All right," Ben said, rising to his feet and walking to a large wall map in the office. "Gentlemen, let's get down to nuts and bolts."

Emil Hite stood in the bedroom of his quarters in the Ouachita Mountains of Arkansas and looked out over his growing kingdom. Not so little anymore, he thought. Growing daily.

On his bed lay a young girl, sleeping after her first initiation into sex. Her breasts were still developing and her pubic hair was sparse. She was just the way each weEmil liked his female sex partners: from twelve to fifteen. Younger than that and they screamed and cried too much; older than that and he felt inferior, inadequate in the act.

To say that Emil Hite was a bit twisted mentally would be putting it most subtly.

Emil walked back to the bed and caressed the soft skin of the child, smiling as he did so. Lovely. Lovely little children. Too bad they had to grow up and become such bitchy women.

His kingdom of followers now numbered almost fifteen hundred, and was growing daily. Not with the numbers of the past, but several came straggling in almost every day. And Emil had found the mutants responded — in their own peculiar way — to kindness. Ugly fucking brutes. But they did make great watch . . . watch*whats?* Things. That would do. They made their homes on the fringes of the mountains, some of them actually constructing shacks of tin and scrap metal and wood. Emil had found that among the mutants, just as in normal human beings, there were varying degrees of intelligence. Some of them, Emil felt, might even be trained to do menial jobs — if he were so inclined to do that — which he wasn't.

A knock on the door of the cabin meant that Emil's lunch was ready, the tray left by the door. Honeybread and fruit and nuts and raw vegetables.

Yuk!

Emil desperately longed for a thick, juicy steak, but that would have appalled his followers, all vegetarians, and he had too good a thing going to screw up this late in the game.

Jumping Jesus Christ, some of the people out there were real fruitcakes. They had built him a throne from where he held an audience twice a week. Emil had to sit very patiently, listening to his followers heap long, boring speeches of love and adulation upon him. And

151

he would smile and nod his head and make the sign of the cross and look pleased while the yo-yos ranted and raved and groveled at his feet.

And Emil had to read his Bible daily, darkly reshaping the passages to suit his own twisted mind and perverted desires.

He sighed, thinking: I shouldn't complain about it. He had it made. Steady tight pussy from young girls and tight assholes from young boys. Love and servants and people to wash him and shave him and rub his feet and back. So he had to preach a couple of times each week.

Sure beat the hell out of selling used cars in Chattanooga, Tennessee.

The young black woman fought the hard hands that gripped her arms, dragging her to the van parked on a side street in the small Iowa town. She fought the men, but her efforts were fruitless. One of the men could not resist this opportunity to squeeze the woman's breasts, causing her to scream in pain as he gripped them brutally. The other men laughed at this.

"You can't do this to me!" she screamed. "I'm a human being, not an animal!" She cut her eyes to the few people standing on the littered main street of the town. "For God's sake!" she screamed at them. "Please help me."

The men and women looked away, not wanting to meet the woman's eyes. But they could not close their ears to her panic-filled cries for help.

She screamed as the doors of the van were pulled open. Her eyes rolled in fear and desperation as she spied the banks of medical equipment and the straps on the narrow, white-sheeted table inside the van. A man and woman stood inside the van, both of them dressed in white. They smiled at her.

She fought even harder. "My baby!" she screamed, hoping against hope someone would find the courage to help her. "My baby!"

She was four months pregnant.

"It won't hurt," the white-jacketed woman inside the medical van told her. "I promise you you will get the best medical care. We really don't want to hurt you. But you are going to hurt yourself if you persist in this struggling."

"Please don't do this to me!" she wailed. "You have no right to do this!"

"You are impure," the blond woman told her. "Although that is not your fault, you are imperfect. As with the mother, so goes the child."

The young black woman began cursing the people as they forced her into the van.

She was screaming as she was lifted into the van and placed on the narrow table. Leather straps were tightened on her ankles and wrists. She felt her dress being cut from her. Cool air fanned her naked flesh. She was suddenly immobile.

"Look at the pussy on this one," a man said. "God, what a bush."

The young woman opened her eyes, looking into the hard, pale eyes of the blond woman standing over her. The woman licked her lips.

The young woman felt the weight of a man covering her, his hardness pushing against her dryness. He grunted his way inside her.

She was raped four times within an hour.

"Enough," she heard the blond woman say.

The man on top of her climaxed and withdrew.

Coolness of alcohol touched the young woman's arm, followed by the tiny, brief lash of a needle.

"That's just to put you under for a time, miss," a man's voice spoke. "We promise you as little pain as possible. We're not savages, you know."

Laughter followed that remark.

She felt herself falling, falling. She fought the blackness that promised soothing, inky arms. Lights spun in her head, pinwheels whirled and sparkled. Blackness overtook her and she sank into midnight. There was some pain through her unconsciousness, but the young woman did not recognize it as such. She could feel herself falling deeper.

The midnight darkness began to be tinted with light. When she opened her eyes, she was in a hospital bed, in a clean, white, sterile room. An older black woman was standing over her, looking down. The woman smiled.

"How do you feel?"

"Shitty."

The black face smiled. "So did I. It was a forced miscarriage, honey. And I'll tell you straight out: You will never have any children."

"They?" She could not bring herself to speak the awful words.

"Yes," the older woman said. "It just takes one shot to destroy everything that God gave us women. The same with men. I don't know what's in that shot, but it's a devil's mixture, for sure."

The young woman turned her face to the pillow and

wept hard, uncontrollably, the tears savage, soaking into the pillow.

"Hell, sister, that won't help none. I know. Was you raped, too?"

"Yes," she sobbed.

"I was raped so many times I don't know how many men took me. Look, honey, I thought I'd kill myself after . . . after they give me that shot. But then I got to thinking—why? Then I thought some more, and came up with a better idea."

The young woman looked up at her through a mist of tears. "What?"

"Keep on livin' and think of more ways to stop these Russian bastards."

"That won't help my baby." She turned her face away from the woman.

"You right, it sure won't. But nothing on this earth will. Listen, we can help save some others from what was done to us. Honey, this is just one of a dozen or more hospitals the IPF has set up—and this one, like all the others, is jam-packed full. This place is full of blacks, Jews, Hispanics. Anybody that don't have fair skin is in trouble with these Russian honk bastards, let me tell you that for a fact, honey, and you'd damn well better believe it."

Through her pain, the mental anguish much more severe than the physical, the young black woman asked, "What can we do?"

"That's more like it." The older woman smiled. "All right, we don't do nothin' 'til you get to feelin' better. Right now, though, we can talk. It'll help some, believe me. What's your name?"

"Peggy. Peggy Jones."

"I'm Lois Peters. The IPF put me in here after I was . . . was worked on," she spat out the last. "Made me kind of a den mother, you might say. I'll tell you this: Be careful who you talk to, 'cause they's some black women copped out, agreed to breed with light-skins, anything to stay fertile. I thought about it some—rejected it. You?"

"They didn't even ask me that. I ran and hid for several weeks, but they finally ran me down and caught me. Lois, I'm not going to take this. Someway, somehow, I'm going to fight."

"Good girl. That's the spirit. You gonna make it now, talkin' like that. All right, what do you know about guns?"

"Nothing. I was born in New York City."

Lois shrugged. "Ever'body has their faults, I suppose." She smiled. "That's a joke, honey. Well, we can teach you about guns. OK. Now then, you ever heard of a man named Ben Raines?"

"Are you kidding! Sure, I have. General, president. That's the man who broke away from the union to form his own country. Why?"

"Word I get is he met with the commander of the IPF, a guy name of General Georgi Striganov. That man is, so I hear, one bad dude."

"Sounds like something you'd eat."

Lois laughed softly. "Son of a bitch stick it in my mouth, he'll pull out a nub. Talk is General Raines put the evil eye on the Russian, gave him a double whammy. Said he was gonna fight him, stop him and his IPF from doing this—like what was done to you and me."

"Anybody can," Peggy said, "General Raines is the

man'll do it."

"Damn right. That's the way I feel, too. You get better, honey. It won't take long. And you be careful who you talk to 'round here. Soon as you're up and about, we'll talk some more."

"You'll teach me how to shoot a gun?"

"Somebody will, don't worry. We ain't got all that many guns, now, but we're gettin' some."

"The people in that little town where the IPF finally caught up with me, they just stood and watched them take me away. I couldn't believe it. They just watched, didn't do anything."

"Most of them couldn't do nothing. The IPF come around, gatherin' up all the guns. You too young to remember the way it was back in the mid-eighties, honey. The goddamn government of the United States passed laws that gave the Feds the right to take all the privately owned pistols. That was the worst law Congress ever passed. Ain't no son of a bitch *ever* gonna take no gun of mine—not ever again. I'll die first; but I'll go out shootin'. Believe it.

"Some of the white folks are in favor of what the IPF is doin'. A lot of them hate it. White folks is just like black folks: No two think alike 'bout ever'thing. But General Raines got all kinds of folks in his new Tri-States, so I hear. Ever'body works together. No hate, no KKK, nothing like that white-trash group of people. God! Just think how wonderful that must be."

"Maybe we can link up with General Raines's people."

"Could be. It's a dream to sleep well on."

"Anything we plan on doing, Lois," Peggy said, a new firmness to her voice. "It can't be passive resistance."

"Lord no, child. Them days is gone forever. Let me tell you something else 'bout this General Striganov: He's got folks testin' other folks' intelligence. Lot of fancy machines and words. He's weedin' out what he calls the mental defectives. Anyone under a certain IQ is in bad trouble. They just been disappearin'. The IPF is takin' it slow and easy and quiet on that, not wantin' to stir up a bunch of people. But they're collectin' folks and takin' them away. Where is up for grabs. Nobody ever sees them again after they're taken, so you can guess what is happenin' to them.

"Something else: That evil Sam Hartline was in here this mornin'. Just after you come out of the operating room. I heard him tell one of the orderlies that after you got all better, he wants you in his stable."

Peggy looked at the older woman. "Just what in the hell does that mean?"

"You a beautiful woman, Peggy. Young, light-skinned. You could pass, you know that?"

"I've thought about it."

"Sure you have. Don't blame you. But Hartline wants you for one of his women. He's an evil he-goat, honey. Likes to hurt women. And he's built up real bad, if you know what I mean.

"Son of a bitch will never get me!"

"Just settle on down, now. Think about it. You be the first black gal he's put his evil eyes on. Be nice to have someone reportin' back to us on ever'thing he says."

Peggy could not believe what she was hearing. "You actually want me to prostitute myself?"

Lois smiled. "A stiff cock never killed no one I ever

heard of, honey, and women been spreadin' their legs to get information out of men for centuries. My grandmother told me that her grandmother told her that back in the olden days they was called house niggers. Kept them down in the quarters informed as to what was goin' on in the big house. You get my drift?"

Peggy nodded.

" 'Sides, once a man gets it up and hard and in you, you got him in a damn good position to slide a knife 'tween his ribs. You follow me, girl?"

Peggy's smile was grim. "I can dig it, honey."

"I'll talk to you later. For right now, you bes' get some rest."

"How?" The question was bitter.

"Just close your eyes, girl. It'll come. You may think it's the end of the world, but give it some time—it'll heal."

"Yeah," the young woman said. "Just give it time." She closed her eyes as the door to her room hissed open and closed. Peggy was asleep in five minutes. But her sleep was restless and troubled. She dreamt she was hearing a baby screaming. Tears rolled from sleeping eyes to dampen the pillow.

Refugees from the IPF's brutal tactics began drifting into the only known safe havens in the country: Juan Solis's southwest, Ben Raines's Tri-States and Al Malden's New Africa. The stories they told were horror stories.

And in the three areas of freedom, the commanders pushed their troops hard during training. The people, of all races, all religions, realized the urgency of the training. No one complained.

As summer began to wane, Al Malden grudgingly began to realize Ben Raines was not a bigot or a racist, and that if any type of democratic government was to survive, the three leaders had best work together. They maintained daily radio contact, using a scrambler network of codes.

"I was wrong about Malden," Ben told Cecil. "He's not a bad sort."

"I was even further off base with my thinking," Cecil said. "He's coming around. It's the damnedest metamorphosis I have ever witnessed."

"I wish to hell ya'll would speak American," Ike said with a smile. "I'm a Mississippi boy, 'member? We ain't used to them big words."

Cecil groaned and Ben laughed. They both knew Ike was one of the most intelligent people in Tri-States; he just liked to act the redneck part. And did a very convincing job of it.

"I've got over two thousand in here," Juan informed Ben. "I spoke with Mark and Al yesterday. Al said close to that number have drifted into his territory. How about you?"

"Just about the same, Juan. Most of them in pretty sad shape, both mentally and physically. I've found very few fighters among my group."

"Same here," Juan told him. "And Al reports the same."

"Well . . . it seems General Striganov is stepping up his moves, and getting rough with it. I've heard some grim stories."

"Same here. There are some pockets of resistance in Wisconsin, but Hartline and his boys are brutal. No prisoners, except for women, and then they're used pretty badly."

"My LRRPs say Striganov is staying above the line, Juan. What do your patrols report?"

"Same thing. But, Ben—we can't allow this to continue. My wife has just about stopped speaking to me, and Al said Mark's wife has closed the door on him, if you know what I mean. I think that's next with me. How about you?"

Ben knew exactly what he meant. Gale had turned decidedly cold. But Ben could live with that; he understood—or thought he did—how she felt. This was the 1930s and '40s all over.

Ben felt sick every time he thought about the IPF and their selective breeding program. But he was realist enough to know even with the three forces combined, they were not strong enough to smash Striganov's people, not without committing all free forces in an all-out war. And if they did that, leaving only a token force behind, the Russian could—for he had enough people—pull an end-around their flanks and come up from behind, putting them all in a box with no exit.

But Ben knew the free forces had to do something. The time for waiting was over.

"Juan, you know how I feel. Whatever you and Mark decide is OK with me."

"We've got to talk, Ben. Nose to nose."

"To keep Al happy, let's meet in South Carolina. You fly in here and we'll fly east together."

"Done. When?"

"Next week. How about . . . Friday, August second?"

161

"I'll see you then, compadre."

"Tri-States, out."

Ben turned to Ike. "Feel like traveling?"

The ex-Navy SEAL nodded. "We've got to do something, El Presidente, even if it means running the risk of destroying everything we're attempting to build. My wife says she's sick and tired of me pacing the floor at night. And Gale says you're getting hard to live with."

"Yeah," Ben said. "I keep remembering pictures I saw of Dachau and Auschwitz and Buchenwald."

"Yeah, I've seen those same pictures. And it's going to come to that, isn't it, Ben?"

"If it hasn't already and we just don't know about it."

"I thought about that, too."

"The survivors are telling us that Striganov and Hartline have instituted a new program of I.D. papers. Person doesn't have papers is in serious trouble."

Ben nodded. "Yeah, I heard that, too. How about the young people who returned?"

"You were close on that, Ben. Close enough to scare me. 'Bout sixty-five percent made it back. But those who died saved the lives of several thousand."

"I wonder how many died hard?"

Ike shrugged. "And how many just quit."

Again, Ben nodded. "Denise?"

"She made it out. She's all right. Reminds you of Jerre, don't she?"

"In a way." Ben stood up, stretched. "What is the mood of the people?"

"Ready to go, Ben."

"They understand this could destroy everything we

have managed to build?"

"Yes."

"They understand we are going to take heavy losses?"

"Yes. But they love freedom that much, Ben. They know Striganov has to be stopped — whatever the cost. And you know every man, woman and child in this area would follow you up to and through the gates of hell."

Ben did not have to be reminded of that. He sometimes had to fight to push it from his mind. "I'll leave logistics to you, Ike. Whatever you're doing, drop it. I want a complete rundown on equipment: tanks, APCs, howitzers, weapons, ammo — the whole bag, Ike, from pencils to panties."

Ike waggled his eyebrows. "Do I get to inspect the latter on the hoof?"

"How would you like me to call Sally and tell her what you said?"

"Lord deliver me from that!"

"You get in touch with Juan and Mark, have them do the same with their equipment. I'll get Colonel Gray to wind up training. It's too late now if the new people didn't learn the first time. I'll get with Cec, find out how many people we're going to have to leave behind as a rear guard. I hate to do it, but we're going to have to leave the older ones behind to shore up our rear."

"They'll handle it, Ben."

"I know it. I just hate to ask them to do it." He sighed heavily. "Looks like we drop the plows and pick up the guns — again."

"It has to be, Ben."

"Maybe after this, we can all settle down and try to pull together."

Ike nodded his head but looked dubious. "It's a nice thought, Ben."

NINE

Hartline hurt her every time she was chosen to be his woman for the night, but it was a hurt curiously mixed with pleasure. She hated herself when she began to respond to him. And she fought her responsiveness until it broke like a dam within her. She knew she had to win his trust and his confidence, but nevertheless, her pleasure made her feel like a whore.

She knew she was small; nothing could change that. And Sam Hartline was built like a bull in the sex department. She thought those men were only found in porn movies. He groaned and cursed and had to force his way inside her. And she hated herself for loving it. Even when she became wet and willing, he still complimented her on what a nice, tight pussy she had.

First nigger he'd ever kissed, too, he had informed her.

He had, at first, been angry when in the heat of passion Peggy had pulled his mouth to hers and slipped her tongue between his lips. He had pulled back and almost out of her. She thought for a moment he was going to hit her. Then he had looked at her, in the soft light from the night stand and smiled.

Supporting his weight on his elbows, he asked, "How much white you got in you, honey?"

The question was not new to her, having been asked by both white and black men and women many times in her life. "None."

"Bullshit," Hartline said. "You ain't full nigger, baby. No way. I figure you're about half white. At least a third. Your mammy must have done some stepping over the back fence a time or two." He grinned at her.

"I rather doubt it," she replied, an edge to her voice. Her parents had both been professional people, very religious and believing strongly in the bonds of marriage. Her husband had likewise been a good person. They had been married only four months before he was gunned down by the IPF.

Hartline laughed. "Tell me how you love this cock of mine, baby."

It was a game they played. Hartline was proud of his manhood, and liked to be reminded how much man he was.

She told him, profanely and lewdly, the words ugly on her tongue, but nevertheless containing more than a modicum of truth.

"Well, good," Hartline said, a strange glow to his eyes.

Then he brutally shoved himself deep within her.

Peggy screamed in shock and pain.

Hartline ravaged her, with no feeling, no compassion in him, merely taking her as an animal might.

He wiped himself clean with a pillowcase and then

166

tossed it on the bed beside the sobbing woman. There had been no pleasure for Peggy this night.

Hartline said, "For a jigaboo, you got the tightest cunt I ever seen. You must not have done much fucking around as a kid. I thought all you niggers started fucking when you were about ten."

Peggy refused to answer.

"Well, since the cat's got your tongue, I got an idea. Next time you can suck me off."

Then he proceeded to tell her, in the most profane and ugly manner possible, what would happen to her if she bit him. His voice and harsh, ugly words made her sick to her stomach.

But she had absolutely no doubts as to his sincerity.

All that had been weeks ago. Now, Sam visited Peggy more than any other woman in his stable. He seemed loose and relaxed around her, even kind to her at times, in his own peculiar manner. She acted as a docile servant, completely devoted to Sam's every whim and need. And Sam talked a bit more each time he came to her; whatever he said, Peggy reported back to Lois, and Lois to the underground.

On this night, just moments before Hartline was due to arrive at Peggy's small home, provided for her by Hartline, Lois had sent word that Ben Raines was gathering his forces to march against the IPF, along with Juan Solis from the Southwest, and Al Malden's black troops from the Southeast. Peggy was to find out how much Hartline knew about the upcoming invasion.

But how?

"Baby," Hartline said, a very slight and somehow strange smile playing across his lips, "you're not yourself tonight. What's wrong?"

Something in his voice caused her to turn around and look at him as he lounged in an easy chair. His smile was filled with sarcasm. And suddenly she knew — *knew* — he had been playing her for a fool. She had underestimated the man from the beginning. Everything he had told her, and she had told Lois, had been false information. Those people from the local resistance, those people who had been picked up . . .

Her fault.

"You goddamn son of a bitch!" she cussed him.

He laughed at her. "Whatever in the world is the matter, sweetmeat?"

"Bastard!"

He rose from his chair with the fluid motion of a man in superb physical condition, and Hartline was all of that. He walked toward her. "Honey, don't you think I know what a house nigger is? My grandpappy came from Alabama. All us Hartlines fought for the Gray way back then. Seems like you coons would wise up after a time. You shines blew it, baby. Everything that's coming at you jungle bunnies, you folks did to yourselves."

Peggy could not believe her ears, could not believe what Hartline was saying.

"History proves you niggers aren't as good as white people. And history is seldom wrong. That's what's the matter with the world, why it got in the shape it's in. Folks just refused to study the mistakes of the past. They just kept repeating them." He grinned at her. It was not a pleasant sight. "Strip, baby."

"W-what?"

"You heard me, sweetmeat: strip! Get bare-assed. Shuck your clothes. Do it."

Hartline was overpowering to almost all who met him. He was big and tough and quick and mean. He was powerful, immensely strong. And he enjoyed hurting people. Peggy had heard stories about his methods of torture.

"Dealing with male prisoners," Hartline began his lecture to a group of government agents, "is quite different from dealing with female prisoners. Man is and has been traditionally the protector of the home, the strong one. You must handle the male roughly—right from the beginning. You must assault his male pride, his virility, his manhood, his penis power. You take the clothes from him by force and leave him naked and feeling defenseless before you. He will immediately lose much of his arrogant pride.

"With a woman it is quite different. Use physical force with a woman only as a last resort. You order her to remove her own clothing. You demand it. Make her disrobe. By doing that her dignity has, from the beginning, rotted. That is a very important first step in dealing with a woman prisoner.

"Don't allow them sleep. Interrupt a prisoner every few moments while they are trying to rest in their cell. They will be imagining all sorts of dire and exotic tortures lying in wait for them. Lack of sleep disturbs the brain patterns—disrupts the norm, so to speak.

"I will give you gentlemen an example." Hartline motioned toward a man standing by a closed door.

The door opened and two of Hartline's men pushed a young man out into the large meeting room. The man was in his mid-twenties, unshaven, red and bleary-eyed. He was pushed onto the small stage.

"Good morning, Victor," Hartline said cheerfully. "Did you sleep well?"

Victor said nothing.

"Remove your clothing, Victor."

"Fuck you."

Hartline laughed and motioned toward the two burly men. They wrestled the young man to the floor and ripped his clothing from him. They pulled him to his feet to stand naked, facing the roomful of strangers.

"You see, Victor," Hartline said, "you are a baby. I can do anything I wish with you, anytime I choose to do so. Remember that, Victor, it might save you — or someone you love — a lot of pain. Now then, Victor, who is the leader of your cell?"

Victor refused to reply.

Hartline shook his head and clucked his tongue in a scolding manner. "Victor, why are you doing this? You know you're going to tell me — sooner or later."

"If you're going to torture me," the young man said, "get it over with."

Hartline laughed, exposing strong, white, even teeth. "Oh, Victor! I'm not going to torture *you,* my boy. Oh my, no." He cut his eyes to the man waiting by the closed door.

The door opened and a young woman was dragged into the room. Both Victor and the young woman had the same pale eyes, delicate features and skin coloration.

They were brother and sister.

"Rebecca!" Victor yelled. He tried to get to her. Strong hands held him firm. "You son of a bitch!" he cursed Hartline.

The mercenary laughed at him. "Tie him into that chair over there," he said, pointing. "Hands behind the back, ankles to the legs."

Hartline looked at the woman. Something evil and perverted touched his eyes. "Now, my dear, you may disrobe."

"No, I won't," she said defiantly, holding her chin high.

Hartline chuckled. "Oh, I think you shall, Rebecca. Yes, I believe you shall."

He picked up a small cattle-prod and adjusted the level of voltage. He walked to Victor's side, then lifted his eyes to the woman. "Take off your clothing, dear."

"No," she whispered.

Hartline touched the battery-operated prod to Victor's bare arm. The young man jerked and screamed in pain.

"Don't do it, sis," he yelled. "I can stand it."

Hartline laughed and touched the prod to Victor's penis. The man screamed in agony and thrashed against his bonds, his jerking toppling over the chair.

"All right," Rebecca said. "Don't hurt him. I'll do what you say."

"Good girl," Hartline told her.

As she disrobed, Hartline walked around her, commenting on her figure: the slender shapeliness of her legs, the firmness of her breasts, the jutting nipples, and finally the mat of pubic hair.

171

The agents in the room whistled and made lewd remarks. Hartline smiled. "You see, boys. There are benefits to be reaped from all this. Or should I say raped?"

The men laughed.

Hartline ran his hands over the young woman's naked flesh, lingering between her legs, his middle finger busy. He laughed at her embarrassment as his finger penetrated her. He glanced at Victor, now righted in his chair. "The name of your cell leader, young man. For I assure you, game time is over."

Rebecca urged her brother not to tell him. "We're not worth anything to him dead, Victor."

"How astute of you, dear," Hartline said. "But sometimes death is preferable to living."

Doubt sprang into her eyes.

"Oh yes, my dear. I have seen human beings reduced to madmen, every inch of skin stripped from them—and still they lived, begging and praying to die. I have seen, ah, I do so hate to be crude . . . various objects forced into a man's anus, including rather large penises. I have seen what happens to a man when a thin, hollow tube of glass is inserted into the penis and tapped lightly with a club. The pain is quite excruciating—so I'm told."

She spat in his face.

Hartline wiped the spittle from his cheek and chin. "You'll pay for that." He looked at Victor. "Talk to me, Victor baby."

Victor shook his head.

Hartline leaned down and kissed one nipple, running his tongue around the nipple, thoroughly wetting it. He straightened and placed the cattle prod on Rebecca's breast. "One of you will," he said.

The rape had been going on for more than two hours. Victor watched as the tenth man mounted his sister as if she were a dog. He could no longer tolerate her screaming. She was bleeding from vagina and anus.

"All right," the young man said. "I'll tell you what you want to know."

Late that night, a man's front door was kicked in and the man dragged from his bed. Later, the man faced Sam Hartline in an old office building. Somewhere in the dark building, a woman was screaming in pain.

"Mr. Samuelson," Hartline said, "you have certain information I wish you to share with me."

Samuelson shook his head.

"Don't be too hasty with your reply, sir," Hartline said. "Before you make any rash statements, perhaps you should visit your daughter. She's just down the hall, entertaining some of my men." He listened as the woman wailed in pain. "She is, ah, obviously not getting into the spirit of things, is she?"

"I don't believe you," Samuelson said.

He was taken down the hall. The screaming grew louder. He was halted in front of a closed door.

"Believe, Mr. Samuelson," Hartline said with a smile. He pushed open the door, exposing the hideous torture of the man's daughter. "Believe."

Peggy pushed those stories from her, but fear kept

173

them faintly in her mind. Slowly, reluctantly, she began removing her clothing. "Ben Raines will stop you," she suddenly blurted.

Surprisingly, Hartline did not lose his temper or hit her. "Could be," he said. "He's a tough bastard. And those people with him are fanatics. But Raines can't do it alone. Hell, sweetmeat, everybody knows niggers can't fight worth a shit, and greasers can't fight any better. Only chance Raines has is to beef up his own forces with white folks. And he doesn't have the time or the people to do that."

Hartline cupped a breast, smiling as he squeezed. He pinched the nipple between thumb and forefinger, enjoying the look of pain that registered on the woman's face.

"General Raines has a lot of nationalities under his command. Lots of minorities in Tri-States — so I'm told," she reminded him, relief on her face as he removed his hand from her breast.

"Yeah," Hartline once more agreed, "that's true. I think what he did, though, was gather up the cream of the crop."

Hartline slid his hand downward, caressing her satin belly, his fingers dipping into the crispness of pubic hair. "Get down on your knees, yellow gal. Start working that mouth and tongue of yours. Get me wet."

She knelt down, afraid to do otherwise.

"Get me ready for the back door," he concluded with a smile.

She looked up from her naked, kneeling position on the floor. Cold fear touched her with a chilling hand., "Hartline — don't, please. I can't take you there. You'll kill me."

"I never heard of anybody dying from it," Hartline told her with a grin. "But I sure have made more than my share holler, though. You got to be taught a lesson, honey, for your lies. And both of us might as well get some pleasure for it."

Pleasure? she thought. No way. She unzippered his trousers and removed his thickening penis, already massive. It was at that moment she made up her mind. She opened her mouth, worked her lips over the head, took it as deeply as possible, and bit down hard.

Hartline screamed from the white-hot pain and tried to jerk away, but Peggy held on with the determination of a bulldog, with Hartline literally dragging her across the carpet.

He slammed a hard fist against her head and she saw bright lights and shooting stars. Releasing him from her strong teeth, she grabbed his ankles and jerked. His feet flew out from under him and his head banged against the floor. He groaned once and then was still.

She searched him for the key to the dead-bolt locks on the house, locks that had kept her a prisoner, and located the keys. She dressed hurriedly and then kicked Hartline on the side of the head, insuring he would stay out for a few moments longer. She prowled the house, in hopes he had brought some sort of gun with him, but she could find no weapon. She peeked out the drapes and saw the street was dark and deserted.

Peggy Jones slipped out the back door and melted into the night.

"How many personnel can we field?" Ben asked.

"I've got two thousand," Al Malden said. "And that isn't leaving many at home."

"Don't spread yourself too thin," Ike cautioned. "The Russian might try to flank us and then come up from behind."

"Yes," Al said. "There is that danger."

Al Malden seemed a bit more human each time Ben met the man—more likable. And Ben found that he did indeed like the man. He had found a sense of humor that heretofore had been kept hidden.

Al sighed and rubbed his face with his hands. "If we don't stop this . . . this madness, this horror, and stop it right now, there won't be much point of having a home to return to."

All agreed on that.

"I can field about twenty-five hundred," Juan said.

Ben nodded. "By stretching it, I can put three thousand in the field. But I'm wondering if all that force at once is the way to go."

Ike perked up. "You thinkin' guerrilla action, Ben?" That was getting to Ike's liking.

"Yes. Hit and run. Neutralize one town, then move on quickly. But we're going to have to arm the people. And then have the worry of wondering if they'll fight after we do arm them."

"There is a hitch to that, Ben," Juan said. "How about the people who *like* what General Striganov is doing? Those that actually support his policies? What about them?"

"That is one fly in the ointment," Ben said. "There are partisans working up there, right?"

176

"Yes." Mark Terry spoke up. "A mixture of black and white and Hispanic. But they are poorly organized and even worse off when it comes to arms. Radio contact with them is spotty, at best."

Ben could understand that. "And I'd bet they are infiltrated."

"Yes," Al replied. "We're sure of that."

"Name one you can trust."

"Lois Peters," Mark said. "She's put herself on the line dozens of times. She runs an underground railway out of that area. Lot of the people who came to us got there with her help."

"Has she secure communications?"

Both Mark and Al shrugged. "Doubt it," Mark said.

Ben glanced at Ike. "Get a few people infiltrated up there. Tell them to get in, get to Lois—if possible—plant the radio, and then stay low until they hear from us. I don't want any heroics, Ike. It's too early in the game for that."

"Got it." Ike left the room.

Ben looked at each man. "How many of your people have training in a regular military unit?"

"Quite a few, Ben," Juan said.

"I have several hundred," Mark said.

"All right. Start forming them into teams of ten. Juan, on my signal, you'll send your people in from the west." The Mexican nodded. "Mark and Al, your people will go in from the east. My people will go straight up. I'll contact those people we met up in Iowa and tell them to hunt a hole if they're staying, or pull out now."

Ben rose from the table to pace the floor. "People, you are not going to like what I'm about to say, but it

177

has to be this way, or not at all. This is the way the operation is going to be run: no prisoners."

Juan, Al and Mark stirred in silence.

"I'll return to a 1950s slogan that was pretty popular until our government lost its guts: If you're Red, you're dead."

"Ben . . ." Juan began.

"No! Any person willing to switch sides that easily is not to be trusted again. That is something that has been proven time and time over. Those of us who were in actual combat—most of us—whether it was World War II, Korea, or especially Southeast Asia could never understand why those people who attempted to destroy or undermine the war effort were not branded traitors and shot. A person cannot have it both ways; one is either against communism or for it. Against liberty, or one hundred percent for it. You can't be wishy-washy on the subject."

Ben's smile was grim as he looked at Al Malden. "Al, you want all the bigots that support Striganov over in New Africa?"

"*Hell, no!*"

"Well, I don't want them either. Juan, how about you?"

"You have got to be kidding, Ben. A macabre joke, but I get your point." He met Ben's eyes. "My people have traditionally loved life, Ben. If we have a flaw, and that could be called a flaw, that is it. It is going to be very difficult for them to kill wantonly."

"They won't be killing wantonly, Juan—not at all. They will be killing to preserve liberty, as strange as that sounds."

"Yes, there is something dreadfully wrong with that

statement," the Hispanic said, shaking his head. "But, again, I see your point."

"If they can't cut it, Juan, let me have it all up front."

"They will do what I tell them to do," Juan replied, just a touch of stiffness in his tone. "They might not like it, but they will do it."

Ben shifted his eyes to Al and Mark. Al met his gaze with a hard stare. "I will personally hand-pick the people that go in, Ben. I can assure you, they will not hesitate to kill a bigot."

"That's what I like to hear, Al," Ben said with a grim smile.

"You're a cold-blooded son of a bitch, you know that, General?" the black said. He said it with a smile, meaning no offense.

Ben took no umbrage. "I sure am, bro. I damn sure am."

"Pax vobiscum," Emil Hite said to each of his followers at that morning's service. *"Pax vobiscum* and *absit omen."* He didn't have the foggiest notion what either term meant, but they sounded good.

His followers returned his smiles and the love they felt for him shone through their eyes. Those that weren't so stoned they couldn't smile, that is. Or wired.

"Pinxit obiter dictum and whop bop a loo bop a lop bam boom!" Emil proudly announced. He was a little high himself. Damn good grass they grew in these mountains. Shit hit you like a bomb. It was as good as Maui Wowie used to be, back in the good old days

when Emil was selling grass along with well-used cars in Tennessee.

"Be bop a lula," Emil said.

One of his flock gave him a curious glance, shook her head and hurried out. She had to prepare her twelve-year-old daughter for Emil's attentions that afternoon. And that was quite an honor. She wondered if she had really heard what she thought she heard the Master say.

No matter, she decided. Gods sometimes meant one thing while saying quite another. Maybe it was the pot. Or the speed. Or the coke. But regardless, everyone knew Emil the Master was a god. There could be no doubt about that.

And there was no doubt Emil had probably saved a few of the men, women and kids that had drifted into and were now residing in his camp. They had straggled in, half-starved, some of them beaten and sick. And Emil had cared for them.

But early on another thought had come to Emil: What was he getting out of all this good will on his part? The answer was: nothing. The next day he had discarded all manner of conventional dress and had appeared in a robe. Actually, it was a wool army blanket that itched like hell, but it had slits for his arms and head and looked pretty damn good.

He had held out his arms and announced to the few hundred or so men and women that he had just had a vision while praying, and he wanted to share it with them.

Emil had not prayed since he was a child in a local Holy Roller church (actually it was a tent) back in rural Tennessee. But he remembered vividly how that lay preacher could work the folks into a wild frenzy, with many of the churchgoers jumping up and down and staggering around the pews, babbling in the unknown tongue.

And Emil had watched more than one so-called preacher squeezing a goodly number of tits and asses while spreading the word, folks. And Emil figured that ol' boy was probably getting more than his share of pussy, too.

So Emil thought he'd give that act a whirl here, see if it worked with these folks.

It did.

He told them God had spoken to him. He told them God had ordered Emil to look after the survivors and to take care of them, to open his arms and give him succor. (And lots of stiff cock, but Emil kept that thought to himself.) He told them God said if they were to survive, they must band together and live in a commune and follow Emil's orders.

Emil prayed long and hard, with that fucking wool blanket about to drive him nuts. He whipped the people verbally, causing many of them to weep uncontrollably. Emil went to each member and laid on hands, and really poured on the B.S. He hadn't been named the best damned used-car salesman in Chattanooga for nothing. All that morning and well into the afternoon, Emil prayed and preached and led the people in songs. Then he began waving his arms and shouting, babbling, inventing a language he would later tell them only he and God knew how to interpret.

Actually, what he was doing was speaking in carny. Many carnival and circus workers of years back used to converse in pig latin when they did not wish the townies to know what they were saying. But too many citizens could understand pig latin. So someone—it is not known who—invented carny talk. It was not that difficult to learn. Take the sound of "ease" and put it behind the first letter of each syllable. Thus Bill comes out sounding Beaseill. Number would be neaseumbeaser. One can become surprisingly fluent in carny in only a short time. And to someone who has never heard the language, it sounds like a snake attempting to talk.

After a time, one can vary the position of syllables and still be understood by those who speak the language.

Iease ceasean seasepeak ceasearneasey.

Most of the people in the camp were, by this time, ready to believe and accept anything. They had survived a nuclear and germ attack; they had seen subhuman mutants and rats as big as dogs. They had been starved, beaten, many of them tortured and robbed and chased, many of the women sexually assaulted (and some of the men) and brutalized. Only a very few walked out when Emil began his pitch. The rest stayed and became believers. Soon the word went out and every nut and goofball and wacko and banana cream pie in a three-state area was drifting in, eager to join.

And Emil had it made.

He had been a corpsman in the navy, and knew something about medicine. He began visiting deserted towns nearby, grabbing up every book he could find on the subject of doctoring. He studied herbal medicine, and really became pretty good at healing—as long as it wasn't anything too serious. If the medical problem was beyond his rather limited realm of knowledge, Emil would pray, babbling in his personal unknown tongue. Sometimes it worked, sometimes it didn't. When it didn't work, and the patient died, Emil would simply say it was God's will.

And anyone who was dumb enough to join a cult in the first place would believe it.

But, Emil mused on this day, all that was secondary to this communist thing that was shaping up in a rather nasty fashion up north. Emil did not want the communists in this area. Ben Raines was bad enough. Emil was scared to death of Ben Raines. But the communists would really frown on his little scam. They would take away his robes and sandals and steady pussy.

And he would have to go to work. Just the thought of that was appalling.

What to do?

Emil didn't know what to do. But one thing was certain: His little kingdom of wackos would come crashing down around his ankles if the commies ever took over.

Emil thought and pondered and schemed and connived and finally decided he might have to take the problem to his followers and place it at their feet. But that was risky, for Emil was supposed to be the head Pooh Bah, Lord of the Beasts, direct communicator with the Almighty, Master of the Multitudes, and all that happy shit.

Emil sighed and scratched his head. He just didn't know what the hell to do.

"What we have to do," Peggy Jones said, "is get it

together and fight."

"Child—" Lois looked at her—"we gonna fight." She shook her head. "But we need guns and bullets and training. We don't none of us know nothin' much about that sort of thing. We got a few shotguns and rifles and pistols—and that's all. I *know* General Striganov has spies among us, but I don't know who they are. What you're sayin' is all well and good, honey, but we got to keep our wits about us, too."

"You just told me General Ben Raines is sending people in here to help us, right?"

"That's the word I get, yes."

"When and how?"

"That, child," Lois said with a smile, "is something you bes' not know—not at this date. Believe me, it's for the good of everybody you not know."

"Don't you trust me?"

"With all my heart, honey—you know that. But Sam Hartline is an expert at torture. He gets his hands on you, Peggy, you'll tell everything you know and even make up stuff, just to get the pain to stop."

Peggy started to protest, but the older woman waved her still. "Peggy . . . listen to me. You wouldn't want to tell, but you would. Ever'body has their breaking point, you, me ever'body. Sam Hartline would get it out of you or me or anybody."

Peggy nodded her head in agreement. She was very frightened of Hartline. "When will the people from General Raines's camp be here?"

"Soon. I don't know just when, and that's the truth. For now, you stay in this basement and don't you stick your head out for *nothin'*. Sam Hartline has said when he finds you, girl, he's going to torture you for days

184

until you're beggin' him to let you die. And he means it, honey." She smiled. " 'Cause you shore did a number on that white man's cock. You didn't bite it off, but you shore skin it up good."

"I tried to bite it off."

Lois laughed softly, the sound muted in the semi-darkened basement of the old farmhouse. "I shore would have liked to seen it. I really would have. I don't know if I'd've had the courage to do what you done."

"I'm afraid of that man, Lois. I will admit I am scared to death of him. He's . . . twisted all up in his mind. He's . . . he's . . ."

"Evil," the older woman finished it.

"Where is Peggy Jones?" Hartline asked the tortured man.

"I don't know." The man gasped the reply. He spat out a mouthful of blood.

Hartline looked at another man in the room and nodded his head. "Pull out another tooth."

The tortured man screamed and fought the leather straps that held him. At a silent signal from the husky man wearing a blood-splattered butcher's apron, the victim's mouth was pried open.

A man wielding pliers leaned forward, a smile of satisfaction on his thick, wet lips. His crotch bulged from sexual arousal. The screaming in the small room became hideous.

Sam Hartline left the room, disgust obvious on his face when the tortured man passed out from the intense pain. He walked down the hall to another room and opened the door.

A dark-haired young woman was strapped to a table; the table was bolted to the floor. The woman was naked. She was strapped belly-down on the table, her legs spread wide and her ankles attached to straps run through thick metal rings bolted to the floor. Her eyes were dull from the pain and humiliation. She had been beaten, raped and sodomized. Vivid marks crisscrossed her flesh from the savage lashings with leather belts and whips.

Hartline looked at her through cold, emotionless green eyes. "Are you ready to cooperate with us now, Miss Brinkerhoff?"

Tears dropped from the young woman's eyes. They splashed on the cold metal of the table. "I don't know anything." She choked out the words.

A man, naked from the waist down, with a huge erection in his hand, stepped behind the woman. He penetrated her anally with one brutal lunge. She screamed in pain as he worked his way deeper.

"I don't know anything!" she cried.

She was telling the truth. She did not know the whereabouts of Peggy Jones. She had never even heard of Peggy Jones prior to Hartline's mentioning her name. She did not know anything about any resistance movement. She was a newcomer to this area. She knew nothing about any upcoming confrontation between Ben Raines's troops and the IPF.

Her attacker's hairy belly slapped against her buttocks. She screamed in pain and degradation.

Hartline and the other men in the room smiled. All were sexually aroused by the sight and sounds of the attack.

It would have been much easier had Hartline simply

given her a polygraph or PSE test; he could have used any of a number of truth serums at his disposal. But Hartline and the group of questioners — men and women — enjoyed seeing people tortured, enjoyed listening to them scream and beg and pray and promise anything and everything if only the pain would stop.

Hartline became sexually aroused when that happened. Hartline and his group of interrogators shared a great deal in common with Hitler's SS and Gestapo agents. Many SS and Gestapo agents used to enjoy slowly strangling young men to death. Just before the final death throes, the naked victims would usually gain an erection followed by their final climax. The SS or Gestapo agents so inclined could then take the penis in their mouths.

So much for the master race.

Sam Hartline would have been at his dubious glory as an SS or Gestapo officer.

He would have experienced shivers of ecstasy had he been commandant of a concentration camp during Hitler's reign of terror.

Hartline would have been the perfect mate for the Bitch of Buchenwald, that lady (referring only to her anatomical gender) who made lamp shades out of human skin taken from her victims while they were still alive and conscious. Said she just loved tattoos.

Hartline pulled the man away from the woman's buttocks. Blood dripped to the floor from her mangled anus. He picked up a small whip from a rack and began beating her back and buttocks, smiling at her screams.

He beat her for a few moments, dropping her almost to unconsciousness. He ordered a bucket of water to be thrown on her, reviving her.

Smiling as he spoke, Hartline said, when he was certain the woman was conscious enough to understand, "If she hasn't talked in twenty-four hours, take her down into Missouri where the mutants gather. Strip her and tie her to a tree. They'll find her."

"No!" she screamed. She had seen the mutants before.

Hartline tossed the short whip to the floor and turned his back to the woman. He walked out of the room. Her screaming intensified as the perversion gained new heights.

Gen. Georgi Striganov knew of Hartline's inclination toward torture. One of the reasons he wanted the man on his team. Striganov was not opposed to torture, he just did not personally want to be a party to it. He had found, years before, when he worked for the KGB, that drugs were much more effective and a great deal neater. And one did not have to listen to the shrieking and yelling or put up with the vomiting and all that other disagreeable mess that was associated with physical torture.

Georgi had known many men and women who enjoyed administering torture. He had closely observed them during the act: the quickened breathing, the glazed eyes, the sexual aspects of the torture act itself. He did not want to become one of those perverted types of people.

Besides, physical torture made him ill.

The Russian compartmentalized the issues before him, and took from one section of the mind the matter of Ben Raines, placing the matter of Sam Hartline in another niche. A darker corner of the mind, where the mercenary could squat and pick at himself.

Ben Raines worried the Russian. Georgi knew the man was going to make a military move against him. He had placed informants in the ranks of Raines's civilians and Emil Hite's idiot grouping months back — but their information was sketchy, at best. And nothing of any use had come out of the camp of Emil Hite. Which was, according to the Russian's way of thinking, perfectly understandable. In his mind, Georgi had already written off Hite and his foolish band. They might be of some limited use at a future date, but the Russian could not possibly think of how that might come to pass.

What kind of move was Ben Raines planning? When would it take place? And how would Raines go about it?

He didn't know.

He did know his IPF personnel were much stronger in number than anything Raines or Solis or Malden could put together, and they were better trained and equipped, for the most part. So Raines was probably contemplating some sort of guerrilla action. He knew Raines and the ex-SEAL, McGowen, were both trained in guerrilla warfare and highly decorated during the Vietnam war. And Raines was an ex-mercenary to boot.

Guerrilla warfare. That was what the Russian feared the most from Raines, for that would mean his IPF forces would have to be spread all over three or four states, and his selective breeding program would have to be placed on the back burner for the duration.

Things had been coming along so very splendidly — especially that new program his doctors had suggested.

"Goddamn it!" he cursed, slamming a fist on his desk top. "Goddamn Ben Raines."

He picked up the phone on his desk and punched savagely at the buttons. He snarled, "Get me Colonel Fechnor — quickly."

The first intelligence reports back to Tri-States were grim and very much to the point:

"Tell General Raines the IPF is mounting up, getting ready for what looks to be a big push — south."

Ben read the copied message. "Damn!" he said. He turned in his chair and looked at Ike. "Now we don't have a choice in the matter, buddy. It's been decided for us."

Ike nodded. "We'll have to meet them head-on." There was a grimness to his voice. "And they'll have us outgunned and outmanned."

"But we can't stay boxed in here," Cecil said. Like Ike, the black man was spoiling for a good fight. An ex-Green Beret, he had earned his CIB in Vietnam. "They'd sit off our borders and lob heavy artillery in on us, and eventually kill us all."

"Give me your votes," Ben said, looking at Colonel Gray, the only person present who had yet to speak.

"Take the fight to them, General," the Englishman said. "If we are going to die, then let us prepare to die for liberty."

Ben smiled. He knew without asking that would be the reply of all his people. He looked at Ike.

"I'm with him," Ike said, jerking his thumb toward

Dan. "I just can't say it as pretty."

"That line came, in part," Dan said, "from a Romberg opera. When the street rabble were preparing to do battle for King Louis against the crown of Burgundy. They were ultimately successful in their efforts."

"Do tell," Ike said.

"Cretin," Dan said with a smile.

"Smart-ass," Ike responded.

Laughing, Ben glanced at Cecil.

"Take the fight to them, Ben. Let's kick their asses all the way back to Iceland."

"All right, that's it. Pull back your people from Iowa. Those that were meeting with Lois Peters. I hate to leave what resistance there is up there defenseless, but I can't risk losing anybody at this stage of the game.

"Gear up. I want the people mobilized and moving within forty-eight hours. Contact Juan and Al and have them get their troops moving—en masse. Right now. Juan will take his people in from the west, Al from the east; we'll go straight up and in.

"Let's do it people."

TEN

"No!" Ben said. "And that is final, Gale. You are *not* going north with the column."

Out came the chin. "I'd by God like to know why the hell *not*?"

"Because this is war, Gale. War. Full-scale warfare. You have no idea what war is like. It's dirty, bloody, awful, dangerous. Can you get that through your head?"

She glared at him. Rose to her full height. All five feet.

"Can you, Gale?"

He towered over her; she glowered up at him.

"When do we pull out, Ben?"

"*Goddamn*!"

"I better get us packed."

"*Jesus Christ*!"

"Do you want me to pack any long underwear for you?"

Ben stalked from the house, muttering. He was still muttering as he walked up the street. Tina pulled in next to the curb, motioning him into the Jeep.

Ben kissed his adopted daughter and smiled at her. He

had not seen her in several months and had missed her. "When'd you get in?"

"Late last night. I stayed with friends."

Father and daughter looked at each other. Tina touched her father's face with her finger tips.

"I've missed you, kiddo," Ben said.

"How much?" She initiated the game they had played when she was young.

"Oodles and gobs."

"Good. Well . . . I thought it was best if I stayed away for a time. Dad, I have something to tell you."

Ben knew what it was. And he thought Tina probably knew he did. Very little escaped Ben's attention in Tri-States.

"Oh?"

"I met this real nice fellow."

"He better be a nice fellow," Ben said jokingly. He knew the young man was. He knew all about the young man.

"His name is Robert Graham. Bob. We're farming down in Louisiana."

"*We're* farming?"

"Yes. I . . . Dad, I live with him."

Ben had never objected to that. With the world having taken such a beating, marriage was getting rare. Sometimes a few words were spoken, but oftentimes not, they were spoken by a friend of the couple, and not a minister.

Varying religions were now almost non-existent, especially in Tri-States. Baptist, Christian, Methodist, Catholic, Lutheran, Jew, all the others, now were, at least in Tri-States, combined. No longer was there the arrogance of one church maintaining that if one did not belong to

193

that particular church, one was doomed to suffer the fires of the pits of hell.

It had taken a worldwide nuclear and germ holocaust to bring the factions together.

Ben smiled. "Thinking about getting married, maybe?"

"Could be. Just as soon as this mission is concluded."

Ben stiffened beside her. He had lost his wife, Salina, and their son, Jack, back in the battle for the old Tri-States. He did not want to lose Tina. For a few seconds, he was flung back in time.

Just seconds after Salina had kissed him and told him goodbye, she had been bayoneted in the stomach by a paratrooper. Ben had killed the young soldier and then knelt down beside Salina's side. She had smiled up at him, then died.

Moments later, Jack had been killed by a machine gun burst. Tina had lobbed a hand grenade into the machine gun emplacement, killing the gunners.

"What are you thinking, Dad?" Tina brought him back to the moment.

"Salina. Your brother, Jack."

"That's what I thought. Did you love her, Dad?"

"No. No, I didn't. But I cared a great deal for her and was always faithful to her."

"Have you ever truly been in love, Dad?"

"I don't believe I have, honey. Maybe someday." He did not feel any guilt about having said that, for Gale knew that thought there was a closeness between them, physical as well as emotional, Ben did not love her.

She touched his hand, this man she loved as her own father.

"Anyway," Ben said, "who said you were going on the mission?"

She squeezed his hand. "I'm a Rebel, Dad. You taught me to be a soldier. You taught me to love liberty and freedom, to know the difference between right and wrong without having courts to tell you the difference. Everything I value, I learned from you. This is as much my fight as it is yours. Now you want to make something out of that?"

Ben laughed at her stubbornness. "Don't get uppity with the old man, kid," he said jokingly.

"The way you were stalking about a few minutes ago, you looked like you had your back up about something. Want to talk about it?"

Ben shrugged. "I'll never understand women."

"What a sexist remark."

Ben's smile was wry. "You and Gale will get along fine, I'm thinking. And that spelling is G-A-L-E."

Tina laughed aloud. "Does she live up to it?"

"Damn well better believe it."

"I'd very much like to meet her."

"Well, so what are you waiting for? Welcome home, honey."

"We'll split up into three columns," Ben told his senior officers. "Ike, your brigade will take Highway 79 out of here to Memphis, then get on Interstate 55 and head north. Angle slightly west and stop at Warrenton. We'll be in radio contact at all times — everything on scramble.

195

"Colonel Ramos, you'll move up Highway 65 all the way to Interstate 70. Wait there for me. I'm going to connect with Highway 63 in North Arkansas and stay with it all the way to Columbia. We'll bivouac and wait until Al and Juan get their people in position, then we'll hit the IPF with everything we've got. I don't like to think about slugging it out nose to nose, but we don't have a choice this time around, boys. All right, we move out at dawn."

The scene resembled a miniature replay of the staging areas of D-day, back in 1944. Hundreds of vehicles of all types: Jeeps, trucks, APCs, cargo carriers. Just over three thousand men and women, a thousand to a brigade, milling about, creating what would look to the untrained eyes to be mass total confusion. It was anything but. The men and women of Ben Raines's Rebels had been trained well; each person knew his job and would give it one hundred percent. But any staging area sounds chaotic.

Whistles and shouted commands and the sounds of hundreds of boots on gravel and concrete filled the early morning air. Quiet conversations between husbands and wives and kids softened the din as men and women told each other goodbye—perhaps for the last time. One more stolen kiss, a touch, a caress, an embrace.

"Keep your head down, Sid, and we'll be thinking of you."

"You remember to pack extra socks?"

"This one will be the last one, Mary. We'll kick the ass off the Russians and then we can all settle down to live out our lives in peace."

"I'll be back in plenty of time for the harvest. Crops

are sure lookin' good."

And then it was time.

"Second platoon, Able Company, first battalion—over here! Group around me."

"Goddamnit, Lewis, if you can't keep that steel pot on your pinhead, tie the son of a bitch to your pack."

"Fuck you, Sergeant."

"Where in the hell is Sergeant Ward?"

"Right here."

"Your wife just called. You forgot to take your allergy pills."

"Shit!"

"Harrison, what in the hell are you doing with that goddamn chicken?"

"It's our mascot, Captain."

"A *chicken*?"

"First platoon, Dog Company, third batallion—get over *here*, damnit!"

Since many of the roads throughout the nation were in sad condition—with many of them having had no maintenance in almost fifteen years—the battle tanks would not be transported on trucks. The heavy tanks would have to be driven as is, overland. The harsh rumble of the big engines firing into life added to the din. Ben was throwing everything under his command at the IPF, and he knew if he failed (and that was a distinct possibility) General Striganov and his forces would then have much more than just a toe hold in America.

81mm mortar carriers were made ready to roll. 155mm howitzers, M60A2 tanks, M48A3 main battle tanks, and M60A1 main battle tanks, each weighing between fifty-two and fifty-seven tons were cranked up, the huge V-12 diesel engines rumbling and snorting to life in the cool predawn darkness.

Tactical and support vehicles, Jeeps and deuce-and-a-halves, pickup trucks and APCs roared into life. M548 cargo carriers wheeled on their tracks, pointing their stubby bulldog noses to the north, preparing to move out at Ben's signal.

On the tarmac of the airport, Jim Slater and Paul Green and a dozen other pilots checked out their planes one final time, once more went over flight plans and looked over their personal arms and equipment. They knew this was not to be an air war. Although their prop-driven planes were armed, they were not fighter planes. They were cargo and spotter planes.

Ben did have three old PUFFs, of the Vietnam era, each plane filled with electronically fired modern-day Gatlin guns. Each PUFF was capable of killing anything and everything in an area the size of a football field. But they were slow planes, and very susceptible to attack from ground-to-air missiles. One infantryman, armed with a Dragon, an XM47 guided missile, could bring down a PUFF.

Suddenly, as if on silent cue, the area quieted down. Engines idled quietly, conversation ceased as dawn began gently touching the east, gray fingers slowly opening from a dark fist to cast silver pockets of new light over the land, bringing another day to this part of the ravaged world.

Ben spoke into a walkie-talkie. "Spotter planes up. Go, boys."

Moments later, the planes were airborne, their running lights blinking in the silver gray of early dawn.

"Dan?" Ben spoke into the walkie-talkie.

"Here, sir," Colonel Gray called in from miles up the

road.

"Scouts out," Ben said quietly.

Miles north, with Col. Dan Gray in the lead Jeep, the scouts moved out.

"Are we in contact with the teams of LRRPs?" Ben asked.

"Yes, sir," a young woman replied. "They are on the south side of Interstate 70, in place, waiting for your order to cross."

"Send them across," Ben ordered. "Have them link up with Gray's scouts already in the area."

"Yes, sir." She spoke to a radio operator and a state and a half straight north, teams of Long Range Recon Patrol moved out on their lonely, dangerous and dirty job. They would be the eyes and the ears of Gen. Ben Raines.

Ben was handed a steaming mug of coffee. He sipped the hot, strong brew, mostly chicory, and walked the long lines of men and women and machines of war. He knew them all, faces if not names.

"How you doing this morning, Hector?" he asked Colonel Ramos, the C.O. of the third brigade of Raines's Rebels.

"Ready, sir," came the reply from the swarthy Hector.

"Viv raise much hell about being left behind?"

"*A 'sangre y fuego.*"

"And that means?"

"Fire and sword, Ben."

"But wasn't making up fun?" Ben grinned.

The Spaniard rolled his dark eyes and said, "*Si—por cierto!*"

Ben laughed and punched his friend lightly on the shoulder.

Ben walked on up the line. He came to a stunned and silent halt at a familiar figure.

The two men stood for a full minute, glaring at each other.

Ben shook his head and said, "Lamar, you are just too damned old for this trip."

Lamar Chase, ex-navy doctor, was in his seventy-first year. Ben stood for a moment, looking at his friend, remembering the first time he laid eyes on the man.

He had been traveling alone, seeing what remained of the nation, talking to the survivors—those that would talk to him. Many ran in fear upon sighting him. He had driven into Colorado, the malamute, Juno, by his side in the cab of the pickup. Ben looked at the ruins of Denver, the sight of the once-beautiful city almost making him sick.

"Damn shame, isn't it?" came a voice from behind Ben.

Ben spun, the 9mm pistol in his hand. Juno had been off taking a pee.

"Whoa!" The man had held out empty hands. "I'm friendly, boy."

The man wore a pistol on his hip, but it was covered with the leather of a military-type holster. USN on the side of the flap.

Ben holstered his 9mm. "Navy?"

"For twenty-four years. Captain when the war broke out. Chase is my name, Lamar Chase."

The men shook hands. "Ben Raines. What happened here in Denver?"

"Enemy saboteurs hit the base and hit it hard. For

some reason, spite probably, they also placed firebombs in the city, in very strategic locations. Gas mains blew. The winds were just right. And Denver is no more. I was home on leave at that time. Took my wife up the mountains and sat it out."

"I used to have a lot of fun in Denver. I was . . . I took some training up at Camp Hale."

Chase smiled. "Ex-Hell-Hound, Ben?"

"That unit never existed, Captain—you know that."

"Shit!"

Both men laughed. Ben took a closer look at the flap on Chase's holster. USNMC. "You a doctor?"

"Yes. You look like the survivor type, Ben. Let's sit and talk."

The men talked for several hours.

"What do you think about our president, Ben?"

"I used to fuck his wife."

Doctor Chase laughed so hard tears rolled from his eyes. "Beautiful," he finally said. "I needed a good laugh. Come on home with me, Ben Raines—meet my wife and eat a home-cooked meal. I've got something to discuss with you, if you're the Ben Raines I think you are."

He was, and the doctor's ideas were very nearly the same as Ben's.

The men had agreed that the concept of Tri-States could work. And it did work for more than a decade.

"I'd like to see you try to stop me from running my combat hospital, Raines." The old doctor stuck out his chin.

"Look, Lamar, be reasonable. Can't I at least appeal

to your common sense?"

"If I had any common sense, you crazy gun-soldier, would I be a part of anything you planned? Huh? Got you there, Raines."

"Old goat!"

The troops stood back and listened in silence. They had heard it all many times from the general and the doctor.

"You should talk, President-General," he said sarcastically. "I'm beginning to think you plan on repopulating the world single-handedly. Why don't you try keeping it in your pants every now and then? Now go tend to your business while I give my doctors and corpsmen some last-minute instructions on how to patch up people."

"Damned hard-headed old crustacean," Ben fired back at him.

"Oh, butt out, Raines."

"That should be corpspersons," Gale spoke from the silvery background.

"Ye gods!" Chase roared. "Is she coming along? Raines, can't you control that woman?"

"You're a male chauvinist pig, Lamar Chase," Gale said with a smile.

"Damn right I am, sweetie. And proud of it." Lamar stalked off, roaring and bellowing for his doctors and corpsmen to get off the dime and get their asses to their assigned places in this goddamned circus parade.

Ben took Gale's hand and together they walked on up the line.

Ben spoke to his Rebels: a word, a greeting, a sentence, a smile. He was very much aware of the fact that every man and woman present would follow him into hell, and he loved them all for that.

He wondered again—as he had many times since he had made up his mind to commit his people—how many would die because of and for him?

He pushed that from his mind. As far away as he could.

"Ike," Ben stopped and spoke to his long-time friend and buddy.

"Ben."

Ben looked over Ike's brigade. He spotted Jerre and her husband, Matt. He smiled and nodded at them and they returned the silent greeting. Ben always wondered what went on in Matt's head, the young man knowing the children he was raising had been fathered by Ben.

He swung his gaze and spotted his daughter, Tina. A tall young man stood beside her. He smiled at them.

He looked again at Ike and noticed the gray in his friend's close-cropped hair.

And the thought came to him: We are not young. Do we have the years left us to see this war-torn nation rise from the ashes?

I hope so.

"Kick-ass time, Ben?" Ike asked with a gin.

The Medal of Honor winner was spoiling for a fight.

"You ready, sailor?" Ben returned the grin.

"Cast off, mate."

"Then get them mounted up and moved out, Ike," Ben spoke the words that would again shake the nation into warfare. "I'll see you in a few days."

"Let's go!" Ike shouted. "Go—go—go!"

Juan's Solis's troops had rolled out of Arizona thirty-six hours before Ben's column headed north. Al Malden and Mark Terry moved their people in conjunction with Solis. Almost seven thousand fighting men and women were rolling slowly but steadily toward the most hideous threat to humankind since Hitler's nightmarish dreams of a master race.

And all knew that madman's ravings could not, must not, be allowed to again rear its ugly head.

Juan knew it. Al and Mark knew it. Ben knew it. All the troops knew it. Troops of every race and nationality: blacks, whites, Hispanics, Jews, Orientals, Indians, both East and West Indians. If this nation was ever to climb out of the ashes of war and destruction and disease and hunger and lack of faith and hope, it would have to be done without bigotry adding to the seemingly insurmountable task facing those who believe in democracy over slavery, justice over lynch mobs, fairness over prejudice.

This violent confrontation just had to be. The participants had no choice in the matter.

This might very well be their only chance.

The world's last chance.

ELEVEN

The convoys had to move slowly, for the big tanks had a top speed of only thirty mph, and it was essential that the tanks be a part of any assault, for the M60A2 tank not only had a 152mm gun launcher, but also carried thirteen Shillelagh missiles, a .50-caliber commander's machine gun, and coaxially mounted 7.62-caliber machine guns. It was fifty-seven tons of awesomeness, twelve feet wide, almost eleven feet high, and twenty-four feet long. Ben had thirty M60A2 tanks. Ten in each brigade.

The M60A1 battle tank was just slightly lighter, weighing fifty-two-and-a-half tons, carrying a 105mm cannon, plus .50-caliber and 7.62-caliber machine guns. Ben had thirty of them. Ten per brigade.

The M48A3 main battle tank carried the same type of machine guns, but with a 90mm cannon. It was a half ton lighter than the M60A1, but could fire ten rounds a minute from its cannon, and was more maneuverable. Ben also had thirty of them. Ten in each column.

The scant intelligence reports Ben had received had indicated the IPF had no tanks, but did have rolling howitzers and mortars.

Ben smiled a secret smile as he drove in his pickup, Gale sitting by his side. Occasionally she would rest her hand on his thigh. He knew he had the IPF outgunned with his M109A1 155mm self-propelled howitzers. The big bastards, with a crew of six, could sit back and lob shells a distance of eighteen thousand meters, which was close to eight miles. Nothing the IPF had could get close to them. Ben had twelve of them. Four per brigade.

Ninety tanks, twelve self-propelled howitzers. Ben had 320 people tied up in armor alone. He had 250 people as drivers and relief drivers. That left him with just over 2500 ground combat troops.

Gale glanced at him, taking note of the secret smile on his lips. She matched it until curiosity got the best of her.

"What are you smiling about, Ben?"

He shook his head. "I shouldn't be smiling. I was thinking that we have the IPF outgunned. But they have us outnumbered."

"Are we going to win, Ben?"

"No way for me to answer that, Gale."

"Humor me."

"The odds are not good," Ben told it like it was. "I won't lie to you about that."

"Where is that famous Raines confidence?" she asked. "That chutzpa that carried you all the way from trashy book writer to president?"

Ben fixed her with a jaundiced look. "*Trashy* book writer?"

"Well?"

"Oh, I still have confidence, Gale. And I won't harp on this subject, but I do wish you had stayed at home."

"I have a personal stake in this, Ben."

"Oh?" Ben glanced at her from out of the corner of his eye.

"Yeah. I'm a Jew."

"Really? I hadn't noticed."

She called him a perfectly filthy name.

If they could make 175 miles per day, they were doing well, even though the tank commanders were pushing the behemoth machines at max speed. Ben's column spent the first night on the road at the junction of Highways 67 and 63, in a small town in Arkansas called Hoxie. It was yet another lifeless town, the bones of the dead scattered by wind and animals, bleached ghostly white by the past summer's sun. No one among the Rebels paid much attention to the bones. It was a sight they had long grown accustomed to seeing.

But the smaller skeletons still bothered most of the men and women. They would not speak of that emotion, but they would avert their eyes and swallow hard, perhaps thinking of their own lost children, or of their brothers or sisters.

That first night, when the troops had been fed and bedded down, the guards posted, Ben rolled a cigarette — one of the few he allowed himself daily — then slipped into the blankets beside Gale. She turned, coming into his arms.

"Hey, Ben?" she softly whispered.

They were sleeping outside, under a sky that seemed alive with dead worlds, millions of miles away, a black velvet background softening the luster, making the diamond glow seem much more intimate, making the two seem much more alone.

"Yes, Ms. Roth?"

"I'm glad it was you that came along, Ben—up in Missouri, I mean."

"Aren't you afraid people will snicker and point at us?" he kidded her. It was a game they sometimes played. "Maybe they'll think you're my daughter. Or maybe they'll think you're a wanton woman. Or maybe that I'm a dirty old man."

"The latter I'll agree with. Come on, Ben. Don't joke—I'm serious."

"OK. No more jokes."

"I've been thinking about what you said today. We're in trouble, aren't we? I mean . . . what is left of the country?"

"Yes."

"About those odds you mentioned."

"They aren't good, Gale. But I can't be certain of that because I can't get accurate intelligence readings out of the areas the IPF control. Maybe the LRRPs will report back some good news."

"Yeah, maybe. I hate to be a harbinger of doom, but have you thought about what might happen if you—we—can't whip these people?"

"Plenty of thought. North Georgia, for one. That area looks good."

"North Georgia? You got a thing about the South, don't you? Is the Klan strong there?" There was open skepticism in her voice.

Ben chuckled. "You remind me of a girl I knew years ago. She—"

"Was she Jewish?" Gale interrupted.

"Yes."

"I don't want to hear about her."

"We were friends, Gale, not lovers."

"You believe if you painted wings on a pig it would fly?"

"What kind of a stupid question is that?"

"About as stupid as you telling me you were friends with a woman. Raines, you have never been just *friends* with any woman you thought you could screw."

"I think I'll go to sleep on that."

She rudely poked him in the ribs with a finger. "So tell me about her."

"I thought you didn't want to hear."

"I changed my mind already."

"She wouldn't visit the South because she thought she would find blazing crosses in every soybean and cotton field."

Gale waited. "Is that it? Is that all? You got me all worked up for that?"

"I thought it amusing."

"You would. Did she?"

"Did she what?"

"Visit the damn South?"

"How the hell do I know? I haven't seen her in years."

Gale was silent for a moment. "Was she pretty?"

"Positively the most beautiful woman I have ever met."

"Raines . . ."

"You were asking, I believe, about north Georgia."

"So proceed." Definitely a touch of irritation.

"I thought we might settle there, win or lose. Right under the Chattahoochee National Forest. I've checked it out. It would be very difficult for anyone to dislodge a sizable force from that area. I've sent a team into that country; they're in there now, nosing around."

She stirred in his arms. "I'll forgive you for making out with that girl."

"*I never made—*"

"Then you don't think we have much chance of beating these . . . the IPF?"

Ben sighed. "If all the troops we are committing, Gale—if they all were my people, trained by me, yes, we would have a chance."

"Would you please explain that?"

"I'm not putting down Juan's people, or Al's people—I don't want you to think that at all. They are all good people, I'm sure of that. But they aren't professional fighters. A great many of the people in my command are combat veterans, Gale *Every* person in my command is highly trained and disciplined. They are probably the best trained people now under one command—anywhere in the world. With the possible exception of Striganov's IPF.

"But the problem, Gale, is not with the courage or the loyalty of the troops under Juan or Al. That isn't it at all. They just aren't trained. And if something totally unexpected or unpredictable is thrown at them, I don't know how they're going to react. Neither Al nor Mark nor Juan ever pulled any military time. They are going to throw their people into this without any of

210

them having any experience in tactics or logistics."
Ben sighed heavily. "Maybe we can pull it off, Gale. I just don't know."

She snuggled closer to him. "Please hold me, Ben," she whispered.

"My pleasure."

Long moments passed before Gale asked, "What was her name, Ben?"

Ben pretended to be asleep. But seeking fingers soon found a part of him that proved sleep to be impossible.

It began to rain the morning of the second day out, a slow, leaden dropping from the clouds, with thick pockets of fog lying heavy over the land. It only added to the desolation of the ravaged countryside. The rain and fog slowed the column down to no more than a crawl.

The Rebels saw no people. Not one living soul. And no animals. But they did find several carcasses of cows and pigs. Something had been eating on them, something with super strength and a fanged mouth.

"I didn't know they had gorillas in this part of the country," Gale said, shuddering at the sight of the mutilated animals.

"They don't," Ben said grimly. "Just mutants."

"Thanks," she replied. "I really needed that just after breakfast. If you want to call that slop we had breakfast."

"C-rations."

"What's the C stand for: crap?"

"Get in the truck, Gale."

"Whatever the master wishes."

The column stopped at Thayer, in Missouri. The town was deserted. They slowly made their way to West Plains—also deserted. Willow Springs looked as though it had been torn apart by angry, petulant teenagers. With the scouts reporting back to them they felt as if eyes were on them.

"Don't dismount!" Ben quickly radioed back. "Keep on rolling through the town. Get on through and wait for us a few miles northwest of there."

Ben halted the convoy in Willow Springs. When he spoke to Gale, something in his voice told her not to argue with him.

"Stay here," he told her. "And do *not* leave the truck unless and until I tell you to."

She nodded.

Ben looked at her to see if she was feeling well.

Ben motioned for a team to begin moving up both sides of the street, weapons at combat ready. A thick, almost tangible odor hung over the small town. It resembled a scene from a grade B war movie: the sweaty faces of the troops; the hands clutching M-16s, AK-47s, CAR-15s and numerous other weapons of violence and death.

The thirty tanks in Ben's column rumbled quietly on both ends of the town, their noise adding to the idling sounds of the APCs and self-propelled howitzers and heavy trucks.

"Shut them down!" Ben yelled. The order was relayed up and down the street.

The dead town suddenly grew silent, the ticking of cooling metal like out-of-sync clocks.

Ben walked the littered streets, his old Thompson at

the ready, on full auto.

"Sinister," Ben heard one young Rebel mutter, his voice rising above the heavy silence. "And eerie, to boot."

"Possibly," Ben replied, not turning his head toward the source of the words. "Steady now," he called softly. "That smell is of mutants—and a lot of them. Fire only if fired upon. Let them make the hostile move. Pass the word."

"There's fresh crap here on the floor, General," a sergeant called. "Not more than an hour old—if that old."

"They're here," Ben said. "I can sense them. But they're not running away, and they usually run at the sight of this many humans. Them not doing that bothers me."

"They want me," the small voice came from the top of what had once been a hardware store.

All heads looked up at the small figure, looking down at them. Even at that distance, she looked worn out.

"Who are you?" Ben called.

"Nancy Brinkerhoff. Sam Hartline tortured me, then ordered me taken to where the mutants gather. They stripped me naked and tied me to a tree, but I managed to get free. I've been running and hiding ever since. The mutants cornered me in this town. They're all around here, hiding, watching, waiting." There was a note of hysteria in her voice.

"Just calm down, miss," Ben called. "You're all right, now. You're among friends. Let us handle the mutants. Come on down."

"Who are you?" she called.

"Ben Raines."

She began weeping and pointing.

The mutants erupted from the empty stores, screaming and howling in rage and hate. Many of them wielded sticks and clubs and crude spears, sharpened on one end. The stench of them was hideous, almost as much as their grotesque appearance was appalling to the stunned Rebels.

Ben was the first to react.

Leveling his Thompson, he pulled the trigger, holding it back. The stream of heavy .45-caliber slugs knocked the front line of mutants sprawling, blood and hair and bits of bone and guts and brain splattered against the brick of the buildings.

The Rebels reacted just a split-second after Ben fired. The fire-fight was very short, with only one Rebel wounded. He took a spear in his leg. Dead and dying mutants littered the sidewalk and street. Blood pumped from their deformed bodies and leaked into the gutters, clogged from years of leaves and rags.

"Let them rot," Ben ordered the Rebels, his voice strong in the shocked silence that always follows heavy gunfire. "Get Miss Brinkerhoff and let's get the hell out of here."

The brigade was stopped for the night in Cabool, Missouri, some sixteen miles northwest of Willow Springs. Nancy had been bathed and fed and dressed in clean clothing; Doctor Chase had examined her and cleaned and bandaged her cuts. She told her story.

She spoke of what Sam Hartline and his men had done to her. She was blunt, leaving nothing out.

"Those people are perverted beyond imagination," she said. "I suppose I'm — was — very naive. But I can assure you — all of you — that was tortured out of me."

"Where are you from?" Ben asked.

"Chicago, originally," Nancy said. The marks of torture were still very evident on her face and arms. "But my family pulled out of there just after the bombings of 1988." She looked square at Ben. "You know why, General?"

"Yes," Ben said, "I know only too well. My brother was a part of that . . . madness."

"You later killed your brother, did you not, General?" she asked.

"Yes," Ben said softly, "I did. Back in Tri-States."

How hated Ben's system of government was did not come home to the people of the three states until late fall of the first year. Ben had stepped outside of his home for a breath of the cold, clean air of night. Juno went with him, and together they walked from the house around to the front yard. When Juno growled low in his throat, Ben went into a crouch, and that saved his life. Automatic-weapon fire spider-webbed the windshield of his pickup, the slugs hitting and ricocheting off the metal, sparking the night. Ben jerked open the door of the truck, punched open the glove box, and grabbed a pistol. He fired at a dark figure running across the yard, then at another. Both went down, screaming in pain.

A man stepped from the shadows of the house and opened fire just as Ben hit the ground. Lights were popping on up and down the street, men with rifles in their hands appearing on the lawns.

Ben rose to one knee and felt a slug slam into his hip, knocking him to one side, spinning him around, the lead traveling down his leg, exiting just above his knee. He pulled himself up and leveled the 9mm, pumping three rounds into the dark shape by the side of the house. The man went down, the rifle dropping from his hands.

Ben pulled himself up, his leg and hip throbbing from the shock of the wounds. He leaned against the truck just as help reached him.

"Call the medics!" a neighbor shouted. "Governor's been hit."

"Help me over to that man," Ben said. "He looks familiar."

Standing over the fallen man, Ben could see where his shots had gone: two in the stomach, one in the chest. The man was blood-splattered and dying. He coughed and spat at Ben.

"Goddamned nigger-lovin' scum," the dying man said. He closed his eyes, shivering in the convulsions of pain; then he died.

"God, Governor!" a man asked, "who is he?"

Salina came to Ben, putting her arms around him as the wailing of ambulances grew louder. "Do you know him, Ben?" she asked.

"I used to," Ben's reply was sad. "He was my brother."

"That's horrible, Ben," Gale said. "Your own brother hated you enough to want to kill you?"

"He was part of Jeb Fargo's Nazi establishment out-

216

side of Chicago," Ben explained. "To this day, I don't know why or how he changed so radically in his thinking." He looked at Nancy. "You want to continue?"

"Yes," she said. "My father took us—my mother, my sister, my brother—and went west, into Iowa. We settled in Waterloo. We survived," she said it flatly. "But it sure wasn't any fun doing so. Never enough to eat, cold and tired most of the time that first year or so. But it gradually got better as things began to settle down. My mother died in '93, my father died a year later. My older sister raised my brother and me. We lived through Logan's . . . reign in office. My older sister always talked about heading out to Tri-States, but somehow we never did get around to doing that. Then Tri-States fell and after that the country seemed to fall apart. I was seventeen when . . . the troops invaded Tri-States.

"We got through the horror of Al Cody and VP Lowry and all that . . . awfulness, all the hate and the discontent. Somehow.

"One day my sister and my brother went out to look for food. I was sick and they didn't want me to go 'cause the weather was bad and I was just beginning to get better. I had pneumonia." She sighed. "That was last year. They never came back. Then one day the rats came. I never saw anything—up to that point—so . . . so horrible in all my life. And I thought after having lived through the bombings and the roaming gangs of thugs and all that, I could handle anything. I must have a mental block about the rats, because I really can't recall much about them. I know I panicked. I ran. I ran blindly. I don't know how I survived, but I did. In a manner of speaking."

Tears ran down the young woman's face and Gale reached out to take her hand and hold it.

"I can't ever have children. The IPF doctors . . . gave me a shot. Me, and hundreds — maybe thousands — of other women, and men, too. Orientals, Hispanics, blacks, Jews, Indians." She wiped her eyes and shook her head. "There is some sort of armed resistance movement north of Interstate 70, General. That was why they were torturing me. Or so they said. I think those people just like to torture people. I know they do. I heard some of them say so. I saw . . . I saw several of the men masturbating while they watched me being tortured. They . . . they would stand in front of me, where I was strapped down, and . . . ejaculate in my face."

When Gale looked at Ben, the rage of five thousand years was printed invisibly across her face. It seemed to say: Five thousand years of persecution is enough. This time, stop it forever.

"All right," Ben said.

The other men and women gathered around looked at each other in confusion, not understanding what had just silently transpired between the man and woman.

Ben swung his eyes from Gale, returning them to Nancy as he saw her rub her arm. His arm picked up the numbers tattooed on her forearm.

J-1107.

"The J stands for Jew?" Gale asked, a husky quality to her voice.

"Yes," Nancy replied. "B for black. O for Oriental. H for Hispanic. I for Indian. M for mental defective. I've seen other letters but I don't know what they represent."

Ben felt sick to his stomach.

Gale was silently weeping.

Ben looked around at the silent circle, more than one man had tears in his eyes.

Nancy resumed her horror story. "Sam Hartline and his men took me, tried to make me tell what I knew about the resistance movement. But I didn't — still don't — know anything about it, other than that it exists. They . . . really had a good time with me," she said, keeping her eyes downcast. "I . . . don't know how many times they raped me or how many men. And women. The women would strap . . . would strap huge penises on and . . . rape me. There is something terribly perverted about many of those people — maybe all of them. I was raped in every way possible. Over and over. It got so I could sometimes block it out.

"They beat me, shocked me. They attached wires to my breasts and my . . . my genital area. The voltage was never strong enough to knock me out. It just hurt so bad. They forced objects up my . . . you know. I know they are doing some kind of experimental medical work up there in Minnesota and Wisconsin. Like the Nazis used to do way back then. But I don't know what kind of experiments. Something to do with the mutants, I think. Mutants and humans.

"They kept questioning me, but I think they knew I was telling the truth. They just wanted to see how much I could take. I guess I'm stronger than I thought. What could I tell them? I didn't know anything. I think I would have told them anything. Anything to stop the pain and the humiliation. The pain." She shook her head.

Nancy held up her left hand. All her fingernails were gone.

"I'm not a coward, but a human being has limits," she said. "They finally stopped. Just quit. I thought I was dreaming. Maybe dead. I didn't know a person could hurt so much in so many places. I don't even remember the ride down to Missouri. When I woke up tied to that tree, I was naked and cold and hungry and sick. They left me with a little reminder of them. The men, I mean. They had attached a dog collar around my neck and defecated on me."

Ben was then conscious of a pain in his right hand. He had clenched his fingers into a tight fist.

"I managed to get loose from the tree and found an old farmhouse and cleaned up. I wrapped up in an old quilt and walked down the road until I came to another house. I found some old clothes there. I found a gun and some bullets on a dead man and taught myself how to shoot the thing. I'm not very good at it, but I sure scared the shit out of some mutants, I know that. I hit a couple of them. Then they began tracking me."

She lifted her eyes, looking at Ben. "They—the mutants—have some kind of intelligence, and some sort of communications system. They have to have that, because they were always one jump ahead of me."

"Interesting," Doctor Chase said. "That confirms what I thought all along."

"And that is?" Ben glanced at him.

"The mutants have leaders, pack leaders, den leaders, if you will, who possess more intelligence than the others. And they have organized them; they have their own form of pecking order."

220

"And the males like human women," Gale added.

"How ghastly," Colonel Gray remarked. "I believe I could have gotten on quite well without that knowledge."

"And me," Gale said. "Gross!"

"Best to know the type of enemy we are facing," the doctor said. "And it appears we have more than one enemy."

Chase did not look or act his age. His wife, a woman forty years his junior, could well attest to that. She had just borne him a child.

"What can you tell us about the IPF, Nancy?" Ben asked.

"Not a whole lot," she admitted. "But I did hear the men talking some when they weren't torturing me. Something about some new people coming in from Iceland. I kept fading in and out, but I think — no, I'm sure — they said several battalions." She looked at Ben. "Does that help any?"

His smile held no humor. "Well, yes and no, Nancy. I don't know the size of their battalions, but we'll call it twenty-five hundred personnel per battalion. Let's call several three. That would mean we now have approximately seventy-five hundred more troops to contend with."

"My Lord," Colonel Gray said after a soft whistle of alarm.

"Yeah," Ben said. "I hope He is on our side in this upcoming fight."

"We've been thinking that for five thousand or more years," Gale said. "Believe me, sometimes I have serious reservations."

"Let's not tempt fate by becoming sacrilegious at

this stage of the game," Ben said.

"For the first time in a long time," Nancy said, "I feel a little bit of hope for the future. I feel like I've found a home."

"Right." Gale once more took her hand. "Believe me, I need all the help I can get with this bunch of schlubs."

"Ben," Doctor Chase said, "have you ever considered taking a hickory stick to her tush?" He jerked a thumb toward Gale.

Gale glared at him. "I didn't know you had turned to wife-beating, Lamar."

"Only when she needs it, baby." Chase grinned at her.

Nancy laughed at this exchange, her first laugh in weeks.

Ben patted her gently on the shoulder. "You're safe, now, Nancy."

"Yes," the young woman said. "But I keep thinking about all those poor people north of here who are anything but safe."

"We're going to do our best to stop the Russians," Ben told her.

"I really hope God is on our side," Nancy spoke to no one in particular. "I really, really do."

TWELVE

The column covered only seventy-five miles the next day due to numerous equipment breakdowns and the worsening condition of the roads. The terrible roads contributed to the mechanical problems. The mechanics stayed busy, cussing as they worked frantically, for they realized they had no time to waste. Each hour meant someone in the IPF-controlled areas was being tortured and killed.

Before limping into Rolla, Ben told Colonel Gray, "Take a full platoon in there, Dan. If you find any of the IPF or any civilian who has tossed in with them — kill them."

The Englishman smiled coldly and knowingly, saluted and pulled out. The ex-British SAS officer was one of the most savage fighters in Ben's command.

The first thing Colonel Gray observed just outside of Rolla was the body of a black man. He had been hanged by the neck and his features were horribly disfigured. A crudely lettered cardboard sign was hanging about his neck: "NIGGERS — STAY IN

YOUR PLACE."

Sgt. Mac Cummings, a young black, swallowed audibly. "My momma used to tell me they'd be days like this, but she didn't tell me they was goin' to come in bunches."

Colonel Gray said, "When — or if — we find those responsible for this, Mac, you may lead the firing squad."

"My pleasure, sir."

A team lowered the body and a medic inspected the stiffened corpse. "Colonel," he called, "this man's been tortured and castrated."

Sergeant Cummings made a low sound of anger and spat on the ground.

"Scouts out," Colonel Gray ordered. "Heads up and steady on, now, lads."

"And lassies," Cpl. Anne Lewis reminded him with a smile.

"I could never forget the lassies." Dan grinned.

"What do you want us to do with the body?" a medic asked.

"Leave it," Dan said tersely. "It will be a pile of rotting bones in a month."

Sergeant Cummings's face registered no emotion. He knew they didn't have the time to bury the body; and what the hell difference did one more rotting body make at this stage of the game? But he had never gotten accustomed to the necessary callousness.

One mile up the pitted and weed-grown highway they were stopped by a barricade stretching from shoulder to shoulder across the highway. A sign on the blockade read: "NIGGERS SPICS JEWS & ALL OTHER NON-WHITES STAY OUT."

"I have just about taken all this crap I am going to tolerate," a young Jewish Rebel said. His words were laced with venom.

"Calm yourself," Dan told him. "Les, get General Raines on the horn and inform him of this development and ask what he wants us to do about it."

The radio operator was back in a moment. "General Raines says to assess the situation, sir. If you think we can handle it, proceed."

"Thank you, son. Sergeant Cummings? Inspect that barricade for explosives. If it is not touchy, please remove it."

"You put your black hands on that blockade, nigger, and you'll die!" A hard voice shouted the warning from the woods alongside the highway.

A shot cracked in the morning calm. The sounds of a body hitting the forest floor drifted out. One of Colonel Gray's scouts stepped from the timber, a smoking pistol in his hand.

"I found another one back in the woods always," the young man said. "I cut his throat."

"Thank you, Jimmy," Dan replied, as if thanking a waiter for a fresh cup of tea. "Well done. I take it the timber is secure?"

"Yes, sir."

"Good."

Dan's walkie-talkie barked. He listened as the message spewed forth. "We got a fight on our hands, Colonel," the forward scout reported. "The citizens are armed and hostile and waiting for us. The man who appears to be in charge says this is as far as we go. No nigger-lovers welcome in here. Told me to tell you to turn around and get the hell out."

"How perfectly inhospitable of him," Dan muttered. "One would think they were void of manners. How many people involved?" Dan asked the scout.

"Couple hundred, sir."

"Pull back," Dan ordered the LRRPs. "Take coordinates for the mortar teams."

"Roger, sir."

"Tell *me* to get the hell out!" Dan muttered. "Halfwits probably never even heard of Lord Byron."

Col. Dan Gray had come to Ben after serving first with the British Special Air Service and then, after the bombings of 1988, with the American Special Forces. His small company of Rebels were known as Gray's Scouts. They could aptly be compared to a cross between Tasmanian devils and French foreign legionnaires, with a little bit of spitting cobra tossed in. They were experts at behind-the-lines, guerrilla-type action, experts with the knife, piano wire, brass knuckles and just plain ol' dirty fighting.

Tina Raines had trained and seen combat with Gray's Scouts. And Col. Dan Gray had given her the highest compliment one soldier could give another: "That lady," said Colonel Gray, "is no lady."

Ben was at the site in half an hour. The barricade had been torn down. Dan quietly and succinctly brought the general up to date.

Ben listened, the anger in him growing as Dan spoke. "Thank you, Dan." He turned to the young man who had headed up the LRRPs into Rolla. "Are

226

the people united in there?" he asked, jerking a thumb toward the distant town.

"Yes, sir—all the way. They told us they wanted a pure race of people, free of color. There is a Jewish girl hanging by the neck just down the road. We asked them about it; they admitted doing it. Said she got uppity with some of their women. We asked them what they meant by 'uppity.' Said the Jewish girl was unhappy about being a servant. So they hanged her. Real nice people, General."

"Yes. Just lovely," Ben said. "How about the minorities that used to live around here?"

"They were either handed over to the IPF, run out or killed."

"I see."

"General," the young LRRP said. "They, ah, the men in there—they took turns raping the girl before they hanged her."

"They told you that?"

"Yes, sir. Seemed proud of it. Said she had real good pussy."

Ben was profoundly glad that Gale was not present during this conversation. He turned to his artillery officer. "Shell it," he told the man. "Shell and burn it. Blow the goddamned town off the map."

"Yes, sir," the officer said. He began speaking into his headset.

Down the highway, the rumble of tanks and mortar carriers getting into position reached the men by the once-barricaded highway. First to whistle and part the air overhead were the 152mm and 155mm cannon shells. 81mm mortars joined the barrage, the projectiles humming overhead. Ben's big self-propelled howitzers began pounding the small city with HE and incendiary rounds. The earth began to shake as the explosions ripped the town. Unit commanders began synchronizing the attack; there was not one full second free of the blasts of artillery, not one full second when an explosion was not rocking and pounding and burning and destroying the coordinated areas.

The limited skyline of the small city was now reduced to burning skeletons of buildings. After five minutes, Ben shouted the order to cease firing.

"Tanks in," he ordered, his voice quiet in the shocked hush after the rolling thunder. "Infantry behind. Roll it."

Gale and Nancy stood beside Ben's pickup truck. Neither of them had ever heard anything to match what they had just experienced. War movies were OK, but this had been the real thing. Both their hearts were pounding furiously. Their mouths were dry. Nancy was the first to speak.

"He doesn't believe very much in diplomacy, does he?"

"Only the final kind," Gale replied, removing her fingers from her ears.

"I'm certain there were probably young children in that town."

"Probably so."

"That doesn't bother you?"

"Sam Hartline was once a child."

Nancy closed her mouth.

Heavy tanks rumbling past them stopped any further conversation for a time. Soon the rattle of automatic weapons drifted through the still air as the mopping up began.

Gale took this time to observe Ben, something she did often, and enjoyed doing. The man was as calm as a professional gambler with a royal flush in a high-stakes poker game. Nothing ever seemed to rattle him. Ben sipped at a cup of coffee — or what now passed for coffee — and munched on a biscuit. He seemed so relaxed he could be watching a croquet match on the greens in England.

Black, ugly smoke from the fires set by the incendiary rounds began pouring into the sky, the flames licking close behind the clouds. With no fire department, the town would soon burn itself out, destroying the ugliness the IPF had spawned.

After an hour, the gunfire had ceased, the tanks had rumbled back to position within the convoy. Far up the highway, Rebels were walking prisoners back to face Ben Raines.

The prisoners did not look overjoyed at that prospect.

They were a beaten and sullen bunch, with no fight left in them. They faced Ben — twenty of them — with downcast eyes. Their hands were behind their necks, fingers interlaced. There was one woman with them, a rather attractive woman. She looked at Ben with frank eyes.

"I give great head, General," she said. "Let me live and I'll do anything you want. I like it up the ass, too."

"Shut your fucking mouth," Ben told her.

"You dirty whore!" snarled the man beside her. "This is one time your pussy won't get you out of trouble."

She laughed and spat in the man's face.

"I ought to hang every one of you," Ben told the

229

group. "Slowly. If torture was my forte, that is what you deserve—then I should hang what is left of you."

A man lifted very frightened eyes. "General . . ."

"Shut up!" Ben roared at him. He turned to a lieutenant. "How many children were found?"

"Twenty-two, sir. The rest of the kids are up at some sort of special school, run by the IPF."

"They are being brainwashed," Katrina spoke. "Depending on the time they have spent there, it is very probably too late to save them." She looked at one man who appeared better fed and in better condition than the others. "How long have the children been at the school?"

"Long enough," the man said with a smirk on his thick, wet lips. "I know you—" he stared at her—"you was here some months ago."

"That is correct," Katrina replied.

"Yeah," the man said. "I heard about you. You're the turncoat. Sorry goddamn traitor to your people."

Katrina lifted her AK-47 and pulled the trigger once. The single shot took the man in the center of the chest. He flopped on the ground and died.

"He was a pig," Katrina said. "He made some very filthy comments to me one day. Exposed himself to me and asked me to lick his . . . asked me to lick it." She looked at Ben. "Am I to be punished for shooting him?"

"Hell, no," Ben said.

"Katrina," Colonel Gray said. "Would you be interested in joining my little group of men and women?"

"The scouts and LRRPs?"

"Indeed."

"I would be honored."

Dan smiled. "The little bird has sharp claws, General."

"Quite," Ben agreed. "How old are the children you found?" he asked the scout.

"Very young. Infants, mostly."

"Take them back to the convoy. We'll raise them. I won't have these bigots preaching hate to young children."

"You ain't got no right to take our kids." A man stepped toward Ben.

Ben butt-stroked the man under the chin with his Thompson. Teeth and jaw cracked and popped under the impact. Blood flew from the man's shattered mouth. He dropped to the ground like a stone and was still.

Ben looked at Colonel Gray. "I don't care what you do with them, Dan. I do not wish to ever see any of them again."

"Yes, sir." He looked around him. "Sergeant Cummings?"

"Sir?"

"Take care of this little matter, won't you?"

"Yes, sir," the black sergeant said. "I will give it my immediate and personal attention."

"I rather thought you would," Dan said.

The Jewish Rebel stepped forward. "Like a little help, Mac?"

"Join the party," Mac replied.

"Dan," Ben said. "Roll the convoy on through. We'll stop up the road at Vienna." He looked at Sergeant Cummings. "We'll see you and your squad in about an hour, Mac."

"Yes, sir."

231

"I wonder what is going to happen to those people?" Nancy whispered to Gale.

"Don't even think about it," she was told.

"Hello, sweetmeat," Hartline said to Peggy.

She whirled around, her eyes wide with fear as she gazed up the basement steps to the open door. Hartline's bulk filled the doorway. She looked around for a weapon—*anything*. But there was nothing. Her heart was pounding so heavily she thought she might faint.

"I told you I'd find you, baby," Hartline said, a cruel smile on his lips.

"How?" Peggy managed to gasp out the one-word question.

"How?" Hartline smiled the question. "How was easy, sweet pussy. This is how." He stepped down into the basement and waved his hand. A human form tumbled down the steps, bouncing sickeningly on the steps. Lois Peters. Or what was left of her.

The woman was naked. Her toenails and fingernails had been ripped from her. Her fingers had been broken. Her feet had been burned black—lumps of seared meat. Her teeth had been savagely pulled out. Her breasts had been mutilated. Peggy looked at the woman's pubic area and was sick at the sight. Lois looked as though she had been raped by some sort of huge monster. Blood streaked her thighs.

She was dead.

Hartline's eyes were cold and savage-looking. The smile hadn't left his lips. "Before I'm through with you, sweetmeat, you'll be begging me to go ahead and kill you."

Peggy rose to her full height. She spat in Hartline's face. "I'll never beg to you, you son of a bitch."

"Oh, I think you will, pretty thing. I really think you will."

Two years before, Sam Hartline and his men, backed by FBI agents with warrants charging several newspeople with treason for refusing to cooperate with the congressional mandate to submit all news copy for review and censorship before airing, entered the Richmond offices of NBC. This was to be the test network.

Hartline, carrying an M-10 SMG, shoved the elderly security guard away from the doors, knocking the man sprawling, and marched into the executive offices. Hartline jerked one startled VP of programming to his feet and hit him in the mouth with a leathergloved right fist. The man slammed against a chair and fell stunned to the floor.

A news commentator rushed into the room. "Here now," he shouted. "You can't do that."

One of Hartline's men socked the man with the butt of his AK. The man's jaw popped like a firecracker. He was unconscious before he hit the carpet, blood pouring from the sudden gaps in his teeth.

"Where is the bureau chief?" Hartline said. "Or whatever you call the boss. Get him in here, pronto."

A badly shaken young secretary stammered, "It isn't a him—it's a her. Ms. Olivier."

"Well, now." Hartline smiled. "That's even better. Get her for me, will you, darling?"

Before the secretary could turn, a voice, calm and controlled, spoke from the hall. "What is the meaning of this?"

Hartline lifted his eyes, meeting the furious gaze of Sabra Olivier. He let his eyes drift over her, from her eyes to her ankles and back up again. She felt as if she had been violated. "You're kind of a young cunt to be in charge of all this, aren't you, honey?" he asked.

"Get out!" Sabra ordered.

The words had just left her mouth when Hartline's open palm popped against her jaw, staggering her. She stumbled against the door frame, grabbing at the doorknob for support.

"Dear," Hartline said, *"you* do not order *me* about. *I* will tell *you* what I want, then you will see to it that my orders are carried out. Is that clear?"

"You're Sam Hartline," Sabra said, straightening up, meeting him squarely, no backup in her. "Vice President Lowry's pet dog."

Hartline never lost his cold smile. He faced the woman, again taking in her physical charms: black hair, carefully streaked with gray; dark olive complexion; black eyes, now shimmering with anger; nice figure; long legs.

Sabra turned to a man. "Call the police," she told him.

Hartline laughed at her. "Honey, we *are* the police."

Sabra paled slightly.

The man on the floor groaned, trying to sit up, one hand holding his broken and swelling jaw.

"Get him out of here," Hartline ordered. "Toss him in the lobby and have that old goat down there call for an ambulance to come get him." He looked at Sabra.

"We can do this easy or hard, lady, it's all up to you."

"What do you want?"

"For you to cooperate with the government censorship order. And no more taking the Rebels' side in this insurrection."

"No way I'll submit to censorship," Sabra said.

"Then you want it hard," Hartline said, the double meaning not lost on the woman, as he knew it would not be.

Her dark eyes murdered the mercenary a dozen times in a split-second. Her smile was as cold as his. "I never heard of anyone dying from it, Hartline."

"Oh, I have, Sabra baby. I have."

Hours later, Sabra Olivier's spirit shattered. "All right," she said to Hartline. "Stop it — stop your men. I'll cooperate."

The moaning and the screaming of her female employees had finally broken her reserve. As Hartline had known it would. And he had not touched Ms. Olivier — yet.

The students at the University of Virginia, after hearing of the takeover of the NBC offices and studios in Richmond, had marched in protest. But this was not the 1960s and '70s, with constitutional guarantees protecting civil disobedience. Now all police were federalized, and the FBI was nothing like that old and solid organization of the past.

The students were met with live ammunition and snarling dogs. Many were killed. Hundreds more were arrested, and in the process, beaten bloody. VP Lowry ordered the university closed.

Hartline smiled and nodded to a man standing by the door to the office. Within seconds, the screaming and sobbing ceased.

"You see." Hartline smiled at her. "That wasn't so difficult, was it?"

If looks could kill.

Sabra watched, a curious look in her eyes, as a minicam was brought into her office, carried by an agent. She did not understand the smile on Hartline's lips.

Hartline pointed to a TV set behind her desk. "Turn it on," he told her.

A naked man appeared on the screen. One of her anchormen. She knew with a sudden start this was live action, not taped. "What is the meaning of this?" she demanded. "I told you I'd cooperate."

"Insurance, Sabra baby," Hartline replied. He picked up a phone from her desk and punched a button. "Do it," he ordered. He looked at Sabra. "Watch, darling."

She swung reluctant eyes toward the screen. A cattle prod touched the man's naked buttocks. His scream chilled her. The prod touched his thigh, then his genitals.

"Stop it!" Sabra shouted.

The man screamed and ground his teeth in pain. Several teeth broke off, bloodying his mouth.

"Goddamn you, Hartline!" Sabra yelled. "Stop it."

"You'll cooperate with us?"

"I said I would, Hartline."

"Anything I say?"

"*Yes!*"

"I have your son ready to perform for us. Would you like to see that?"

"God*damn* you!"

236

Hartline laughed. He spoke to the minicam operator. "Start rolling it." He unzipped his pants. His flaccid penis hung out. "Come here, Sabra baby. This one is for VP Lowry. And if you ever fail to obey an order, if you ever let any copy air without government approval, this tape gets played—in its entirety—on the six o'clock news."

"You goddamn low-life, miserable son of a bitch!" Sabra cursed him.

"Strip, baby. Take it all off while facing the camera. Let's give Lowry a really good show. That's it. Play with your puss a little bit. Good, good, now you're getting into the spirit of things."

Naked and embarrassed and trembling with anger, Sabra faced the mercenary.

He hefted his penis. "In case you have it in mind to take a bite of me, Sabra baby, bear in mind your son is now bent over a table just down the hall. You get hinky with me, he gets gang-shagged. Understand?"

She nodded.

"Kneel down here, baby. On your pretty dimpled knees. You know what to do. You probably sucked cocks getting to where you are in the network anyway."

She took him as the camera recorded it all.

Just as Hartline climaxed, the semen splattering the woman's face, Hartline laughed. "It's just so fucking easy when you know how. Just so fucking easy."

The tiny hamlet of Vienna was deserted, completely void of any type of life, human or animal.

"Strange," Ben muttered, conscious of Gale's eyes

on his face. "I don't recall ever seeing anything like this." He ordered scouts out to give the place a quick once-over.

Gale put her hand on Ben's thigh. "This place scares me," she admitted.

Ben, as usual, kept his emotions in close check. At least outwardly. Inside, he felt a little shaky. This place was, he concluded, a place of death—but somehow much different from all the other towns he had seen.

A Rebel jogged toward the pickup, his words breaking into Ben's deep thoughts. "You gotta see this, General. It's unreal."

Ben, with Gale in tow, followed the Rebel on foot to a weather-beaten old frame church. The church had once been painted white. Now the paint was almost gone, the wood rotting from years of abuse from the harsh elements of sun and wind and cold.

"The door is locked, sir. From the inside. I looked through the window around here at the side. But you both better brace yourselves for what you're about to see. It's tough, sir."

The scene grabbed at Ben's guts. Fifty or so people—or the skeletons of what had once been people—filled the pews. Many of the ladies still had rags of what had been their Sunday hats perched on their white, bony skulls. About half of the worshippers still sat upright, grinning grotesquely and staring through sightless eyeholes at the bones of a man who sat in a chair directly behind the rotting pulpit. He would wait forever to deliver his Sunday sermon.

"Look at the watch on that guy's . . . wrist," the Rebel said, pointing to a nearby skeleton.

Ben rubbed at the dirty windowpane and stared.

The watch was a LCD type and was still silently exhibiting the time in the House of the Lord, to pews full of bones.

"What happened, Ben?" Gale asked in no more than a whisper, almost breathlessly. "I mean, how could this be?"

"I can't answer that, honey," Ben said, his eyes still fixed on the scene before him.

"I can," Lamar Chase said.

"Jesus Christ!" the young Rebel blurted, jumping about a foot off the ground.

"Naturally, he can," Ben said dryly, but with a grin.

Lamar glanced at the badly shaken young Rebel. "I warned you about keeping late hours, son. Bad on the nerves."

"Yes, sir," the young man said, grinning, red-faced with embarrassment.

"It was airborne," Lamar said. "At least some strains of it."

"Airborne, Lamar?" Ben said. "The plague?"

"What the hell do you think I'm talking about?" the doctor said. "Gonorrhea? Yes, the plague. The only answer I can give is there must have been several strains of it. Very short-lived. What are you going to do with these . . . remains?"

"Leave them right where they are," Ben told him. "I can't think of a better resting place than this, can you?"

"Yes," Doctor Chase said with a sour grin. "Don't die."

"Little sweetmeat," Hartline said, stroking the unwilling flesh of Peggy. His touch made her skin crawl as if covered with thousands of lice. Somewhere in the old warehouse-turned-interrogation-center for the IPF, a human being was wailing in agony. Gender was not identifiable by the hoarse yowlings.

Hartline raised his head at the sounds, a smile on his handsome face.

"That would be Mr. Linderfelt, I should think," he said. "Would you be at all interested in knowing what is being done to him, sweetmeat?"

"No. I'm sure it's horrible and perverted. What are you going to do with me, Hartline?"

"Oh my, sweetmeat, that does present a dilemma. Yes, it does. Quite a dilemma. You see, I just haven't made up my mind as yet. How about you calling the tune, dear."

"Your humor is sick, Hartline. Just as sick as the rest of you." She struggled against the leather straps that held her to the operating table. She was naked, her legs spread wide.

Hartline's right hand was busy between her legs, his middle finger working in and out.

He laughed at her struggles.

"Let me tell you what is being done with Mr. Linderfelt, dear."

She screamed and fought against the straps. She struggled until her slender body was bathed in sweat, light bronze shining under the harsh lights that hung above her. Hartline stood and watched her, a smile on his lips. She finally ceased her futile writhings and glared up at the mercenary.

"You see, my dear Miss Jones," he said, returning his hand to its busy work between her legs, "it was I who finally convinced General Striganov he was making a terrible mistake by sterilizing all the minorities, inferiors that you are. I said to Georgi, 'Georgi, just think what we can do for the generations of scientists yet to come. What a contribution we could make in the field of genetics.'"

A woman began screaming down the long hall in the sectioned-off warehouse. The woman was howling in pain and fright, begging to someone not to do this to her. To kill her. To please have mercy on her. That this was inhuman. She just could not . . .

Her scream changed in timbre, ending in a series of heavy, painful grunting sounds.

"Hartline . . ."

"Be quiet, dear. What is happening to . . . whatever *is* that woman's name? It escapes me at the moment. No matter, as I was saying, it won't happen to you. You have already been — how to subtly say this — *spayed* like the dog-bitch you are."

He threw back his head and howled out his laughter.

Something in the warehouse growled.

Peggy had heard that sound before. The realization of what was taking place in the experiment rooms struck her with all its savagery. "Hartline . . . you didn't! I mean, you can't be serious?"

"Oh, but we are serious, sweetmeat. Really. Look at it this way: We are making real contributions in the field of genetics. It is as I told Georgi: 'Take the inferior races and start a program of breeding them to the beasts. Male mutant to female human inferior. Female to male human inferior.'

"That is what is currently happening to our Mr. Linderfelt and to Miss, ah, yes, Llado. That is that greaser's name. We have to give the human males large injections of aphrodisiac in order for them to cooperate—large doses of Valium work wonders in many cases—and it is really working out well, I believe. Our doctors don't, as yet, know the gestation period for the female mutants, but it is very fast, we believe. It should produce some interesting offspring, don't you think, my dear Miss Jones?"

"You're savages!" Peggy whispered. "Nothing but dirty, filthy monsters."

Hartline looked hurt. "Oh, not true, not true. If everything works out as planned, we shall have a race of beings with some degree of intelligence, able to perform menial jobs, thus freeing the more intelligent for other work. It's science, my dear, that's all."

He freed her from her bonds and forced her to a low table, strapping her on her belly, legs spread wide, her bare feet on the cold floor, her buttocks elevated. She knew what was in store for her.

"I believe, my dear," Hartline said, removing his trousers, carefully folding them and hanging them on the back of a chair, "we were in the process of doing something when you turned savage on me. Were we not?"

He was naked from the waist down, his penis already swelling in anticipation of the assault.

Peggy did not reply.

She felt grease or oil being spread between the cheeks of her buttocks.

"Yes, we were," Hartline said, positioning himself.

Peggy began screaming.

By maintaining daily radio contact, Ben learned that Ike's and Hector's columns were having as much equipment trouble as his own. Ike had been forced to halt at St. Genevieve in Missouri for major repairs. He reported to Ben that the city contained survivors, but they had, so far, shown no interest or inclination in fighting General Striganov. They would take whatever form of government happened along.

Ben resisted an impulse to tell Ike to shoot them.

Hector's column was bogged down in Warsaw, Missouri while his mechanics worked frantically on the engines and transmissions.

The troops from North and South Carolina had been halted in Illinois.

Juan was the only one to have reached his objective and was digging in for the fight.

But the IPF was having no problems.

The rumble of Jeeps and heavy trucks grew louder to the small team of LRRPs hidden by the side of the road in central Iowa. The column of IPF forces stretched for miles.

"Must be four or five battalions," a LRRP said to his buddy.

"At least that. And they've got more heavy guns than we first thought. We got them outgunned, all right, but they've got us outmanned." The LRRP picked up his mic and called in, speaking softly.

"At least five battalions of infantry heading south in trucks. We counted forty of the six-bys pulling cannon. 105s."

"Tanks?"

"Negative on tanks. Here comes another convoy. Hang on."

The LRRPs counted the heavily loaded trucks—those loaded with men and those loaded with equipment. They radioed back to Ben's HQ.

"Three more battalions rolling south."

"Acknowledged. Maintain your positions and stay low."

"If I got any lower my buttons would be in the way."

The radio operator took the bad news to Ben.

"Seven or eight battalions," Ben read aloud the hastily scrawled message. "Damn! General Striganov knows he's got to defeat us; once that is done, he's home free. Get me Ike."

Colonel McGowen on the horn, Ben said, "Ike—we've got six thousand troops coming at us, buddy. They're in central Iowa now. Whatever you have that will roll, get the wheels turning north and assume your positions. Get ready for hell, partner. We've got to have time to dig in, so move them out *now!* The clock is ticking. Interstate 70 is the stopping point for the Russians. We've got to hold them. The personnel you leave behind can catch up ASAP. I'll be talking with Hector in a moment. Roll it, Ike . . . and God go with you."

"Ten-four, Ben. Luck to you, ol' buddy."

Ben spoke briefly with Colonel Ramos, telling him to move out and dig in. No sooner had he released the talk button than Mark Terry was on the horn.

"We are engaging the IPF in central Illinois, Ben. And we are meeting heavy resistance. We are holding."

"Dig in and slug it out, Mark. Don't let those people break through and come up behind me. I can't spread my people out any thinner. General Striganov is throwing some six thousand troops in my direction."

"Jesus," Mark said. When he again spoke, his voice was calm, the sounds of gunfire heavy in the background. "I have instructed my people not to surrender, Ben. I can only hope they will obey to the last man. Good luck to you."

"The same to you, Mark."

The connection was broken.

Ben turned to tell the radio operator to get him Juan Solis on the horn when the Mexican's voice came through the speaker.

"We are looking at some two to three thousand troops, Ben. We have the Missouri River to our backs and we are not going to surrender. It's up to you, Ben. Good luck."

His company commanders, platoon leaders and squad leaders had gathered around the communications van. They looked at Ben in silence.

Why is it always up to me? Ben thought. Why me? All I ever wanted was to be left alone and to live out my remaining years in peace.

Why me?

"Move out," Ben told his people. "We've got to stop the advance of the IPF. Good luck."

THIRTEEN

*Lord God of Hosts, be we
us yet,
Lest we forget—lest we forget.*

—Kipling

The bridges crossing the river at St. Louis were long gone, and Ike had left personnel at Memphis, Caruthersville, Cairo, Cape Girardeau and Chester, with orders to blow the bridges if any IPF forces attempted to cross and come up from behind. Ike began spreading troops from St. Peters, Missouri west to Warrenton. Ben would spread his personnel from Warrenton to Columbia, and Hector would cover the area from Sweet Springs east to Ben.

They were all spread thin, with very few troops left in reserve. It would be a tiring campaign, with little time for the troops to rest. And they would be outnumbered almost three to one.

But Ben's Rebels had something going for them the IPF personnel had never known in all their lives: a belief in God Almighty and freedom.

When Ben's column reached the outskirts of Columbia, he met with Colonel Gray. After the two men shook hands, Dan brought Ben up to date on the latest developments his scouts and LRRPs had radioed in. Ben said, "I want to meet with General Striganov one more time, Dan, even though it will probably do no more than buy us time. When I am doing that, you take your scouts and LRRPs and circle behind the IPF people; begin a guerrilla campaign against them. No holds barred, Dan, I want as much blood and terror and demoralization as possible. I don't have to tell you how to play dirty."

The Englishman's grin was decidedly nasty. Now the game was getting to his liking. The men once more shook hands. "Good luck to you, General, and Godspeed."

"To us both, Dan," Ben said.

Ben turned to his commanders. His message was brief.

"Dig in."

The thin line of defense of democracy stretched some 140 miles—and it was stretched thin. Much too thin, Ben knew. But Striganov knew, too, that to punch one hole in the line of defenders would accomplish very little, for Ben would simply order his people to tighten up, swing ends around, and then trap the

Russian's spearheaders in a box.

No, the Russian would be careful, very careful, for he had read every book Ben Raines had ever written — read them many times — and had teams of psychiatrists study the writings and give personality profiles on the man. Georgi had reached the conclusion that Ben Raines was a madman. A man who would fight to the death for a mere principle. That, to the Russian's way of thinking, certainly and irrevocably constituted insanity.

And Ben Raines did not like to lose. Ever. He was — if his major characters were any indication of the author's true personality, and Striganov knew that to be true in most cases — the type of man who would resort to any tactics to win, if it took him a lifetime to do so.

So Striganov concluded this battle was to be of the classic style, the classic-fought duel between armies, the two forces slugging it out, wearing the other down, with Interstate 70 the no man's land.

But the Russian knew, too, that it was only a matter of time for the Rebels. He felt sure and confident in that, for he had Ben Raines's Rebels outmanned. Yes, he knew the mission would be costly in human life and limb. But his perfect people were not being thrown into this battle; they were safely tucked away back in Minnesota, back at the warm and comfortable breeding farm.

Striganov smiled as he sat in the cushioned back seat in his armor-plated and bullet-proofed car in the center of the convoy heading south to Interstate 70 and Gen. Ben Raines and his foolish, idealistic Rebels. He was proud of what he and his people had accomplished in so short a time. They had sterilized several thousand inferiors, had disposed of several hundred mental defectives, and were coming along splendidly with their breeding programs. But just look what he had to work with: those lovely people of his command, the cream of perfection. The women were so fair and blond and beautiful and intelligent; the men so tall and fair and blond and handsome and intelligent — both genders pale-eyed, of course.

All families of the perfect people had been researched carefully for flaws. And so far, the children born to the IPF over the past decade . . . perfect. Not one defective. All beautiful. Selective breeding would work, even that idiot Hitler had known that.

Striganov stirred restlessly in the back seat. He poured a glass of wine and dipped a cracker into black caviar, chewing slowly, savoring each bite.

But that fool Hitler had almost destroyed any hope of the revival of a *Мастер Раса*, a *Meister Rasse*. It was one thing to let a race die out naturally — more or less — but to destroy them with ovens and gas and starvation . . .

That was unthinkable. Barbaric. Savage. It served no useful medical purpose. For even defectives could be used in experiments. True, Hitler did once have a few experiments going, but his were not on the grand scale of the IPF.

Striganov really never thought that what he was doing was just as terrible and barbaric and horrible — perhaps even more so. The Russian actually believed — had convinced himself — he was doing humankind a service, not a disservice. What he was now putting into effect had been his lifelong dream, ever since as a child he had read and absorbed the rantings and ravings of that only-sometimes-lucid little paper hanger.

Yes, the little man had had—at times—some good ideas and thoughts. But Striganov was so very glad the man had not succeeded. For his own theories and ideas were so very much better.

A master race, a fully workable caste system—that was the ultimate achievement. A world whose leaders and thinkers and breeders at the top level would all be fair-skinned and blue-eyed and handsome and intelligent.

How could anyone wish for more than that?

But suddenly a frown crossed the handsome features of the Russian. For there was only one flaw in an otherwise perfect master plan.

Ben Raines.

"Ben, do we send troops in to help Juan and Mark?" Lieutenant Macklin posed the question at a briefing before the battle. "They won't have a prayer without some support from trained combat troops."

"No." Ben stood firm in one of the most agonized-over decisions he had ever had to make. "That is what Striganov is hoping I'll do. Hoping I'll further weaken this thin line we're maintaining."

"Do they know this, Ben?" Hector asked.

"Yes. The leaders do. And I'm sure most of the line troops sense it as well."

"It could backfire, ol' buddy," Ike reminded Ben.

"I know it—only too well," Ben admitted the weakness in the plan. "Unless we can defeat the IPF here, those on the west side might punch through and come

250

in under us with so much force we couldn't close the pincers on them. I know that. It's going to be a slugging match, people. We'll be taking and losing and retaking the same ground—on both sides of the line—twenty times before we're through. I think Striganov knows—just as I know—this is going to be the stand-up-and-slug-it-out type of battle. And he knows, as I know, we are going to both inflict and take heavy losses."

But Ben was worried as he glanced at Ike, and Ike knew it. Knew what Ben was thinking: neither ex-SEAL nor ex-Hell-Hound was an expert in this type of fighting. Both of them were trained—and highly so—in the art of guerrilla warfare: that dirty cut-slash-run type of unconventional warfare. The men had defended the original Tri-States in the West, and done it well but they had been forced out. Not because of lack of courage, simply because of superior manpower thrown at them by forces of the United States government, when Hilton Logan was president and his hate for Ben Raines had finally erupted into bloody warfare.*
And it was superior manpower they were again about to face.

Ben rose, signalling the meeting was over. He shook Ike's hand, then Hector's. "Showdown time, gang. Let's win it and get the hell back home. We got crops to harvest in a few weeks."

Ike and Hector and Mary smiled, nodded and walked away. Mary was part of Ben's HQ's company.

*See *Out Of The Ashes*.

Ike went to the east, Hector to the west.

To war.

But only one of the two men would return from the final battle.

PART TWO

PART TWO

ONE

Gen. Georgi Striganov, in full battle dress, stood on the north side of Interstate 70. Ben Raines, in full battle gear, stood facing the Russian from the south side of the concrete strip. As if on silent command, the men walked across their two lanes of concrete to face each other, median strip separating them. Each man had requested this one final meeting before they began man's most awesome means of settling disputes: war.

"You're looking disgustingly fit and well, General Raines," Striganov said. "It pays for men our age to keep in shape, *da?*"

"I will agree with that, General."

"Nice to know we can agree on something, General Raines." His eyes drifted to Ben's old Thompson SMG. "My word, General. Where did you ever find that antiquated weapon?"

"I've had it a long time, General," Ben replied. "It's an old friend."

"Friends can sometimes disappoint a person, General—let one down, so to speak. If one depends upon them too much."

"It hasn't yet."

"Pray that it doesn't." Striganov smiled. "My people are, to use one of your quaint Western expressions, kicking ass to the west and the east. I think you sacrificed those people, General Raines, and I think you know you did."

"Perhaps. But in war, no one is indispensable. Not you, not me."

"You don't believe the latter any more than you believe a mule can fly, General. General? This does not have to be. Join me and let us work together."

"Toward a master race?"

"But of course, General Raines. Why not?"

"Because I believe what you are doing is more than evil, it's monstrous."

The Russian shrugged that off. "Yes, I keep forgetting you were once married to a half-black wench, weren't you?"

Ben said nothing.

"And now a Jewess shares your bed."

Ben remained silent, thinking: He's got people in Tri-States, and he just gave that fact away. I wonder why? Slip of the tongue? "That is correct, General. But I don't think of people in race categories. They are just human beings."

The Russian spat contemptuously on the ground. "What a noble thought," he said, his voice full of open scorn. "Fortunately for me, I do not share your misguided philosophical meanderings. I saw some time back that the pure white race is the master race, the most intelligent of all the races—by far. And General, you are, I believe, too intelligent a man not to see that.

You are just idealistic at a time when that is a luxury that you cannot afford."

"I will admit to being somewhat of an idealist," Ben said. "Personally, I think it is an admirable trait to possess—if one keeps it in perspective."

The Russian studied the American. He should have ordered snipers to accompany him and shoot Ben Raines. That would have solved a great many problems. But Striganov had always prided himself on being an honorable man, and he fully believed he was just that.

A great many people would have cheerfully called him anything but honorable.

Striganov shrugged his muscular shoulders. "Perhaps. I am sorry it has to be this way, President-General Ben Raines, for I think in many ways we are quite alike. But . . ." Again he shrugged.

Ben stood tall and silent, watching the Russian study him.

"I shall conduct myself and my troops as gentlemen during our upcoming confrontation, General Raines, carefully observing all the articles of war."

"I won't," Ben bluntly informed him.

The Russian laughed heartily, with good humor. "Ah, I fully expected that of you, General. But you see, there is a method behind my plans."

"You are hoping, if there is someone around to write it, that history will treat you much more kindly than it shall treat me."

"I knew you were an intelligent man, Ben Raines. Yes, of course that is it. Quite correct and very astute of you. You will have that despicable Englishman, Gray, and his people moving about behind my lines,

257

slitting throats and blowing things up and engaging in all sorts of subhuman guerrilla tactics. But I and my people shall be gentlemen at all times. So I believe history shall paint you as the savage, not I."

Ben had to laugh at the Russian's sincerity. "Do you really believe all that shit, General?"

Striganov looked amused that Ben should doubt it. "But of course! Not only for a gentlemen's war, but in the fact I am purifying the white race. Surely you will be big enough to admit a great many people support what I am doing?"

"A much greater number find it appalling and disgusting," Ben countered. "And kindly include me among them, and everyone who fights alongside me."

"Then I must conclude they are short-sighted or misguided people," the Russian said with a smile. "And since I really don't believe you are short-sighted, President-General Raines, you must fall in the latter category."

Ben laughed at him, the laughter bouncing off the Russian.

"I shall give you a few more hours to mull over your reluctance, General Raines. If you have not seen the error of your decision, 0600 tomorrow shall be the beginning of your Armageddon."

Ben smiled. "A very interesting choice of characterization, General Striganov. Armageddon. Of course, you represent the evil?"

The Russian did not take offense. "If that is how you choose to view it, President-General. But I believe history will view me in a much gentler light."

"If you win, General Striganov, history probably will view you in that manner — a lie, of course — since

258

there will be only your *Herrenvolk* to write it."

Again, the Russian laughed. "But of course. You see, Ben Raines, I planned well, did I not?"

Ben had to grudgingly admit the Russian had indeed planned very well. But he'd be goddamned if he would compliment the bastard for doing so.

"When I take you as my prisoner-of-war, General Raines, I give you my word you will be treated with the respect due a man of your position."

Ben's reply was very much to the point. "When I take you as my prisoner of war, General Striganov, I'm personally going to shoot you."

The Russian threw back his head and laughed loudly, uproariously. "Oh, I do like you, Ben Raines. It is such a pity that we cannot be good and close friends. There are so few truly intelligent men left to converse with on matters of importance. So, Ben Raines, do be sure and give your Jewess a great big kiss for me, *da?* Good morning, sir."

He turned his back to Ben and walked across the two lanes of concrete and onto the shoulder of the interstate. He was soon down in the ditch and then lost from view as he entered the woods.

Ben returned to his troops. Gale breathed a huge sigh of relief upon sighting Ben. "I just don't trust that bastard, Ben."

"He said to give you a great big kiss from him." Ben grinned.

Gale spat very unladylike on the ground. She fixed Ben with a dark, angry glare. "How would you like a fat lip, Raines?"

"I think I'll pass," Ben said with a laugh.

He sobered as he looked at his personal contingent

of Rebels. He knew them all from the hard days. Captain Seymour. Lamar Chase. Jane Dolbeau, the blond Canadian who everyone knew was in love with Ben — everyone that is but Ben. Steve Mailer and Judith Sparkman. James Riverson. Carla Allen. Lynne Hoffman. Judy Fowler. The survivors. Men and women who had followed Ben through it all, who believe in him.

He could not let them down.

He saw Roanna Hickman watching him as he walked away. She hurried to catch up with him.

"Just had to deal yourself a hand in this battle, eh, Roanna?" Ben said.

"I'm still a reporter, General. There may not be any networks left, or any big daily newspapers, but I'm still going to ply my craft — someday, somebody will read it."

"I hope so, Miss Hickman. You were a very good reporter."

She smiled. "Coming from you, General, that's as good as receiving the Pulitzer."

And for a moment, both of them were caught up briefly in the grips of memory.

Sabra Olivier had called Roanna into her office*, intercepting the reporter outside the door and leading her to the washroom. As she had seen in countless TV

---

*See *Fire in the Ashes*.

shows and movies, Sabra turned on the water in the sink to cover any noises of conversation.

Knowing Sam Hartline as she did, Sabra would not put it past the man to bug the ladies' room.

"Roanna, you know all about Hartline. I've never pulled any punches with any of you. But what do you *really* think of him?"

"I'd like to cut the bastard's cock off and stuff it down his throat," Roanna replied without a second's hesitation.

Sabra was mildly shocked. She had never heard Roanna be so crude. "He got to you, Roanna?"

"Oh, yes." The brunette's smile was more of a grimace. "From behind. Said he'd been watching and listening to my stories for a long time, didn't like what I'd done about mercenaries. Wanted to give me something to remember him by. He did. I walked funny for three days. The son of a bitch."

"How many other women?"

"Sabra, it's not just the women. Some of his men are twisted sexually—really bent all out of shape in the head. I don't know what you're planning, but be careful, you're dealing with a maniac in Hartline. He's a master of torture. He's got most of the people in the networks frightened out of their wits; men and women—old, hard-line, tough reporters tremble at just the mention of his name. All of us wonder how it got this far out of line so quickly."

"Yes, I was wondering the same thing a few moments ago. Roanna, look, I've got to get someone in Ben Raines's camp, and I've got you in mind. I think I can convince Hartline it's for the best. You do a story on Raines; I'll do one on Hartline. I'll make him look like the coming of Christ. We'll do little three-minute segments each week, but they'll be coded with messages for Raines."

"Sabra . . ."

"No! It's something I believe we've got to do. I'll accept some responsibility for what's happening — what has happened to this nation; it's partly our fault. Hartline . . . visits me twice a week. Lately I've been accepting his visits as something I have no control over. He thinks I'm enjoying them. He's an egomaniac; I can play on that. Really build him up. It's amazing what a man will say when he's in bed with a woman. We'll work out some sort of code to let Raines know what is going on, or what is about to happen. Are you game?"

"You know what will happen to both of us if Hartline discovers what we're doing?"

"Yes. Very well."

"All right," Roanna said. "Let's do it."

"What kind of game are you playing, Miss Hickman?" Ben asked her.

They were seated outside, a cool but not unpleasant breeze fanning them. Roanna sat beside Dawn — the two women had known each other for years — the women facing Ben and Cecil and Ike.

"No game, General," Roanna said firmly. "Game time is all over. We're putting our lives on the line this go-round. For the women, our asses, literally."

She brought them all up to date on what Hartline was doing and had done.

"If this is true," Cecil said, "and for the moment, we shall accept it as fact, Ms. Olivier is playing a very dangerous game."

262

"And you, as well," Ike looked at Roanna.

"More than you know," Roanna's reply was filled with bitterness. "Sabra's husband said if she saw Hartline again, he was leaving. She couldn't explain what she was doing, for fear Hartline would torture the truth out of Ed — that's her husband. Ed walked out the day before yesterday, took the little boy, left the daughter behind. I wish it had been reversed. Sabra's told me Hartline is looking at Nancy . . . you know what I mean."

"How old is the girl?" Ike asked.

"Fifteen. Takes after her mother. She's beautiful."

"Hartline is, ah, somewhat perverted, is he not?" Dawn asked.

Roanna snorted in disgust. "To put it quite bluntly, Dawn, he's got a cock like a horse and doesn't care which hole he sticks it in."

"Jesus Christ, lady!" Even Ike was shocked, and to shock a Navy SEAL takes some doing.

Ben resisted a smile and said, after looking at the reporter for a moment, "You have any objections to taking a PSE test, Miss Hickman?"

"Not at all," Roanna replied. Then she smiled, and her cynical reporter's eyes changed. She was, Ben thought, really a very pretty lady. "What's the matter, General, am I too liberal for your tastes?"

"Liberals are, taken as a whole, just too far out of touch with reality to suit me," Ben said, softening that with a smile.

"I'd like to debate that with you someday, General. Yes," she mused, "that might be the way to go with the interviews. Hard-line conservative against liberal views."

"I'm not a total hard-line conservative, Miss Hickman," Ben informed her. "Although many have branded me as that: unfeeling and all that other garbage. How could I have been a hard-line conservative and advocated women's rights, abortion, the welfare of the elderly and children . . . and everything else we did in Tri-States?"

"Yes," Roanna said. "There is all that to take into consideration. But you did shoot and hang people there." She fired the reporter's question at him.

"We sure did." Ben's reply was breezy, given with a smile of satisfaction. "And we proved that crime does not have to exist in a society."

"But not to the satisfaction of everyone, General."

"But to ours, Miss Hickman, and that was all that mattered."

"Still miss the hustle and bustle of big-city living and reporting, Roanna?" Ben brought them both back to the present.

"Yes, and I'm looking forward to the day when it will return."

"It will never return, Roanna." Ben dashed her dreams with a splash of hard reality. "Civilization, as we have known it, is over."

"I have running chills up and down my spine when you say that, General."

"It's truth time, Roanna—and I have spoken the hard truth."

"But you can't know that for certain, General. That must be a personal opinion, nothing more."

"It's over, Roanna. From this moment on, either learn to adapt or die."

"I believe I shall continue to cling to my dreams, General."

Ben's smile was sad. "Your option, Roanna. But while you're clinging to them, use the other hand to cling to a gun."

"Goddamn jungle bunnies fight better than I thought they were capable of," Sam Hartline remarked to one of his field commanders. "I just didn't believe the niggers had it in them."

The men stood on a bluff overlooking the scene of two days of very fierce fighting between Al and Mark's troops and the IPF and Sam's mercenaries. The IPF and Hartline's mercenaries had been unable to punch through the black troops dug in on a far ridge, a small valley between the opposing forces.

"For a fact," the young mercenary replied. "For a sure fact. The niggers got more guts in them than I figured."

Hartline suddenly laughed, an idea shaping into solid form in his twisted mind. "I got an idea," he said. "Oh hell, yes—a damn good one, too. Max!" he called. His X.O. walked over.

"Yeah, Sam?"

"Get on a plane and go back to Wisconsin, with a side trip to Minnesota. I want you to bring me fifty of the best-looking coon gals we got—including Peggy Jones. Then round up about fifty or seventy-five old niggers, the older the better."

The executive officer looked at Hartline, a curious glint in his eyes. "What have you got cookin' in that brain of yours, Sam?"

Hartline laughed. "Just a damn good idea, Max—a

sure-fire way to shorten this little action. I'm going to strip the nigger gals buck-assed naked and tie them on the front of the APCs full of our troops. We'll mix in the old niggers with our troops coming up with and behind the APCs. I just don't believe the coons on that ridge over there will shoot their own kind. I think we can drive right through them and put them all to rout. Yes, indeed. Be fun to see the expression on their monkey faces, too." He turned to another merc. "Pat, I want you to go back with Max. Round up fifty or so good-lookin' senoritas and about seventy-five or so old greasers. Take them all over to the west front to Colonel Fechnor; tell him what I'm planning but to wait for my signal, and don't tell Striganov. He'd nix the plan. We'll coordinate this. I think, by God, we can shorten this fight considerably."

"I like it, Sam," the X.O. said. "Oh yeah, I like the hell out of it."

"I seen me a spic gal last week," Pat said. "Must have been about thirteen or fourteen. She looked prime. Little titties just buddin' out. Nipple just a-stickin' out of the raggedy blouse. You mind if I get me a taste of that pussy 'fore I send her west?"

"Hell, Pat, I don't care. I imagine she's been spayed, don't you?"

"Probably so. She sure looked old enough to bleed to me."

"Sure, go ahead. Make her suck your cock before you fuck her. Those little spic gals can suck a cock best I ever seen."

Staying south of the interstate, using state and county roads, Ben made one final inspection of his troops on the eve of the battle. They were stretched far too thin. But it was the best Ben could do. Two things his troops were not short on were ammunition and weapons. Stretched out all along the 140 mile battle front were .50-caliber machine guns mixed in with M-60 machine guns. Each squad had two of the big .50s and all the ammo they could use.

Working around the clock, they had fortified their positions, digging bunkers and sandbagged foxholes; mine fields were carefully laid, using thousands of the deadly Claymores. Mortar pits were dug, sandbagged and camouflaged. Supplies were brought up and cached.

The Rebels had done all any of them knew to do. They were ready. Now came the hardest part: the waiting.

Cecil was commanding a battalion that was dug in Columbia. Ben knew there would be some wicked street fighting there, much of it hand to hand. Ben had tried to talk Cecil out of taking command, but the black man would not be deterred from the job.

"You're too damned old for this job, Cecil," Ben told him. "Let a younger man have it and back me up at HQ. I guarantee you, you'll see all the combat you'll want to see there."

"I seem to recall I did a pretty damned good job at this in 'Nam," Cecil responded.

"Goddamn it, Cec, that was almost thirty years ago! Tell me about it, man—I was there too, you know?"

Cecil looked around him, his beret placed properly on his head, like the Green Beret Cecil had been. It was worn unlike Ben's black beret, which he still wore in Ranger fashion: cocky.

"Ben, some of these kids weren't even born when you and I did our thing in 'Nam. Damn, Ben. No, they're going to need a calm head here."

"A calm *gray* head," Ben said sarcastically.

Cecil smiled. "I matured early for my age."

Ben laughed, knowing he was not going to sway his old friend, and moved on down the line of Rebels.

He received the thumbs-up signal from each squad or platoon or company he passed. They were ready. These men and women nicknamed Raines's Rebels by the press years back. They were ready for a good fight. They knew the odds were hard against them, knew casualties would be high and that many would die. They knew only too well the price of freedom came high—it never came cheaply.

They were ready to die for freedom. Theirs and anyone else's that might be threatened.

Ready.

Back at HQ, Ben told Gale, "You will stay with Chase at the hospital. You're a nurse, and that is where you'll be needed. And I will not have any static from you about it. Is that clear?"

She smiled sweetly at him. Very sweetly. Too sweetly. "I have already made arrangements to do just that, General, sir. And I didn't need you to tell me about it. Thanks just the same."

That night, on the eve of the battle that would, although neither the Russian nor the American knew it, forever split the nation and plunge the ravaged country into a sickening slide toward barbarism, ignorance and tribal law, Ben and Gale engaged in the gentlest and most deeply satisfying love-making of their relationship. And Gale sensed with a woman's insight on such matters that she became pregnant.

And she knew she wanted this child more than anything else in the world.

When Ben was asleep (she could never understand how the man could quietly drop off when faced with such a monumental task as that which lay before him) she rose from their blankets to stand some distance away from Ben's sleeping form, to stand looking up at the cloudless star-filled heavens. She spoke to and asked questions of her god, and seemed satisfied with the silent words that filled her head. As she turned to return to Ben's side, she was startled to see a figure standing by a huge tree, gazing at her. She looked around her, curious to see if anyone else had noticed the man.

No one had, although the guards were plainly in sight all around the encampment — and that really piqued her curiosity.

Gale walked to the shadowy umbrella created by the huge limbs of the old tree and stood facing the man. She had, she concluded, never seen anything quite like him.

She studied him in silence, as he was silently studying her. "How did you get in this area without being shot?" she asked.

The old man smiled. His smile seemed to light the area around them. "You would not understand if I chose to tell you."

"Oh yeah?" Gale looked more closely at the old man. He wore robes and sandals and carried a big stick. A staff, the word popped into her brain. His beard was long and very white. He looked older than God. "What do you want?"

The man looked at her more closely; his eyes seemed amused, then sad, or so it appeared to Gale. Finally, he said. "No, you are not the one. But you will help the man in his struggles. That will be seen to. You have my word."

"What!" Gale reached the conclusion that this guy was not playing with a full deck of cards.

Ben and Ike and Cecil had told her about the many cults that were springing up around the torn nation. She had seen some with her own eyes during her wanderings prior to meeting Ben. This nutso had to be one of them — what else?

"I am known as the Prophet."

"Swell," she said dryly. "And I'm Mary. Man, you'd better be careful when you leave here. Someone could shoot you."

His smile was gentle and knowing, and rather, Gale thought, condescending. "I have no fear of death, child."

"That's nice, 'cause frankly, it scares the hell out of me."

The old man chuckled, a deep sound from his massive chest. "You have a sense of humor. Good, you'll need it." The old man glanced up at the sky, as if he had suddenly received some silent message.

Gale looked up, feeling rather foolish as she did so.

"As wars go," the old man said, "this one will be small in magnitude. But it will be enormous in its ramifications. What follows will be the beginning."

"Beginning of what?"

"The beginning, child."

Gale was now one hundred percent certain the old boy was at least three bricks shy of a load. Best humor him. "Right."

"The strugglings you will all endure will be, of course, right and just and moral, but they will, I must tell you, appear futile."

Gale shook her head. Maybe the guy had found some old acid and was tripping the light fantastic in his woolly head. "Hadn't you best be getting on back to the ward?"

The old man smiled indulgently. "I must now tell you goodbye, child."

On impulse, she put out her hand to touch his arm, but her hand seemed to freeze in midair. She fought to move her hand. It seemed stuck.

"No," he said gently. "That is not permitted."

"Are you the reincarnation of Houdini?"

"I am the reincarnation of no one, child. But I am, I can assure you of that."

"Am, eh, you're what?"

But he was gone.

Gale's arm fell to her side. She lifted it, looked at it. She shook her head. Looked around her. The old boy was nowhere to be seen.

"It was a dream," she muttered. "Had to be, I'm dreaming, sleepwalking. Couldn't be anything else."

She returned to the warmth of the blankets and the soled and comforting shape of Ben. When the first shell from the IPF exploded at 0600 the next morning, Gale forgot all about the man who called himself the Prophet.

For a time.

271

TWO

It was an artillery duel for the first two days of the battle, with the combatants never catching sight of each other. For the most part, the infantry troops had little to do except stay alive and maintain their sanity under the almost-constant pounding of the big shells.

For those who had never experienced shelling, it was a frightening, numbing experience. The ground seemed to shake constantly, and it appeared that any-place one sought in safety was the wrong place.

Both the Rebels and the IPF had to constantly shift the positions of their artillery, with the exception of Ben's big self-propelled 155s, which could sit back miles from the front and lob destruction and terror into the IPF's positions with terrifying pinpoint accuracy. Ben was no gentleman at war; he used chemicals, anti-personnel, high explosive, incendiary, and beehive rounds.

Ben kept his tanks in reserve, carefully concealed and camouflaged, even though the crews and commanders were chafing to get into the fight. Ben wanted something with which to fall back on when the situation began to deteriorate, as he knew it would. That, he knew, was only a matter of time.

The third, fourth and fifth days were ground troops days, with the infantry troops slugging it out, taking, losing, regaining and losing the same ground a dozen times.

On the sixth day, the IPF attempted to cross the interstate at six locations, sending huge numbers of troops across the concrete in what appeared to be a kamikaze-style rush of bodies.

Five sectors of the Rebels held, but the IPF broke through one line, allowing more troops to pour through and set up positions west, east and south, in the form of an open-ended box. Hector Ramos's troops were cut off, battling lopsided odds, fighting for their lives.

In western Iowa and central Illinois, the dawning of the new day brought a fresh horror to the men and women of Juan Solis's and Al Malden's troops.

A man's scream brought Mark Terry on a flat run from his bunker, running hard up the hill to the first line of defense. A man squatted behind sandbags, his face mirroring his horror and revulsion. He seemed unable to speak. He could but point to the valley.

Hartline's men had been unusually silent for several days, with no attempt to push past their battle lines. There had been only sporadic sniper fire from the west to keep the troops from New Africa alert — a lead reminder that Hartline's mercs and the IPF had not forgotten them.

The sentry found his voice as he handed Mark binoculars and pointed to the valley. "Nobody could be that low," he said, his voice choked with anger and frustration.

Mark felt his guts churn and his breakfast fight to lunge from his stomach as he lifted the long-range glasses to his eyes. Like the sentry, he was, for a moment, speechless. He felt the blood rush from his head, and for a moment, thought he would pass out from the sheer horror of the sight in the valley below.

"The dirty *bastards!*" he finally found his voice.

Al had joined him on the ridge, pulling field glasses to his eyes. "Oh, my God!" he blurted. "Oh, my God—no!"

The IPF and Hartline's troops were on the march, moving up behind armored personnel carriers. On the front of each APC, strapped to the sloping front of the carrier, a naked woman was positioned, her legs spread wide, ankles and feet secured to the lugs near the base of the M113. Her arms were out-flung, wrists tied to the headlight brackets. The machine gun mounted to the front of the APC was only inches from each woman's head, guaranteeing a savage muzzle-blast burn to the side of the woman's head.

When the troops on the ridges saw what was coming up behind the APCs, to a man, they openly, unashamedly wept.

A hundred or so old people were being herded in front of and mixed with the mercenaries and the troops from the IPF.

The elderly black men and women were crying from fear and humiliation as they stumbled along, prodded by the rifle barrels of the mercs and the IPF troops.

The elderly men and women had been stripped naked and were barefooted.

The IPF troops and Hartline's men were moving ever closer, and so far no shots had been fired from the troops on the ridges. All eyes were fixed unbelievingly on the scene before them. Weapons had been forgotten, hanging loose in their hands.

"They have to be stopped." Mark was the first to speak, his words hoarse-sounding, pushed from his tight throat. "We have to stop them; there is no one else to do the job."

Up and down the thin and battle-weary line of defenders of liberty, the troops looked first at each other, and then to Al and Mark for orders. But for many, the decision had already been made in their minds.

From the lead APC, still much too far away to be heard by any of the resistance fighters, Peggy Jones was screaming.

"Fire!" she screamed. "Shoot your guns! For God's sake—*shoot!*"

The IPF troops in the APC laughed at her words.

"I can't fire on those people," a man said, tears in his eyes. "I can't shoot, I might hit some of the old people or the women. I can't do it."

"Fire!" Mark screamed the command. "Goddamnit, people, they have to be stopped regardless of the cost. Fire, goddamn you!"

The enemy moved closer.

Now the troops on the ridges could hear Peggy's screaming, very faint, but audible.

"Shoot," she screamed. "For God's sake, shoot!"

The machine guns on the front of the APCs began singing their lethal songs, spitting out lead. One woman's hair caught fire from the fierce heat of the muzzle; her screaming was hideous.

"Pick your targets," Al yelled to a rifle squad. "Shoot around the old people."

The snipers tried, but the troops in the APCs were crouched low, and almost impossible to hit. Bullets struck one naked young woman in the stomach; she cried out in pain. Several old people were struck by the lead from the men on the ridges. They fell to the earth, screaming in pain and confusion. A Jeep ran over one; an APC crushed the legs of another. Yet another elderly man tried to grab the rear of a Jeep. He was dragged over the rocky ground for several hundred feet until life and strength left him.

Most of the guns on the high ground fell silent. They could not be blamed for that.

"Fall back!" Mark yelled, knowing his position was nearly hopeless. "First and second companies regroup. First company to the right flank, second company to the left, come in behind them."

But it was too late; Hartline's men and the IPF were too close. They had already begun executing an end-around sweep. The defenders on the ridges were cut off.

"Goddamn you!" Peggy yelled her rage at the men on the ridges. She tried to anger them into firing. "Can't you niggers do anything right? You have to leave everything up to whitey?"

Hartline's mercs thought that hysterically amusing.

The APCs and Jeeps were roaring up the small inclines, the ring-mounted .50s on the Jeeps and APCs spitting and hammering out death.

Al Malden lifted his M-16 and shot one machine

gunner in the face. A second later a hard burst from an M-60 spun him around and tore his chest open. He danced grotesquely and then fell to the cool earth, his blood soaking into the ground.

The mercenaries and the IPF troops crested the ridges and were over the top as the troops who had pulled the flanking maneuver sealed off much of the rear escape route. The black troops fought well and bravely, but the better-fed, better-trained and better-equipped IPF and mercs soon overwhelmed the small force on the ridges.

Mark Terry shot the driver of one APC in the head and dropped a grenade into the carrier. The grenade exploded, sending bits of human flesh and brains flying out of the APC. He slashed at Peggy's ropes, freeing her. He jerked her toward a Jeep, bodily picking her up and throwing her into the back seat. A bullet slammed into the fleshy part of his shoulder, spinning him around and dropping him to the ground. He pulled himself into the driver's seat with his good arm and jerked the Jeep into gear, racing back to the main encampment, to his command post. But Hartline's flankers were well ahead of him, and he could see the battle was almost over. Hartline's men were shooting the wounded in the head.

Cursing, Mark floorboarded the Jeep and headed for the timber. Driving deep into a forest, away from the battleground, he pulled over, off the old dirt road, and switched off the engine.

Mark removed his field jacket and gave it to Peggy. He could see that the woman had been beaten and tortured. Despite that, she was still beautiful.

Mark poured raw alcohol onto his shoulder wound

and bandaged it hurriedly. Peggy crawled into the front seat beside him.

"We're beaten," she said flatly.

"Not yet," Mark said grimly. He slammed the heel of his hand against the steering wheel. "Goddamnit!" he cursed. "I just didn't count on Hartline doing anything like that."

Her bitter laugh lifted his eyes toward her. "You can count on Hartline doing almost anything," she told him. "He is brilliantly insane and perversely twisted; and so are a great number of his men."

"You sound like you know him well."

The sounds of battle were coming to a close, with only an occasional shot being fired far in the distance. Mark felt like a traitor for running out on his men. But there was still a chance he could regroup some of his people. But it was a slim one and Mark knew it. And he didn't know if he wanted to see those who refused to fire. He thought he might try to kill them.

The taste of defeat was brass-bitter on his tongue. The word coward kept coming to him.

But Mark knew he was no coward; he had faced too much adversity in his life to be a coward. He just wished he could have done more.

As if reading his thoughts, Peggy said, "That battle was lost before it began back there, and Sam Hartline knew it. Said as much. There was nothing you could have done to change any of it. What is your name?"

"Mark. Mark Terry."

"I'm Peggy Jones. Yeah, I know Sam Hartline." The words rolled harshly from her tongue. "I was his . . . house nigger for a time, reporting back to Lois Peters, and she to the resistance. But he knew what I was do-

278

ing all along and the information he gave me was deliberately false. I . . . got away from him—don't ask me how—but he finally tortured Lois until she gave away where I was hiding. I can't blame her for that. He tortured her to death. It was . . . terrible what he did to her. I will never get that picture of her out of my mind.

"Then," she sighed, "he had a high old time with me. I . . . really don't want to say what he did to me. It was sexual, most of the time. I will never be able to bear children. The IPF people . . . fixed me." She lifted her arm and pulled back the sleeve of the field jacket, showing Mark the tattoo on her arm. "Hartline and a lot of his men and the IPF people as well are perverted. They enjoy inflicting pain; and Hartline likes to do it in a sexual manner. And that is all I'm going to say about that."

Mark touched her hand. "You don't have to say anything, Peggy. Some of the refugees that came into our area told us a lot about Hartline. What the women said was . . . sickening."

Her eyes, filled with the horror of what had been done to her, touched his eyes. "We need to get to a safer place, Mark, and I need to fix up that shoulder of yours."

Something deep within Mark, something very soft and gentle, moved slightly, touching him in a manner he had never known before. He was unsure of the origin or the meaning. "Yeah," he said softly. "Right. And . . . Peggy?"

He looked at him. "Yes?"

"People do adopt kids, you know."

He put his good arm around her and she put her

face against his chest and wept.

"Holy Mother of God!" Juan whispered. "That isn't warfare — that's *evil*."

He stood gazing in disbelief and shocked horror at the line of APCs coming at them, naked women and naked young boys and girls roped to the front of the carriers.

"Take a look at what is coming up behind them," a soldier said, his voice hushed with shock in the early morning.

Juan lifted his binoculars to his eyes. After a moment, he lowered them and began cursing, long and passionately, in his mother tongue.

"What do we do, Juan?" The question came out of the knot of company commanders standing behind him. It was a question Juan did not want to hear, but one he knew had to be answered.

After a moment that seemed like an eternity to Juan, he said, "We stop them; we have no choice in the matter." There was a deathlike quality to his reply.

"Juan, we can't —"

"Yes, we can!" Juan whirled around, his face tight with anger as he recalled Ben's words: "If they can't cut it, Juan, let me have it all up front." And Juan's reply now returned to haunt him: "They will do what I tell them to do. They might not like it, but they will do it."

God, Juan silently implored the Almighty, let my people have the courage to do this awful thing.

"We have to stop them!" Juan shouted the words.

A company commander lowered his binoculars,

tears streaming from his eyes, rolling in rivers down his cheeks. "The little ones are all crying," he said, his voice breaking under the strain. "The—"

"Stop it!" Juan shouted.

". . . Old people are naked and barefooted. Must be two—"

"Goddamn it, fire!" Juan screamed. He looked up and down the line of the first defense. "Fire on them, goddamn you!"

". . .Or three hundred of the old people." The man appeared to be in shock.

Juan slapped the man, the force of his open-handed blow rocking the man's head back, bringing blood to his lips.

Juan jerked up a rifle, firing at the mercenaries, the IPF, the young and the old. A few more defenders joined him. But most did not. They could not.

The forces, under the command of Colonel Fechnor, drew closer.

Juan's men began backing off the small ridge, bucking under the awfulness of what lay before them, growing nearer with the screams and cries of the young and the old.

"You have no place to back up *to*!" Juan shouted at his men.

Over the rumble of the APCs and Jeeps, the sounds of the children's weeping drifted to the men on the hill. About a third of Juan's first line of defense stayed by his side, fighting at his orders. The others drifted back, not out of cowardice, but because they loved life so much they could not bear to fire on the very young and the very old.

"Cobardes!" Juan screamed at the backs of his men.

"Chacals!" But he knew those men were not cowards or jackals. They simply could not bring themselves to fire on helpless old people and babies.

"Fall back to the river!" Juan yelled to those men who elected to remain by his side. Far in the distance he could see trucks rolling toward the bridge at Blair. He turned to his radio operator. "Order them to stop," he told the woman.

She shook her head. "I have them now, sir. They say they are not defeated or running away. They say they will defend our homelands, but they will not kill women and babies and old people."

Alvaro, Juan's brother, hurried to his side. "Juan, we have about one minute before we meet eternity."

The screaming and the crying of the children lashed to the front of the APCs was now very clear. The old people were stumbling, almost down from exhaustion. They were being prodded forward by rifle barrels.

The taste of the defeat was ugly on Juan's tongue. He gave the order he knew must he must give to save at least some of his forces. "Fall back!" he shouted.

As Juan rode in the Jeep, crossing the bridge over the Missouri River, he muttered, "God help Ben Raines."

THREE

Ben listened grimly to the reports from the Rebel's LRRPs. He stood in his command bunker and cursed. When he ran out of obscenities, he looked at the woman manning the radio.

"Sorry about that," he apologized.

She grinned. "I haven't heard such cussing since the time my daddy caught me in a hayloft with a kid from down the road."

Ben felt some of the anger leave him and he grinned at her. "I bet that was quite a moment."

Her grin widened. "It was worth it."

Ben laughed. "OK. Get on the horn and tell Colonel McGowen to cut and run. Head south. Instruct Colonel Ramos to break through his south lines and do the same. Order all forward units to hunt holes and get in them and keep their heads down until they receive orders from me to resume guerrilla activities. No last-ditch stands for any unit. No heroics out of anybody. Pull back. We'll regroup along Highway 60 in southern Missouri, from Springfield to Poplar Bluff. Pull back with all speed."

"We're retreating, sir?"

"No," Ben told her. "We are executing what the marines used to call a strategic withdrawal. Get to it, Sergeant."

"This isn't as much fun as the hayloft," she said.

Chase walked into the battle-scarred bunker. "I've got badly wounded people, Ben. To move them at this time would be endangering their lives."

"Move them," Ben said. "It can't be avoided, Lamar. We don't have a choice."

The doctor looked at the man for a long moment. Then he nodded his head. "All right, Ben. I'll start pulling them out now." He turned to leave.

"Lamar?"

The doctor turned around.

"I'm sorry, Lamar."

"I know, Ben. I'm sorry, too."

Gen. Georgi Striganov was furious. The deaths of the old people, the young women and the children did not bother him as much as what it had done to his self-image. The Russian perceived himself as a fair and just person. History might well paint him as an evil person for condoning something like this. That bothered him more than anything.

"I gave no orders to do anything this monstrous!" Striganov raged at Sam Hartline and Colonel Fechnor. "Killing old people and little children."

"Only a few old niggers died," Hartline said. "One nigger woman took a round in the guts and one got her brain cooked when her hair caught fire. There were a few greasers killed over in Iowa. No big deal. Anyway, if you have to yell at somebody, yell at me," Hartline told him. The deaths of the young and old bothered him about as much as swatting a fly. "Colonel Fechnor was assigned to my command and he was only obeying orders like any good soldier."

Col. Valeska Fechnor breathed a silent sigh of relief. He would have to think of some way to repay Hartline for getting him off tenterhooks. This could have turned into a very ugly scene.

General Striganov calmed himself slowly by taking deep breaths and clenching and unclenching his fists. He turned away and gazed out the front of the open tent. He would have to tell his historians that it was the mercenary who ordered the old and the young used in such a horrible manner; let future generations know that he, personally, had nothing to do with anything so monstrous.

"Anyway," Hartline said with a smile, "we won, didn't we? Raines is pulling his people back, turning tail and running. So the victory is ours."

"Ben Raines is most definitely *not* turning tail and running," the Russian told the mercenary. "He is merely executing a perfectly logical military option. I would do the same if the situation was reversed. One battle does not win the war. And do *not* attempt to do with Ben Raines what you succeeded in doing with the inferior minorities. General Raines would not hesitate to shoot. He would not like it, he might weep while giving the order, but he would shoot. Don't ever think otherwise."

"Yeah," Hartline agreed. "You're right about that, I guess."

Striganov withered him silent with a cold look. "I am almost *always* correct, Sam. And never again do anything of today's magnitude without first consulting me. Is that clear?"

"Clear as rain," the mercenary said, the scolding bouncing off him. Hartline had a hide of iron.

"Yes, sir," Fechnor said crisply.

"Very well," Striganov said. "The matter is closed. We shall count our dead, give them a proper soldiers' burial, then map out strategy for the upcoming campaign against General Raines. And it will not be an easy one. Do not — either of you — delude yourselves into believing otherwise. Unless we are lucky enough to kill Ben Raines — *in combat* — his people will fight forever, constantly a thorn in our sides."

"Have some of your people down in Tri-States ambush him," Hartline suggested.

"No," Striganov said. "I will not stoop to Raines's level of fighting. Not yet, at least. Besides, you can bet Raines will ferret those people out when he gets back. If he gets back. I was arrogantly wrong when I admitted to him I was aware of his Jewess bed-partner. My mistake. I shall be big enough to admit it. All right, now then, how great were the losses of the black people?"

"Fifty to sixty percent," Hartline told him. "Maybe seven to eight hundred got away. Certainly no more than that."

"Their leaders?"

"Al Malden is dead. Mark Terry got away. Took Peggy with him and cut out."

"Peggy?" Striganov questioned. "Who is Peggy?"

"No one of any importance." Hartline waved

the question aside.

"The Mexicans?" The Russian glanced at Colonel Fechnor.

"They fared a bit better. My men have counted some five hundred dead. We took less than two hundred prisoners. The rest ran away like cowards."

"Pursuit?"

"None. My men stopped at the Missouri River. As you ordered."

"Good. Very good, Colonel. I commend you." He walked to the tent opening. "Now, gentlemen, let us honor our gallant dead."

Ike was furious when he met with Ben. Ben let the ex-SEAL blow his tanks until he wound down. Ben then waved his friend to a seat.

"I was plenty pissed too, Ike. But then I got the whole picture from a survivor out of Malden's command." He told Ike what the IPF and Hartline's mercs had done.

Ike sat in horrified silence for a few seconds. "Ben . . . that's the worst goddamned thing I ever heard of. Jesus Christ! Kids and old people." He shuddered his revulsion. "I will admit my guys pulled some pretty raunchy shit in 'Nam, but nothing like that."

"It's low, buddy, I'll sure go along with that. Well, it's done, and nothing we can do about it. Let's get down to hard facts, buddy: How many people did you lose?"

"Too goddamn many. I lost just about twenty-five percent. Another ten percent wounded so badly they're out of action for weeks—maybe months.

Equipment fared a lot better. We got ninety-five percent of our howitzers and armor out."

"Thirty-five percent of your command, then?" Ben questioned, a deep and very personal sense of loss touching him. He knew every man and woman in every unit.

"At least."

"Don't feel too badly, Ike. My figures are just about the same as yours. Cecil's bunch took one hell of a pounding, too. He lost almost forty percent. And I hate to see Hector's losses when he comes in."

"I know he took a beating. When Hec's left flank caved in—wrong choice of words—was overrun—he lost an entire company right there. Last radio contact I had with him, he told me he took some heavy losses. Striganov really threw some people at him. Hec told me he was outnumbered four, five to one."

"I've sent out scrambled messages for any survivor to the east to come across at Cairo. That's why I asked you to leave people there. I got a hunch they'll be in pretty bad shape. Chase is sending medical teams over there to assist."

"You heard Malden's dead?"

"No. I hate that. We were beginning to be friends. Mark Terry?"

"I just heard he was wounded, but managed to get out. He rescued one young woman from the front of an APC."

"They'll be drifting in pretty soon, I imagine. I hope so. We're going to need all the warm, breathing bodies we can muster."

"Plans?"

Ben shook his head. "I don't know what we're going

to do, Ike. I want a fully attended meeting of the minds as soon as everybody gets in."

"I wonder if the Russian knows how really weak we are?"

"I doubt it. And he must not find out. If he threw everything he had at us right now, he'd hammer us into the ground."

It was a downhearted and beaten group of men and women that straggled southward toward Cairo, Illinois. Although they did not speak of the horror, the picture of the naked women lashed to the front of the APCs and the old people stumbling along, frightened and humiliated, was a mental scene none could erase from their minds.

And for many, the thought nagged at them: Was I acting cowardly by refusing to shoot?

It was a question that many would never resolve to any degree of satisfaction.

Mark and Peggy encountered the first group of troops from New Africa at Du Quion, Illinois. Mark, his resentment toward them still a hot fire within him, at first would not acknowledge their presence. He drove past them without speaking, waving or even looking directly at them. Outside of the deserted town, he pulled over, conscious of Peggy's unwavering stare on his face.

He parked on the shoulder, sighed and then cut off the engine. He turned to face her. "What is it you want me to do, Peggy?"

"I want you to go back and rally your people. The fight isn't over, Mark. The fight can't ever be over until the Russian and Hartline are both dead and the dream of . . . of the master race is dead with them."

"Those people back there are cowards," Mark said, jerking his thumb in the direction from which they had just come.

"Oh, Mark, they aren't any more a coward than you are. And in your heart you know that's true. They're confused and troubled and I'm sure they feel they let you down."

"Let me down? Hell, they did let me down! And not just me. They let Ben Raines down. And there is something else, Peggy. I keep replaying that awful scene in my mind, over and over. And I keep asking myself this: If those people lashed to the front of those APCs, thoses people being herded in front of the troops, if those people had been white instead of black, would my troops have stood their ground and fired?"

"Oh, Mark! How could you even think such a thing? That's—"

"No, Peggy, let me finish. This is something—what I'm about to say—I argued and debated with Al many times. And I think, I believe, the events of the day before yesterday prove me right. There is still a lot of hate among the races in this country; and it is not one-sided as Al used to preach. I'm sorry he was killed; he was coming around, getting his head on straight. The nation, if there is to be a nation, cannot exist the way we were going. I mean, Hispanics in one part of the country, blacks in another, whites in yet another. Damn it, Peggy, that isn't democracy. Our young people aren't — weren't — getting an accurate picture of life. I'm not African—I'm an *American*. I don't speak Swahili—I speak English. Al could never understand,

I could never make him see, that I didn't give two hoots in hell about the internal politics of Uganda. I was too concerned about what was happening in *this* nation. I don't want to wear tribal robes and stick a bone in my nose. Jesus Christ. That was part of the problem with many whites refusing to accept blacks.

"Look at Cecil Jefferys; he's never had any problem in his entire life being accepted—anywhere. And do you know why? I'll tell you why: He dressed well; he spoke proper English and insisted his kids do the same. He didn't try to excuse bad grammar by saying it was part of the black culture. He knew, just as I know, that is pure bullshit. Bad grammar is bad grammar. Period. I cannot for the life of me conjure up any image of Vice President Jefferys doing any shuckin' and jivin'."

Peggy laughed aloud at the expression on Mark's face.

"You mean Mr. Jefferys calls a spade a spade?" she said with a grin.

"I'll have to remember that one," Mark said, returning her smile. "Cecil will get a kick out of that. Yes, that's true, Peggy. He calls a spade a spade. Cecil, as does Ben Raines, knows there are classes of people: just as there are bigoted, ignorant rednecks in the white race, there are ignorant, bigoted niggers in the black race." He smiled at her. "Sorry, Peggy—I didn't mean to preach at you."

"No, it's all right. I like what you've said. Go on."

"All right, I'll lay it all out for you. I'm linking up with Ben Raines. I think that's what we have to do if any of us are going to make out of this situation. Those people back there—" he jerked his thumb—"if

291

they want to live under those rules, those conditions, those ideas that Ben and Ike and Cecil put forward — then fine, that's what we'll do. I'll put what happened on the ridges out of my mind, forgive, if not forget, and we'll join Ben Raines and try to beat this IPF thing. Those that want to go on back to New Africa and stick a goddamn bone in their noses . . . well, to hell with them."

Her dark, serious eyes never left his face. "You must think Ben Raines hung the moon and the stars in the heavens, Mark."

He shook his head. "No, I don't think that at all, Peggy. Ben Raines is just a man, with faults like all the rest of us. And I don't agree with all he says. As a matter of fact, I hated him at first. Until I began to wise up to what he was saying: no free rides. And then he began to make sense to me. His Tri-States worked, Peggy. It really worked. All races lived there, honey. *All races.* And Ben Raines did it. He made it work."

"I've never met the man. But I have seen his picture."

"He's . . ." Mark paused, searching for the correct words. "Ben Raines is impressive. He . . . exudes power and confidence. And something else, you may as well hear it from me: A lot of people believe Ben Raines sits awfully close to a higher power."

Disbelief sprang into her eyes. "And what do you believe, Mark?"

Mark sighed, many different emotions surging through his mind. "I . . . don't know. I don't want to believe that. But I've heard so many stories about him. And I know that many of them are fact. Peggy, the man's been shot two dozen times; he's been stabbed, blown up, shot off mountains and fallen God knows how far. Name it, and it's happened to Ben Raines. But he *won't die*."

A frightened look replaced the doubtful look in her eyes. She again searched his face. "Mark, are you sure of what you're saying?"

"Yes." His reply came quickly and quietly and surely. "I am positive."

"Then I think we should join your Mr. Raines."

And the legend of Ben Raines surged forward.

Mark and Peggy stood by the side of the road and waited for the troops to reach them. When they drew close, Mark stepped into the center of the weed-filled, cracked old road. He held up his hand.

The convoy stopped and the troops got out to face Mark.

Some four hundred men and women stood facing him; many would not meet his hard eyes.

"Here it is," Mark spoke firmly. "As far as I am concerned, New Africa is no more." He noticed only a few stirring at his words. "Those of you who wish to follow me, you're welcome. Personally, I am linking up with Ben Raines and his people. If he will have me, I will live where he lives, and live under his rules. Do not think that Ben Raines would have behaved as I did a few days ago. If Ben Raines had ordered you to shoot, and you refused, you would not be standing on this highway this day, for Ben Raines would have personally shot you for disobeying an order. I'm not that hard; I should have done that, but I couldn't. Ben Raines would have done it without blinking, and so will I if it ever occurs again. You will never disgrace my command again — and live to speak of it. Ben Raines is hard; that's why he is a survivor and you people are slinking along the road with your tails tucked between your legs like whipped dogs. And if you're not afraid to fight, if you think you can obey orders, and if you love freedom and liberty, follow me. I'll take you to Ben Raines."

Juan Solis, his brother, Alvaro, and several hundred followers pulled into Ben's new command post and base camp six days after their defeat. Juan walked up to Ben and the two men shook hands.

"These are all I could convince to join me, Ben," Juan said. "When my troops witnessed that . . . awfulness, it seemed to take the fight out of many of my men. I told them they were making a mistake."

"Don't they know that eventually General Striganov will move against them?"

Alvaro shook his head and said, "We tried to tell them, General Raines. Both of us. But they were too numbed by what happened for it to sink in. I am afraid that for many of them, when if finally does sink in, it will be too late."

"Mark Terry pulled in yesterday with about five hundred troops," Ben said. "He told me if I'd have them, they want to join us, not temporarily, but on a full-time basis. New Africa is, according to Mark, no more. He gave quite a speech to his people, so I hear. Said we were wrong—all of us—in living the way we were. You and I have spoken of that, Juan."

The Mexican shook his head. "Yes, and to a point I agree with Mark. I am very disappointed in my people, Ben. I can understand what they did—their refusal to fire—but I cannot forgive it. I simply cannot. So, Ben Raines, we are here. I will not return to lead a people whose men have lost their *cojones*. I, and these hundred who follow me, now wish to pledge our loyalties to you, General. You lead; we shall follow and obey."

And again, Ben asked the silent question to which he had yet to receive a reply: Why me?

FOUR

The IPF had not come out of the battle with Raines's Rebels smelling like the proverbial rose. They had lost more men than all three brigades fighting against them combined. But Striganov could better afford the heavy loss of personnel and equipment, for he had fresh troops coming in from Iceland, and still more behind those in reserve. If he chose to go in that direction.

But the Russian general who dreamed of a master race did not choose to go that route. He knew, now, the fierceness of President-General Ben Raines. He knew, now, that those who followed Ben Raines would follow him and fight to the death. And he knew, from scouts' reports, contingents from the Mexican and black brigades had once more linked up with Raines, and those racially inferior people had also pledged to fight to the death alongside Raines's Rebels.

Well, Striganov mused, let them fight and let them die. Their struggles would be in vain. The Russian had no doubts about that; nothing clouded his mind; nothing within the Russian suggested that his dream of a master race would be unsuccessful. He felt, from studying history, that if Hitler had not committed so many troops to the Russian front, the little paper hanger would have won the war and chased the Allies right back into the English Channel.

But Striganov was no Hitler. The Russian knew he was not insane, and would make no such costly errors in judgment.

He gave his orders. "Prepare to move out. We move in two days. Leave only a token force behind to guard our perfect people and the other breeding stock. This time we throw it all at General Raines."

They met in Ben's suite of rooms at a motel in Poplar Bluff. Cecil, Ike, Hector, Juan and Mark.

"All right, boys," Ben got the ball rolling. "I'm open for suggestions as to our next move. Let's toss it around and see what we come up with."

"Looks like to me," Ike said, "we're damned if we do and damned if we don't. Any move we make is going to cost us in blood."

"Yes," Mark said. "I agree. If we elect to cut and run, try to set up a stable government anywhere, Striganov will just find us and we'll still have to fight."

"Root hog or die," Juan mused aloud. "I believe we are in this to the death. I cannot see any other way." He looked at Cecil.

Cecil sighed and then nodded his head in agreement. "Even if we could make some sort of peace arrangement with the Russian, none of us would be able to live with our conscience, not knowing what was taking place with so many people. I think it would drive me insane knowing Striganov was putting his master race plan into operation, with all the horrors therewith, and we were sitting back safe, allowing it to happen."

"I felt physically ill when I first saw that tattoo on Peggy's arm," Mark spoke softly. "I believe that hit me harder than seeing the young women and the old people that day on the ridge. It . . . it drove it all home to me."

Ike drummed his finger tips on the meeting table. "What bugs me is that we can't get an accurate picture of just how many troops Striganov has. If we knew that, then we could make some firm plans."

"No way yet of really knowing that," Ben said. "But I'll wager he's got two divisions to back him up—at least."

"Felt like he was throwing that at me," Hector said with a very slight smile. "But I know he wasn't."

Hector had been wounded in the side and in the arm, but his wounds were more painful than serious. What was more agonizing to Colonel Ramos was the fact he had taken such awful casualties: Almost seventy-five percent of his troops were either dead or wounded, with many of the wounded not expected to live.

"They were tryin' to flank you, Hec," Ike said. "Come up under us. Their intelligence was bad; they thought you had the smallest force, when in reality, Ben had the smallest troop contingent." He looked at Ben. *"Two divisions, Ben?"*

"Yes. But I don't believe they are all stateside; I

think they're still coming in from Iceland. And there is this to consider: Russian divisions have always been smaller than American divisions. But even with that knowledge, I'd make a guess Striganov has between eighteen and twenty thousand troops. After all, people, Striganov's had better than a decade to work this out."

He expelled his breath and rubbed a hand across his face, as if trying to erase the worry he felt. "I think we're back to plan one, boys. We just don't have the people to stand up and slug it out with the Russians."

Colonel Gray stepped into the room. "Sorry I am late, gentlemen," the Englishman said. "But I wanted to debrief the last group of LRRPs that came in. General, they report the Russian is gearing up to throw it all at us the next go-round. And the rumors they heard, plus some actual radio transmissions our intelligence people decoded, clearly state the massive push coming at us very soon."

Ben nodded. The news did not surprise him. It was what he would do if he stood in the Russian's boots.

Colonel Gray poured himself a cup of coffee, tasted it, grimaced and said, "My word."

The men laughed and Cecil said, "Ben, you said back to plan one. What did you mean?"

"I believe we're too small a force to stand up and do anymore nose-to-nose slugging it out with the IPF. Add the fact that we've taken substantial losses in troops—it wouldn't take Striganov long to overrun and destroy us. That's my belief. So . . . I think we've got to go to a guerrilla-type operation: hit and run, and I mean hit hard. Cut and slash and demoralize. If it can be mined, mine it; if it can be blown, blow it up.

We've got snipers who can knock the eye out of a squirrel at three hundred meters—use them as long-distance shooters. Give me your thoughts on those ideas."

"I don't see that we have a choice," Ike said.

The rest of the men agreed.

Ben spoke to Cecil. "Order the heavy howitzers into hiding with the main battle tanks. Send the PUFFs into hiding. We can't risk losing any of them and with this type of operation, we'll have to depend on speed to survive. I want *them* to come to *us* this time. This is perfect country for ambushes and throat-cuttings: rolling hills and lots of brush.

"Gentlemen, start breaking your commands into small, highly movable teams. I want destruction and terror and confusion. Ike, get word back to Tri-States that I want all the Claymores, C-4, mines and dynamite we have in storage sent up here ASAP. Go over the use of high explosives with all your people. Hec, get your people to cleaning up the airport here at Poplar Bluff—we'll use that strip.

"Colonel Gray, send fresh teams of scouts and LRRPs back north with all the equipment they can carry. Tell them to start cutting throats. Have them determine which route the IPF will be taking and mine those bridges. We've got some good electronics people with us; they can rig those explosives so our LRRPs can lay back two, three miles and blow the bridges, with maximum killing effects and less danger to themselves.

"I want fresh teams on the way to replace weary teams at all times. I don't have to tell you men what a strain guerrilla warfare is; you all know a man tires

300

mentally and physically very quickly. And I don't want any heroics." He looked each man square in the eyes. "I mean that. For a number of reasons. Just being a part of any guerrilla action is heroic enough. And you all know that for an iron-clad fact.

"We've got the edge over the IPF in this type of action, even though we're heavily outnumbered. Most of our people have been fighting, in one way or another, for years. This is our type of war. But tell your people if they think they can't cut it—no pun intended," Ben said with a smile, and the men all laughed in rough soldier humor, "to step forward now. Don't endanger their buddies' lives.

"We will neutralize our zones of operation. If the people are IPF supporters—kill them. We went over this before, but I feel it best to hash it out again. The people will either be one hundred percent for what we are attempting to do, or one hundred percent against us. There will be no middle ground. We don't have the time or the personnel for a political debate. Anyone could turn our teams in. If you're Red, you're dead. That's the way it has to be, and that's the way it is going to be from this moment on. Do I make myself clear?"

"Perfectly, General," Colonel Gray said. He smiled. "Put quite forcefully, I should say."

Ben looked around the table. There were no questions from any man.

"All right, boys," Ben said. "I want the first teams equipped and moving north by late this afternoon. That's it, people, let's move it and shake it."

Cecil held up a hand, signaling that the meeting was not yet over. "Ben, I have to ask the question that is on all our minds."

Ben looked at him.

"Your part in all this guerrilla action will be to oversee the project and direct from this base—is that correct?"

"Not necessarily." Ben braced himself, for he knew what was coming. And he was going to have no part of it.

"Whoa, now, partner." Ike swung his eyes to Ben. "Like it or not, someone has to run things from this side of the battle line. You know that and you know who that person is."

Colonel Gray sat without entering the conversation. He knew very well no one would be able to keep General Raines out of the field. The man had entirely too much old war-horse in him for that. Middle-aged or not.

Juan looked horrified. "General Raines, you can't be serious. I mean, you can't be thinking of leading a team into the field."

Even Mark was upset, his face registering that discomposure. "General, your place is here. That you would even consider—"

Ben silenced them with a look and wave of his hand. "My place, gentlemen, shall be wherever I'm needed and can do the most good. If I feel the need to go into the field, I shall do just that." He stood up. "And that settles the matter. Do we have any further questions concerning this operation?"

There were questions by the score on each man's tongue, but they checked any vocal arguments. They all knew better than to cross Ben when his mind was made up.

"Tina is well-trained in this business of guerrilla warfare," Colonel Gray asked the question without it being put as such. "I know, I helped train her."

"Then by all means, use her," Ben said, no expression on his face. "No one among us is indispensable."

Only one man, the thought jumped into the brain of the men who sat looking up at Ben Raines.

But no one spoke the name aloud.

"Move out, gentlemen," Ben said softly. "And good luck to you all."

FIVE

I have passed the Rubicon; swim or sink, live or die, survive or perish with my country — that is my unalterable determination.

— John Adams

"It ain't our fight," the burly man told the young captain from Raines's Rebels.

"Mister —" the captain stood his ground, the ground in this case being just below the Great Smoky Mountains National Park in north Georgia — "if you think it isn't your fight, if you think the IPF won't be in here after you and your family, you'd better think again."

The man spat tobacco juice on the ground. "When or if this Russian and his troops get here, we'll fight. But not before."

"By then it may well be too late," he was told.

"Mayhaps you be right in that," the man replied in the peculiar mountain dialect that many families still used after centuries. "But me and mine been gettin' by in these mountains for more years than there was a nation, sonny boy. The Russians come in here and they'll find us to be not so hospitable as we is to you and your soldiers . . . sonny boy."

The young captain met the mountain man's stony gaze with a look just as unflinching and unyielding. "Mister, you call me sonny boy one more time, and you're going to be eating on the butt of this AK-47. And after I butt-stroke you, I am going to stomp your fucking guts clear out."

"He looks and acts like he might just be able to do it, Abe," a man called from the porch.

Good-humored laughter broke from the knot of men gathered around the troops.

Humor touched the burly mountain man's eyes. "I do believe you'd try your best to whup me, wouldn't you . . . Captain?"

A grin touched the corners of Capt. Roger Rayle's mouth. "Yes, sir, I sure would."

The mountain man laughed and shook his shaggy head. "All right, Captain. Come on up to the porch. Folks been a-bringin' in food all morning. We eat and talk about this thing. We don't get much outside news 'round here. Be nice to find out what's happenin' in the world and with these Russians."

Abe stopped dead in his tracks and slowly turned around when Captain Rayle said, "A resurgence of Nazism, sir."

Abe stared at him for a long moment. He blinked. "Resurgence. Good word. I believe that means—and you tell me if I'm wrong—these Russian people, the IPF, they doing the same thing that Hitler feller done back in the thirties and forties to the Jews.

305

Am I right?"

"Yes, sir. You are exactly right. And they must be stopped."

By now the crowd around the stone and wood house had grown to more than a hundred men and women. They stood silently.

Abe said, "My daddy was a paratrooper in that war. He helped liberate a concentration camp. Don't rightly recall just where it was. He told me he had seen some ugly sights in his life, during the war. Hadn't never seen nothing to compare with that. Said them people was the poorest lookin' bunch he'd ever seen. Made him sick, so he said. Couldn't keep nothing on his stomach for a week or better.

"Now, as for me, I don't know many Jew folks. Them I have known, I didn't much care for. Too pushy for my tastes. But my personal opinions don't matter much when it comes to another man doing a deliberate hurt to a human being 'cause of race or religion. I just don't hold with that. What is this IPF bunch doin' to folks?"

"They are taking everyone not of a pure white race — blacks, Hispanics, Asians, Jews, Indians — and operating on them so they cannot reproduce offspring. They are tattooing I.D. numbers on them. They are torturing them and conducting medical experiments on them. If a person does not have a high enough I.Q., regardless of race, he is being disposed of."

"Killed, you mean?"

"Yes, sir."

The man spat another stream of tobacco juice on the ground. "All this is fact?"

"Yes, sir."

A long, lean, lanky man set his coffee cup on the porch railing and stood up. "Abe," he said, "don't you be startin' no meetin' 'til I get back here, now, you hear?"

"Where you be goin'?"

"To get my kin and my gun."

Raines's Rebels got in the first bloody, savage lick of the newly declared guerrilla war. The column of IPF troops and equipment was on a bridge in south central Iowa, crossing the Des Moines River when hundreds of pounds of carefully hidden high explosives were electronically detonated. One full company of troops was killed when their trucks plunged nose-first into the cold, dark waters of the river. Fifty were killed when the bridge exploded, hurling men and equipment and assorted arms and legs high into the air, to plunge and sink into the river.

The LRRP teams had allowed several IPF trucks to cross the bridge before activating the charges, cutting them off from the main convoy. The IPF troops were chopped to bloody rags of flesh and splintered shards of bone by mortar and heavy machine gunfire from the Rebels hidden in the thick brush that now grew alongside the roads and interstates of the once-most-powerful nation in the world.

By the time the IPF could backtrack and cross the river, coming up to the point of ambush, the Rebels were long gone, fading silently and quickly into the countryside, their gruesome jobs efficiently and effectively done.

Colonel Fechnor, who was commanding the troops spearheading the assault south, smiled a humorless grimace of grudging respect for the men and women of the scouts and LRRPs, and for Gen. Ben Raines.

This one action—even if there were no more, and Fechnor knew there would be many more—had succeeded in its initial objective: slowing down the advance of the IPF. Now every bridge, no matter how small, would have to be inspected and inspected very carefully. Fechnor *knew* the Rebels would have ambush teams at every bridge and overpass along the way. If just one out of every five teams Fechnor sent out returned, he would consider that good odds.

No, Fechnor mused, this President-General Ben Raines was not going to roll over like a whipped puppy and give up. If Raines went down at all, it would be with a snarling, biting, savage action.

For the first time—the very first time—Colonel Fechnor felt that just maybe the International Peace Force had bitten off more than they could chew or swallow safely.

But, Colonel Fechnor thought, mentally shaking off the thought of defeat, he could not think that— that was treason. He was a soldier, and as a soldier he obeyed orders. He did not question whether they were right or wrong. He simply obeyed. Fechnor was the epitome of the universal soldier.

A type found in all armies. The type without which no army could exist or function. Without them, there could be no wars.

Fechnor ordered his dead buried. He stood with an impassive soldier's face as this was done.

Then the colonel made his second mistake of

that day.

"What do our scouts report on the conditions in Ottumwa?" he asked an aide.

"The city is deserted, sir. They say it is a ghost town. They don't know where the people went. First reports of several weeks ago stated the city had several hundred residents."

They probably left to join Ben Raines, the colonel said to himself, and he was right in that assumption. "Very well. No need to change course. Drive right on through the city."

Ottumwa was anything but a ghost town.

Colonel Gray's people had sealed the bypass around the city with old semi-rigs, carefully placed so it looked as though there had been a terrible accident months before and the wreckage never cleared.

There was about to be just that. But what was about to occur to Col. Valeska Fechnor's IPF troops was to be anything but an accident.

The old highway ran through the center of the once-thriving little city, and on both sides of the main drag of town, waiting behind dusty and broken windows, crouched on rooftops and hidden in ground-level old stores, were the trained troops of Gray's Scouts. They waited, hands gripping weapons, their only movement the shifting and blinking of eyes.

"Convoy approaching the city limits, sir," a forward-placed LRRP radioed back to Dan Gray.

"Received," Colonel Gray's aide radioed back. She turned to Dan. "Convoy coming in, sir. And it's a big one."

"Good, good." Dan smiled and rubbed his hands together. "Excellent, dear. Now we shall teach the bloody arrogant bastards a hard lesson about life. Or," he laughed, "the loss of it."

She returned the soft yet hard laughter of the professional fighter.

The lead scout APC cautiously turned the corner and swung onto the main street.

"Hold your fire," Dan whispered into a walkie-talkie. "Let them get clear; our lads south of the main area will bloody their knives on the scouts."

Colonel Fechnor felt it first. An experienced soldier, he felt that anticipatory tingle on the short hairs of his neck. He looked around him. His entire convoy stretched out behind him on the main street of town.

Where were the dogs? he thought. There should be mangy dogs slinking about. Birds, too. But the street was void of all life.

Suddenly, Fechnor knew he had been suckered.

Sitting ducks! he thought. "Floorboard it!" he yelled, startling his young driver. "Get the hell off this street and out of town." He grabbed up his mic. "Ambush!" he shouted. "Ambush!"

The driver jammed the pedal to the floorboards and the car shot forward just as a building exploded to Fechnor's right. A second later the building on the opposite side of the street blew, just as two buildings far down the street erupted in rubble-filled fury, effectively blocking both ends of the street and sealing the IPF column.

Fechnor's armored car just barely escaped the carnage only heartbeats away.

"Cut to the right!" Colonel Fechnor screamed.

310

"Head to the west."

The frightened young man obeyed instantly as the sound of automatic weapon fire and grenades reached their ears.

The taste in Colonel Fechnor's mouth was sour and ugly as his frightened young driver found Highway 34 and roared toward the west. Toward safety, the young man feverishly hoped.

On the main street of Ottumwa, the troops of the IPF were being brutally slaughtered, many of them taken by such surprise they were unable to fire their weapons before slugs chopped them to death.

Using M-16s, M-16A2s, .50-caliber and M-60 machine guns, AK-47s, anti-tank rockets and grenades, the Rebels cut and slashed at the IPF personnel. Screams from the frightened and the wounded and the dying echoed off the buildings, mingling with the yammer of rapid fire and the booming of grenades and rockets. The air was filled with gun smoke and concrete dust from the shattered buildings. Small fires had broken out, the smoke adding to the confusion of the ambushed IPF troops.

The fire-fight was over in five minutes. Those men and women from the IPF who had managed to jump from the trucks and run inside the buildings, seeking safety there, were riddled with bullets from the Rebels waiting for just such an action.

Col. Dan Gray's Scouts and LRRPs took no prisoners. Teams went to each fallen IPF member to deliver the *coup de grace:* a bullet to the back of the head.

"Gather up all the weapons and equipment," Colonel Gray instructed his people. "Every piece of equipment that is workable, every vehicle that will run, anything we can possibly find some use for, take it. We'll head south and cache it."

The smell of blood and urine and relaxed bowels from the dead that littered the shattered streets was foul in the air.

And the dogs had returned, warily, sniffing at the dead.

"What about the bodies, Colonel?"

Colonel Gray looked at the dogs, then carefully smoothed his trimmed moustache with a finger tip. "Leave them. The dogs appear hungry."

The sounds of the long, blacksnake whip cutting into flesh was followed by the cries and screams of the man being beaten and the sobs of the naked woman who was being forced to watch. The woman was held by two men: occassionally one or the other of the men would carelessly reach out to fondle some part of her nakedness. She had resigned herself to this humiliation and no longer struggled when one of them touched her. In the background, a huge wooden cross had been erected, its butt jammed into a hole in the ground and secured. It was blazing, sending shimmering waves of heat into the coolness of the autumn air.

Tears streaked the woman's face. "Please stop," she implored the men. "You're killing him. For the love of God — stop it."

"Naw, we ain't neither," a white-robed man casually informed her, not taking his eyes from the naked man being beaten. "We jist markin' him up some; teach him a lesson furst, then we'll get to you, seein' as how you lak' niggers so much." He laughed. "Yeah, we got a right nice treat in store for you, missy."

The long, leather whip whistled and sang its painful tune as it hummed on its way to impacting with bare flesh. The impact was a cracking slap, blood leaping from the cut. The young man screamed as the pain tore through his body. He sagged against the post where he was bound. His crotch rubbed against the rough wood of the post.

"Lookee there!" another white-robed man called as he laughed. "Nigger-lover looks lak' he a-tryin' to fuck that there post. Hunch agin' it, boy!"

The woman averted her eyes from the sight of her husband.

"Ol' Henry there is an expert with the blacksnake," one of the men holding her said. He reached across and pinched a nipple. The woman bit her lip to keep from crying out. The man grinned at this. "For a nigger-fucker, missy, you got nice titties. Yep, I seen ol' Henry make a whuppin' las' for near'bouts three hours once. I believe that were back in ninety-six. 'Course hit were a nigger buck we was whuppin' then—bigger and some tougher than your little man. Built up better, too. I can see why you like nigger meat so much; your man ain't got no cock on him at all. Never could make that nigger beg. So after we whupped him rawer 'an a skinned pig, we strung him up." He pointed to a tree. "Rat over there. We choked him to death. Took 'bout a hour. That was fun, watchin' that nigger dance. We lowered him a dozen times, let him suck air. Man was lak' an animal." He grinned lewdly. "Had him a cock lak' a horse. Way you lak' nigger meat, missy, you'd have cummed jist a-lookin' at that nigger's whork."

313

The woman shook her head and sobbed out her reply. "I have never had sex with a black man. Only with my husband."

"You a lie!" another man told her, walking up to the nude woman. His robes were satin, much more ornate than any of the others. "You nothin' but white trash, woman. We caught you travelin' with niggers."

"We were only helping them escape!" the woman screamed. "I've told you people that. Why don't you believe us?"

" 'Cause you a lie, 'at's why." The man turned away from her. He looked for a moment at the beating, then called, " 'At's enuff, Henry. Don't want to kill the boy. Cut him down. You, Richie, you go get that nigger buck, drag his monkey ass out to the circle."

A slender black man was dragged into the circle of robed men and women. He was naked. His eyes were blazing with fury and shame. "You people had no right to do this," he told the Klansmen. "This man and woman were merely helping me and my wife to escape from the IPF."

That got him a crack across the mouth from the Klan spokesman. "Shut your nigger mouth, boy. You stay in your place, you hear? 'Round here, boy, niggers talk when spoken to."

The horsewhipped man was cut from the whipping post and dragged into the center of the circle. "Dump some water on his ass," the spokesman said. "We want him to watch this."

A bucket of creek water was poured on the sobbing, bleeding man. He struggled to sit up on ground and at the same time cover his nakedness.

"You wastin' your time a-tryin' to cover that little

thing of yourn," a man leered at him. "You must have to stick it up your wife's asshole afore she even knows you got anything in her."

That brought hoots of laughter from the circle of men and women. More than one Klan woman had her eyes on the genital area of the naked black man.

" 'At there's not a bad idea," the spokesman said. "Luther, you go get Big Jim and brang him over here. We'll have us a show 'fore we let the nigger buck and the white bitch have at it."

Within moments a huge white man entered into the circle of the white-robes. That the man was mentally deficient was obvious at first glance. His eyes were dull and his face wore the slackness of the near-insane.

"Big Jim," the spokesman said. "I want you to shuck outta your pants. Now, you go on and do 'er now, boy, show us all your equipment."

Big Jim dropped his ragged jeans to the dirt. He wore no underwear. Many of the Klan women licked their lips at the sight of his enormous penis.

"Go git the nigger's wife," a man was ordered.

A well-shaped and pretty light-skinned woman was dragged naked and weeping into the circle.

"That'un got more'n her share of white blood in her," Henry said. "Big Jim gonna have him a high ol' time with her, awright."

"Missy," the spokesman told the white woman. "You crawl over there and jack off Big Jim; git him up good and hard."

She refused at first. Several hard slaps across her face changed her mind. Reluctantly and with revulsion on her face, she complied.

Big Jim soon became more than enormous. He was

deformed. The woman released him and was dragged back to the hard hands that held her.

"Tear that nigger gal's pussy up, Big Jim," the spokesman said with a laugh.

The young black woman's screaming soon echoed around the circle gathered around the burning cross. When Big Jim left the woman, she was huddled in a ball of hurt on the dirt. The grinning man was pointed out of the circle. He left carrying his pants.

"Position the nigger-lover," the spokesman ordered the men holding the woman.

She was forced to her hands and knees. The black man was told, "Git it up, shine. We gonna watch and see what you got that this nigger-lover laks so much."

"I will not!" the black man said.

The Klansman grinned. "How'd you lak' for me to call Big Jim back in here and have him fuck your wife unnormally?"

The man hissed his revulsion at the thought.

"Will you let us go after we . . . do that?" the naked white woman asked. "If we . . . have sex, will you promise to let us go?"

"We'll let you go alive. Shore we will."

"Do it, Jimmy," she told him, all resistance gone from her. She sagged in defeat. The cries of the black woman were still very much in sound and fury. The woman was bleeding. "Do it, Jimmy," she repeated. "If you don't, they'll torture and kill us all."

"You bes' listen to the woman, nigger."

"Why are you doing this to us?" Jimmy asked, anguish in his voice. "We haven't done a thing to you people. Why?"

"You be a nigger, boy, and that there is reason enuff.

This area is pure 'round here—for miles and miles. Pure white. No nigger, no greasers, no spics, no wops, no Jews, or nobody else lak' 'at 'round here—and they ain't never gonna be neither. Now don't none of us know nothin' 'bout this Russian ya'll keep flappin' your gums about, and I don't really care. But it sounds lak'—if they is such a feller—he's on the right track with his thinkin'. Now you get that cock of yourn up hard and dog-fuck this white bitch. Then ya'll can leave here. When you do git gone, pass the word: No niggers allowed in here."

"I . . . can't get an erection under these circumstances," Jimmy said.

The Klansman kicked the white man in the side. He fell to his back and screamed in pain.

"White boy, you lak' niggers so much, you crawl over here and suck this black bastard hard. And you either do it, or I'll have your balls cut off."

His wife's tears dropped to the dusty ground.

Jimmy stood trembling in rage and humiliation and helplessness.

His wife sobbed on the ground.

The bloody young man crawled toward the black man.

The circle of robed men and women began laughing.

SIX

"We're going to have trouble in central Illinois, Ben," Cecil said. "We're getting more reports stating a strong Klan resurgence in that area. And they are getting nasty with it."

Main Command Post, Poplar Bluff, Missouri. Ben sighed and looked up from a map.

"How many and how strong?"

"Field reports show the IPF is sending in teams to talk about an alliance with the Klan, and the Klan is buying their garbage."

"Shit!" Ben spat the word. "God, that's all we need at this time."

"Lots of hate, Ben. I think even more so than back in eighty-eight.

Ben rubbed his face with his hands. He blew out a long, sighing breath. "It's time for some good news, Cec. What's the word out of north Georgia?"

"Hostile at first. But Captain Rayle said in his last report the people are getting stirred up about the IPF. Most are willing to see us come in. Captain Rayle says they'll work with us."

"Good. I want those mountain people on our side. I just can't help remembering the reception I got in the Smokies back in eighty-nine."

"Oh?"

The first of May, 1989 found Ben in the middle of the Great Smoky Mountains, sitting in a motel room in a deserted town, eating a cold, canned meal.

These mountain people, he concluded, were weird. He couldn't get close enough to any of them to say a word. At a little town just south of Bryson City, a man made the mistake of taking a shot at Ben. Ben had reacted instinctively and spent the next few, long hours watching the man die from a stomach wound.

"Why did you shoot at me?" Ben asked. "I wasn't doing a thing."

"Outsider," the man had gasped. "Got no business being here. We'll get you."

"Why? Why do you want to 'get me'?"

But the man had lost consciousness and Ben never learned the answer to his question — at least not from the man he'd shot.

Sitting in the motel room, Ben was filled with doubts and questions. Where had all the people gone? The people of Atlanta? What was the use of spending years writing something . . . ?

His head jerked up as Juno growled softly, rising to his feet, muzzle toward the door.

"We don't mean you any harm, mister," a boy's voice said. "But if that big dog jumps at me, I'm gonna shoot it."

319

Ben put a hand on Juno's big head and told him to relax. He clicked on the recorder. "So come on in and sit," he invited.

A boy and girl, in their mid-teens, appeared in the door. They looked to be brother and sister. Ben pointed to a couple of chairs.

The boy shook his head. "We'll stand, thank you, though."

"What can I do for you?" Ben asked.

"It ain't what you can do for us," the girl said. "It's what we can do for you."

"All right."

"Git your kit together and git on outta here," the boy said. "They's comin' to git you tonight."

"Who is coming to get me—and why?"

"Our people," the girl told him. She was a very pretty girl, but already the signs of ignorance and poverty were taking their toll, affecting her speech and features.

The poverty and ignorance of her parents, Ben thought.

Root cause—in the home, passed from generation to generation, parent to child.

When will we ever learn? But . . . is it too late now? He thought not.

"I've done nothing to your people," Ben said.

"You kilt our uncle," the boy said. "Ain't that doin' somethang?"

"Your uncle shot at me for no reason. All I was trying to do was catch some fish for my supper."

"Our roads, our mountains, our fish," the girl said.

"I see," Ben's reply was soft. "And you don't want any outsiders here?"

"That's it, mister."

"If you feel that strongly, why are you warning me?"

The question seemed to confuse the pair. The boy shook his head. " 'Cause we don't want no more killin' around here. And if you'll leave, there won't be no more."

"Do you agree with your people's way of life?"

"It ain't up to us to agree or disagree," the boy said. "The word's done been passed down from Corning. And if you stay here, mister, you gonna die."

"Who or what is a Corning?"

"The leader."

"Ah, yes." Ben smiled, but was careful not to offend the young people, or rib their manner of speaking or thinking. "Let me guess: This Corning is the biggest and the strongest among you all. He is a religious man—or so he says—and he has a great, powerful voice and spouts the Bible a lot. Am I right?"

"Mister" —the girl's voice was soft with awe— "how'd you know all that?"

Ben looked at her. She was pretty and shapely and ripe for picking. "And I'll bet this Corning—I'll bet he likes you a lot, right?"

She nodded her head. "He's taken a shine to me, yeah."

"No doubt." Ben's reply was dry. How quickly some of us revert, he thought. Tribal chieftain. He stood up and the kids quickly backed away, toward the open door. "Take it easy. I won't hurt you. Are you going to get into trouble for coming here, warning me?"

The girl shook her head. "We come the back trails. We know where the lookouts is. You leavin'?"

"Yes, I'll be gone in half an hour."

She stood gazing at him. "We're not bad people, mister. We jist don't want no more of your world, that's all. Why cain't ever'body just live the way they want to live, and then ever'body would git along?"

Why indeed? Ben thought, and once again, the Rebels entered his mind. He felt compelled to say something profound. Instead he said, "Because, dear, then we wouldn't have a nation, would we?"

She blinked. "But we ain't got one now, have we?"

Then they were gone.

"Wonder what happened to that cult?" Cecil asked.

"Died out, hopefully. Maybe someone bigger and stronger than Corning came along and killed him. That's the way it usually happens, I guess." He stood up and stretched. "Any word from Dan?"

Cecil grinned a warrior' smile of satisfaction over hearing of an enemy's defeat. "Not since yesterday. That is one randy Englishman. His bunch completely destroyed a full column of IPF troops. Wiped them out to a person."

"For a fact, Cec, Dan does not like to be bothered with prisoners. Those SAS boys were randy as hell." Ben grinned. "Besides wiping out an entire column, they demoralized the hell out of a bunch of other IPF troops." Ben's grin grew wider. "I can't help but wonder what happened to that colonel who was commanding the unit."

"Dan said he turned tail and ran."

"Well, he got his tit in the wringer for that, I'm betting."

Cecil gave Ben a mock grimace. "God, Ben! I'm

glad Gale isn't here to hear that crack."

Ben laughed. "Me, too."

General Striganov at first could not believe his ears. He stared at Colonel Fechnor for a full moment. "The entire battalion!" the general finally roared. He rose from his chair to face a still-badly-shaken Fechnor. "I can't believe this. You lost an entire battalion?"

Colonel Fechnor's driver stood by the colonel's side. The young man was trembling from fear and exhaustion: fear at General Striganov's rage, and exhaustion from the long and sometimes-harrowing drive north, all the while imagining all sorts of dire repercussions from the general. Much to his regret, what he envisioned was coming true.

Fechnor stood at full attention, no give in him at his general's rage. "Yes, sir," he replied. "First a bridge blew, then we were forced to wait and regroup. Then we were ambushed in Ottumwa. I—"

"*I* am not interested in excuses!" Striganov roared. His face was red with fury. "Excuses are a weak man's forte. You are not a weak man, Fechnor. Fechnor—" he visibly calmed himself—"you are a trained, experienced combat veteran. You were decorated for your work in Afghanistan, for bravery as well as for common sense. We've been together since you were a mere lieutenant. What in the name of everything we hold sacred has happened to your courage?"

"There is nothing the matter with my courage, General," Fechnor flared, forgetting to hold his tongue. "My scouts reported the town deserted. I am forced to accept their findings—as any field commander must.

323

We approached the city with all due caution. My people fought well. But in vain. As for me—"

"You ran." Striganov stated the damning fact flatly, considerable heat in his voice. "You should have remained there, fighting and dying with your people."

The colonel met the general's stare, refusing to back down. "What you say may be true, General. If so, I am ready to accept and face whatever punishment you deem necessary, including, of course, the firing squad. I—"

Striganov waved him silent. He ordered the driver to leave the room. The young man almost fell over his feet in his haste to obey. Both men were forced to smile at the young man's antics. They both remembered their own youth, and their fear and awe of superior officers. The eyes of the two senior officers of the IPF met and held, and understanding passed between them in silent messages.

"Don't be ridiculous, Valeska," Striganov said. "I have absolutely no intention of putting you against a wall. I spoke in haste; you should not have stayed and died. You are my most experienced and valuable field officer. I cannot afford to lose you; you know that. I apologize for losing my temper. Your scouts are to blame for not thoroughly checking the city. They should have—as you did—sensed an ambush." Striganov returned to his chair and sat down heavily, sighing deeply. He remained thus for a time, brooding silently. Finally he looked up, catching Colonel Fechnor staring at him. The colonel was still standing at attention.

"Stand at ease, Colonel," Striganov said. "No," he amended that order. "Relax, make yourself comfortable. Have some tea. I insist."

Colonel Fechnor relaxed and walked to the tea service, pouring a cup of tea. He sugared and creamed the beverage and returned to sit in a chair facing General Striganov's desk, carefully placing cup and saucer on the desk.

"Valeska," the general said softly, "do you believe in any sort of supreme being?"

The question caught Fechnor off-guard. He thought for a few seconds, then said, "Why I . . ." He paused, not sure how to reply.

"Truthfully, now, old friend," Striganov said with a very slight smile, as if sharing some secret with the man, a confidence only the two of them knew. "We have no one listening to report our conversation back to the Central Party Headquarters."

Fechnor returned the slight smile. "Yes," he said. "One does tend to forget the old ways no longer apply, *da?*"

"Old habits are difficult to break," Striganov agreed.

"Yes," Fechnor spoke after a time. "Yes . . . I do believe there is something . . . something—I don't know what—after death. Good or bad," he said with a shrug of his shoulders. "Yes—I simply cannot believe that all the world, with its trees and flowers and animals and . . . beings just evolved. I have felt that way for a long time. Since maturity." Colonel Fechnor felt better for having said that.

"I see." Georgi spoke the words so softly Valeska had to lean forward and strain to hear them. The colonel waited for his commander to drop the other shoe—if he had another shoe to drop. He did.

"Yes," Striganov said. "I find that interesting, Valeska. For I, too, have felt for some time there just might be some truth to the belief in a higher power. Although I do not profess to know what type of higher power—I don't believe anyone does. I ..." He paused, choosing his words carefully. "But I do believe ... I have this thought, this theory, that President-General Ben Raines stands—quite unknowingly, I think—very close to this ... this higher being. *If* there really is some sort of ... supreme being."

Col. Valeska Fechnor could but stare at his commander. He could not believe the words his ears had heard.

Striganov's smile held more than a touch of amusement. "Oh yes, Valeska. Your ears have not deceived you. But I repeat: I do not believe Ben Raines knows of his ... closeness. If my theory is correct, that is. However, I do not think Ben Raines is always viewed in a favorable light by—" he grimaced—"by whatever it is that we believe might exist as some higher power or order."

Colonel Fechnor sat stunned in his chair, the excellent tea in front of him forgotten, cooling its fragrance. "Are ... are you saying, Georgi, that we are locked in combat with—*God?*"

Georgi lifted his eyes to meet Fechnor's amazed look. "In a manner of speaking, yes. If one believes in God. But if there exists such a person or thing or being—whatever—He is not known for direct interference or intervention. Lately I have studied the babblings of the Bible. I have studied them quite closely, over a period of months. Of course, it goes without saying I reject most of the writing as a figment

326

of someone's imagination, but . . . parts of that book disturb me. The New Testament is quite bland and un-interesting—it's the Old Testament that intrigues me, fascinates me. Since you used the word, let us maintain the usage: Why would *God* interfere so directly and openly in the Old Testament and not in the New? I find that contradictory. Very much so." Suddenly his features hardened. "And the goddamned Jews just persist in surviving. No matter what happens to them, no matter five thousand years of attempting to wipe them out, the bastards manage to survive. Through thousands of years of persecution—they survive. And now Ben Raines shares his bed and blankets with a Jew bitch." He shook his head. "I do not believe it was an accident."

Fechnor waited for a moment, then said, "What is at the base of all this, General? I gather it centers around the Jewess. What about her?"

Striganov drummed his finger tips on his desk. "Kill her," he said.

"The advance of the IPF has halted in southwestern Iowa," Cecil reported to Ben, a puzzled look on his face. "And I don't know why and neither do any of our intelligence people."

"Striganov is up to something," Ben replied without hesitation.

"That is our consensus," Cecil said, sitting down. "Without solid proof, of course. Dan Gray's LRRPs report the eastern column stopped at Muscatine and Dan says his people have reported the center column halted at Oskaloosa. Everything has stopped dead in its tracks."

Ben looked around him at the roomful of men. "Anybody care to venture an opinion as to why?" he asked.

No one would venture an opinion. The Russian's action was confusing to all of them.

Gale took that opportunity to stick her head into the motel room Ben was using as an office.

"Give your Jewess a great big kiss for me, *da?*" The words of the Russian popped into Ben's consciousness. Maybe, he thought.

But what would Striganov hope to gain by harming her? Ben silently asked.

He could find no answer.

"Come on in, Gale," Ben told her.

Gale smiled. "Am I intruding on this all-male gathering?"

"Honey." Ike returned the smile. "As pretty as you are, your presence could never be considered any sort of intrusion."

"Ike," she said, looking at him, "you are so full of shit as to be unreal."

"I do so love a plain-spoken woman," Ike replied, taking no umbrage at her remark. Ike could take it as well as dish it out.

"Ben," Gale said, turning to him, "I just spoke with some stragglers that wandered into town. They came from California. They told me about seeing and talking with some old fellow who called himself the Prophet."

Ben nodded his head; he had not thought about the strange-appearing old man in some time. "A lot of people have seen that old guy, Gale. I've seen him—

Ike, a number of others. Why? What about him?"

"Who is he, Ben?"

As Ben began to talk, telling her what he knew of the old man, memories flooded him, taking him back to Little Rock, more than a year before.

Little Rock was a dead city. Twelve years of neglect and looting had reduced the once-thriving city into blackened girders, stark against the backdrop of blue skies and burned-out buildings. Dead rats lay in heaps, stinking under the sun, fouling the air of the dusty streets.

Ben drove by a high school that somehow looked familiar. Then he recalled that troops had been sent to this high school in the 1950s to integrate it.

He told Rosita as much, but she did not seem impressed.

"Doesn't history interest you, Rosita?" he asked.

She shrugged her indifference. "It don't put pork chops on the table, Ben," she replied with her usual air. She was one of the few who dared to speak to Ben in such a manner.

"What?"

Her smile was sad. "Ben—I can't read much."

"Dear God," Ben muttered. He glanced at her. "You must have been about eight when the bombs came, right?"

"Pretty good guess, Ben. I was nine."

"How much schooling since then?"

"Lots of lessons in the school of hard knocks," she replied, going on the defensive.

"Don't be a smart-ass, short stuff," Ben said with a

grin to soften his words.

"OK, Ben. I'll play it straight. Not much schooling. I read very slowly and skip over all the big words."

"You don't understand them."

"That's right."

"You know anything about nouns, pronouns, adverbs, sentence construction?"

"No." Her reply was softly given.

"Then I will see to it that you learn how to read, Rosita. It's imperative that everyone know how to read."

"I got by without it." She pouted.

"What about your children? Damn it, short stuff, this is what I've been trying to hammer into people's heads. You people are make or break for civilization. I don't understand why so many of you can't—or won't—see that."

He stopped the truck in a part of the city that appeared to be relatively free of dead rats. They got out and walked.

"So I and my *ninos* can learn to make atomic bombs and again blow up the world, Ben? So we can read the formulas for making germs that kill? I—"

"Heads up, General!" a Rebel called.

Ben and Rosita turned. Ben heard her sharp intake of breath.

"Dios mio!" she hissed.

A man was approaching them, angling across the street, stepping around the litter. It was the man in the dreams Rosita had been having. Bearded and robed and carrying a long staff.

The man stopped in the street and Ben looked into the wildest eyes he had ever seen.

And the oldest, the thought came to him.

"My God," someone said. "It's Moses."

A small patrol started toward the man. He held up a warning hand. "Stay away, ye soldiers of a false god."

"It is Moses," a woman muttered, only half in jest.

Ben continued to stare at the man. And he stared at in return.

"I hope not," Ben said, and *his* reply was given only half in jest. Something about the man was disturbing. "Are you all right?" Ben called to him. "We have food we'll share with you."

The robed man said, "I want nothing from you." He stabbed his long staff against the broken concrete of the street. He swung his dark, piercing eyes to the Rebels gathering around Ben, weapons at the ready. "Your worshipping of a false god is offensive." He turned and walked away.

Rosita stood in mild shock, her heart hammering and racing wildly.

Gunfire spun them around. Then the radio crackled with the news a patrol had found a family unit of mutants and the mutants had attacked them. The Rebels had killed them all. Ben and his patrol went to the building that had housed the mutants and were wondering what to do with the only survivor, a small mutant child.

"Here comes nutsy," a Rebel called into the basement.

"Who?" Ben looked up, then realized the Rebel was referring to the old man in robes.

The old man appeared at the shattered basement door. "I am called the Prophet," he spoke.

He pointed his staff at Ben. "Your life will be long and strife-filled. You will sire many children, and in the end none of your dreams will become reality. I have spoken with God, and He has sent me to tell you these things. You are as He to your people, and soon—in your measurement of time—many more will come to believe it. But recall His words: No false gods before me." The old man's eyes seemed to burn into Ben's head. "It will not be your fault, but it will lie on your head."

He turned away, walking back into the street.

The Rebels stood in silence for a few moments, until a Rebel from the outside stuck his head into the doorway.

"Sure is quiet in here," he said.

"What did you make of nutsy?" he was asked.

"Who?"

"The old guy with the beard and the sandals and the robe and staff."

The Rebel had seen no one answering to that description.

"Well, where the hell have you been?"

"I been sittin' outside in the Jeep!" the guard replied indignantly. "And there ain't been nobody wearing robes or sandals and carryin' a stick come out of this building. What the hell have you people been doing—smokin' some old left-handed cigarettes?"

Later, Ben spoke with Buck Osgood, who had just pulled in from Arizona. He told Ben he had seen some old man who called himself the Prophet.

"When did you see him, Buck?"

"Ah, last week."

"In Arizona?"

"Yes, sir."

"What date, Buck?"

"Ah, the ninth, sir."

"Time, approximately?"

" 'Bout noon, I reckon."

"That's the same date and time I saw him," Ben told the young sergeant.

Buck looked at the general strangely. "I didn't know you were in Arizona on the ninth, sir."

"I wasn't," Ben said. He met the man's eyes. "I was in Little Rock."

Gale paled at the telling of the story, one hand going to her throat. "Ben—I saw him and spoke with him the night before the IPF shelled the camp alongside Interstate 70."

Ben leaned back in his chair and studied her. He sighed. The mystery man was beginning to disturb him. Who was he? What did he want? What did he represent? And why did he keep popping up?

"What did you two discuss, Gale?"

She repeated the conversation almost word for word.

Lamar Chase leaned forward, listening intently.

Ike and Cecil sat open-mouthed.

Hector crossed himself.

When she had finished, Ben said, "I don't want you to leave this camp, Gale. Not for any reason—not on your own. I'm going to have guards with you at all times."

"Ben, why are you scaring me like this?"

"I'm not doing it deliberately, Gale, believe me. I just have this feeling Striganov might try to grab you or harm you; he might think he could get to me that way. I want you to be very careful from now on, Gale. Very careful."

She sat down, a worried look on her face. "All right, Ben. From what I've heard about Sam Hartline, I don't want to fall into his hands."

"You won't," Ben assured her. "Just do as I say and don't argue about it."

"That'll be the day," Lamar said dryly.

Gale stuck her tongue out at him.

"The beast is impregnated from the sperm of a human male," the IPF doctor informed General Striganov. "And the Mexicans, the blacks, and the Jew bitches are pregnant from the sperm of the male mutant. I believe gestation time is going to be very short."

Striganov smiled his pleasure and approval. "Give me an educated guess as to gestation time," he pushed the doctor.

The doctor shrugged and lifted one eyebrow. While in Iceland he had discovered old George Sanders movies and had begun emulating the late actor's mannerisms. "X-rays show the fetus developing very rapidly. I would say no more than sixty days, at the outset." He held the X-ray up to the light and clipped the print in place.

General Striganov studied the picture. The shape of the baby was very clear, depicting a form more human than animal, but still clearly showing animal characteristics. The Russian leader again nodded his pleasure. "Very good, doctor. Now—cease, at once, all sterilization projects on the women remaining in our camps. I want them fertile for the mutant experimentation. I will issue orders for teams to fan out, to gather more women, as many as possible. I believe — if all works out, and I see no reason for failure — we just might have stumbled upon a new race of workers, doctor. I think, doctor, we are going to go down in history as great men." He smiled and rubbed his hands together. "Yes indeed, doctor. A pure master race with subhuman workers at our command. I like that concept, don't you?"

"Very much so, General," the doctor replied, his smile as large as that creasing the general's face. "Perhaps the Jews and other inferior minorities have finally found their true niche in life, *da?* Copulating with mutants!" He laughed.

Both men found that hysterically amusing. They were laughing as they walked out of the office and into the hall.

But to the women who were desperately attempting to devise a method of aborting the half-human fetuses they carried in their bodies, and to the men who had been forced to copulate with the female mutants, it was anything but amusing. The women could not put into words their feelings at being strapped onto specially built tables and experiencing the horror and pain of the male mutants jamming their sex organs deep into their bodies. The hideousness of the sex act was so disgusting, that if given a choice, all would have chosen death over the mating. Several women had gone into such deep shock they had died. Several more had tried to kill themselves. Another was mauled so badly when the male mutant became excited during the act, she would carry the physical scars forever.

But the women could think of no way to abort

themselves of the monsters that were forming inside their bodies—growing, taking shape, at almost unbelievable speed. The women were under constant supervision; a member of the IPF medical teams was at their sides at all times. The women were never left alone, not even when going to the bathroom. The chosen women would birth the half-mutant children, and if the IPF doctors had their way, there would be many of the half-mutant offspring.

In selected and carefully padded rooms in what had become known as the warehouse, the wailing and screaming of the women being sexually introduced to male mutants could be heard throughout the day and night. To keep the big male mutants happy and content, many of the sterilized women were "given" to the mutants—always under careful supervision so the big males would not kill the women when they became excited while copulating.

The screaming seemed to never stop.

And the human men chosen for the experiment were experiencing nightmares of such hideous magnitude many of them had to be sedated before sleep. And to make matters worse for the men, many of the female mutants had grown fond of their human sex partners; so much so the beasts were not content unless they could be with the men at least part of the day and night, touching and stroking and caressing them.

The men and women of the IPF found that most amusing.

"You do know what fightin' is all about," Abe Lancer said. He spoke from the ground, where Captain Rayle had tossed him during a hand-to-hand combat session. "I'll be gittin' up now," Abe said. "Take me a rest. You 'bout wore me plumb out, Captain."

Captain Rayle extended his hand and grinned. The mountain man accepted the hand warily, then returned the smile as he was helped to his feet.

"All of President Raines's people trained like you?" the man asked Roger.

"Quite a number of us. The general insists on his people being able to take care of themselves."

Abe rubbed his aching and bruised shoulder and grinned ruefully. "I would have to say, Captain, you folks do know that, all right."

The crowd of mountain people and flat-landers from down in Georgia had watched in silence and some disbelief — at first — as the smaller, lighter and much less powerful Rebel captain had tossed the big mountain man around like a rag doll, bouncing him off the ground time after time. Abe had been unable to land even one blow.

Captain Rayle and his small contingent of Rebels had been surprised at the number of survivors they had discovered in the area, and delighted at the number who accepted them. Almost a thousand men and women had volunteered to be trained by the small detachment of Rebels.

But the civilians needed no training in marksmanship, however. There was not a man among them who could not punch out the center of a Prince Albert can at three hundred yards with a rifle.

All the Rebels had been touched by the naivete of the country people and amused and mildly shocked by the open frankness of the people. And all had been genuinely welcomed into the homes of the people.

Ben had deliberately mixed the detachment, including blacks and Jews and Hispanics and Orientals; he wanted the people to see exactly what his philosophy was all about.

"We ain't got nothing agin' black folks — or anybody else, for that matter," one man had told Captain Rayle. "We live side by side with black folks and work ever' day with 'em. Long as a man pulls his weight and don't want something for nothing and don't try to mess over another person, anyone is welcome to come here and live. The one thing we ain't gonna put up with is no goddamn welfare state. If a man or woman is able to work, by God they gonna work; they ain't gonna lay up on their backsides and do nothing 'cept eat and git fat at somebody else's labor." That much was the Rebel's philosophy. "I 'member how it was — how it got — 'fore the big war of eighty-eight: lazy-assed trashy women of all colors layin' around and fuckin' and havin' babies that the taxpayers had to support; goddamned sorry, trashy men too lazy to work, sayin' a certain kind of job was beneath 'em. Piss on those people. We ain't gonna have none of them in here. No way. Now they ain't nobody who is sick gonna go hungry or cold in this area; we'll look after 'em folk — see to it that nobody lacks for comfort. But them that can work is gonna work.

"It's a small community as communities go. We all know who is tippy-toein' around, liftin' what skirt and when. Woman gets in a family way, the man responsible is gonna support the child. And we don't give a good goddamn how much more work the man's gotta do. He's gonna do 'er.

338

"I ain't sayin' I hold much with mixed marriages, but me and mine kinda figure that really ain't none of our truck. Man or woman wants to wake up in the morning time and look at ugly—that's their business."

"Had many cases arose where a man refused to support a child he fathered?"

"One, to date. Feller admitted he got his jollies with the lady—said she should have tooken some measures to don't have no kid. Refused to help with the child."

"What happened to him?"

"He come up shot one night," the man replied noncommittally. "Dead."

The Rebel smiled at this very final type of justice. "Klan strong in this area?"

The man fixed him with a baleful look. "I ain't got no use a-tal for that bunch of white trash. Never did have. Don't know nobody that do. Wouldn't have 'em around me if I did. Don't know no one that would. That answer your question?"

The Rebel laughed. "Sure does."

Captain Rayle radioed back to Ben, requesting that medical supplies and medics be sent into the area. Soon trucks began rolling in, some of them diverted from the battle area. The trucks brought in not only badly needed medicines, but also a few doctors and teams of highly trained medics to beef up the few medical people that had survived the plague of the previous year. They were welcomed.

Ben had given Captain Rayle his orders personally, in a private meeting back in Tri-States. Roger had the mapped-out coordinates for what Ben had called the last chance for his dream, and it was in that area that Captain Rayle and his people were working, fanning

339

out, attempting to make contact with all those who survived. They began finalizing the boundaries. The Alabama line would be the western boundary, from Burke up in Tennessee down to Bowdon in Georgia, on the Alabama line. The line would run straight east to Orangeburg in South Carolina, then take a ninety-degree turn to Columbia, angling gently northwest, following Interstate 26 as the guiding line up to Ashville. From there, the north boundary would be a line straight east, connecting with Burke to close the area.

"Get your defensive positions quietly laid out," Ben had instructed. "Study what we did in the old Tri-States back in eighty-nine and ninety. Use that as a guidebook. When we get as many of the people out of the areas controlled by the IPF as possible, we'll be coming in. To stay," he added, with more than a touch of grimness to his comment. "I hope."

There were tears in her eyes, spilling down to roll in silver rivers over her cheeks as she read the message, then reread it. Ben sat quietly and watched her. Gale looked at him through a blurry mist. She wiped her eyes and threw the message in a wad onto his desk.

"That is the most monstrous thing I have ever heard of, Ben," she said, considerable heat to her comment. Her dark eyes flashed fire through the mist that tinted them multicolored.

She had just read about the IPF's experimentation programs with minority men and women. The report had been sent to Ben by LRRPs and verified by people who had managed to escape the area controlled by the

IPF.

"Yes," Ben said.

"The man is a reincarnation of Hitler!" she spat out the damning accusation.

"I concur, Gale."

"And his doctors and IPF people are no better than the fucking Gestapo!" she shouted at him.

"Yes, I agree with that."

"He has to be stopped, Ben."

"Yes."

"Well?"

"Well, what?" Ben knew what was coming at him and he dreaded it.

"Stop them, Ben!"

Ben rose from his chair and took her into his arms, holding her, touching her, smoothing her hair. "Gale, I don't have the manpower to do that." For once she didn't attack the statement as being sexist. "Striganov has me outgunned and outmanned, and in many instances, the American people are supporting his actions. I—"

She pulled away from him and glared up at him, about a hundred pounds of mad. "Don't tell me that, Ben. Just don't you attempt to hand me that crap! You're Ben Raines. You pulled—single-handedly— this nation back together in eighty-nine. You formed your own government within a government and made it work. You can do anything, Ben. Everyone who follows you says you can do anything. And I believe it. Yes, now I believe it. You're forgetting, I spoke with the Prophet, and I've talked with people who were in that mutant basement when he singled you out, spoke directly to you. You've been chosen, Ben. You—"

Ben looked down at her and laughed, a harsh, sarcastic bark of dark humor. "You, too, Gale? Come on! Of all the people I thought would reject the notion that I am something more than a mortal, I thought you would be that person. Gale, I'm flesh and blood — nothing more than that. I cut myself shaving, I stub my toe sometimes, and cuss when I do. I bang my shin on coffee tables. I don't sit on the right side of God Almighty; and I don't receive any special instructions from him. I—"

"I'm pregnant," she announced.

Ben stood for a moment, looking at her. He blinked a couple of times.

"Aren't you going to say anything?" she asked.

"Well . . . ah . . ."

"For a writer, Ben, you sure have a way with the English language."

"I can do without your smart-ass remarks, Gale."

"Big deal."

"Ah, are you certain about this?" he asked.

"I'm certain. I was certain the night it happened. And it happened the same night I spoke with the Prophet. It will be twins."

"Gale . . . you *can't* be certain about that."

"I know."

Ben shook his head. "You mean you know you can't be certain?"

"No. I know I'm certain."

"Well . . ." He hesitated for a moment. "I'm . . . glad."

"I can see you leaping up and down from joy," she commented dryly. "Are you going to move against the IPF?"

"I am moving against them, Gale. In the best way I know how."

She put her hands on her hips and stood her ground. "It isn't enough."

Ben fought to keep his patience, but knew whatever he said was going to be wrong to her ears. And he didn't want to speak the words. For what was happening in the IPF-controlled territory was sickening to him, although, he knew, not to the extent it was to Gale.

"It's the best I can do, Gale, without launching a full-scale invasion into IPF territory."

She hung on with the tenacity of a pit bulldog. "Then it appears to me that would be what you would have to do. Now."

"No, Gale."

"Why not, Ben?"

Ben took a deep, calming breath. It didn't work. "Because it would be too costly in terms of human life. My people's lives."

A funny-odd look slipped into her dark eyes. She smiled. Ben took a step backward. He had seen that look before. "What are you thinking, Gale?"

"Why don't you put it before your people, General Raines," she challenged him. "Or are you afraid they'll say go in and fight and stop this horror?"

"Gale, that is what I want to do. Believe me. But I have a responsibility to *all* those who follow me."

She glared up at him. "You talk about human life, Ben. Human life?" She softened her tone, coming to him, touching his arm. "Oh, Ben, you don't understand what is happening up there." She waved toward the west. Ben pointed in the right direction: north. She made a face at him. "I don't believe you really understand. Not at all. Not all the terror and horror and suffering. Human beings are being used as lab rats and guinea pigs. They are being tortured. Horrible, terrible, perverted, disgusting acts are being perpetrated upon them. Human life, Ben? How about human suffering? Rape and degradation and God only knows what else. I can't believe you can just sit back and allow this to continue."

"Gale, honey, listen to me. I don't want you to misinterpret this, but my group is, I believe, the last shot civilization has if any type of democratic social order is to prevail. Civilization—"

She spun away from him, her eyes flashing fire and fury. She balled her hands into small fists and hit him on the shoulder. "Fuck civilization!" she screamed the words at him. *"Civilization!* Goddamn it, Ben. Do you think General Striganov is *civilized?* Do you think what that monster is doing to men and women and children can be called—by any stretch of the imagination—civilized? You're living in a dream world. You're talking about law and order and speaking in terms of productivity and education. But I'm talking about *survival!* The God-given right of any race of people to exist in peace. That's what I'm talking about, Mr. President-General Raines." She jabbed a finger against his chest. "And you, sir, and your people, are the only ones left on the face of this earth—that I know of—who have the might to uphold and maintain and guarantee that right. And that is, I believe, your *duty!*"

She stood before him, chest heaving from her fast speech. The room was still and silent after her outburst.

Ben looked at her for a moment. Then he looked toward the closed motel room door. "All right, people," he called. "You can all come in. I know you're out there listening."

The door swung open slowly and Ike and Cecil and Doctor Chase stood there, grinning sheepishly.

"Cec," Ben said. "Get in touch with the tank commanders. Tell them to roll the tanks back up here and get in position to move north. Then get in touch with the heavy artillery, same orders. Contact Tri-States. I want every man and woman and teen-ager that can handle a weapon up here— *pronto!* Those that are too old for actual combat can start stripping the area clean, loading it up on trucks, and moving it over to Captain Rayle's area in Georgia.

"Ike, move one full combat company over to Georgia, just in case the Russian figures out what we're doing and sends people in there. Roll the convoys day and night, push them hard— I want all the combat troops up here in thirty-six hours.

"I don't want any of you people to get your hopes up too high about this operation. We're not going to beat Striganov. We are too few against overwhelming odds. But I think we can hurt him badly enough to make him stop what he's doing. Or at the very least give us the time to rescue as many people as possible. And I want to hurt him badly enough to give us the time to rebuild over in Georgia, give us the time to fortify our positions so he'll think a long time before launching any attack against us. I won't say we'll never have to move again. We probably will. History proves that for every group of people who attempt to start some form of orderly society, there is always some other group or groups that want to destroy it. But we have to try and try and keep trying. We must never give up. Never.

"We are going to take heavy losses in this campaign; prepare your people for that. That's it, gang—move out."

He looked at Gale. "All right, Gale. We'll give it our best shot."

She kissed him on the cheek. "Of course you will, darling. I knew that all along."

SEVEN

Jimmy Linfort and his wife, Helen, along with John Demoss and his wife, Lisa, staggered down the weed-filled, old two-lane highway. They were naked, but it was difficult to tell that because all four of them had been tarred and feathered before the Klansmen had dragged them to the town limits and kicked them out, warning them never to come back. And to spread the word: No niggers or nigger-lovers allowed. Before they had tarred and feathered the four of them, half a dozen Klansmen had raped the white woman and assaulted the black woman anally, forcing their husbands to watch the humiliation. They had then forced the white man to rape the black man while the robed circle of men and women laughed.

"You sucked his black cock, boy," a Klansman yelled. "Only fair you git some brown on that little thing of yourn."

Then they tarred and feathered the four of them.

As they staggered away from the city limits sign, one man said, "They look lak' big, ugly ducks,

347

don't they, boys?"

The four of them were heading for the Missouri line on Highway 54, planning to cross the Mississippi at Louisiana, Missouri. When they felt they were far enough away from the Klan-controlled territory, the four of them stopped at a deserted old farmhouse, found some gasoline, and began the job of cleaning up. And that was painful, for a lot of hide and hair came off with the tar and feathers.

They primed an old pump until clean water came gushing out, and bathed. For the first time in days, the four of them felt some degree of safety as they dressed in old but clean clothes.

A slight noise from the back yard spun them around, fear leaping into their eyes, hearts hammering. But fear changed to compassion when the saw the source of the noise: several children, ranging in age from eleven to fourteen. A black girl, a Spanish girl, and a Jewish boy and girl.

All four children, the adults would soon learn, had been beaten, tortured and sexually assaulted many times.

"We won't hurt you," Helen said, kneeling down, opening her arms to the kids.

But the young people were hesitant to come forward, distrust evident in their eyes.

"Where are you from?" Jimmy asked.

The oldest boy looked at the adults for a moment, then pointed to the north. "We escaped from IPF country."

"We found some canned food," Lisa said. "We'll share it with you. Are you hungry?"

They all nodded that they were.

And food broke the barrier of fear and distrust.

It was only after dinner that evening, in the lamp and candlelit old farmhouse by the side of the road, that the young people melted enough to talk. The oldest, Leon, told the adults of their ordeal.

"People from the IPF came and got our—" he indicated his younger sister, "parents. Our mother and father. Later on that day, a man slipped through the alley by our house and called out to me to get my sister and get out—run. I grabbed up some clothes and food and got Amy and ran, slipped out the back door just at dark. I later heard that our parents had been killed when they escaped from the IPF and tried to organize a resistance force. The same thing happened to the other kids' parents. We hid out in old houses and in the woods and stuff like that. We only traveled after dark. One afternoon I fell asleep and Amy went walking, looking at flowers growing wild. Some men grabbed her and raped her. Did other stuff to her. She was bleeding when I found her."

Helen looked at the small child. She seemed so frail and helpless, clinging to her brother. "How old are you, Amy?"

"Twelve," the child whispered, keeping her eyes downcast.

"Jesus," Jimmy said.

"They hurt me," Amy said simply.

Her brother swung his gaze to his sister, then looked back at the adults. "That's the first time she's spoken of it since it happened. The first words she's said in months."

Amy crawled over to Lisa and let the woman hold her. There were no tears on the child's face, no emo-

349

tion evident in her eyes. Just a childlike, stoic acceptance that what had happened could not in any way be changed.

"We met a lot of kids on the run," Leon said. He appeared to be the spokesman for the young group. "They all had pretty much the same story. We've been on the run for—" he was thoughtful for a moment—"I think about five months. We have all had things done to us that . . ." For a moment it looked as though he might weep, then his slender features hardened as he toughened. "Things that we would all rather forget . . . but I know that none of us ever will. Ever." He dropped his eyes and was silent.

"Stay with us," John told them all, going to the young group, putting his arms around a young girl. "We're going to arm ourselves. We'll take care of you. We promise."

Leon looked gravely at the four adults. His sudden and small smile was grim. He reached into his knapsack and pulled out a large revolver. It seemed too big for his small hand, but he looked as though he knew how to use it. "Yesterday," he said, "a man tried to take one of the girls. He opened his pants and exposed himself to me. Wanted me to suck him. Said he had some buddies just down the road he wanted us all to meet. I knew what kind of men his buddies would be. He put his hand between Amy's legs and felt her . . . there. Then he tried to fondle me. I shot him in the face. Right between the eyes. Killed him. So maybe we'll go with you people—maybe not. It all depends."

The adults could not understand the reluctance. "Depends on what?" Jimmy asked.

"Which direction you're going. We're going over to

350

Missouri to find Mr. Ben Raines. If that's the direction you people are heading, OK, we'll tag along. But you people better find yourselves some guns, because it looks like you've all had a bad time of it. And you'd better not be cowards—none of you. Because if you are, you won't make it. Somebody will rape you all—men and women—and then they'll kill you, after they use you and torture you. You all better remember that."

The four adults looked at this frail-appearing but obviously tough young boy, scarcely into his teens and already having killed a grown man in defense of his charges. And ready to kill as many times as need be. The knapsack was open, and all could see the haft of a hunting knife. They had no doubts that Leon would use that knife as well as the pistol.

"You are a very tough and capable young man," Helen observed. She was just a little bit in awe of the boy.

"I'm a survivor," Leon cleared it up. "And so is Mr. Ben Raines—among other things, that is." He did not attempt to explain that last bit. "The IPF or anyone else will never take me or my sister alive—not ever. Some big men grabbed me . . . about four months ago. I heard them coming and hid Amy. They took me, stripped me, and used me like a girl. I couldn't walk for three days. No one will ever do that to me again."

"We'll start looking for Mr. Ben Raines first thing in the morning," Jimmy said.

"All right," Leon said. "We'll look together. But first we'll find you all some guns. There's lots of guns around. You just have to know where to look for them."

"None of us has ever fired a gun before," Jimmy said.

Leon leveled old/young/wise eyes on the group of adults. The words that came from his mouth, rolling from his tongue, were harsh, and older than his young years. "Then you'd all damn well better learn how."

They had gathered in southern South Dakota, some three hundred young people, ranging in age from eight to eighteen. They came from the west side of the Mississippi River. The youngest to be armed was twelve. They had all seen horrors through young eyes; all had experienced some form of sexual abuse from the perverts that now roamed the land with impunity, with only slightly more immunity than when law and order prevailed—or so the myth went before the great war wiped out all forms of social order, liberal *and* conservative.

All the young people had endured and survived physical abuse. Many had been on their own for years. All had toughened during this period of violent upheaval. All were wise to the ways of survival, these young people, and they had fought off the cruel advance of perverted men and women many times during the years of young youth past. Play was something they knew nothing about. A good time was a full belly and a warm place to sleep. Happy was being safe for a few hours. Most did not know the meaning of love.

On the other side of the river, the east side, in Indiana, yet another group of youths had gathered, almost identical to the grouping on the west side of the Mississippi. The two groups had maintained radio contact for months now, in preparation for war. Now they waited for word that Ben Raines was moving against the IPF. They would join Ben Raines in that upcoming fight.

Both groups were armed with a mishmash of weapons: from .22-caliber rifles and pistols to AK-47s and M-16s and shotguns. Some carried Molotov cocktails: bottles of gas with a rag stuffed down the neck— homemade bombs. Others carried grenades hooked onto web belts. All carried at least one knife, and they had used the sharpened blades more than once.

The thugs and perverts and two-legged slime that are always lurking in the gutters and who seem to survive any tragedy had learned to give these bands of young people a very wide berth. They had learned that very painfully over the years, leaving dead along the way, stiffening reminders of the harsh lessons one must learn in life's classroom.

The young people were of all races, all creeds. None of them paid any attention to whether the boy or girl next to them was white or black or tan or yellow or purple with antennae for ears. They were of like mind: to fight the IPF to the death, for many had lost brothers and sisters and mothers and fathers to the cruelty of the IPF. But first they would wait until Ben Raines started his push north. They all thought he would, for Ben Raines, so the legend went, was a Godlike man— and all the young people felt him more God than man. And they knew Mr. Ben Raines would win this fight, for gods do not know defeat. The young wanted to help Ben Raines, and then join his free society. Wherever Mr. Ben Raines wanted to settle would be just fine with them.

For they all worshipped Ben Raines.

They had first seen and then helped erect shrines to Ben Raines, wherever they happened to wander throughout the ravaged land.

Like their counterparts to the west, the eastern-based young people also worshipped the legend called Ben Raines. None had ever seen the man in person, but most carried small pictures of him, carefully sealed and protected in plastic.

And like their counterparts to the west, each young person had his own personal horror story of sexual abuse and perversion and torture and hunger and shame and loneliness.

A young girl who at age eight had been raped repeatedly then tossed aside, left to die in a ditch by the side of the road, but had been found by other young people and cared for.

A young boy of ten who had been used as a girl by older men.

A young black who had been tortured and then left for dead . . . simply because of the color of his skin.

An Indian boy who had been stripped naked and sexually abused, then beaten and left for dead.

An Oriental who was found hanging naked by his ankles from a tree limb, almost dead from being whipped, nursed back to health by the caring young.

The stories were almost the same in their horror.

But now the young people—a modern-day Orphans' Brigade, east and west—were organized, armed, and ready and willing and able to fight. They had all been bloodied, now they were ready to spill

354

someone else's blood . . . for the right to live free.

They waited. Waited for the man-god they worshipped.

Ben Raines.

In the extreme northern regions of Michigan, in the deep timber, more than eight hundred men and women had gathered. They had done so quietly, attracting no attention to their congregation. The men and women were all over fifty, many of them in their seventies, some in their eighties.

They had gathered together for protection, coming to this area when word spread through the grapevine of the coming together of the elderly.

The men were all armed, and well-armed. Almost all were veterans of the early days of Vietnam. Some from the Korean War, a few from the Second World War. They were ex-marines, ex-Green Berets, ex-navy, ex-air force and ex-AF Commandoes. They were ex-SEALs, ex-Rangers, ex-LRRP, ex-grunt. All had killed, many with wire and knife and bare hands.

"Has President Raines got a chance?" a man asked.

"Slim to none," was the reply. It came as no surprise to any of the men.

"I don't feel right sitting up here in safety while Raines and his people take it on the chin for us," came another opinion.

"Who said we were going to do anything like that?" Gen. Art Tanner (ret.) spoke from the fringe of the gathering. "Let's gather at the lodge and talk this out."

The men gathered in the huge meeting room of the

once-famous ski lodge. They waited in silence as Tanner mounted the stage and spoke through a bull-horn.

"All right, boys," Tanner said with a grin, the thought of once more seeing action making his blood race hotly through his veins. "You all know why we came here. Let's get down to it and map out some hard reality and plan our strategy. Let's take it from the top. We're getting old, boys. Hell, we are old. We're not young bucks anymore, all full of piss and vinegar and a constant hard-on. We've all got to face up to the fact that our legs and lungs aren't what they used to be. Anyone here want to take off on a twenty-mile forced march with full pack and combat gear to prove me wrong?"

No one did, but it galled the men to have to admit they weren't the men they used to be. No one had to say a word; it was very evident on every face in the room.

" 'K," General Tanner said. "Now we know where we stand physically. But on the plus side, we know things the young bucks don't know. We know planning and we know patience. We know the weapons we carry and we are all well aware of our personal capabilities in the field — what we can and can't do. That is something that comes only with age.

" 'K. There are four hundred and fifty of us old coots. We'll divide up into three short companies of one hundred and twenty-five each. Support and HQ will number fifty. The other twenty-five will act as LRRPs, scouts and forward observers. Those will be the youngest of us." He laughed and the meeting room shook with male laughter. "The youngest here being fifty-three, I believe. Mere child."

Again the room rocked with laughter.

General Tanner waited for the laughter to subside and finally held up his hand. " 'K. Now then, how many here have pacemakers?"

A dozen hands went up, some of them reluctantly.

" 'K," Tanner said. "You people will be part of HQ's company. Now then, how many here have bad backs, arthritis severe enough to limit walking or running, or any other debilitating illness that would keep you out of the field?"

Another dozen hands went up, some of them gnarled and twisted from arthritis.

"You'll join HQ's company," Tanner told them as his eyes swept the room. He found a man sitting quietly and unobtrusively, as if attempting to avoid notice. "Now, goddamn it, Larry!" Tanner shouted. General Tanner was stone deaf in one ear and hard of hearing in the other. His normal tone while speaking was that of a top sergeant addressing troops. In a hurricane. "You only have one leg. You got the other one shot off in Laos back in sixty-two. What the hell good do you think you'd be in the field?"

"I'll be as good as any other man," the veteran said. "I can still do the bop." He stepped out into the aisle and did just that, ending the dance with a little soft-shoe routine.

The men in the room applauded.

"All that is very commendable, Larry," Tanner said. "But what if you break that wooden leg?"

"I'll use my dick!" Larry retorted. "It's long enough."

The men exploded with laughter.

"Yes, Larry," General Tanner said dryly. "That

would be one solution to the problem, providing a man your age could still get it up!"

It was a full two minutes before the laughter died away.

"You got me there, General," Larry shouted, a grin on his red face. "I'll join your HQ's company and shut my mouth."

"Fine. Step over there with the others." His eyes found another man. "Jesus Christ, General Walker!" he roared. "You were with Merrill's Marauders in Burma during World War II. You're eighty-five if you're a day."

"You give me a Springfield, by God," the old man stood up erect, white-maned head held proudly, "and I'll show you kids I can still cut the mustard."

"Fine, General. That's good. I'm sure you can, too. But I just don't know where I could locate a Springfield."

"Well, why the hell not!" the old general roared. He was as hard of hearing as General Tanner.

"Because the army quit using the goddamned things about sixty fucking years ago!" Tanner returned the verbal sound and fury.

"Why the hell did they do that!" Walker roared. "Oh—yeah. I remember. No matter. That was still the best weapon the army ever had."

"General Walker," General Tanner said patiently. "I would be proud and honored to have you join my HQ's company. Your knowledge of tactics is unsurpassed, and your—"

"Boy," Walker cut off the sixty-five-year-old retired general. "If you get any sweeter, you're going to give the whole bunch of us diabetes."

Again the laughter.

"Speaking of that," Tanner said when the laughter had faded away.

A half dozen men stood up and joined the group that was making up headquarters company.

" 'K," Tanner said. "All right, boys. We've been scrounging and stealing and gathering up equipment all summer. Get on back to your billets and pack up your gear. Kiss your wives and girlfriends goodbye. We move out day after tomorrow. Scouts out at 0600 in the morning. Dismissed — and good luck."

"Ah, sir," Emil Hite walked up to the wounded Rebel who seemed to be in charge of the loading of equipment. The Rebel had his left arm in a sling and the right side of his face was heavily bandaged. "May I be so presumptuous as to inquire why you have all these people racing willy-nilly about, creating all this confusion?"

The Rebel officer looked at the cult leader. The contempt he felt for the man was ill-concealed in his eyes. "What business is it of yours, weirdo?"

Emil ignored that slur upon his appearance. "Because if you people are leaving this area, I would like permission to move my poor band of followers in here."

The Rebel laughed at him. "Why, sure," he said. "I don't see why not. Maybe some of what we did here will rub off on you. Just as soon as we're gone, just slide on in."

Emil looked around him. He took in the neat fields and gardens, the homes that had been repaired and painted and restored, the neatly trimmed lawns and carefully maintained sidewalks.

"I thank you from the bottom of my heart, sir," Emil said. "And on behalf of my people, they thank you for your consideration." Emil's mind was racing. He thought: Why, with an idyllic setting such as this, he could attract hundreds, perhaps even thousands more followers into his fold. Just think of all that new pussy! Emil hid his smile and resisted an impulse to rub his hands together in glee. Instead, with his left hand in one pocket of his robe, he scratched his crotch.

"Ughum, bugum, bisco," Emil said.

The Rebel looked at him. "Flaky son of a bitch!" he muttered.

The Rebel began yelling out orders, his grating voice causing Emil to flinch. The man reminded him in a very painful manner of his old drill sergeant. A most disagreeable fellow. Emil hoped one of the bombs that fell back in eighty-eight landed right on that bastard's head.

"Once again," Emil. "I wish to thank you on behalf of my simple flock of worshippers." Somehow, Emil thought, that never came out just right.

The Rebel looked at him and laughed.

"Juggy, muggy, be bop a lula," Emil said.

"Joe Cocker to you, too," the Rebel said, then turned his back and walked away.

"Fuck you," Emil muttered. "And fuck the horse you rode in on, too." But he was very careful not to say that too loudly. The Rebel was huge. And very mean-looking.

Emil shuffled away, his robes dragging along the

ground. He caught the toe of one sandal in the hem and almost tripped himself. He ignored the laughter coming from the wounded Rebels.

"Bless you, my children," Emil said to them.

One of them gave him the finger.

No matter, Emil thought, shuffling away, being more careful where he put his feet. After this, he would be even more revered by his people.

For a very short time.

EIGHT

"The route has been cleared of all mines?" Ben asked Colonel Gray.

"All clear, sir," the Englishman replied.

Ben turned to Ike. "How about the troops, Ike — they ready?"

"Eager to go, Ben."

Ben looked at Cecil. "How about your people and the supplies, Cec?"

"Ready to go, Ben. We have supplies for a three-month campaign."

"We'd better get it done a hell of a lot sooner than that," Ben said grimly. He glanced at Doctor Chase. "Medical teams ready?"

"Yes," the doctor replied softly, for once not retorting with a smart crack.

To Hector: "I wish you would reconsider, Hec. You were hit pretty hard and not that long ago."

"My command, Ben. Where they go, I go," the Mexican replied. "Besides, you're forgetting, I have a personal stake in all this."

Ben nodded. He glanced around him in the predawn darkness. A heady feeling of *deja vu* swept over him. He had done this before. God, how many times? The massive convoy was silent in the darkness. All motors off. Dew glistened wetly off the camouflaged metal of Jeeps, tanks, half-tracks, APCs, rolling artillery, mortar carriers, deuce-and-a-halves, tanker trucks and off the helmets of troops and the metal of their weapons.

A messenger walked up to him, a flashlight in his hand. "Dispatches, sir. I found them to be . . . well, rather unusual."

"Read them to me, son," Ben said.

"Yes, sir. This one is from the north, up in Michigan. It's from General Tanner and General Walker."

"Iron-Legs Walker? Captain March or Die, from Merrill's Marauders?"

"Yes, sir."

"My God. The man must be pushing ninety!"

"Yes, sir, that's the one. And General Tanner used to command the Eighty-second down at Bragg."

"Go on," Ben whispered. He shook his head. "Jesus God."

"Mr. President," the Rebel read the first dispatch under the narrow beam of a flashlight. "Have four hundred and fifty of us old soldiers moving out this a.m. in simultaneous advance with your troops. Do not fear for us. We have lived our lives and lived them well. We have seen the rise of America, and have witnessed her downfall, as well as predicted that downfall. Now it is up to you to put this nation together once more. We believe you are the only man capable of doing that monumental feat. But first we must rid ourselves of General Striganov and his IPF people. We

363

will dig in at various spots along the Iowa line, just as soon as our scouts report the IPF crossing into Missouri. You will have young people on both your flanks. If we have any sort of luck, we will have the IPF in a closed box. I call the young people the Orphans' Brigade, if you remember that from the Civil War. It fits them well. They're all tough little monkeys and they'll more than hold their own. Don't spend too much time worrying about them. We will be shoving off at first light. Good luck and Godspeed, Mr. President."

"Dear God," Ben said, with more than a touch of awe in his tone. "Most of those old boys must be in their sixties and seventies."

Ike had a large lump in his throat and was afraid to speak.

Cecil looked as though he was fighting back tears.

Chase cleared his throat several times.

Hector was openly weeping.

The messenger's hands were shaking as he unfolded the second dispatch. "The next two messages are almost identical, sir," he said. He read: "There are three hundred and twenty five of us to the west, Mr. Raines, and some four hundred to the east. We will be moving out at 0600. We will try to link up with your people on the lower west and east borders of the battleground, putting the IPF in a box when we do. We have no parents, no homes to return to. We are now part of your society, Mr. Ben Raines, and we will follow wherever you choose to lead us. Good luck, sir."

Ben fought back tears. His voice shook when he spoke. "Children, all children. What are their ages, Sergeant?"

The sergeant cleared his throat. Had one hell of a lump building there. "I believe, sir, their ages range from eight to sixteen or so."

"Eight!" Ben's reply was almost a shout. "Those are babies."

"Yes, sir," the sergeant said.

Ben shook his head in disbelief and walked away from the small group just as Juan and Mark walked up. They had stood in silence as the sergeant read the messages. They had heard it all.

"Ninos," Juan said. "Little children with guns. Brave little boys and girls."

"What kind of war is this to be?" Mark pondered aloud. "Little children facing grown men. It's shameful."

Just before Chase walked away to join his medical teams, he said, "I used to hope I'd make it to the year 2000. Now I'm not so certain I'm entirely happy about it."

Ben found Gale in the lightening darkness and put his arms around her. "This time, lady, you don't argue with me. You're assigned to the field hospitals in the rear."

"I know, Ben," she said softly. "I won't argue about it."

"We might not see each other for days, Gale," he reminded her.

"I know that, too," she said, pressing against him, taking comfort from the bulk of the man.

"If conditions start going from bad to worse," Ben said, "I'm sending you to Georgia, to Captain Rayle's command. And I don't want any static out of you about it."

"There won't be, Ben." She looked up into his face. "Ben, I want you to know I think you are a fine, good man. You could have walked away from all this, but you didn't."

"Yeah." He smiled down at her. "But then I would have had to listen to you bitch about it for the next fifty years."

"You got that right, buster."

He kissed her mouth and then, grinning, patted her on the butt. She slapped his hand away. "OK, babe—take off. I'll see you whenever and wherever I can."

She returned the kiss and, grinning, patted him on the butt. She broke free of his arms and walked away into the dim light of early morning, the faint silver from the east picking up pockets of lights in her short-cut, dark hair. The mist hung about her in the Missouri morning.

She looked so small and vulnerable.

Ben walked back to the main column and gave the orders. "Crank them up," he said.

The morning was filled with the coughing of powerful engines fired into sudden life from the cold metal.

"Colonel Gray?"

"Sir?"

"Scouts out?"

"Yes, sir."

"Hector?"

"Sir?"

Ben held out his hand and the man shook it. "Luck to you, Hec."

Hector's teeth flashed white against the olive of his face. "See you after we kick ass, Ben."

Ben nodded. Both men knew the odds of them kicking the ass of the IPF were hard against. He looked at Cecil, held out his hand.

"Luck to you, Ben," the black man said, gripping the hand.

"Take care, old soldier."

Cecil walked away to join his command.

Juan and Mark shook hands with Ben and the two of them left to link up with their respective commands.

Ben looked at Ike. The ex-navy SEAL grinned boyishly. He said, "Here we go again, El Presidente. Seems like we just got through doing this."

"I know the feeling," Ben replied. "Ike, we've got to make the first punch hard enough to knock them down. Then we've got to stomp them while they're down. We've got to make this as dirty and vicious as we know how. And we're going to take a lot of casualties doing it."

"It's worth it, Ben—you know that. None of us could have lived with ourselves if we'd turned our backs to this."

"I know. I was only delaying the inevitable." He held out his hand and the two friends shook hands.

"Luck to you, old warrior," Ike said.

"Luck to you, old friend," Ben replied.

The men walked away in opposite directions.

Ben stood in the center of Highway 67 just as dawn hit the horizon, casting his shadow long down the highway. He looked toward the north and lifted his hand, pointing a finger straight north.

"Let's go!" he yelled. "Go, go, go!"

PART THREE

Be ashamed to die unless you have won some victory for humanity.

— Horace Mann

ONE

Thousands of tons of men and machines and instruments of war and destruction lunged forward from southeast Missouri. At the same time, young boys and girls moved forward from South Dakota and Indiana. To the north, old soldiers were telling their wives and sweethearts goodbye.

"You're entirely too old for this nonsense, Sonny," a woman said, kissings her husband of forty years goodsbye. "But I am so proud of you for doing it."

The veteran of the early days of Vietnam kissed his wife and grinned at her. She patted the top of his bald head as he said, "Honey, I think civilization will either begin or end within the next few weeks. That is my firm belief. I can't sit back and watch it all go down the tube."

She smiled at him. "I want you to come back to me, Sonny. But I can't help but remember what the Spartan mother told her son as he was leaving for the wars."

"Either come back behind your shield, or on it," the husband said.

371

"I love you, you crazy old soldier."

"Love you, baby."

The aging warrior picked up his rifle and walked away before his wife could begin weeping.

"Tanner, you old goat," the retired general was told by his wife, "how many damn times do I have to tell you goodbye?"

"Hopefully, this is the last time, camp-follower," he said with a grin.

"Yes."

"You know the drill, lady, should I not return from this campaign."

"Up into Canada to the cabins. There the rest of us old gals will live out our lives in peace," she repeated in rote, a dry tone to her voice.

"The cabins are well-stocked. You're no slouch with a garden. You'll have adequate medical supplies to last you for years. You all should get by quite nicely."

"But I want to get by with you at my side. So come back to me, Art."

"I shall certainly try, Becky."

He kissed her and was gone.

"Take care of yourself, honey," the man said.

"I shall. And you come back to me."

"Do the best I can."

"Look, old girl, this is something that must be done, you know that."

"Of course I do, Lewis. And don't get amorous, old man," she said with a smile, removing his hand from her rump. "We don't have the time for that. You just do your duty and come back to me."

"You got your high blood pressure pills, Bob?"
"Right here in my pocket, honey."
"You come back to be me, lover."
"I'll be back."
But he would never be back.

"After thirty-five years in the military," a wife told her husband, trying her best to maintain a brave face, "you'd think I'd be used to this."
"Last time, honey."
It would be the last time she would ever see him.

The men moved out.

"Ben Raines is on the move," Hartline informed the Russian commander.

Striganov lifted his head from a report he'd been studying. Disbelief was evident in his eyes. "What did you say, Sam?"

"I said Ben Raines is on the move. Scouts report columns advancing at full speed, heading straight at us from the south."

"His logic escapes me," General Striganov said, a puzzled look on his face. "His people took a terrible battering at the hands of our troops. What does he hope to gain by this action?"

Hartline shrugged his big shoulders. "I haven't the vaguest idea. But that's moot, isn't it? The fact is, he's moving."

"Yes, you are correct. Moot. Mobilize the forces for a push south. Meet General Raines head-on. Have those troops I left in southern Iowa begin marching toward Raines. Engage the Rebels and hold them until we get there with reinforcements. This time I intend to finish the matter."

Hartline started to speak, then hesitated, a curious look on his face.

Striganov caught the hesitation. "Is something the matter, Sam?"

"Yes . . . I think so. Our intelligence shows a group—or groups—of armed people moving toward us not just from the south—that's Raines's bunch of Rebels, we know who that is—but also from the west, the east and from the north."

"Who could it possibly be?"

When Hartline explained who it was, the Russian began laughing. "Children and old men!" he howled out his mirth, pounding his hands on his desk. "Little babies and senile old men. I love it. Hartline, you have made my day. I find this hysterically amusing. Hysterically!" He sobered as abruptly as he fell into laughter. "Very well, our . . . enemies," he giggled, "have been identified. So send two companies to spank the children, one east and one west, and one company to point the old men back to their rocking chairs. I don't want to spare any more men than that."

"Ah . . ." Hartline looked at the Russian, a strange

374

look in his eyes. "I don't know, Georgi. Don't sell these groups too short; they're all well-armed and very dedicated."

"Bah!" Striganov verbally brushed aside the warning. "Do not concern yourself with trivialities, Sam. Old men and children are no match for my people. You have your orders; carry them out and then take your men south to meet Raines. I'm counting on you to crush Ben Raines. That will be all, Sam. Good luck."

The Russian returned to his paper work.

Outside the office, Hartline stood for a moment, his handsome features a study in concentration. He muttered, "I think you're making a bad, big mistake, Georgi, but it's your show."

The members of the forward IPF forces were in a joking mood as they moved west, north and east to confront the "children" and the "old men." This would be no more than a lark for them—a pleasant outing in the fall of the year. And it would be far easier than fighting Gen. Ben Raines and his Rebels. Those people fought like madmen.

One man stepped away from the parked column in northern Iowa, close to the North Dakota line, to relieve himself in the woods. When he did not return in a few moments, another man was sent in to find him. The troops of the IPF waited for the second man to return. He did not return. The woods remained still. Silence greeted the troops.

The IPF section leader, using his hands, ordered his people to fan out and to search the timber. "Nockopee!" the section leader whispered hoarsely, motioning his people to move quickly.

A shout reached the small group of forward scouts. In a rush, they ran into the woods. They stopped abruptly at the sight that lay before them on the ground.

Both men who had entered the timber now lay on their backs, their arms flung wide. Blood soaked the cool ground under and around them. Both men had an arrow embedded deeply in their chest. Weapons and all ammunition and equipment had been removed from the men. Their boots were gone. One of the men had a hole in his left sock, the big toe sticking through.

The section leader ordered his people back, making no noise, speaking with motions of his hands. He turned. An arrow hissed through the air and drove through the man's skull, the point coming out just above one ear. He fell silently to the ground without uttering a sound.

The still and calm woods began to clatter and roar from the sounds of gunfire. The IPF found themselves surrounded, with no place to run, death facing them from all directions. The men and women of the IPF had little chance to use their weapons, because there appeared to be no visible targets.

The deadly and bloody ambush was completed in less than one minute. Young people began drifting out of the deep brush and timber into the blood-soaked clearing. The young people stripped the bodies of uniforms and weapons and ammunition. They took all the equipment they could find.

The leader of the young people was dressed in buckskins and jeans, moccasins on his feet. He was tall and rangy and well-built, his dark hair hanging to his shoulders. His name was Wade. He did not remember what his last name had been. His parents and his brothers and sister had died in a house fire back in ninety. He had been alone, on the road, since he was eight years old. And he had survived. His weapon for this day—he was quite proficient with any type of weapon—was a huge bow, and he was an expert with the longbow. Wade could not read or write well, but he could survive.

"Strip the people of their uniforms," he ordered his young charges. "Wash them free of blood at the creek. Dry them well." To another group of young: "Hide their vehicles. They will be useful when we ambush the others." He smiled and his smile was savage. "I think they misjudged our strength and our dedication to Mr. Ben Raines. I think the IPF people made a mistake." He laughed. "I *know* they made a mistake."

He walked to a small clearing and stood in a narrow beam of sunlight pouring through the thick stand of timber. Nature had managed to renew what man had destroyed. Huge stands of timber now flourished throughout the nation, in lovely contrast to mindless and short-sighted land developers, greedy farmers and stupid loggers; for between the factions, they had managed, in only seventy years, to rape the land, paying scant attention to the warnings of environmentalists and, in many cases, common sense.

Wade laboriously and with much silent lip movement, studied and read a map taken from the section leader of the advance party of the IPF. Finally he looked up, a smile on his lips.

"We will ambush the main column here," he said,

thumping the map. With a finger he traced a red line drawn on the plastic map cover. "They are sending one company of men. That is approximately two hundred people. Twenty-five trucks carrying the men and equipment and several Jeeps for the officers and senior sergeants." He again consulted the map. "Yes," he said, "this will be the perfect spot to catch them in a cross-fire. They are one day behind their scouts. Let's get ready for them."

The forward troops of the IPF made camp in Indiana on their first night toward destroying the force of the eastern-based "children."

Most of the fed and sleeping IPF members would never wake up from their slumber. Those that did would know only a few seconds of intense pain before the bullets of the "children" mangled them into that dark and endless sleep.

Just before the first changing of the guards, moonlight flashed silver on sharpened blades. A very slight grunt as cold steel slid between ribs on the way to the heart; a gurgle as a throat was cut, blood leaping free and thick and steaming in the darkness; a short gasp as black wire looped around a soft throat, shutting off the air. Eyes bugged and tongues turned black and swollen in death.

Then the camp was once more silent.

The men who waited to replace the guards slept on, sleeping through the tap on the shoulder that never came.

The "children" positioned themselves.

"Now!" a young voice called out from the darkness.

For a full sixty seconds the air reverberated with the sounds and fury of gunfire. Most IPF personnel never got a chance to crawl from sleeping bags and blankets. They were shot to death, jerking and bleeding rags of flesh and bone, blood-splattered.

The young people watched and waited in silence. Occasionally, a shot would split the air as someone in the IPF camp moaned and stirred in pain. The shot would still the moaning.

The leader of the eastern-based young people, a young man of eighteen, named Ro, gave the quiet orders to move into the bloody encampment. Like his counterpart to the west, whom he had never met but had spoken with by radio, Ro was dressed in buckskins and jeans, moccasins on his feet. He was quite good with a bow, but on this night he used a twelve-gauge shotgun, loaded with slugs.

Ro did not know his last name, or even if the name Ro had been given him by his parents, whom he did not remember. He was called Ro—that was all the name he knew. He was a survivor.

"Take their uniforms," Ro ordered. "And gather up the weapons and ammunition. Wash the clothing in the river and dry it. Hide their vehicles and bring me any maps you find."

A ragged young boy of ten scampered down the embankment and began picking through the gore with others of approximately his age—although none of the young people really knew how old they were. The blood and the gore and stink of relaxed bowels and bladders seemed not to bother the young boys and girls as they conducted their grisly search.

The bodies were stripped down to their underwear

and left where they had fallen and died. Birds and animals would eat them.

"Food here," a young girl called to Ro.

"We'll eat now," Ro told them.

The young people had learned what the Indians of America had known for centuries: Eat when you can, sleep when you can, drink when you can.

With the blood of the dead IPF members still soaking into the cool, grassy earth, the young people sat and squatted and began to eat among the men sprawled in grotesque death. All present had been born into the horror of war and its aftermath, and had lived through a police state by depending on their guile. Social amenities were few; the young people gnawed at their meat and hard biscuits, eating with their fingers. Their eyes constantly flicked from left to right, much like an animal when he eats, aware that someone or something was always waiting to steal the food should guard be relaxed. When the young boys and girls finished eating, they wiped their hands on their clothing and one by one melted back into the deep timber and brush to seek a place to sleep: a deserted house, a culvert, a thicket. In the morning they would plan another ambush.

The combat company of IPF personnel that rolled northward to "point the old men back to their rocking chairs" drove straight into hell. The American veterans allowed the scouts to pass through the ambush site, after blocking all other roads in the area, then wiped out to a person the entire company of the IPF. They then captured the scouts and hanged them by the side of the road.

Just before they hanged the scouts, one of the Russians muttered under his breath.

"What'd that Russian bastard say?" General Tanner asked.

"I said," the IPF scout replied in perfect English, "that the old bee can still sting."

"Damn right," General Tanner told him. "Hang them," he ordered.

Tanner flexed the fingers of his left hand and then rubbed his aching shoulder. Damned arthritis was acting up again.

When the first reports reached the desk of General Striganov, the Russian could not believe it. Three full companies destroyed—wiped out to a person. Not one man had escaped. It was incredible that children and old men could have done it. Striganov just did not believe it. It had to be a trick of some sort. Little children and senile elderly men do not destroy three companies of highly trained troops.

The thought came to him: Perhaps Sam Hartline lied to him?

No, he immediately rejected that notion. Hartline would have no reason to do that; that would be detrimental to the mercenary's own goals.

President-General Ben Raines must have planted the false information about the children and old men and then had his own Rebels beef up the children and old men. Yes, that was certainly it. Striganov felt better now that he had worked it out in his mind. He leaned back in his chair and smiled.

Well, Striganov pondered the small problem, no point in mentally berating oneself about it; no point in flailing one's mind with whips of defeat. It was done and over and that was that. But the mild irritation that for the first time his people were in a box nagged at him. Not a box with a very substantial lid on it, to be sure, but a box nonetheless.

And that irritated the general. Striganov liked for everything to be done neatly and orderly; he did not like irritation. It was . . . well, unsettling.

But, he thought, putting his hands behind his head, everything else seemed to be going quite well. No — not *seemed* to be going well — it was going well. The inferior minority women who had been forced to breed with the male mutants were swelling with new life. The mutant females who had copulated with the inferior minority men were likewise swelling with pregnancy. The areas controlled by the IPF were coming along quite well, and the people, while not content — many of them — were beginning to adjust to the rule of Hartline and the IPF. True, there were still pockets of resistance scattered about, but nothing that Hartline had not been able to contain, and contain it quite brutally. Fear was the great ruler, and Sam Hartline was very good at instilling fear.

Crops had been harvested and winter wheat planted in those areas suited for farming. Factories were now open — not too many, but there would be more as time passed.

Put people to work. That was the great pacifier. Idle minds and idle hands always meant trouble.

But for now, Striganov must deal with the problem of Ben Raines and his Rebels. And the old men. And the young people.

"Shit!" General Striganov spat out the American profanity. All was not progressing as smoothly as he would have liked.

But he had no doubts as to his success. Failure never entered his mind. Never. True, he would have to shelve his plan to kill the Jew bitch; and that had been a good plan, Striganov reckoned, one that would have sucked Ben Raines out into the open, seeking revenge. Or so Striganov thought. But the Russian did not know Ben Raines as well as he thought.

"Hello, baby." Hartline smiled at Jerre. "My, you are a fine-looking cunt."

Jerre remained silent for a moment. She knew why Hartline had kidnapped her, but she also knew the mercenary had grossly underestimated Ben Raines if he thought Ben would drop whatever he was doing and come to her rescue. She knew Ben was somewhere in Virginia, moving his Rebels toward Richmond, to seize the government from President Addison and Al Cody. Ben had told her several times: "No one in my command is unexpendable, Jerre. Person gets taken prisoner, we'll come after him if at all possible. But I won't risk losing a hundred people just to save one."

And she knew Ben meant it.

"Where am I?" she asked Hartline.

He had laughed. "About a hundred miles from Ben Raines. You're in Virginia, baby. Didn't you have a nice flight out here?"

"Not particularly. Some of your men kept feeling me up. Where are my children?"

"They got away, so I'm told. Big, blond fellow took them. Friend of yours, maybe?"

"Yes. Matt. Good. Then I know that my babies are safe."

She seemed satisfied with that.

Hartline sat looking at her. He seemed puzzled. He didn't understand these followers of Raines. Even though he had broken half a hundred of them with physical torture, and raped and sodomized a half a hundred more, they always seemed to look at him as if he were the loser, not them.

Her smug expression angered the man. He reached out and slapped her hard across the face. She slowly brushed back her blond hair and continued staring at him.

"What's with you people, anyway?" he demanded. "You sluts and losers seem to think Raines is some sort of God. What kind of fucking special society did you people have, anyway, to make you think you're so much better than the rest of us?" He was shouting at her. "Answer me!"

Jerre realized she was dealing with a psychopath — at least that. And she had best walk softly in his presence.

"We don't think we're better," she replied. "But we do believe we had a good society."

"Perfect one?"

"No. I don't think that's possible with humans being the carpenters of that society."

"Isn't that profound?" Hartline said, his voice ugly with sarcasm. "Did you make that up in your pretty little head?"

"No. Ben Raines did."

"I'm sick of his name!" Hartline yelled at her. "You hear me? I don't want you to say it around me, you understand that?"

"Yes."

He changed as quickly as the flit of a fly. He was now calm, smiling at her. He reached out and cupped a breast. "That's nice, Jerre baby. I bet you could give a guy a ride, couldn't you?"

"I . . . don't know how you want me to answer that."

"You like to fuck?"

"I like to make love."

"Tell me about love, baby."

"Are you serious?" she blurted. Then realized that was a mistake.

He slapped her.

Through her tear-blurred eyes she watched as the mercenary unzipped his pants and took out his heavy penis. She was pushed from her chair to the floor, on her knees.

"Kiss it, baby," Hartline ordered. "Just pretend it's a pork chop and lick it. Unless, of course, you're a Jew. Then you can pretend it's a bagel."

He thought that funny and laughed.

Jerre bent her head.

With the death of President Addison, and the wounding of Ben and his appointment to the office of the president, Ike, Captain Gray, and Matt led teams into the Midwest to rescue Jerre. Hartline got out just in time, but his mercenary army had been routed.

Jerre and Matt returned to the West Coast, and Ben

began the awesome job of rebuilding America from the ground up.

Then the rats came, bringing with them the plague.

A year later came Striganov and the IPF.

General Striganov punched a button set into his desk top. Seconds later, an aide stuck her head into the room.

"Sir?"

"Have my equipment laid out and my car made ready. Tell my guards to prepare for a move south. This time I shall personally see to it that President-General Ben Raines is destroyed."

"Yes, sir," the young woman replied.

But she was not so certain about the mission of the IPF as she once had been. So much of what she had heard about Ben Raines was disturbing. So many of the Americans believed the man to be a god—and that disturbed her. She had been taught from birth that the Christian God did not exist. Now the Russian woman was beginning to have doubts about the validity of that philosophy. President-General Ben Raines had been shot so many times, had been stabbed and blown up—still he would not die. Or, the thought chilled her, could not die. He had single-handedly fought and killed a massive mutant, and had come out of that fight without a scratch on him. And there was that story circulating about him having spoken to some sort of God's messenger. That filled the young woman with dread. It caused her—and many more of the IPF—to suffer bad dreams during her sleep.

No, the young woman did not look forward to traveling south with General Striganov. She wished the IPF could have just stayed in Iceland and lived in peace. But she was more than just an aide to the general. She was his sex partner upon command. And she was a soldier, and she had her orders, and she would obey.

Like a good soldier.

TWO

To the north, to the west and to the east, the IPF was running into more trouble than even the most cynical among them had anticipated. To the north, even though Striganov had sent four companies of IPF to fight the "grandfathers," as the Russian had referred to the old soldiers, the IPF found they could not punch through the lines of the old men. The "grandfathers" were holding firm.

The old soldiers knew warfare and knew it well. Thousands of hours of actual combat lay among the men: They were experts in the art of ambush; experts in tactics; experts in producing and deploying explosives; experts in long-range sniping and experts in guerrilla tactics; experts in building and camouflaging hidden bunkers.

As one IPF commander put it, "The old bastards are there one minute, then they are gone the next. They just vanish. You never know where they might pop up: behind you, in front of you, at your flanks, snapping and biting like a small dog. Then they cut a throat or two and disappear. I hate these old men. I hate this country."

And the IPF troops, for the very first time, met the horror of true guerrilla warfare. The men and women of the IPF became fearful of entering the dark timber, for they had found the areas mined with Claymores. And the deep timber and brush contained deadly swing traps and punji pits.

On the fourth day of fighting in the north, what was left of the four companies of the IPF found themselves in the unenviable position of having themselves surrounded, with no place to run, no place to hide, facing either surrender or death.

To the west and the east, the young people fought just as cunningly, but with much more savagery. For most of the young had been on their own for years, and they had learned the hard facts of postwar: If one is to survive after a holocaust, one had best learn how to kill—silently, stealthily, and without mercy or pity. Most could just barely read and write, but all—boys and girls—were experts in the art of survival. Those that did not learn the art of survival while very young . . . usually died.

The boys and girls were small—due to years of bad diet—but they were quick, for they had lived their lives on the fringes of civilization, learning the savage lessons on how best to avoid the mutants and the sudden explosion in the population of bears and wolves and bobcats and mountain lions. Just as Ben Raines had learned back in 1988. . . .

I've got to search the town for survivors! the

thought came to him just before he went to bed. Surely there will be somebody left alive.

The next morning, after shaving and showering and eating a light breakfast, he took his coffee outside and stood for a moment by his small house in the country. He viewed the silent scene that lay before him. Birds still sang and dogs still barked in the distance, and that puzzled him. A nuclear war that would kill humans and leave the animals alive? Not likely. So it had to have been some type of germ warfare. He had to find out what happened.

He went to several stores in search of a worldwide radio. But the stores had all been looted. He finally found one at the Radio Shack. He sat on the curb outside the store and studied the instructions on the operation of the radio. He turned it on. No batteries.

"Wonderful, Ben," he muttered. "Marvelous presence of mind."

With fresh batteries in the radio, Ben worked the dial slowly, going from band to band. Sweat broke out on his face as he heard a voice from the speakers.

The voice spoke in French for a time, then went to German, then to English. Ben listened intently, a feeling of dread washing over him. "We pieced together the story," the voice spoke slowly. "The whole story of what happened. Russian pilot told us this is what happened—from his side of the pond, that is. They—the Russians—had developed some sort of virus that would kill humans, but not harm animals or plant life. Did this about three years ago. Were going to use it against us this fall. Easy to figure out why. Then they learned of the double cross; the Stealth-equipped sub. That shot their plans all to hell. Everything became all confused. If we had tried to talk to them, or they with us, or the Chinese, maybe all this could have been prevented. Maybe not. Too late now. Some survivors worldwide. Have talked with some of them. Millions dead. Don't know how many. Over a billion, probably. Maybe more. Ham operators working. It's bad. God in heaven — it's bad."

This message was repeated, over and over, in four languages.

"A goddamned tape recording," Ben said.

A snarling brought him to his feet, the .45 pistol in his hand. A pack of dogs stood a few yards away, and they were not at all friendly.

Ben leaped for the hood of his truck just as a large German shepherd lunged for him, fangs bared. Ben scrambled for the roof of the cab as the dog leaped onto the hood. Ben shot the animal in the head, the force of the heavy slug knocking the animal backward to die in the street.

The dogs remembered gunfire. They ran down the street, stopping on the corner, turning around, snarling and growling at the man on the cab of the truck. Ben emptied his .45 into the pack, knocking several of the dogs spinning. Ben slapped a fresh clip in the pistol and climbed down. He got his .45-caliber Thompson SMG from the cab.

"From now on, Ben," he said. "That Thompson becomes a part of you. Always."

And now the young of the new century found themselves facing an animal explosion, with many of the animals mutant in size and nature. Flesh-eaters. And the young, without benefit of parental guidance and formal education, without adults helping to shape their minds and lives and actions, and teachers to help shape the mush of their minds into facts, became even more savage than the usual child, for without education, training, discipline and love, we would all be savages.

This then was the shaping of the future generations of the world. The less than auspicious start of the long, slow drift downhill into ignorance and barbarism.

Unless one man could stem the tide, plug the dam, rejuvenate the fountain of knowledge. And do it all in time.

Ben Raines.

But this tragedy—that was all foreseen and forewarned, from Orwell to Meade—was not confined to the land that was once known as America. And to place the brunt of the blame solely on the young would be grossly unfair. For the same was occurring worldwide. In the once-civilized land called England, home of the Magna Carta and the birthplace of law, the Druids were once more flourishing, with the survivors of that once-beautiful and civilized land now robed and hooded, gathering at Stonehenge to ponder the mystery of centuries. And to worship there, all praising and calling to an unknown god. And to sit in caves, painting themselves blue with dye from the berries of wild plants, tracing dark and mysterious lines on their bodies in some ritual of a religion that until only a few years ago had been an evil and unknown memory in the dim reaches of their brains, only now springing forth to sit and snarl and pick at themselves in the real but confused light of consciousness.

In France—or what was left of that germ and nuclear-torn country—the people had gathered and again broken off into formations of Burgundy, and Orleans, and Bourbon and Brittany; and, God save King Louis, into groups of Celts and Normans and Chouans and Gaul and Huguenots.

In Germany, there was not much left, for that country had taken the brunt of much of the nuclear warheads. But a few survived, and they raised their heads out of the rubble and ashes and roaming mutants and thought: There is no God, not the God we were taught to believe in and worship and praise. For if God did exist, He surely would not have permitted this. And there, as in so many other once-prosperous and reasonably civilized nations, statues and man-made Baal-like places and objects of worship began to spring up throughout the countryside, in basements and caves and underground burrows now inhabited by human beings; they would be called the Children of the Darkness. And they would worship the Prince of Flies, the King of Beasts, Lord of Filth—Satan.

Around the world, in Peru, India, Italy, Holland, Hawaii, all around the war-torn globe, many of the survivors began worshipping a false god, in the mistaken belief that they had displeased him or her in some manner, and it was now time for them to make amends . . . in some way.

In many cases, the amends were of the sacrificial nature—human beings.

Civilization was crumbling. Not yet dissolved—many years would pass before that would happen, many more battles involving Ben Raines and his descendants. Civilization was not finished, but well on its way if something or someone did not step forward to take the reins of responsibility in a firm hand, provide direction and leadership and replace myth with truth, ignorance with knowledge, hate with love and compassion and justice.

But that man had his hands full at the moment.

It was the third full day of fighting. Why the phrase came to Ben, he could not understand, for he had no idea yet that the enemy was beaten. But Perry's message to General Harrison leaped into his mind: We have met the enemy, and they are ours.

I hope, Ben silently thought.

At that moment, a mortar shell burst very close to Ben's bunker. The ground shook with a fury, sending bits of dirt and dust floating down into the hastily dug and sandbagged bunker. Ben did not flinch. He continued gazing at the battleground through field glasses.

Lt. Mary Macklin and Sgt. Buck Osgood could but look at each other and shake their heads. Ben Raines's courage was unshakeable and unbelievable.

A sniper from the IPF lines began shooting, several slugs whining through the small opening in the reinforced sandbags.

Ben calmly turned and spoke to Mary. "Mary, have someone neutralize that long-distance shooter, will you?"

Mary's hands were shaking as she rang up the mortar teams and called in the coordinates Buck gave her.

Mortar rounds began fluttering overhead as several

teams walked the rounds in, both from the north and the south.

The sniper was neutralized.

Ben was certainly no coward, though he did know the taste of fear on his tongue. But also knew that to show any cowardice in the face of fire would be highly demoralizing to his people. Therefore, he did not.

"Get me heavy artillery on the horn, Mary," Ben ordered.

The colonel on the line, Ben spoke into his headset. "Let's do it again, Bert. And this time let's give them everything we've got. 105s, 155s, 90mm, 152s, 81mm, and Shillilaghs. Keep pounding them until the metal gets so hot rounds are in danger. Keep pounding them until I give the order to stop. We've pounded their brains out for two-and-a-half days, let's give them some more. Commence firing in one minute."

It was as if the battered troops of the IPF knew something hot and heavy and lethal was in the wind, for the battleground fell strangely silent as Ben's troops dug in deeper for the barrage.

The booming began from the rear of Ben's Rebel lines. Within seconds, the landscape in front of them was transformed from a peaceful country scene to one out of the mind of a raging psychopath in the final grips of destructive madness.

Huge trees were flung into the air, as if ripped from the ground and hurled about by a giant child in a fit of temper. Vehicles and human beings were ripped apart and thrown high into the air amid an assortment of arms and tires and legs and fenders and severed heads and axles.

"Order all troops to prepare for chemicals," Ben

spoke into his headset.

The countryside became quiet, with only the moaning of the wounded and the smoke to remind anyone of the battle just past.

The battle just seconds away would be much quieter, but much hideous in the pain and suffering it would wreak.

"Now," Ben said.

Moments later, the air was once again filled with the sounds of incoming death, as chemical warfare began from the side of the Rebels. The faint screaming and shrieking of the IPF troops could be heard as the acid and mustard and modified nerve gas touched living tissue and burned and ravaged and destroyed the flesh and the eyes and the organs of the IPF troops across the ripped and smoking and wasted no-man's-land.

"High explosives," Ben ordered. "Every third round white phosphorous."

Then the screams of the IPF personnel began in bone-chilling earnest as the WP rounds began dropping, the burning shards of phosphorous searing the flesh and burning to the bone and beyond.

Then the Shillelaghs began seeking targets, the missiles destroying anything they were locked onto during their fiery journey.

As the bearded, robed old man called the Prophet had told Gale, "It was not a war of great magnitude."

But it was enough for the IPF. With a bitter taste in his mouth, and an oath on his lips, General Striganov ordered his people to retreat.

Just seconds after Ben saw what was happening through his binoculars, he jerked off his headset and ran out of the bunker, startling Mary and Buck. Ben yelled, "Spearheaders — go — go — GO!"

With Colonel Gray's Scouts and the LRRPs leading the way, the Rebels charged across the no-man's-land, screaming their rage and fury at the retreating forces of the IPF.

"Keep the rounds in front of the IPF!" Ben yelled back to the bunker. "Call it in. Drive the bastards back to meet us."

The heavy artillery and mortar crews lifted their cannon and tubes and adjusted klicks. A barrage of explosives landed in front of the retreating IPF troops, forcing them to turn around and face the advancing Rebels charging toward them.

Six thousand troops of Striganov's IPF had initially faced the men and women of the Rebels on the four sides of the battleground. Just over three thousand IPF troops had been killed in the first few days of fighting. As the IPF were slowly pushed and forced into a small valley just north of Highway 136 in northern Missouri where they took the heaviest casualties to date. The Rebels closed the pinchers and began the final slaughter of the master race.

It was not quite Gen. Georgi Striganov's Armageddon, but it was to be the last battle for more than ninety-five percent of the troops facing Ben Raines's Rebels.

Many of the surviving IPF troops were already leery about fighting the Rebels, for they had heard all the stories about Ben Raines's supposedly supernatural powers, about him being something of a god, about his abilities to face death down.

Of course, ou.wardly they scoffed and made jokes about that. But for many, inwardly, they weren't so certain.

When the troops of the IPF turned to face the advancing Rebels, fear sprang into their hearts. For the "pure master race" of supermen and superwomen found themselves facing blacks, whites, Indians, Jews, Hispanics, Orientals and practically every other race of people known to exist on the face of the earth.

And they saw pure hate in the eyes of the Rebels. They saw the silvery glint of cold steel affixed to the weapons, the long bayonets gleaming in the cool fall sunlight. For most of the IPF troops, that would be the last thing they would ever see.

The IPF was forced to fight rage against what they stood for, love of country and a fierce dedication to justice and personal liberty, and an almost fanatical loyalty toward Ben Raines. And the IPF knew, to a person, they were beaten.

Miles away, heading back north to safety, Gen. Georgi Striganov sat slumped in the cushioned comfortable security of his armored car. He had tried to direct the operation from the rear, knowing that it was a mistake, but one he felt he had to make, one his advisors had practically insisted upon. He was safe, yes, but his best troops had been wiped out.

His thoughts were as ugly as the bitter taste lying sour on his tongue.

Using the radio in his armored car, Striganov called in to his HQ. "Evacuate west," he said tersely. "Until I arrive, Colonel Fechnor is in charge. I want plan B put into effect at once. Move all personnel and equipment west into the Oregon, Washington and Northern California areas. Order all troops from Iceland to commence their sea journey to America—utilize the long route for safety. Transport the experimental minorities with care, for the females are not far from birthing. Put the evacuation plan into effect immediately."

The Russian sank back into his seat. "Goddamn Ben Raines," he cursed. "Goddamn his soul to the pits of hell!"

To hell! he thought. To hell? He shook away the thought of any punishment after death. He didn't believe in that myth.

Or . . . did he?

"What do you want done with the prisoners, General?" Colonel Gray asked Ben. It was a useless question, for the Englishman knew perfectly well what Ben's reply would be.

Ben looked at him. His smile was grim: a slight upturning of one corner of his mouth. His eyes were bleak. "Shoot them," he said.

The Englishman nodded and turned away.

"Gather and inventory all weapons and equipment," Ben ordered. "We're going to need it."

A thin cover of smoke lay over the little valley of death. Bodies were piled on top of bodies as the Rebels moved into the carnage, stripping the dead of anything they might find useful.

"Tell our engineers to bring earth scrapers in here," Ben told Lieutenant Macklin. "And scoop out mass graves for the IPF."

She walked away, happy to be leaving the immediate area, for the stink of the dead and mangled bodies was ugly to her nostrils.

Ike appeared at Ben's side. Ben glanced at him. The

stocky ex-navy SEAL had come through the fight unscathed. Ike wore a long face.

"What's up, Ike?"

"Hector's dead, Ben. He took a round right through the head."

Ben sighed heavily. Another friend lost. Hector Ramos now joined all the others who had died to defend liberty. "I'm sorry, Ike. Hec was a friend of mine, too. Have him buried apart from those bastards." Ben jerked his thumb toward the piles of dead IPF troops. Something told him that Ike was not through with his report. "All right, ol' buddy. Drop the other shoe."

"OK, Ben, but it ain't good. Prelims show we took a thirty percent loss. Another four hundred too badly hurt to fight. We lost twenty tanks to suicide teams from the IPF, six mortar carriers. One long tom completely out of it, another that will have to have major repairs. One PUFF was shot down, all aboard dead. Two spotter planes down—crews still missing, presumed dead.

"In other words, we've got about eighteen hundred troops still able to fight?"

"That's stretching it, Ben. Make it fifteen hundred. Be more like it. And some of them are more badly wounded than they want us to know."

"Very well," Ben said, mentally tallying up the troops still able to fight. "So what it boils down to is this: Pursuit is out of the question."

"Nil," Cecil said, walking up. He had commanded the west flank. "The last intelligence report we received stated that Striganov had at least another six to eight thousand troops in reserve—but not all of them on American soil. We may have the spirit and the

400

cause, but Striganov simply and flatly has us out-gunned and outmanned the way we are."

"Stopped dead in the water," Ben mused. "At least for a time." He was thoughtful for a moment. "I'm betting Striganov and his people won't stay in the North. I'm betting he's already given orders to pull out and relocate. But where?"

"To the west," Juan said. He and his people had just pulled in from their positions on the west side of the Mississippi River, just above that area defended by Ike's Rebels. "Or to the south. I think those are the only two logical moves left him. You said some time back, Ben, the Russian would probably have eyes and ears out and know we are planning a move to the east. He couldn't move into the once-heavily-industrialized Northeast, for those areas—many of them—will be hot for another thousand years. He certainly would know the work you people did in the new Tri-States, the building and the cultivation of crop-lands. He might go there, but I'm hunch-betting he's pulling out to the west."

"California, Oregon, Washington areas, maybe," Ben said, more to himself than to the others. "Putting as much distance between us as possible, knowing we would be very much overextended by attacking his people with that much of a supply gap between us."

"Yeah," Ike said, spitting a stream of tobacco juice on the ground. "And with three thousand miles separating our base camp from the Russian, we'll be in a hell of a bind as far as supplies went. You're right, Ben."

Ben thought of Gale, and how she would take this news. "Mary?"

Lieutenant Macklin stepped forward. "Sir?" She had delivered Ben's orders to the engineers and returned.

"Mary, have Colonel Gray send out teams of LRRPs. Stay well south of the IPF column but give us daily radio communiques as to their progress. Juan, radio your people in New Mexico and Arizona, warn them the IPF is heading west. Maybe that news will help them find their courage and get them to fight."

"Don't count on it, Ben," Juan warned.

"I'm not. Mary, have Colonel Gray ask for volunteers for a hit and rescue mission on Striganov's HQ up north. I want it mounted quickly, while the IPF is in a mild state of panic and confusion, getting ready for a massive pull-out west. I want them to rescue as many of the captives as possible.

"All right, people, here it is. We are going to stay put for a time. Let Striganov think we're here to stay in this area. It just might confuse him. I doubt it, but there is always a chance. Let's get to the job of burying our dead."

Ike stood by Ben's side as the others left. The two men stood side by side, gazing out at the smoke drifting up from the torn landscape.

"Kinda reminds you of things past, doesn't it, Ben?"

"Yes," Ben replied quietly, his thoughts flying back over the years. "Yes, it does."

The battle for Tri-States took thirty-five days. Just over a month of savage fighting. Ben's people quickly resorted to guerrilla tactics and scattered. Ben's Rebels hit hard and ran, and they booby-trapped everything.

The government troops who stormed Tri-States soon learned what hell must be like. Everything they touched either blew up, shot at them, bit them or poisoned them.

Earlier, the medical people in Tri-States had discovered packs of rabid animals and captured them, keeping them alive as long as possible, transferring the infected cultures into the bloodstreams of every warm-blooded animal they could find. The day the invasion began, the rabid animals were turned loose on the government troops. It was cruel. But isn't war always?

The government troops began their search and destroy missions. They entered hospitals and nursing homes but the patients had been armed. The very old and the very sick and dying fought just as savagely as the young and strong and healthy. For those people who chose to live in Ben Raines's Tri-States wanted only to be left alone, to live their lives as they saw fit. And they would fight to the death for that right. And did.

Old people, with tubes hanging from their bodies, some barely able to crawl, hurled grenades and shot at the government troops who had invaded them. And the young men in their jump boots and berets wept as they killed the old people. Tough marines cried at the carnage.

Many of the young government troops threw down their weapons and walked away, refusing to take part in any more killing. Not cowardice on their part — these young men would have fought to the death against any threat to liberty, but the people of Ben Raines's Tri-States had threatened no one's liberty. All they wanted was the right to live and work and play in peace and personal freedom—and to govern themselves as they saw fit, infringing on no law-abiding citizen's rights.

Many of the young government troops deserted to join the Rebels; many were shot by their own officers for refusing to fight against a group of Americans whom they believed had done no wrong.

The universal soldier syndrome came home to many of the government troops: without us, you can't have a war.

And the children of the Rebels, they fought as well and as bravely as the older, more experienced Rebels. Some as young as ten and twelve stood with weapons and fought it out with the government troops . . . wondering why, because they thought *they* were Americans. The children hid with sniper rifles and had to be hunted down and killed. A battered and bleeding little girl might just hand a medic a live grenade and die with him.

Rightly or wrongly, Ben Raines's decision to school the young of Tri-States in the tactics of war had been driven home. They had been taught for as long as Tri-States stood—nine years—to defend their country, their beliefs, and that is what they did.

The hospital finally had to be blown up with artillery rounds; it was unsafe to enter because the patients were armed and ready to die for Ben Raines and his form of government. Everywhere the U.S. troops turned, something blew up in their faces. With thousands of tons of explosives to work with, the Rebels had wired everything possible to explode.

Tri-States began to stink like an open cesspool. The

U.S. troops were forced to kill every warm-blooded animal they saw. There was no way of knowing what animals had been infected, not in the early stages. The government troops became very wary about entering buildings, not only because of the risk of a door being wired to blow, but because the Rebels had begun placing rabid animals in houses, locking them in. A dog or a cat is a terrible thing to witness leaping at a person, snarling and hissing and foaming from the jaws.

U.S troops could not drink the water in Tri-States. Doctor Chase had infected it with everything from cholera to forms of anthrax.

There were no finely drawn battle lines in this war, no safe sectors for the U.S. troops. The Rebels did not retreat in any given direction, leaving that section clean. They would pull back, then go left or right and circle around, flanking the government troops, harassing and confusing them, slitting a throat along the way. For the Rebels knew this territory. For nine years they had been training for this, and they were experts at their jobs.

The bloody climax came when the government troops could not even remotely consider taking prisoners; they could not risk a Rebel, of any age or sex, getting that close to them.

Then the directive came down the chain of command, beginning at the White House, from the mouth of President Hilton Logan: total extermination.

For many, this was the first time for actual combat. The first time to taste the highs and lows of war. And there are highs in combat. The first taking of a human life—all the training in the world will not prepare a person for that moment.

Sometimes in combat, the mind will turn off, and a soldier will do things to survive without realizing he is doing them or remembering afterward. Rote training takes over.

Fire until you hear the ping or plop of the firing pin striking nothing. Fresh clip in. Resume firing, aiming at the thickest part of the enemy's body. Your weapon is jammed. Clear it, cuss it, grab one from your dead buddy. Fire through the tears and the sweat and the dirt.

Sometimes a soldier will fire his weapon until it's empty and never reload, so caught up is he in the heat and horror. He is killing the enemy with imaginary bullets.

You can't think. Too much noise. Don't even try to think. Kill the enemy. An hour becomes a minute; a minute is forever. God, will it never end. No! don't let it end. The high is terrific. Kind of like a woman moaning beneath you, approaching climax.

One soon learns the truth: You didn't cum—you shit your pants.

And when did it start raining red? Thick red.

You imagine yourself indestructible. *They* can't kill *you*. Laugh in the face of death. Howl at the Reaper. A man running for cover is decapitated by a mortar round. The headless, nonhuman-appearing thing runs on for twenty more yards, flapping its arms in a hideous silent ballet, the music provided by machine guns, the applause the sound of screaming. In your head. It's you, but you don't know that. Look at the headless man. Fascinated. It falls down. Still.

Someone else is trying to stuff yards of guts back into his belly. He falls down, screams, dies. Good. At least it shut the son of a bitch up. His guts are steaming in the cool air.

God, you shot a woman. It's a good hit. The cunt falls funny, kind of limp and boneless.

Then the thought comes to you: How long has it been since you've had any pussy?

What a time to be thinking of that.

Turn to speak to your buddy, just a few feet away, in a ditch. That red rain you felt? That was his blood. He's still alive, but just barely. The blood is really gushing out. No time to worry about the dying. You've got to concentrate on staying alive.

Eyes smart and sting from the smoke and dust of battle. Get it all together, pal, 'cause here come the enemy. Close.

There is that dude from Bravo Company, the one who used to brag about all the pussy he got. He won't be getting any more. Took a slug right between the eyes. All that yuk leaking out of his head.

Suddenly, too quickly, you're mixing it up hand to hand. This is stupid; the enemy looks just like you. His mouth is open, his eyes are wide with a combination of fear and excitement, and he is dirty and smells bad. Your eyes meet. Brains send the message. Kill.

You're off your knees. (How did I get on my knees? What the fuck was I doing, praying?) Legs support you. You're going to be all right.

Squeeze the trigger. The enemy is dead. No, he isn't! The goddamn rifle is empty! Slam the butt of the M-16 into his balls. He doubles over, puking. Bring the butt down on his neck and pray the goddamn plastic stock doesn't break. If it's from Mattell, it's swell. Hear the neck pop. He's dead. A fresh clip in the weapon.

Shoot him just to be sure.

Turn in a crouch, trying to suck air into your lungs, can't get enough air. Another Rebel has just killed that guy . . . what's his name? Third platoon. You notice the strangest things. The guy needs a shave. Force your bayonet into the Rebel's back. (When did you fix the bayonet on the lug?) Damn—it's not as easy as in the movies; the guy is screaming and jerking around and pissing on himself. Oh, shit! The bayonet is stuck in the guy's back. Blow it free. There it is.

Suddenly, you're on the ground, flat on your back. How'd that happen? Am I hit? Oh, God! Don't let my balls be gone!

"Get up, you yellow son of a bitch!" a sergeant is yelling.

Is he yelling at me? Hell, I'm not yellow. I just killed a couple of Rebs. Damn, Sarge, I didn't get down here deliberately, you know. The sergeant takes a slug in the back. Must have gone right through the spine. He falls funny. You can't remember his name.

Get to your feet to face the enemy. What is this, a replay? You just did this.

Some troops have captured a Rebel woman, pulling the pants off her. Aw, come on, guys! She's screaming as they mount her. They're hurting her. That's not right, guys; we're not animals.

"Want some pussy, Jake?"

They're talking to you, stupid. "No." Turn away. Don't have to look at this.

The woman is really screaming in pain.

A man is on the ground. A Rebel. Some government troops are sticking him with bayonets.

"Beg, you motherfucker!" they yell at him.

"Go to hell!" the Rebel shouts his defiance.

The Old Man said no prisoners. So the Reb is shot. But they didn't have to shoot him *there*. He's screaming in pain.

It's quiet. You look around you. Is it over? Yeah—almost. HolyMotherofGodJesusFuckingChrist-Almighty! Look at the bodies. All the blood and stuff. Oh, Lord—the sergeant is walking around, shooting the wounded Rebels in the head. Someone tells you that you're now a sergeant. Battlefield promotion. Somehow it doesn't seem like such a big deal. You want to scream: "But I don't want the promotion!" Then suddenly there is a .45 in your hand an you're stepping through the gore and sthe pain and sthe moaning and sthe pistol is jumping in your hand, ending the moaning and the screaming ands the pain.

No prisoners.

That was the rule on both sides of the conflict.

That woman Reb was still screaming. They were sodomizing her. And calling out crudely as they did so.

You walk away from the sights and sounds of the rape. You could tell them to stop and they would have to. You're a sergeant. But you don't want to lose the respect of your men this early in the game. What the hell? She's only a Rebel. The enemy.

All around you the enemy is lying dead on the ground. And that woman is still screaming. Wish she would shut up.

A Rebel is still alive, shot hard in the chest. He's looking up at you, defiance in his eyes. You shoot him in the head and try not to look at the wedding band on his left hand, third finger. Maybe that was his wife the guys are screwing up the ass.

Don't think about that.

Rationalize the situation. Look, you say silently to the dead man, don't blame me. I'm just following orders, man.

The enemy is defeated, most dead, and it's just too quiet around here. Somebody say something. But everybody you look at averts their eyes. Guys are breathing too hard; somebody tosses his breakfast, puking on the ground. Someone else is praying. The Lord's Prayer. You feel like laughing. Man . . . you think *God* is listening to this shit?

"It's too goddamned quiet!"

You spin around. "Who said that?" you demand in a harsh voice.

Nobody will answer.

Our Father which art in Heaven . . .

A Rebel is moaning in pain.

Hallowed be Thy name . . .

You point to the Rebel. "Shoot him!" you order.

Thy kingdom come. Thy will be done . . .

Bam!

The gunshot is so goddamned loud.

In earth, as it is in Heaven . . .

There is a guy from your platoon, kneeling, holding a tiny, blue-colored bird in his dirty hand.

Give us this day our daily bread . . .

The bird is dead.

And forgive us our debts, as we forgive our debtors . . .

Everybody gathered around to look at the bird. No one speaks. It's quiet.

And lead us not into temptation . . .

There isn't a mark on the bird. No blood. Seems

410

funny to see something with no blood on it. Wonder what killed the bird?

But deliver us from evil . . .

"Hey, Sarge?"

"Yeah?" Your voice sounds funny. Odd.

For thine is the kingdom, and the power . . .

"You know what, Sarge?"

And the glory. . .

"What?"

Forever . . .

"We won."

Amen.

THREE

Gale was silent for a time that evening of the IPF's first major defeat on American soil. Then, after an hour had passed, with Ben leaving her alone to work it all out in her mind, she came to him.

She stood looking at him for a moment before speaking. "We did the best we could, didn't we, Ben? I mean, the fighting?"

"Better than I thought we'd do, Gale. Better than I could ever imagine, in fact."

"You're not just saying that?"

"No."

"Your people — our people, the Rebels — they knew they would suffer losses, didn't they?"

"Yes."

"But still they laid their lives on the line for people they had never met?"

"That is correct."

There were tears in her eyes as she said, "Then I won't nag you about it again, about doing anything else."

"It isn't over, Gale. We haven't given up. I have teams moving to the north right this minute, to rescue as many people as possible. But what we have to do is recoup and rest, plan our next move carefully. We'll eventually beat Striganov—I'm sure of that—but we just can't do it now."

"We'll always be fighting, won't we, Ben? I mean, fighting somebody or something?"

"It looks that way, Gale."

She wiped her eyes and kissed him. "Well . . . least I feel reasonably safe when I'm around you," she said with a smile, some of her spirit returning.

He put a big hand on her stomach. "How is the kid doing?"

"Kids, Ben," she corrected.

"Right. Twins."

"They're fine."

He smiled at her. "Ever been to the Great Smoky Mountains?"

"No."

"It's lovely. You'll like it."

"When do we pull out?"

"In a couple of weeks. We'll let the more seriously wounded get fit to travel. And we'll probably be joined by General Tanner's people and by the kids. Should be interesting."

"Know what I want to do right now?" she questioned. There was a smile on her lips and her dark eyes sparkled with mischief.

"Play Monopoly?" Ben said with all innocence.

"That's one way to describe it. How many times do you think you could make me pass Go?"

He thought about that for a moment, then leaned

down and whispered in her ear.

"Oh my, Ben! Well . . . if you can do that, then I'll just have to think of something nice for you. Have any ideas?"

He again whispered in her ear.

She drew back as if in shock. "Pervert!" she said, but with a smile.

General Tanner's "grandfathers" pulled into Ben's base camp. The old warriors were jubilant as they met with Ben and the others and each congratulated the other on their shared victory over the IPF.

The teams began returning from the north, returning with men and women who told horror stories about their treatment at the hands of the IPF. They told of the mutant breeding farms, of being forced to have sex with the monsters, and of those women who were heavy with mutant children having been taken to the west.

"How many did the teams miss?" Ben asked.

"About half of us," he was told.

It sickened Ben, but he was fully cognizant of the fact there was nothing he could do—not at this moment.

"You did all you could, Ben," Gale told him, and that made him feel better. "Someday, perhaps. But I've come to realize that you can't shoulder the troubles of the world alone, honey."

It made him feel better, but still left him with an ugly taste in his mouth.

Standing alone outside his headquarters at dusk, Ben looked toward the setting sun and murmured,

"Someday, Striganov, I promise you. Someday, I'll find you and kill you."

Behind him, Gale heard the promise and shuddered as a hard chill of fear shook her. She wondered if she would be permitted to live that long? She hoped so. She knew Ben did not love her, knew that for a fact — her woman's intuition told her that. But she felt him to be content with her, and she had enough love for the both of them. Of course, she would never let him know that, she thought with a smile, as the chill of sudden fear left her.

She stood in the shadows of the motel and looked at the man, so tall and strong as the rays of the setting sun silhouetted his shape, making his shadow appear fifty feet long, making the man fit the image so many thought him to be.

And did she feel that way as well?

She didn't know. And she was afraid to question her mind too closely on the subject.

She turned and slipped quietly away.

"Here comes the Orphans' Brigade," Buck said, sticking his head into Ben's quarters. "General, you got to see this to believe it."

"That bad?" Ben questioned, getting up from behind the desk. He put on his beret and headed for the open door.

The columns of young people were still about a mile away from the HQ. They were marching steadily. Ragged and dirty and appearing malnourished, the kids marched with their heads held high.

Ben, with Gale by his side, watched the young

415

people. One column was marching in from the northwest, the other from the northeast.

"Damnedest thing I believe I've ever seen," Ben said, his voice not much more than a whisper.

"Oh, Ben," Gale said, taking his hand. "Some of them are just children. Babies."

"Don't you believe it, Miss Roth," Buck said. "Those kids — most of them, so I hear tell — have been on their own for years. They're tough little guys and gals. And the way it was told to me, most of them would as soon kill you as look at you."

"Buck, I can't believe that," Gale replied, her heart going out to the little ones in the columns.

"Believe it," Ben told her. "They've had no schooling, no parental or adult guidance, no discipline other than what they impose on themselves. A sort of tribal law, I should imagine. They have had but one thought all their waking years, and that is to survive. Yet another sad fact of postwar."

"They look so helpless," Gale muttered.

"Bear in mind," Ben said, "those two columns of kids helped destroy four battalions of trained IPF personnel. And they took no prisoners."

"Colonel Gray mentioned that they looked helpless," Mary Macklin said, joining the growing group. "He offered one little girl a candy bar and she bit his hand to the bone." Mary smiled at the mental picture. "His LRRPs said the colonel then became quite ineloquent."

Gale looked at Mary. "Poor little girl," she said.

"Then that poor little girl grabbed his rifle, kicked him in the shins, and took off into the woods with the AK." She said it all with a straight face. But there was a definite twinkle in her eyes.

Gale looked shocked at the telling.

"How old was the girl?" Ben asked.

"Eight," Mary said.

Ike walked up and looked at the approaching young people. The leading edge was only a few yards away. The young people stopped and were looking at the adults looking at them.

"Aw," Ike said, "look at them poor, little kids. Makes your heart ache, don't it? Me and Sally got to take in a few of them to raise."

Ben smiled.

Ike walked into the street and stood smiling down at the first few young people. He felt his heart soften as he looked at the ragged and dirty little kids. The stocky ex-SEAL knelt down beside one little, dark-haired girl.

"Howdy, honey," he drawled in his best Mississippi accent. "My, you sure are pretty. How'd you like to come live with me and my wife?"

The little girl, no more than nine or ten, pulled a pistol from a holster and pointed it at Ike. Ike paled in shock. She said, "How'd you like to eat lead, fatso?"

Ben had to struggle to keep from laughing at the expression on Ike's face. It was very difficult to get anything over on Ike, and Ben knew this story would fly around the camps of the Rebels. Ike would never live it down.

Gale glanced at Ben. *"Ben!"* she hissed. "Damn it, it isn't funny."

Ben groaned, suppressing a chuckle.

"Now, darlin'," Ike said, very carefully getting to his feet. "There just ain't no call for nothin' like this. I don't mean you no harm."

"Yeah?" the cute little girl asked belligerently. "That's what them guys told me last year, too. I believed 'em. You know what they done to me?"

"I'd really rather not hear about it, if you don't mind," Ike said.

"I guess you and your wife is gonna love me and hug me and give me food and pretty clothes and all that shit?" the little girl demanded Ike answer.

"Well, ah, yes," Ike said, after wincing at her language.

"That's what them men told me, too," the girl said. "So I believed 'em. They took me to a house and raped me—all of them. They hurt me real bad. Then Wade come along and him and his people killed them men. I believe Wade. I don't know you, so I don't believe you and I don't trust you. I got my reasons, mister."

Ben stepped forward as the HQ appeared to swell with the arrival of more young people. "You can believe him, girl," he said. "Ike is sincere in wanting you to come live with him and his wife. Ike and Sally are good people."

The ragged little girl with the pistol in her hand swung old/wise/young eyes to Ben. She holstered the .38. "Maybe," she said, suspicion in her voice. "I don't know you neither, but you look familiar. Who you is, mister?"

"Ben Raines."

The little girl reached into a leather pouch on her belt and removed a plastic-covered picture. She compared the picture to the man then turned to face the large knot of young people, now hundreds strong. "It's him!" she called.

The little girl fell to her knees and every boy and girl in the column followed suit. Ben stood open-mouthed, astonishment evident on his tanned, rugged features.

"What the hell?" Ben muttered.

Wade crawled toward Ben. Clearly embarrassed, Ben tried to motion the young man to his feet. But the young man would have none of that.

"Get up!" Ben whispered hoarsely. "What are you doing?"

With his eyes downcast, Wade called out, "All praise Ben Raines."

"What!" Ben whispered, aware that his people were looking strangely at him.

"All praise Ben Raines," the hundreds of young people echoed.

Ben lost his temper. "Now just a damn minute!" he yelled. "Everybody here — off your knees. Get up and face me."

Ben handed his Thompson to Ike and the eyes of the young people all followed the shifting of the old SMG. More than a few sighed audibly. They now viewed Ike in a different light.

Ben motioned the young people up from their prostration, feeling a bit foolish as he did so.

Reluctantly, and with fear on their young faces, the kids rose to their feet.

"You young people do *not* worship *me!*" Ben said, his voice carrying over the crowd. *"Nobody* worships me. I won't have it. It's silly. Where in the world did you young folks get such an idea?"

"It . . . it is written," Wade stammered out the reply. The seemingly fearless young man now seemed genuinely afraid standing facing Ben.

Ben looked hard at the young man. "Written? Where is it written that I am to be worshipped?"

"An old man told us," Wade said. "I mean . . . he didn't exactly say it like that, but he talked real funny—old-time like. And he said that to worship a false god was a sin in the eyes of the Lord. I told him that maybe that was so, but that there wasn't but one man I would ever bow down to, and that was Mister Ben Raines."

Ben nodded, and to the young people, the nod appeared sagely. Irritation flashed across Ben's face. "Was the man's name the Prophet?"

The crowd of young people drew back, as if much afraid. They knotted together, touching, seeking comfort by physical contact.

"Yes," Wade said, standing his ground, but looking very much like he would rather cut and run.

Ben looked at the young spokesman. "What did he say or do when you told him that?"

"He . . . said that perhaps you . . . Ben Raines . . . might be the man to do the job at hand. But that on your head would lie the . . . the con-con—" he struggled with the unfamiliar word—"the consequences should you try but fail."

"All right. Now tell me this, young man. What do you think the old man meant by that?"

A look of confusion passed over the young man's face. He finally shrugged his shoulders. "That you are a god—what else?"

"He was wrong," Ben said. "And you are wrong in thinking you should worship me."

"No, sir." Wade's reply was softly given, just audible

to Ben's ear. "No, sir, I don't think so. And none of the people who are with me think so, neither. Mister Ben Raines, I have traveled all over this land," Wade stated. "I have been to both big waters, east to west. I have been from Canada down to Texas, and I have personally seen with my own eyes what some people have built in reverence to you."

Ben stirred. Those rock and stone monuments he had heard about but never seen. He did not know how to reply to Wade. A strange emotion moved deep within him. Stirred, turned, then became still as Ben took a deep, calming breath.

Wade said, "You have many, many followers, Mister Ben Raines. We are but a few of them. You have people who revere you living in small pockets all over this nation. But for the most part they are afraid to leave the safety of their tunnels and caves."

Tunnels and caves! Ben thought. We have people in this nation who are living in tunnels and caves? A society of darkness?

Wade said, "Those people would join you, sir. But they are afraid."

Afraid of whom? Ben thought. Or what? "When did all this start?" Ben asked.

Again, Wade shrugged his shoulders. "I . . . don't know, Mister Ben Raines. Right after the war come to us, I reckon. Long time, judging from the age of some of the tributes to you."

"How did you and your . . . group avoid President Logan's relocation efforts and Al Cody's agents all these years?"

Wade smiled. "We know the ways of the mountains and the deep timber, Mister Ben Raines. We are as much at home in the wilderness as you are in your house. Have you ever tried to capture sunlight or a moonbeam and hold it in your hand?"

Ben returned the smile. He liked this young but very tough and capable young man. He felt Wade and his people would be good allies. "No, I haven't attempted to do that, Wade. I should imagine it would be very difficult."

"Yes, Mister Ben Raines. Very difficult."

"We are going to the east, Wade. Moving over into Tennessee and Georgia and North Carolina. Would you and your people care to join us?"

"That is why we are here, Mister Ben Raines. And that is why Ro and his people have come."

"Ro?"

Wade pointed to the second column of boys and girls. And to a tall young man who stood at the forefront. "Ro."

Ben nodded and stepped toward Ro. He extended his hand, but the young man backed away, refusing to accept the gesture of friendship.

"It is not permitted, Mister Ben Raines," Ro told him.

"What is not permitted?" Ben asked, an edge to his voice as he became slightly irritated.

Ro looked at him and smiled a secret smile. "It is as the old man said: You do not yet know who you are. But still, it is not permitted."

He bowed and turned to his people. He said something Ben could not understand. The language sounded very much like pidgin English.

Dear God, Ben thought. Have we reverted to this — already!

Ro turned again to Ben. "We accept your invitation to join your following. We will follow you wherever you lead. For now, where do you want us to camp?"

"Bed them down, Buck," Ben said. He looked at Wade. "This is Sergeant Osgood. He'll show you where to bunk and then we get you bathed and fed and clothed and have our medical people look you over."

"We are at your command, Mister Ben Raines," Wade said. He turned to his group and spoke to them in the same pidgin English Ro had used. The young people turned, falling into a loose formation. Ben stood and watched them march off, following a clearly embarrassed Buck Osgood.

"I feel like a damned pied piper," Buck said.

The same strange ritual was conducted by Ro, making Ben feel more set-apart than ever. He knew, felt a very dangerous precedent being set, or had already been set on this day. But how to combat it? He didn't know. But he knew he had to come up with something very quickly.

"For a god," Gale said, walking to Ben's side, "you have some pretty good moves in the sack, Ben. Did you learn all that on the slopes of Olympus?"

Ben almost choked on his cigarette. "Jesus, Gale! I didn't find it amusing."

"I didn't either, Ben. What are you going to do about it?"

He shook his head. "I don't know."

"Tunnels and caves, Ben?"

"That's what the young man said." He looked at Cecil and Ike and Juan and Mark. "Any of you people ever hear about a subterranean culture that worships me?"

"Nothing, Ben," Cecil said. But Cecil could never lie worth a damn.

"Umm," Ben said.

Chase had joined the group. Ben looked at him. The doctor, like the others, remained noncommittal.

"It's a big country, Ben," Ike said. "It doesn't surprise me to learn there are groups who hold you in high regard."

"Being held in high regard is one thing," Ben replied. "Being looked upon as possessing some supernatural power is quite another. And I don't like it." He looked hard at his friends. "None of you gave me an answer to my question, boys—why?"

"I tried to tell you, Ben," Doctor Chase said. "Tried on several occasions. But you always brushed it off as having little or no importance. I got tired of trying."

"We have all tried, Ben," Cecil said. "But you refused to believe it or even discuss it with us. Now it's coming home, as we all told you—or tried to tell you—it would."

"You people are behaving as if the problem is all my fault," Ben said peevishly.

"No." Doctor Chase picked up the anger in Ben. His words were softly spoken. "I think it is just time for this to occur, Ben. And I warned you about that, too." The doctor walked away, without going into more detail. He knew he didn't have to

"It'll pass," Ben said firmly. "By God, I'll see to that personally."

"Good luck, El Presidente," Ike said. And he got a hard look from Ben for the words. " 'Cause you're sure gonna need it."

A subterranean society did indeed exist in what was once known as America, South America, Central America, Asia Minor, Africa, Asia—all around the globe. The People of Darkness, as some called them, spanned the war-torn globe. They lived in tunnels and caves and underground repositories and old mines. They came out to work carefully hidden vegetable gardens and to hunt for game. They did not venture out before dawn or after dark. For where they lived—or existed—many of whom having lived there for more than a decade, the animal population explosion was very real.

Some mutants, those more animal than human, had on occasion bred with bear, and the results were truly hideous to behold. They were very dangerous. But perhaps the most dangerous were the offspring of mutants who had kidnapped and bred with human women. They not only possessed the strength and fury of the animal, but also the cunning and intelligence of their human side.

The mountain lion now roamed the land, in greater numbers than ever before; the wolf had reclaimed his rightful spot in the scheme of the animal world. As had all predatory animals. Some, like the mutant/bear, whose genes contained the radiation and germ contamination, produced monsters in their litters, bigger and stronger and much more deadly than the pure species.

And these stalked the deep timber and deserted villages and towns at night.

The people who lived in the caves and tunnels had long ago given up on modern technology and weapons and what was once considered the acceptable mode of dress. They wore the skins of animals and the soles of their feet were as tough as shoe leather. And they did not worship God.

Some of them worshipped Satan, with all the horror that went with that. Some worshipped some form of higher entity; but for the most part they did not believe He was all-powerful. No true all-powerful God would have permitted the world to turn into such as it had now become.

No, blind faith was almost universally unacceptable.

But Ben Raines, now—he was real, and that weapon he carried was real, and Ben Raines was doing something to correct all this misery and awfulness. So, many of them reasoned, Ben Raines must be in touch with some higher power. And if that was true, then Ben Raines was the man-god here on earth.

In a manner of speaking, the older and wiser among them cautioned.

So around the fires against the night, in hundreds of caves and underground mini-communities around the nation that was once known as America, Land of the Free, Give Me Your Huddled Masses, and all that crap, the men and women of the People of Darkness talked of things past and what they hoped for the future.

And of Ben Raines.

"Counting the kids who just came in, Ben," Cecil said. "We can put about twenty-four hundred troops in the field."

"Against Striganov's ten thousand or so."

"Yes."

"All we can do is wait for the day to come when we are strong enough to move against the IPF."

All agreed that to try that now would be suicide.

"Are you going to marry Katrina and Roy?" Cecil asked. "That's the talk around camp."

"They came to see me. But I'm not a minister, Cec."

"You married Ike and Sally back in eighty-nine."

"That was a mock ceremony and you know it."

Cecil shrugged. "Ministers seem to be in short supply, Ben. And, whether you've noticed, or not, getting shorter."

Ben said nothing. But he knew Cecil was working up to something.

Cecil said, "And those we've talked with seemed to have misplaced their faith."

"Stop dancing around what's on your mind, Cec. It isn't like you. Come on, let's have it."

Cecil made up his mind. It might be the wrong direction to take — might be very bad advice — but Chase and Ike and Juan and Mark and Colonel Gray and all the others in positions of authority in the Rebels had agreed it was worth a shot.

"Maybe it's up to you to put the faith of the people back on the track, Ben."

"You better explain that," Ben said. There was a deadly quality to his tone.

Cecil met his angry eyes. "Maybe what the kids believe isn't such a bad idea."

"I don't believe I'm hearing this!"

"Ben . . ."

"Goddamn you, Cecil. Stop it!"

"No, I won't stop. And I won't allow you to make me angry. People have lost their faith in God. And a nation cannot exist as such without that faith, and you know it. Ben, if this nation ever gets whole again, it will be your doing. And only yours. No one is asking that you set yourself up as some little tin god on a make-believe throne. But if a strong belief in you is what it takes to help repair this country—then so be it."

Ben sat back in his chair. He was stunned speechless. That this ex-college professor, this highly educated man, this man he called friend for many years . . . could even dream of such a monstrous idea. It was inconceivable.

It was ludicrous.

"Chase agrees, Ben," Cecil said.

Ben sat in silence.

"Ike agrees, Ben."

Ben looked at the man, not believing what he was hearing.

"Juan and Mark and Dan agree, Ben."

Ben found his voice. "You want me to walk out of that goddamned door and not come back, Cec?"

"You know I don't, Ben."

"Then don't you ever bring this up again, Cec. By all that's holy—no pun intended—I'll take Gale and clear out. I mean it."

"It just may be too late, Ben. I think you have given that some thought, too. Am I right?"

He had, but he was not going to give up without a fight.

"Sometimes, Ben, an unwilling or reluctant god is preferable to the people."

"We won't speak of this again, Cecil. I'll forget you brought it up."

Cecil's eyes were sad. "Yes, we'll speak of it again, Ben. Whether you like it or not, whether you want to or not. But we will speak of it again."

Cecil walked from the room.

EPILOGUE: THE DAWANING

Ben had made it clear to Gale the subject was closed. She respected his wishes and did not speak of the matter of gods.

As they stood in the predawn darkness, listening to the sounds of engines coughing into life, she looked up at Ben.

"A new land, Ben? A place where we can live in peace and raise our children?"

"I hope so, Gale."

She knew he was just saying that because it was what she wanted to hear.

"Colonel Gray?" Ben called. "Move the people east."

"Yes, sir."

THE REBEL

Ben looked to the west, toward the dream of a master race.

"I'll kill you someday, Striganov," he muttered, as

Gale stirred beside him. "Tattoo that on *your* arm."

THE RUSSIAN

Striganov stood with the sun just looming over the horizon. He stood looking toward the dream of a free society.

"I'll kill you someay, Ben Raines," he said. "That is a promise."

"Sir?" Colonel Fechnor said.

Striganov turned. "Yes."

"The women have begun birthing the half-mutants."

"Oh? How do they look?"

Fechnor smiled, the sun gleaming off his steel teeth. "Magnificent, sir. They are truly a sight to behold."

THE PEOPLE

The ragged and dirty little girl stood holding onto the hand of her big brother. She was six. He was nine.

They stood looking toward the east.

"Are we going now?" she asked.

"Yes."

"To find this man?"

"Yes. It's a long way, but we'll make it."

"And then everything will be all right? We won't be hungry or cold or afraid anymore?"

"That's right."

They started walking down the weed-filled, old two-lane highway.

"This man," she said, "he must be somebody really special."

Her brother looked at her. "The people back in the caves said he was."

"What is he?"

"They said he was God."

"I've heard of that person," she replied. "I wish we were there now. I'm hungry."

"Maybe I can kill us a rabbit and we'll cook it."

She wrapped her thin coat around her. "Does God have a name?"

"Ben Raines."